SCANDAL

A REGENCY HISTORICAL ROMANCE

Carolyn Jewel

cJewel Books
Petaluma, California

Carolyn Jewel

Books By Carolyn Jewel

HISTORICAL ROMANCE SERIES

The Sinclair Sisters Series
Lord Ruin, Book 1
A Notorious Ruin, Book 2

Reforming the Scoundrels Series
Not Wicked Enough, Book 1
Not Proper Enough, Book 2

OTHER HISTORICAL ROMANCE

In The Duke's Arms
(from the Anthology *Christmas In The Duke's Arms)*
One Starlit Night
(novella from the *Midnight Scandals* Anthology)
Midnight Scandals Anthology
Scandal
Indiscreet
Moonlight, A short story
The Spare
Stolen Love
Passion's Song

PARANORMAL ROMANCE

My Immortals Series

My Wicked Enemy, Book 1

My Forbidden Desire, Book 2

My Immortal Assassin, Book 3

My Dangerous Pleasure, Book 4

Free Fall, Book 4.5 (a novella)

My Darkest Passion, Book 5

OTHER PARANORMAL ROMANCE

Alphas Unleashed, Anthology *Dead Drop*

A Darker Crimson, Book 4 of the Crimson City series

DX (A Crimson City Novella)

FANTASY ROMANCE

The King's Dragon, A short story

EROTIC ROMANCE

Whispers, Collection No. 1

CHAPTER ONE

Havenwood, near Duke's Head, England,
NOVEMBER 2, 1814

The first thing Gwilym, Earl of Banallt, noticed when he rounded the drive was Sophie perched on the ledge of a low fountain. Surely, he thought, some other explanation existed for the hard, slow thud of his heart against his ribs. After all, he hadn't seen her in well over a year, and they had not parted on the best of terms. He ought to be over her by now. And yet the jolt of seeing her again shot straight through to his soul.

He was dismayed beyond words.

Beside him, Sophie's brother continued riding toward the house, oblivious.

She heard them coming; she left off trailing her fingers in the water and straightened, though not before he caught a glimpse of the pale nape of her neck. Just that flash of bare skin, and Banallt couldn't breathe. Still seated on the fountain's edge, she turned toward the drive and looked first at her brother and then, at last, at him. She did not smile. Nor, he thought, was she unaffected.

Nothing at all had changed.

"Sophie!" Mercer called to his sister. He urged his horse to the edge of the gravel drive. Banallt took a breath, prayed for his heart to stop banging its way out of his chest, and followed. He wasn't afraid of her. Certainly he wasn't. Why would he be? She was a woman and

only a tolerably pretty one at that. He had years of experience dealing with women. "What luck we've found you outside," Mercer said,
leaning a forearm across his horse's neck.

Anxiety pressed in on Banallt, which annoyed him to no end.
What he wanted from this moment was proof she hadn't taken possession of his heart. That his memories of her, of the two of them,
were distorted by past circumstance. They had met during a turbu-
lent time in his life during which he had perhaps not always behaved
as a gentleman ought. They had parted on a day that had forever
scarred him. He wanted to see her as plain and uninteresting. He
wanted to think that, after all, he'd been mistaken about her eyes. He
wanted his fascination with her to have vanished.

None of that had happened.

Banallt still thought he'd do anything to take her to bed.

Sophie lifted a hand to shade her eyes. "Hullo, John."

She was no beauty. Not at first glance. Not even at second glance.
Bony cheeks only just balanced her pointed chin. Her nose was too
long, with a small but noticeable curve below the bridge that did not
straighten out near soon enough. Her mouth was not particularly
full. Thick eyebrows darker than her dark hair arched over eyes that
blazed with intelligence. The first time he saw her he'd thought it a
pity a woman with eyes like hers wasn't better looking. Not the only
time he'd misjudged her; merely the first.

She stood and walked to the edge of the lawn. Behind her, nearer
the house, mist rose from emerald grass, and above the roof more
fog curled around the chimneys to mingle with smoke. Havenwood
was a very pretty property.

"My lord." Sophie curtseyed when she came to a halt. Her smile
didn't reach her eyes. Banallt saw the wariness in the blue green

depths. She didn't trust him, and she was still angry. Considering his reputation and their past interactions, a wise decision. She knew him too well. Better than anyone ever had.

Banallt relaxed his hands on the reins. Really, he told himself, his situation was not dire at all. He preferred tall women, and Sophie was not tall. In coloring, his bias had always been for blondes, and she was a brunette whose fine-boned features added to one's impression of her fragility. Delicate women did not interest him. She was in every way wrong for him. Havenwood might be a gentleman's estate, but despite the wealth and property, despite the fact that Mercer had important connections, the truth remained that Mercer and his sister were only minor gentry. Sophie's marriage had most definitely been a step down for her. His dismay eased. He would get through this ill-advised visit unscathed. He would tell her good morning, or afternoon, or whatever the hell time of day it was, express his surprise at seeing her, and be on his way, having just recalled an important engagement.

"You haven't changed," he told her. Good. He sounded stiff and formal. It was not in his nature to abase himself to anyone. Not even to Sophie Evans. His Cleveland Bay stretched its nose in her direction, remembering carrots and sugar fed from her hand, no doubt.

"You've met?" Mercer asked. His mount danced sideways, but he settled his gelding quickly. He was a competent horseman, John Mercer was. And far too alert now. Mercer was a dutiful brother looking out for his sister. Well. There was nothing for it. Banallt was here after all, and Mercer had reason to be suspicious.

"Lord Banallt was a friend of Tommy's," Sophie replied when Banallt did not answer. She pressed her lips together in familiar disapproval. Sophie had seen him at his worst, which was quite bad indeed. Legendary, in fact. Heaven only knew what was going through her mind right now. Actually, he thought he knew. It was not much to his credit.

"I didn't realize," Mercer said. Now he had the same wary eyes as his sister. The line between connections that were tolerable and connections that were not was sometimes all too fine. Mercer must have been wondering if that slender gap had been breached. A widowed nobleman with a long-standing reputation as a rake was one thing. A gentleman might overlook a scandal or two in the career of such a man. But a rake with a heretofore unknown acquaintance with one's sister was altogether different. Particularly when said sister was already well connected with scandal.

A look passed between Sophie and Mercer that made her mouth go thinner yet. If she was unhappy living with her brother, Banallt thought, this was something in his favor— *if* he went through with the madness that had begun flirting with him the moment he saw Sophie sitting at the fountain. That same compulsion had brought him here, all the way from Paris by way of London.

"We met once," she said. "Only once in eight years."

"Twice, wasn't it?" Banallt said in a lazy voice. If she was lying to her brother, which she was, then he had hope that she would not dismiss him out of hand. In fact, he had visited Rider Hall exactly four times. Three times that her late husband had known about.

"Was it?" she replied. Her voice could have frozen hell at noon twice over. He knew that voice well, and hearing it again made him want to smile. So many memories. She was the first woman ever to arouse his intellectual interest. Suffice it to say he typically admired women for other attributes than the quality of their minds. Perhaps his downfall had begun the moment he heard her speak with crisp indifference for his consequence. She spoke her mind. She wore her hair differently now, smoothed back from her forehead with fewer curls than he remembered. How like her to do so little to enhance her looks. "I don't recall."

"Sophie," her brother said with eyes that narrowed as he looked at her. But Mercer was no match for his sister's chill. No one was. "I should think you'd want to mention that."

She rolled her eyes. "John, for goodness' sake." Her familiar no-nonsense tone fit perfectly with her features. Prim. Modest. Completely unremarkable. She was like a governess scolding some young charge.

Banallt stared at her, more fascinated by her than he'd been by any other woman. His obsession with her bubbled up from wherever it was he'd tried to lock it away. He had been in the intimate company of women of undisputed beauty, but not one of them, not even the most exquisite, had made his stomach drop to the bottom of the earth as did one glimpse of Sophie.

"What does it matter," Sophie asked her brother, "if I met Lord Banallt before you did or, for that matter, whether we met one time or three?" She threw a hand in the air, and Banallt felt smugly certain she recalled exactly how many times they'd met. "Or even a dozen?"

"Mercer," Banallt said. He shifted on his saddle. "I'd no idea your sister was Mrs. Thomas Evans." The lie rolled from his tongue like warm butter.

The thing was, Mercer was right to be suspicious. Banallt and Sophie were both lying, for one thing. For another, any woman who confessed to knowing him stood a good chance of having been to bed with him. John Mercer was not fool enough to think his sister would be excluded from the likelihood. Well. And so. The truth was he wished Mercer's suspicions were well-founded.

"That much I understand, my lord." Mercer smiled. "It's my sister's silence I wonder at. You're all anyone has talked about since first we heard of your arrival at Castle Darmead. For pity's sake, she practically lived at Darmead when we were children. Your hair would curl, my lord, if you'd heard even half the stories she told about you and your ancestors."

Sophie shrugged as if the talk—more like gossip—was a matter of no importance. Her attention was on her brother, which gave Banallt an unrestricted view of her inelegant nose and the slant of her sharp cheekbone. Today's cold and foggy weather suited her; the gray brought out the bronze in her dark hair and gave the faintest pink to her cheeks. Had he not come to Havenwood to discover whether the unthinkable had, indeed, befallen him? He was far more than bewitched. Damn the world to hell and back for it, too.

"Sophie," Mercer said. "Let's serve tea in the conservatory, shall we?"

"As you like, John." She spoke coolly, and Banallt didn't know if she did so to allay her brother's suspicions, unfounded though they were as to any past sexual connection, or whether because she was bitterly displeased that Banallt had come to Havenwood. God knows she was justified in thinking him here for no good purpose.

Banallt urged his horse up the drive ahead of Mercer so as not to reveal his uneasy state of mind. Whatever else he did, he owed her an apology. Would she forgive him? And if she did not? He might well regret his decision to come here. He'd made a mistake. They'd never have met, not in a thousand years, if she hadn't been married to that bounder Tommy Evans. Met they had, and Christ, he'd fallen hard. Precisely, he thought, because she was so unexpectedly the opposite of everything. The opposite of his expectations, the opposite of his desires, the opposite of any woman ever to flit into his imagination.

She was still dainty. Still slender. Still with eyes that made a man think of nothing but looking into them a moment longer. Still wary and reserved. He knew her as he had never come to know any other woman. He knew she longed for love and that her life up to now had not been one to make her think she would ever have it. He still wanted to take her into his arms and swear she would never want for anything again. None of which he had ever done, despite the fact that he never had considered a woman's marital status an impediment to an affair. Nor his own, either. Her opinion on the matter was quite the opposite.

Rather than catching up to Banallt, Mercer stayed behind to say something further to his sister. Banallt heard the tension in their voices but not the words themselves. He gave his Cleveland Bay the signal to stop when he heard Mercer riding after him. Damn. A man of his experience of life was too old for butterflies. The question now was whether Mercer had been tasked with sending him on his way. He mastered himself, and the control felt comfortable, like a favorite coat. From the corner of his eye, he saw Sophie cross the lawn, heading toward the house.

"Sophie never mentioned she knew you," Mercer said when he'd caught up.

Banallt gave Mercer an icy stare. "Should she have?"

"You tell me."

"Like any good rake, Tommy Evans kept his mistress in London and his wife in the country." He tried to recall whether Sophie had ever talked about her family and concluded he'd known only that she had an elder brother who lived at Havenwood. "London was where he preferred to be. In those days, so did I."

Mercer said nothing, and Banallt didn't know what to make of the man's silence. How unfortunate that Mercer was easily as intelligent as his sister.

"I was in Kent twice, as I recall. Perhaps three times. I met your sister then, when Evans brought me to Rider Hall to hunt." They had not, to his memory, done much hunting, unless one counted choosing a whore at the local bawdy house as hunting. More like shooting fish in a barrel.

"I see."

Banallt sighed. Mercer most assuredly did not see. "Forgive me if I am blunt. But Evans was more interested in whoring and gaming than in his domestic bliss. As was I. In those days," Banallt said.

"But you met her."

So, Mercer did suspect they'd been lovers. He wished they had been, because then he'd not be here, making a fool of himself.

"Naturally, we met. I thought her—" What was he to say? Heartbreaking. And then intriguing, and at last, utterly beguiling. "—charming." He had not for a moment expected Tommy Evans's wife to be anything but a foolish, empty-headed female of the sort that kept a man in London month after month. He had arrived at Rider Hall a rake unfettered by scruples of any kind, blissful in his ignorance that his life was to be set on end.

"There's scandal attached to her," Mercer said. The bitter way he spoke made Banallt look sharply at him. Mercer had a knowledge of Sophie's past that Banallt did not. He knew a different Sophie, a woman Banallt had but glimpsed through a door left ajar, then swiftly and decisively closed. He envied Mercer the knowledge. Deep waters here, treacherous to navigate. "Were you aware they eloped?"

"Evans mentioned something about that." Crowed about it. He'd eloped with an heiress. Some dull and starry-eyed seventeen-year-old who was his before they crossed the Scottish border into Gretna Green where the laws were so amenable to eloping couples. Even if they'd been caught, he'd have been forced to marry her. Respectable heiresses did not run off in the night with men to whom they were not married.

"It was a scandal here."

"Elopements generally are," Banallt said. Poor Sophie. She'd squandered her love and her money over the anvil. Tommy put her away in Kent and dedicated himself to spending seventy thousand pounds sterling as fast as he could.

"And then there was Evans's death," Mercer said, opening that distant door again and offering another glimpse of Sophie. Banallt was fiercely opposed to learning anything to Sophie's detriment. "If he was an acquaintance of yours, I'm sure you heard."

"No, actually. I've only recently returned from Paris. He died while I was away." His curt reply seemed to satisfy Mercer. Thank God.

When they got around the corner of the house and were heading for the stables, Mercer pulled up. Banallt did the same. He knew what was to come, and, like Mercer, he did not care to have the servants overhear. This was a discussion best had quickly and in privacy. One of the grooms came out of the barn but retreated when he saw them in conversation. Mercer leaned forward. "I know your reputation, my lord."

Banallt waited to hear if he was to be sent away. His mount, well-trained beast that it was, remained utterly still. There was no defense possible for his past. He'd been warned off more than once in his life, and by men with more reason than Mercer to be angry and fearful. But Mercer surprised him by meeting his eyes directly, and for that Banallt liked him.

"You've come to Duke's Head for the first time in your life." There was steel in Mercer's voice. Another groom turned a corner from the rear of the stables, glanced their direction, and disappeared inside the outbuilding. "People talk about a thing like that."

Banallt cocked his head in acknowledgment. Mercer had no choice but to connect Banallt's presence here with his sister. He was right to do so.

"I hope," Mercer said softly, "that scandal does not come down on us again."

Oh, well done. Mercer's oblique warning ranked among the best he'd ever had from a concerned relative. More than oblique enough to be taken for concern about Sophie's behavior rather than his. Banallt said, "My wife has been dead for some time now. I have no heir and no desire to see the title go elsewhere. A man in my circumstance must put his mind to marriage." That, he thought, was rather well done of him.

Mercer's green eyes were unforgiving. "From among the young ladies of Duke's Head?"

From where they'd stopped, Banallt could see servants moving inside the conservatory. He was amused that Mercer could not bring himself to ask the obvious. Well. He'd had enough of warnings and insinuations. He met Mercer's eyes. "I did not come to Duke's Head on a lark."

"I thought not."

Banallt took a breath. One never liked to show one's hand too soon. But there it was. "I intend to marry your sister."

Mercer's eyes widened, but he had something of Sophie's fortitude. "My lord." He inclined his head. "Just so we are perfectly clear, are you asking for my consent or my blessing?"

"Either will do." His heart thudded again. If only the matter could be resolved so easily. What he wanted, though, was for Sophie's too-intelligent brother to stay the hell out of his way.

Mercer leaned forward then resettled himself on his saddle. The leather creaked as he did. "They say you're likely to be raised in the peerage."

"I am quite content with my present title," he said. If he went from earl to marquess or even higher, then he was content with that, too.

Mercer frowned, and for an instant, Banallt saw him as the young man Sophie had spoken of. But only for an instant. Mercer returned to what he was: an impediment to something Banallt desired. "Suppose you marry Sophie."

"Yes," he murmured. "Suppose I do."

"Setting aside my conviction that such a marriage would make no one happy, least of all my sister, my nephew might be a marquess or perhaps even a duke."

"Or merely a lowly earl."

"With fifty or a hundred thousand a year in his pocket."

"Closer to a hundred thousand," Banallt said. Triumph flashed through him. He urged his horse toward the stable. "Console yourself, Mercer, by writing her a settlement to ease your conscience."

"I'm sure you've bought women for far less," Mercer said.

Well, yes, actually. But having Sophie as his wife was worth any price.

CHAPTER TWO

Banallt watched Sophie from the doorway of the conservatory. She stood with her weight on one leg, speaking to a white-haired servant, the butler, he surmised from the man's clothes and bearing. Mercer wasn't a dolt as so many brothers were about their sisters. Once they'd come to the house, Mercer had conveniently remembered business that would delay him in joining Sophie and Banallt for tea.

Someone at Havenwood was fond of roses. Beyond the beds of flowers, white, red, and pink, an orange tree grew toward the ceiling. She turned her head toward him. Her eyes widened when she realized he'd come without Mercer. Just that one look from her and all his pent-up and repressed feelings for her returned in force: his anticipation of her company; his delight in her intellect, her wit, her eyes; the way his body clenched when he was near her.

No, nothing at all had changed.

Banallt walked in. The butler said something to a footman, who nodded and picked up an empty tray. He had the feeling he'd just been thoroughly dissected by a pair of blue green eyes. And found wanting. The footman left on the butler's heels, leaving the field to him. His roguish instincts reared up. Such an enchanting setting for seduction.

The scent of roses hung in the air. If not for the gloomy sky, he might have imagined himself in a summer garden. Damask roses filled a Chinese vase on the table. An excellent touch, he thought.

The damask rose itself was farther away, blossoms open in the afternoon light. Watercress sandwiches were layered on a plate, while on another were cakes iced in green, pink, and blue and decorated with frosted yellow ribbons. Quite the grand step up from her previous situation.

"You should not be here," she said when he stopped just short of her. She walked away from the table and stood behind a bench that faced the lawns. He joined her, breathing in the scent of her hair. Outside, only slightly distorted by the glass, the garden gave way to lawns that sloped away from the house. Emerald green became lost in the mist twisting through the bare-branched trees far distant. She gripped the topmost rail of the bench.

"Is it possible you're still angry with me?" he asked. "After all this time?"

"Why have you come here?" She did not look at him.

He hated the fact that he could not interpret the emotion that flashed over her face before her expression stilled. "Castle Darmead has been in my family for more than five hundred years. It's time I visited." He took one of her hands in his and rubbed the inside of her wrist through her glove. She still didn't look at him, but she didn't object to the contact, either, and that was something.

"Why didn't you wait another five hundred years?" she said in a low voice. "Why now, Banallt, when I have only just begun to put my life back together?"

"I am a changed man, Sophie." He tugged on her hand and drew her with him to sit on the bench.

"I expected never to see you again." Her tongue flicked out to touch her lower lip. "I wanted never to see you again."

After they sat, he kept her hand in his and continued to draw a circle on her wrist. "I was out of the country when I heard Tommy had died."

"Yes. You were in Paris," she whispered. "With the Bourbon king." She bent her head and stared at the ground and the tops of her slippers, and Banallt found himself confronted with the naked back of her neck.

"What happened?" he asked.

"Didn't you hear?" She straightened but didn't look at him.

"Yes. But I should like to know the truth."

"It was very sudden," she said.

He wanted to ask if her heart was irreparably broken. Did she still grieve for her bastard of a husband? Instead, he said, "I am very sorry for your loss. I know you loved Tommy. And I'm sorry, Sophie, that I was not there to comfort you."

"I knew you'd been sent to Paris."

"When I returned to London," he said, still rubbing her wrist, but more slowly now, "I went to Rider Hall to pay my respects."

She looked at him, and, as ever, he felt a shock at the beauty of her eyes. Thick, thick lashes framed her almond eyes. And the color, my God, a lucid blue green, an astonishing shade sparked to life by her formidable wits. A man could lose his soul in her eyes. A man had. "Did you really?" she asked.

"The house was full of strangers, and you were gone."

"I was here," she said. "Home at last."

"So I learned." The silence stretched out, and Banallt was content to let this one settle between them for a while yet.

"I'm sure the new owners were surprised to see you at their doorstep," she said.

"They were alarmed," he replied. "They have three daughters."

She laughed, and that made him smile. When he first knew her, she rarely laughed. And when she had begun to, his heart had already long, long traveled far from anyplace safe. She turned toward him, still smiling. "Horrors," she said.

"You may well imagine."

She straightened his cravat and then pulled back. Too late. The gesture was done and fairly shouted between them. He kept his smile. Whatever she said, whatever lies she told him now, he knew the truth. She was not indifferent. He said, "Once, you consoled me when I was in need of sympathy. I promised myself that if ever you were in similar need, I would come to you instantly. To my eternal regret, when it happened, I could not."

Sophie touched his cheek with the tips of her fingers. "Oh, Banallt," she whispered. Her hand fell away from him before he could capture it. "How you break my heart."

"Sophie..." Her words echoed back to him. She had spoken them just so on that day. Exactly so. He was not over that heartbreak, and he found himself obliged to master himself for the second time in a single afternoon.

"You should not have come here."

"Your brother invited me."

She gave him a look. "How could he not when Duke's Head's most famous resident is at last at Castle Darmead?"

He leaned forward. The scent of orange water filled his senses. She was no longer married. Sophie was free, and he had been widowed for over two years, waiting, he knew in his soul, for Sophie.

They heard voices in the distance, and the moment for intimacy, if ever it had existed except in his imagination, passed. He moved away and leaned a shoulder against one of the wooden support beams. Cold air through the glass chilled his shoulder.

"Everyone says you came here to find a wife." She hurried on before he could say anything. "You should, you know. Marry again."

"The line must be secured before much longer. I have relatives whose chief occupation is calculating the odds of their inheritance."

"I'm sorry to hear that." She gave a shrug. "One's family should be a refuge from the world. As John was for me when Tommy died."

He let that pass, though he felt the unvoiced accusation despite knowing she didn't blame him. She hardly could. He'd not even been in Britain when Tommy died. "You should have written to me, Sophie." Yes, that was anger in his voice. He tamped down the reaction, but really, she had promised she would tell him if ever she was in need, and she hadn't done so. "You should have told me. I would have left Paris if you had written to me."

She swallowed. "His creditors descended," she said softly. "And I soon had nowhere to go. Nowhere but back here." The corner of her mouth tightened. She kept her gaze on him. "But you, you could go anywhere to find another wife."

"I do not intend to marry the wrong woman." He pressed his lips together. "Not again."

She let out a long breath. "The young ladies of Duke's Head will be as dazzled by you as I was by Tommy."

"Dazzled?" He pushed off the beam and took a step toward her. His recollection hadn't exaggerated her intensity, nor her fathomless eyes, nor the way she held herself so straight; all that was just as he'd dreamed every night since they parted so badly. And he hadn't misremembered how deeply he wanted her, either. God knows *that* had not changed. "You're not going to suggest I marry some girl fresh from the schoolroom, are you?"

"Why not?"

"I'm thirty-three years old. I've no interest in girls who can be dazzled."

Sophie tilted her head like a curious sparrow, a motion he knew for the deception it was. Well. She'd always been stubborn and stultifyingly good at hiding her emotions. "Are you asking me to make you a recommendation, my lord?"

He crossed his arms over his chest. "Why not?"

"Indeed," she said. "Why not? Shall I tell you why not?"

"Please do."

"Because there will be gossip, Banallt. Simply because of who and what you are."

He lifted his hands palms up. "Gossip is inevitable whenever a man like me makes it known he's looking to marry. Are you holding me to account for the gossip others spread? That's unfair of you."

"You are being willful, Banallt." She had to tilt her head back to look at him. He felt a rush of desire for her. Damn, but nothing at all had changed. "If you stay here, there will be gossip. Your reputation invites scandal. Your temperament assures it."

Rain spattered on the window glass. The gloomy day had at last descended into outright wet. The conservatory door opened, and Banallt grabbed Sophie's wrist to prevent her from walking away. "The hell it does," he said in a low voice.

"You forget," she said, "how well I know you."

"Sophie," he said in a low, dark voice. "I came here to marry you, not some silly girl I've never laid eyes on. You."

"Don't, Banallt," she said.

"I am not Tommy."

"No, you are not Tommy." She was angry now, and Sophie in anger was always magnificent. "You're worse than Tommy ever was."

"You're wrong." He continued to grip her hand. "And even if I was, that's done now. I'm not the man you knew."

"I am no longer young and no longer naive." She shook her head. "I won't marry a man who would never be faithful to me. I can't. I won't live like that again."

"Sophie."

"No." She lifted her chin to look into his face, and Banallt obliged her by lowering his. "I would rather die than marry the man my husband wished he could be."

And then Mercer came in and Banallt had no choice but to release her wrist, and Sophie spun on a heel and walked away. "I'm sorry, John," she said to her brother in a voice of awful deadness. "I've a terrible headache. Do forgive me."

All Banallt could do was watch her leave him. Again.

CHAPTER THREE

Three years earlier. Rider Hall, Kent,
AUGUST 17, 1811

Sophie's heart slammed against her ribs when the front door opened with a crash that rattled the windows. Her first thought was that someone had broken in. It was half past two in the morning, and the servants had gone home hours ago. Nan, the maid of all work and the only one who lived in, was fast asleep. Even if she was up and about, the girl was incapable of making that much noise.

Downstairs, something crashed to the floor. A painting falling from the wall?

"Damn me, I'm killed!" a man yelled. She heard more thrashing about and then the screech of something heavy being dragged or pushed across the marble floor.

She bowed her head to her desk and concentrated on steadying her breathing. Not a house cracker, but Tommy. Her husband, whom she had not seen in nearly a year. Her hands trembled as she put away her writing, hiding it deep in a bottom drawer. Tommy. After all these months apart. And instead of joy at his arrival, all she could think was, why?

"Where's a bloody lamp?" Tommy shouted from downstairs. But then his feet clomped and shuffled on the stairs. He was singing

"Whisky, You're the Devil," but the words didn't make any sense until he got to the chorus.

Her knuckles hit the ink bottle when she reached for the cap, and she lived a moment of pure terror while she juggled the cap and the bottle both. But no harm was done, except to her racing heart. She capped her ink and put away her pen without cleaning the nib. Those, too, went inside a drawer. Tommy's singing became louder and then stopped. He was home and in no fit condition. A welcome thread of anger pulsed in her.

"Sophie?"

The door rattled, covering the *clack* of the desktop closing. She turned the key just as the door to their room crashed open. Tommy swayed in the doorway, staring at the empty bed. He squinted. This time, she thought for just a moment, things would be different.

"Sophie? Where the devil have you got to?"

"Here, Tommy."

Her husband, as angelically handsome as ever, turned his head toward her. He squinted again. "Sophie?"

He wore a green coat and the gold watch she'd given him on their second anniversary. Several fobs she didn't recognize hung from it now. He had on soiled white gloves and a beaver hat. His neckcloth was askew. He wavered on his feet. Sophie hurried to him, but she was too late. He lurched toward the bed and tumbled face-first onto the mattress. At the bedside, she could smell the drink on him.

She was unable to rouse him. She felt a pang of guilt for thinking perhaps that was for the best. He was her husband, after all, and she ought to be glad he was here. With some effort, she got him onto his back and then levered his legs onto the mattress. She rescued his hat from the floor. His gold-buckled shoes were new and shined to a blinding polish. Was that what they wore in Town these days? When she unfastened his coat, she smelled a flowery perfume. Nothing at all had changed. She managed to undress him down to his shirt and breeches, and then she gave up. Tommy outweighed her by too much to hope she could move him. Besides, he was snoring now. He wasn't going to wake up until late tomorrow morning—with a headache and a murderous temper. She pulled the duvet over him and hoped he would not take a chill.

"Tommy!" cried another masculine voice, deeper than Tommy's and more commanding than Tommy's had been. The owner of that voice was in the hallway, for heaven's sake. "You whoreson, where are you? It's bloody dark here."

Sophie tightened the sash of her dressing gown, picked up her lamp, and left her room to find the devil himself had taken possession of her hallway. A man with startlingly pale skin stood with his arm draped around the shoulder of a woman whose gown glittered with silver tissue. The woman put an ungloved hand to her blond hair and smiled at Sophie with eyes whose vagueness might have been due to exhaustion. Or drink.

As for the man, the words *cold hauteur* must have been coined directly from his face. One black eyebrow rose when he saw her. He was about Tommy's age. Late twenties, possibly thirty, and pale, though not from ill health. He seemed paler still because hair the color of ink hung thick about his temples, long enough to reach his collar. She'd thought Tommy's clothes were fine, but this man's put his to shame. Tall and broad shouldered, he wore clothes so beautifully cut he fair hurt her eyes. The woman tucked herself tightly against his side.

"What have we here?" the man said, laughing into his companion's neck. He turned his head again and looked her up and down not once but twice. "A wee faerie?"

"No," Sophie said.

He studied her some more. "My God, you're a dainty little thing. Why is Tommy hiding you away here?"

"You are under a misapprehension, sir—"

And then, just like that, he stood straight. His arm fell from the woman's shoulder. "Ah," he said in a different sort of voice. "The fog of Bordeaux has been penetrated at last." He closed his eyes and kept them shut to at least the count of three. When he opened them, his voice was as cold as his eyes. "Mrs. Thomas Evans, I presume?"

"Yes." She was near enough now to see his eyes. Black rimmed his irises, the color bleeding slowly into a solid and unrelenting gray eerily flat of expression, or rather, she thought, the color, like silver gone to tarnish, made them impervious to reflection of his interior thoughts.

"Tommy failed to mention his wife lived here."

If she'd been in a better mood, Sophie would have laughed. The man actually sounded personally affronted to have found her here. "Since my husband did not warn me of his arrival, let alone that he would be bringing guests, we are equally inconvenienced, wouldn't you agree?"

Some emotion, quite possibly irritation, flickered over his face but was quickly tucked away behind the coldness of his eyes. "Touché, Mrs. Evans. May I ask where your esteemed husband has gone?"

She pictured Tommy, flat on his back and gently snoring. "He is…asleep, sir."

"Ah."

"I am at a disadvantage," she said, lifting her lamp. His hair flashed blue black in the light. "You know who I am, while I have no names to put to you or your companion."

He bowed, though Sophie had the impression he had to concentrate to perform the motion. So he *was* drunk. "Lord Banallt, at your service, ma'am."

Her heart stuttered at the familiar name. *Lord Banallt.* The universe was perverse indeed. Of all the noblemen Tommy might have brought home, he'd brought this one. A man who could buy and sell Tommy twice over. A man whose name she'd grown up hearing and about whom she had made up all manner of silly, romantic fantasies. "The Earl of Banallt?" she asked. As if he could be any other.

"The very same, ma'am." Lord Banallt put his arm around the woman again and walked her away to whisper in her ear. Sophie's hearing, however, was excellent, and Lord Banallt's voice was not as low as he likely fancied. "Forgive me, kitten. Maeve," he murmured. Sophie heard the drink in his low, soft voice. But with that smoky note, no wonder Maeve was melting against him. "You cannot stay here." She made a sound of protest and squirmed into his embrace. "My love, my heart. She's Tommy's *wife.* I'm desolate, I promise you." He kissed the top of her bare shoulder. "King will drive you to the nearest inn."

Sophie's practical nature took over. "It's too late at night to send her away, my lord."

Lord Banallt lifted his head and looked at her, surprise etched on his face. And yet she saw nothing in his eyes. Nothing at all. She shuddered to think of the kind of life that gave a man such empty eyes.

She walked past them and opened the door to one of the other bedrooms. "You'll both need rooms, of course," she said.

"You are most gracious, Mrs. Evans." Lord Banallt bowed.

"Separate rooms," she said to forestall any chance he thought she condoned *that* sort of behavior under her roof. "Ma'am?" She looked at Maeve and prayed she would not object to being separated from her lover. What was Tommy thinking, bringing Lord Banallt and this woman here to Rider Hall? But then she remembered the perfume on Tommy's clothes, and she was angry twice over. "My apologies. There was not time to air the room." She went inside with Maeve. The earl followed, which worried her. She had no intention of letting him stay. While she lit another lamp, however, Lord Banallt made himself useful and started a fire in the hearth. She was surprised he knew how. "I'll send my girl to help you, ma'am," she told Maeve.

"Thank you," said Maeve. She spoke in a cultured voice, in the accent of a woman who'd been respectably reared, yet she was certainly not sober. Lord Banallt had brought an expensive whore with him. Into her home. Her heart contracted to think of Tommy spending time in the company of a man who kept women like Maeve in gowns that cost the very moon and stars. "You're kind, Mrs. Evans," she said.

"You're welcome," Sophie said. She hated that she sounded stiff and pompous, too.

Maeve reached for Banallt's hand as he passed her on his way from the hearth. He stopped. "Banallt," she said in a voice that made his name both a protest and an enticement.

"Have a pleasant night," he said while Sophie opened the cedar trunk at the foot of the bed and took out two extra blankets. It was

August, but the room hadn't had a fire for weeks and the air was not only cold but musty. She could not help the staleness, but the cold she could remedy.

When she looked up from the trunk, Lord Banallt had his arms around Maeve's waist, and Maeve was plastered against him. The woman ran her fingers through Banallt's thick, black hair. In response, he bent his head and brushed his lips across hers. Sophie saw his mouth open. She looked away, but not before his hands tightened around the woman's waist. And not before she saw him sway on his feet. Her belly tightened as he made a low sound far too intimate for a moment that was not private.

Sophie closed the chest. Loudly. The couple broke apart, and she pretended she'd not seen anything. She placed the blankets on the bed. "If you'll come with me, my lord."

Banallt followed her out, one hand smoothing his hair. Nan, Sophie's maid of all work, stood in the hall, a cloak drawn tight around her shoulders and gloves on her hands. She held up her lamp. "Mrs. Evans?" she said. Her attention went to Lord Banallt and her mouth dropped open.

"Thank goodness you're up, Nan." She smiled with relief. "I don't suppose anyone could sleep through that racket. My husband is here unexpectedly, with Lord Banallt and—"

"Mrs. Andrews," Banallt said from nearer to her than she'd thought he was.

"Can you do for Mrs. Andrews?" Nan was twenty years old, a pretty girl and utterly reliable. Without her assistance, managing Rider Hall would have been an overwhelming responsibility. "She's just in there, and I expect she needs assistance."

"Yes, ma'am." Nan's eyes constantly shifted to Lord Banallt. So-phie now had a new worry. Nan was a very pretty girl. Too pretty to find work at other homes where the ladies of the house preferred less temptation before their husbands. Sophie shot Banallt a look and was not reassured.

"Nan," Banallt said. Oh yes indeed, he had noticed Nan and her pretty face. Nan, in the act of knocking on Maeve's door, froze at the command in his voice. "My valet is in the barn attending the horses. His name is King. You will recognize him from his crooked nose. He's ugly as sin but putty in the hands of a pretty girl. Give him a smile, and tell him he's required after all. Direct him to my room, if you would."

Nan curtseyed. "Milord."

Sophie opened a second door farther down the hall—inconveniently far, she hoped as she went in. She found a lamp and lit it while, again, Lord Banallt bent over the hearth to start the fire. "At least you make yourself useful," she said.

"I've no desire to freeze to death."

She pulled sheets off the furniture. Rider Hall so seldom had guests that Sophie kept most of the rooms closed up. Done with the fire, Banallt stood at the grate. He put a hand on the mantel to steady himself. She wondered how much he'd had to drink. To think this was the man she had once imagined as the hero of so many stories. "Sit down, my lord, before you fall and break your head."

He threw himself onto a chair and let his legs sprawl out. "I'm foxed," he said slowly. "More foxed than I thought." He ran his hands through his hair. "My head's spinning."

"Overindulgence will do that."

"You have a very tart tongue."

"You're drunk."

"Well," he said. "And so."

"I disapprove of spirits."

"Whereas I cannot live without them." He let his head fall back against the chair. "I am not a happy drunk, Mrs. Evans. I hope that tomorrow you will have the kindness to recall nothing of my condition."

She stopped with her arms full of sheets. "Leave Nan alone, and I'll have no cause for complaint."

"She is pretty." He nodded to himself. "And she has a lively eye. I wonder that you hired her."

"Tommy is never here." She dropped the sheets onto a chair.

Once again he looked her up and down. His eyes were unpleasantly cold. "You're not a'tall what I expected."

"A crone?" she said.

He smiled, and it transformed his face, giving it all the warmth he'd previously lacked. He took her breath. "Bent over and crippled in both legs."

"With a long, hooked nose." She skimmed a finger along her nose, and Banallt's gaze followed her motion. "Pie-eyed and shrewish, too."

"But famously deep in the pockets."

"Yes," she said. "Tommy has described me to the last penny."

He clasped his hands on his head and stared

hard at her. "I am not too drunk to fathom the *entendre* in those words of yours. You're a clever girl," he said slowly. "Not a girl. A woman. A clever woman." He shook his head. "No good ever comes of clever women."

She wanted to laugh. To think here sat the man whom she'd given the role of knight in shining armor! Her imagination was far more pleasant than reality. As she'd done for Maeve, she took blankets from the chest at the foot of the bed. He stood again and walked to the fireplace where he leaned an elbow on the mantel and rested his chin on his palm, facing sideways so that he watched her. Sophie felt their rapport slip into intimacy, as if they were lovers who'd parted amicably and were now comfortable in friendship. Well. Was he not the very man she'd imagined meeting since she was ten and overheard her mother telling some visitor that, yes, the Earl of Banallt owned property just two miles distant? How strange that she should meet him now. So many years later and so far from home.

"I continue to struggle, Mrs. Evans, with the notion that you are Tommy's wife. You were described to me as—well, nothing like you."

"You said yourself you've had too much to drink. I expect tomorrow you'll see me clearly and find your opinion in accord with my husband's."

"I'm not that foxed, ma'am." He considered her again with a slow perusal she found more than faintly insulting. And—something else she couldn't name. "Are you certain you're not an imposter?"

"Quite."

"You've the finest eyes I've ever seen on a woman. Bar none. And that, madam, is saying something. Your eyes are lovely."

"Thank you." She was in the process of spreading one of the blankets on the bed, and while she was doing that, she discovered he'd moved toward her without making a sound.

"Mrs. Evans." He spoke in a different sort of voice. A voice that sent a shiver up her spine. It was the voice he'd used to whisper to

Maeve. The kind of voice Tommy never used with her. She froze with one hand on the edge of the blanket. "Perhaps," he said in that caressing, silken voice, "you would care to join me in this lovely bed?"

She turned around, the backs of her legs touching the mattress. "I am a married woman."

"And I am a married man." He crossed his arms over his chest and looked at her with those awful eyes, gray with that odd rim of black. She felt quite certain she would never be free of the heat of his gaze. "What could be more natural than for us to be lovers while I am here?"

"You've had too much to drink," she said.

He smiled. "Yes," he said. His voice fell, and it wasn't deliberate; it just was. "But I assure you, it won't affect my performance." Banallt touched her cheek, and she slid away from him, unpleasantly aware of the intensity of his eyes on her. He gripped the bedpost and leaned sideways, trapping her. "Darling, don't go."

"Let me pass." She stared at him. Heavens, he'd trapped her in the darkness of his eyes, and there wasn't any way out. His eyes enfolded her in layers of silver tarnish.

"Say yes," he said. His voice fell to a whisper. "Let's have a wicked, wicked affair while I am here." He took a step closer.

With her heart galloping out of her chest, Sophie slapped him as hard as she could.

CHAPTER FOUR

Havenwood,
MARCH 11, 1815

N apoleon has escaped from Elba."

Sophie gaped at her brother. From his expression she knew the matter was serious. She mentally repeated the words to herself before the meaning penetrated. "Oh my dear heavens. When? How?"

John clasped his hands behind his back and paced. "Does it matter? He's believed to be making his way to Paris. He may be there even now." He watched her sideways as he walked. He looked so like their mother, intent and lovely and so earnest about his feelings, Sophie felt her throat close off with tears. "What matters, Sophie, is I am needed in London. Even if I were not wanted in the House, Vedaelin wishes me to be in London."

"Of course," she said calmly. The Duke of Vedaelin was John's patron, the man who had gotten him started in his political life. John was a member of Parliament now, thanks to the duke. "You must be in Town."

He stopped in front of her chair and frowned at her. She kept her knees together, hands clasped on her lap. "I know this inconveniences you, Sophie."

"I hardly think, John, that the escape of Bonaparte is an inconvenience only to me."

Her brother looked away and then back. "A bachelor alone, trying to entertain?" He drew in a breath. She knew what he was getting at, but John needed to come around to things in his own time. "I shall bungle everything. But you, Sophie, you can manage a household. Havenwood's never run better since you came back."

She kept her face still. "I should be delighted to be of assistance to you, John."

A look of relief crossed his face but was quickly replaced by calculation. As if he'd ever been in doubt that she'd go to London with him. "We'll leave first thing tomorrow morning."

"Of course. I'll see to everything."

"Excellent, Sophie," he said. She rose, expecting John to move. He didn't. "Banallt will be in London." His gaze pierced.

Did he think she would refuse to go? Or that she didn't realize Lord Banallt would be in London at the same time they were? As if they would travel in the same circle as the Earl of Banallt. "London is a large city. I doubt we shall see him."

"And if we do?"

She shrugged. Banallt knew her feelings. If they should happen to see each other, she believed he would respect them. "Then we shall say good day to each other. Perhaps remark on the weather. And that will be that."

"Sophie," John said softly. "What happened between you two?"

"Nothing." And if it had, what then? She was under no obligation to tell John anything about the years she'd lived cut off from her family.

"A man like him doesn't come to a village like Duke's Head because he fancies a change of scenery."

"He came to see Darmead, of course."

John touched her cheek. "No one lives a perfect life."

She didn't want to be reminded of all the ways her life had been imperfect. "I imagine not."

"I remember when you were a brat in pigtails, and all too soon a foolish girl."

Sophie pulled her head back, and John's hand fell away from her cheek. Anger welled up, but she had no choice except to choke back every bitter word that leaped to her tongue. If she lived to be a hundred, Duke's Head would still be gossiping about her. *See that old woman? Yes, that one. She eloped, don't you know, with a fortune hunter. By the time her father caught up, it was too late. A scandal. Oh yes.*

"You grew up," John said. You were eight years married and are now a widow. You still look seventeen to me, but I accept you are a grown woman with a right to her own mind and her own mistakes."

"I never, ever betrayed my husband."

"And yet Banallt loves you."

She rolled her eyes when what she wanted to do was jump to her feet and shout at him. "He doesn't," she replied calmly. "Lord Banallt is incapable of that emotion, I assure you. He only ever took an interest in me because he was bored. And the only reason he didn't lose interest just as quickly was that I told him no. That, famously, is something rare for him to hear."

"After all this time, Sophie?"

"All this time, John, and I am still as you remember. Plain and quite uninteresting to a man who has been to bed with every beauty ever to set foot in England." Anger choked her, at John and at Banallt and at her father for returning her letters unopened. Never read. Her departure never mourned. "Banallt cannot fathom how someone like me would refuse him. It's a game with him, and all he can think is that he must win."

"You're mistaken."

"I know him, John." She clenched her hands into fists. "No one knows him better. He doesn't love me. He just wants to have won."

John said nothing for too long, but Sophie knew better than to speak. She'd only make her unintended revelation even more significant to him. "Then I hope your paths do not cross."

"It makes no difference to me." It was a lie, but as long as John believed her, all would be well.

Organizing the removal kept Sophie up until long past midnight. John's valet and Sophie's maid, Flora, left at dawn with the wagon loaded with their trunks. She and John departed shortly after ten. The remainder of the trunks and a groom with John's horses were to follow later in the day. The Duke of Vedaelin had secured them a house in Mayfair. She found when they arrived that afternoon that it was a narrow two-story building on Henrietta Street.

They located their rooms, washed away the dirt of travel, confirmed the cook knew they would dine in, and then John went out to call on the duke. Sophie stayed behind to oversee setting the house to rights. The house came furnished, but Vedaelin's taste, if that's what the decor represented, was firmly in the previous century.

Downstairs was a front and back parlor, an office for her brother, and a dining room; below, the kitchen and pantry; and above, rooms for her and John, with two guest rooms. Across the street was a mews. They could keep their carriage in Town, and horses, too. At some point, she went through the cards and invitations already left for them. There was nothing from Banallt. How odd that she'd even think of him leaving a card when her acquaintance with the earl was so thoroughly over. She doubted he even knew she was in Town.

She separated the cards and invitations by occasion, noted them in her personal calendar, arranged the cards chronologically then alphabetically, and met with the cook to discuss supper. She had tea alone, as John sent word he was having tea with the duke. In her room, she fell asleep reading the *Court Journal.*

She was fast asleep when John came home. It was on his instruction that no one woke her. She was still asleep when there came a knock on the front door.

CHAPTER FIVE

Number 26 Henrietta Street, London,
MARCH 12, 1815

I s Mrs. Evans at home? Banallt asked the butler who answered the door at Henrietta Street. Ah yes, the redoubtable Charles, with his luxurious head of white hair. Down from Havenwood with his employers.

"Who, may I ask, is calling?"

From the man's expression he knew too well who Banallt was. He suspected as well that Sophie was home. Whether she would see him was another matter. He handed the butler a card. "Gwilym, Earl of Banallt."

The butler opened the door. "Will you wait while I see if she's in?"

"Yes, thank you." He walked in. Truth to tell, he was anxious. His feelings for Sophie were utterly and incomprehensibly unchanged. From the moment he'd heard she and her brother were in London, he had been unable to think of anything but her. Her dismissal of him at Havenwood had failed to cure his affliction. He followed the butler to the front parlor, a dreary room of faded blue and yellow. The only spot of color in the room came from an extravagant bouquet of white roses in a red vase. Roses he had not sent. A card leaned against the vase. Vedaelin had sent the roses. What business had he sending roses to a woman half his age?

Welcome to London, Mrs. Evans. What was the duke after?

He had no idea if Sophie would agree to see him. She was here. In London. As was he. Their town house overlooked a small park, well tended and colorful with early spring flowers on a rare day of blue skies. Voices from upstairs had him turning away from the window. Masculine voices. Footsteps followed, coming closer until, at last, they approached the parlor where he waited like some lovesick boy.

"My lord," said John Mercer. He came in and closed the door behind him. "Good day." He walked to the center of the room. He did not sit down. "What a surprise to see you. I've not been in Town twenty-four hours."

"Mercer." He kept his back to the window. Was Mercer going to pretend Sophie hadn't come with him? Ridiculous. "Is your sister not at home, then?"

Mercer indicated a chair. "Please, my lord, sit."

He raised one eyebrow. Damn. "Ought I?"

"Suit yourself." He had his sister's eyes, but for the color. Mercer's eyes were dark green, but the shape and thick lashes were the same as Sophie's. Mercer focused his gaze on the floor, gathering himself, Banallt fancied. Mercer took a breath, let it out, and lifted his head. "My lord. May I speak frankly to you?"

"If you must."

"Sophie is my sister. My only relation. It is my duty to look after her. When you came to Havenwood and professed to have fallen in love with her, I confess I imagined you meant the girl who ran away with Thomas Evans and broke all our hearts."

"Then you were incorrect."

"She's a girl no longer, I'll allow you that. And yet I think no two could be more unsuited than you and my sister." The edge of his mouth quirked. "It's not her you claimed to love, but some other woman. A woman I don't know and never did. And still don't." He threw himself on a chair, legs sprawled, one hand clutching his hair. "I don't know how best to protect her. You did not see her after you left Havenwood."

"A dilemma for you, to be sure."

"It was worse, my lord, almost worse, than when she first came to Havenwood. After her husband's death." Mercer's gaze was unfocused. Obviously he was privately recalling those days. "She was...so altered then I hardly knew her."

"She was very much in love with her husband."

"I know."

"She mourns him still," Banallt said. "I do understand."

"Actually, I don't think you do." Mercer sat forward, forearms on his spread-apart knees, immune, it seemed, to his glare. "You haven't any idea what she was like as a girl, do you?"

Banallt said nothing. Sophie had told him almost nothing of her childhood.

"Always laughing. She was a happy child. Did she happen to mention to you how much time she spent at Castle Darmead?" Mercer waited a heartbeat. "I thought not. She'd badger the caretakers for information and come home full of facts about the castle and its history. The history of your family." He smiled fondly. "And then she'd work all those facts into stories. No reason she'd tell you about that, but she did. The earls of Banallt always loomed large in her tales. I used to try to trip her up in her facts, but I never succeeded. Eventually I gave up trying. Ripping good stories, too." He sat up straight. "I'm telling you this so that you'll understand why she would be more susceptible to you than anyone else. To your title in particular. Don't misunderstand me, I mean the fact that you are the Earl of Banallt. If you were Prinny himself she wouldn't care half so much."

"Your sister is quite the democrat." He was certain where their conversation was headed. But he did not intend to be so easily discouraged.

"My point, sir, is that however it was you met, you couldn't possibly live up to her girlhood ideal of the absent master of Castle Darmead."

"You underestimate your sister if you think her unable to separate childhood imagination from a flesh-and-blood man."

His eyes narrowed. "Whatever you were to her, I think we both know you didn't come close to being her knight in shining armor."

Banallt barked a laugh. "Me, a knight in armor? She never thought that of me."

"Perhaps not. Yet I know seeing you again has hurt her." He stood up. "My sister has had more than her share of unhappiness, my lord. More than enough. What happened between you two I don't care to know. What I do know is that Sophie assured me she would be unaffected should we have the misfortune of meeting you in London." He lifted a hand. "Hear me out. She insists that's so, but I don't believe her."

Banallt made sure his expression revealed nothing. Mercer looked at him, his curls wild from his hand scrubbing through his hair. Mercer continued. "I want Sophie's happiness, my lord. Do you understand? She deserves that after Evans. What a debacle that was. At least three people saw her the night she ran away with Evans.

Three. And no one said a word. No one warned us, and my father didn't realize she'd grown up and needed watching. To him, she was still his little girl. He never dreamed she felt that way about Evans."

"I think," Banallt said, "you are unaware of how hurt your sister was by her family's refusal to see her." Mercer wasn't blameless in Sophie's unhappiness. "Her husband's neglect she dealt with in her own fashion. But the letters returned to her from Havenwood? Unopened?" Mercer cocked his head, assessing what it meant that Banallt knew about the letters and how she'd felt. "She never recovered from that."

Mercer looked at him from under his lashes. "That's unfair."

"It's unfair of you to judge what you never witnessed. And you, Mr. Mercer, never witnessed your sister's married life. Nor her devotion to an undeserving husband, nor her private heartbreaks. Nor my friendship with her." He was angry but managed to maintain a smooth and even tone. "Which, I do assure you, is all there was between us."

"She turned you away, my lord. Don't overestimate my influence over her. I assure you, I have little to none. I can't make her accept you if she doesn't love you."

"She's a grown woman, not a girl. She can make her own decisions."

"You will only cause her pain." Mercer rocked on his heels. "I'm convinced of that. And I won't have her hurt." He glanced at the flowers. "Not when there's hope she'll meet a decent man."

His heart stilled with icy certainty that their conversation was now headed in a direction he did not wish to follow. "Am I being asked to step aside, or told to?"

Mercer crossed his arms over his chest. "Perhaps you think that during my sister's marriage, we knew nothing of her life. That is far from the case. Your name was connected with Tommy Evans's. I followed your life of scandal because I followed Tommy's. I have more than a small suspicion of the reason Sophie came home so altered. And that reason is closely connected with your name."

"I am not responsible for the state of their marriage. He made her unhappy long before I met her. Long before I met Tommy Evans, as well. I assure you, I am not responsible for his decision to elope with your sister. I didn't know the man until after he was married." Because, quite frankly, Tommy Evans hadn't had the money to enter his circle until after he'd secured Sophie's fortune. "Neither did I influence his decision to live in London while she remained at Rider Hall."

"And yet, as I say, she refused you at Havenwood, my lord."

"Your point?"

He shrugged. "Perhaps you do love her. I can't know what's in your heart. But she does not love you. If she did, she would not have turned you away."

"You say she is not unaffected by me. That observation is correct. When I went to Havenwood, I had not seen your sister in quite a long time." He chose his words carefully. "Not seen nor corresponded with. Am I to have but one chance to convince her of my desire to make her my countess?" He looked Mercer in the eye. "Is that a connection you can afford to turn away?"

Mercer's eyes turned hard. "My lord, I cannot with any conscience at all support your pursuit of her."

He, too, looked at the roses. "Have I a rival already?" he asked.

"No one who's declared himself, if that's what you mean."

Well. And so. He wasn't blockheaded about who this potential rival might be. "I'm to be thrown over for Vedaelin? Yes," he said bitterly. "An earl in the hand may well be thrown over for the prospect of a duke."

"When you came to Havenwood, I thought you two had quarreled." Mercer looked at him from under his lashes. "As lovers sometimes will."

"Sophie was never my lover." And not for want of his desiring that it should be so.

"And yet you make free with her given name." Mercer's eyes flashed. "You look at her as if you want to devour her. With a rake's eyes. Do you think me so rustic I am easily fooled by London manners and a lofty title?"

"This is absurd."

"I was willing to let you apologize and put yourself into her good graces. You did not. Having seen firsthand her reaction to you, I believe you cannot."

"That's something your sister ought to decide." Banallt smothered his outrage. Mercer was a reasonable man, he knew that. As calculating as he was himself. Moreover, he believed he was acting in his sister's best interest. And that, ironically, they had in common. "You say you know she's not the girl who eloped with Tommy Evans. I say you don't understand the woman she is."

"I hope, sir, that if you meet my sister socially, you will do nothing to upset her."

Banallt realized then that Mercer expected him to bring up Fidelia. He should. He ought to bring to bear every weapon at his command. Before Sophie he would not have hesitated. Now?

Threatening Mercer in such a fashion was, alas, too despicable. "We are bound to meet; you know that."

"But you are not bound to acknowledge your acquaintance with her."

He drew himself up. He'd had enough of this arrogant puppy. "That's presumptuous of you, Mercer."

"Lord Banallt." Mercer scowled. "I very much regret to tell you that you are not welcome here. Nor will you be if you call again. I won't have her miserable, and misery is all she will ever have from you." He walked to the parlor door and opened it. "Good day, my lord."

CHAPTER SIX

Cavendish Square, London,
MARCH 14, 1815

The duke's home on Cavendish Square was every bit as grand as Sophie expected. The ducal coronet was carved in the stone above the door. The entranceway was white marble with columns and a staircase to the upper floors. An enormous arrangement of roses spread a delicious scent through the air. A butler dressed in black from his coat to his breeches answered the door and gravely accepted John's coat and hat and Sophie's coat and muff. "This way, Mr. Mercer, ma'am."

They followed a liveried footman into the depths of the house. The servant wore a gray wig and forest green livery worked with gold flowers and silver braid. His heeled shoes clicked on the marble floor. The murmur of conversation grew louder as they proceeded down the corridor.

"John," she whispered when they were shown into a salon with angels cavorting on the ceiling. She came to a halt inside the doorway. Brilliantly dressed men and women filled the room. "You said this was a small party. An intimate one."

Her brother patted her arm. "It is small." He laughed. "For His Grace. There'll be even more guests after we've dined."

"There must be forty people here." In all her life, she'd never been at a party half as large. Before her marriage, she'd been too young to attend her father's gatherings. Judging from the bills that came her way, Tommy did his entertaining in London.

"You see?" His mouth turned up at the corners. "An intimate supper." He raised a hand to acknowledge someone across the room. "Let's find Vedaelin and get you formally introduced, Sophie."

Sophie pushed away her nerves and smiled. She knew the value of an entrance, and while she didn't expect to make a grand one, neither did she wish to be seen as timid or embarrassed. John needed her to make a good impression, and she intended to do so. Her gown was more than appropriate for a woman of her age and station in life, and John had brought their mother's diamonds from the vault at Havenwood. Her mother had let her wear them once and they'd made her feel beautiful. She wasn't an antidote by any means, but she had almost nothing of her mother's looks about her. At least the diamonds helped.

The duke's guests had separated into distinct groups. In one corner of the room several people were gathered around a gentleman playing the mandolin. He was quite good. Others sat on chairs or sofas; still others stood in conversation, some serious, from the looks of it, others not in the least. One day she would write a story in which her heroine came to London. Her villain would be first seen leaning against a wall, examining every female to enter with a haughty expression.

"There he is. What luck! With everyone you ought to meet." John's hand tightened on hers, and she hung back at the pressure of his grip. "This is important, Sophie," he said. "Most of the men you're about to meet run Britain." He touched the tip of her nose. "So, Sophie, please. On your best behavior. No outrageous opinions."

"John, I'm not a child who needs to be reminded of her manners."

"Your Grace," John said when they reached a group of gentlemen standing at the side of the parlor. Sophie scanned the gentlemen for John's patron. She knew the Duke of Vedaelin was fifty-six. She imagined him gray haired or nearly so, soft about the middle, but with a gravitas to tell the world he was a duke. She would not have been surprised to find he still wore a wig. So many older gentlemen did. None of the men here wore wigs, and the portly ones—there were a few—were too young, too old, or not grand enough. She'd looked up the duke in *DeBrett's* months ago when John first began talking to her of his political ambitions, and so she knew His Grace was the third duke, a widower with three sons. His heir was finishing at Oxford, the second son just beginning, and the third recently commissioned to the navy.

"Ah," said a voice from somewhere in the back of the group. "Is that you at last, Mercer?"

The men closest to John and her moved aside, and a whip-thin man whose dark hair was tipped with gray came forward. He had swarthy skin, as if somewhere in his past was an Italian or perhaps a Spaniard. He was a slender man with dark eyes. He had reached that age, that maturity of life in which he seemed ageless as older men so often were. They clasped hands. "Yes, Your Grace," John said. He tugged on Sophie's arm. "I've brought my sister to meet you, as promised."

"Mrs. Evans," the duke said. He reached for her gloved hand. She curtseyed, and when she'd straightened, the duke continued to hold her hand. He didn't look anywhere near his age.

"Your Grace. Thank you so much for the lovely flowers you sent to Henrietta Street."

Vedaelin's smile was warm yet did little to dispel his penetrating gaze. He reminded Sophie of a hawk, and a hungry one at that. John was six feet tall, and Vedaelin was only an inch or two shorter. He was decidedly handsome. "You are the sister of whom I've heard so much."

"Yes, Your Grace," John said. He made the formal introduction and Sophie curtseyed, again, aware the other gentlemen among the duke's companions were staring, some with open curiosity.

"Mrs. Evans," Vedaelin said, taking her hand in both of his. The lines of his face bespoke experience, a man who'd seen too much of life not to understand his place in it and the consequences of the power he wielded. "Shame on you, Mercer. You never mentioned your sister was a beauty."

"What?" John's eyebrows headed for the ceiling. He grinned. "Do you mean Sophie? My sister?" He ended on a note of feigned incredulity.

"Of course I mean your sister. A more compelling woman I've never met." He shot an amused glance at John then returned his attention to her, continuing to hold Sophie's hand. "Or have you another beautiful sister hidden away somewhere?"

Rather than greet her and let her go, which Sophie had expected, Vedaelin brought her into the circle of gentlemen. There were more than she'd initially thought. Two or three had been standing in the shadow of a column, and she simply hadn't seen them when they approached. Her heart tripped, because one of the gentlemen was Banallt, and he was watching her intently.

Her reaction to seeing him shook her confidence. John looked at her, and she realized she'd taken a sharp breath. "What is it?" he asked softly.

"Nothing." Their meeting again was bound to happen. She just hadn't thought it would be so soon. She didn't believe in Banallt's disappointment over her, if even he had been so affected. All the same, her heart beat faster. His effect on her had not altered. Vedaelin began to introduce her.

Male eyes moved from her brother to her. She kept her smile. The contrast between her and John was striking, she knew. He so tall and dark with his curls and green eyes, and she... well. She was quite the opposite. John had always been the beauty of the family.

Though her attention stayed on the duke, or the man to whom he introduced her, Sophie remained aware of Banallt. She'd never seen him in a social setting before. Her previous interactions with him had been exclusively at Rider Hall. He looked splendid and very much at ease.

The earl wore buff trousers tonight, cashmere and very daring. His burgundy coat was cut rather long in the back. His waistcoat was striped gold and cream, his black cravat tied *à la Mathematique* across pure white linen. He'd already tugged on it enough to destroy the symmetry required of the knot. That about him had not changed.

Cabinet ministers, nearly all of them. One of the gentlemen was Major William Haggart of the Guard Dragoons. He was, Sophie knew, a close friend of Banallt's and had already shaken hands with John. He leaned heavily on an ebony cane as he waited to be introduced to her. He'd been wounded at the battle of Salamanca and was lucky, Sophie knew from Banallt first, but later from John, to have kept his leg.

"Major Haggart," she said. "Pleased to meet you."

He bowed over her hand, leaning heavily on his cane as he did so. "I assure you, the pleasure is mine, Mrs. Evans. We admire your brother immensely, you know."

Banallt was the last to be introduced.

She curtseyed to Banallt after Vedaelin presented her. She spoke without any inflection to betray the pounding of her heart. As always, his eyes trapped hers with that dark silver gaze. He did not reach for her hand, nor did she offer hers. Best not to. "A pleasure to see you again, my lord."

He bowed, a slight nod of his head, as cold and haughty as she'd expected of the duke. Seeing Banallt like this, among his peers, disturbed her. It made her feel she'd misjudged him, or that he'd deceived her all this time, pretending to be barely acceptable company rather than a man others held in esteem. "Mrs. Evans."

What a cold, cold voice. She was not used to that from him, either. Silence fell, one of those awkward moments that sometimes happen. She was too aware of John watching her and of Banallt's gaze on her, and she was deathly afraid she'd say the wrong thing. Banallt's face might lack any semblance of warmth, but that didn't stop him from being outrageously handsome. "Are you well, my lord?" she asked.

"Yes, ma'am," he said. He looked bored. Excessively bored. And why wouldn't the infamous Lord Banallt be bored by a woman as undistinguished as she was? She felt she was confronted by a stranger. The man she'd known at Rider Hall was not this man. Not at all. She turned away only to be stopped by a question. "I know you've always wanted see the City. Are you enjoying London now that you're here at last, Mrs. Evans?"

For all his cold demeanor toward her, he wasn't going to pretend they had a small acquaintance. Just as well. Others always knew more than one expected. Best not to make a secret of it. His association with Tommy had been well-known. She turned back. "I've not seen much of Town, but yes, thank you."

She was glad to quickly find herself in the hands of Mrs. Llewellyn, Banallt's cousin by marriage, who was Vedaelin's hostess tonight. Now that was an interesting discovery. Were Banallt and Vedaelin so close, then? Mrs. Llewellyn introduced her to several people, including her daughter and Lord Banallt's goddaughter, Miss Fidelia Llewellyn. She was young, not twenty, and breathtaking. Her hair was raven's wing black, her eyes sky blue, and her skin had the same striking paleness as Banallt's. She was perfect. Everything Sophie was not.

Before she quite knew it, Sophie was left to her own devices. John had been absorbed into Banallt's group, and Mrs. Llewellyn had left her with several other women who were organizing aid for sailors wounded in the war. She was not, she discovered, very good at the sort of small talk necessary for a gathering like this. The weather as a subject of conversation went only so far, and not far at that. She felt separate, ill at ease, a foreigner who did not speak the language. Some of the people she'd met had known her late husband, and she didn't think she was wrong that they thought the less of her because of it.

Not once did she lose her sense of where Banallt was. Never. Before long she gave up trying to fit in and sat near the mandolin-playing gentleman. It was quite easy to pretend she was listening to the music. Her brother remained on the far side of the parlor where Banallt stayed with the Vedaelin group. He leaned against the wall, arms crossed over his chest, precisely like the villain she'd thought of one day sketching in words. One of the other men was speaking animatedly, hands cutting through the air. She'd much rather be listening to their conversation.

She must have stared too hard, because Banallt's focus was on her. The shock of the connection of their gazes reached across the room. He didn't look away but left Sophie to break the contact. He ought not stare like that. He oughtn't. She turned back to the music, but she felt his eyes on her.

At last, though, dinner was called. She'd been paired with Mr. Reginald Tallboys, who was too handsome for his own good with his golden brown hair, short and neatly trimmed, and eyes the color of old honey. He was older than the other young gentlemen here, perhaps thirty, she guessed. Around Banallt's age. Her brother had mentioned him a few times as a man of good sense. He came from an old and respected Cheshire family. He had the good manners to appear delighted to be her dinner partner. John's partner was, of all the miserable luck for him, Miss Fidelia Llewellyn. He could not be very happy about finding himself obliged to converse during the entire meal with Banallt's relative. Banallt himself was partnered with the very lovely Lady Harpenden. Blondes, she recalled, were a preference of his, and Lady Harpenden was a curvaceous blonde. She remembered too well that Banallt never thought a married woman was off-limits. Much the opposite. A perfect match for Banallt, wasn't she?

Mr. Tallboys offered his arm. "Shall we?"

Sophie liked Mr. Tallboys's smile. They walked into dinner and he held her chair for her. When he was seated beside her, she leaned toward him and said, "I've been introduced to so many people tonight, I'll never recall all their names." John would expect her to remember everyone she'd met. "Will you rescue me, Mr. Tallboys, and whisper names to me?"

"I will, ma'am," he replied with an engaging grin. He had one of those smiles that made you smile back without even thinking why.

She and Mr. Tallboys were closer to the head of the table than she'd expected to be. Close enough to easily overhear Banallt's conversation. A servant placed a bowl of clear consommé before her, and when she leaned back, she saw Lady Harpenden lean to Banallt, her mouth by his ear. As he listened to the countess, his eyes settled on Sophie with a dark, unreadable gaze. She looked away. Mr. Tallboys sat on her right, but to her left was an academician, a member of the Royal Society whose name and occupation she'd already forgotten. Mr. Jacob Nolan, an astronomer—so Mr. Tallboys whispered to her.

She was horribly aware of Banallt. Not only was he seated closer to her than she would have liked, he was on the opposite side of the table and perfectly within her line of sight. Mr. Tallboys leaned toward her again and she tipped her ear toward his. "You know Lord Banallt, of course," he said. He'd been going around the table, whispering names and occupations to her. "I saw you being introduced to him tonight."

"Yes." She had no desire to eat. None whatever.

He nodded, very slightly, in the direction of her brother, who was sitting next to Miss Llewellyn. He was smiling, putting on an excellent show of being delighted with the girl at his side. Her brother's manners were faultless. "Everyone thought she'd marry last season. Any number of young bucks wooed her." Tallboys shook his head. "But with her beauty and connections, she might look very high indeed. The woman on Lord Banallt's left is Lady Harpenden."

All Sophie could think was that Lady Harpenden was a lovely blonde who seemed to have no trouble making conversation with anyone around her. She was gay and light and completely comfortable in company so lofty.

"Her husband, Lord Harpenden, is farther down the table. With the dowager countess there. She'll talk his ear off."

"The poor man." She picked up her spoon and pulled it through her soup, though she did not taste it. If she ate anything, she'd be ill.

"The gentleman on the dowager countess's other side is Mr. Underhill. He's a director at the Bank of England. A notorious snooze. If you're introduced, whatever you do don't mention British monetary policy. He'll lecture you until your brains congeal."

Sophie smiled at Tallboys. "I presume you've heard the lecture."

His expression turned so serious Sophie had a strong urge to giggle. "Took me a week to recover." He shuddered. "Nightmares for months after."

She laughed. "Thank you for the warning."

Lady Harpenden let out a peal of laughter. Nearly the entire table looked in her direction. "I suspect she's set her cap at him." Mr. Tallboys chuckled. "Should be amusing to watch."

Sophie set down her spoon and turned to look at Tallboys. "Amusing? Why is that?" She had no right to be angry at Banallt, but she was. Why should it matter to her if he embarked on a sure-to-result-in-scandal affair? "I should think with his reputation she should have no trouble whatever."

"Ah," Mr. Tallboys said. The smile faded from his eyes. "I daresay you're right. But I think all the same she will not succeed."

"Why not? She's quite a lovely woman. Why, she's even a blonde."

"True." He chuckled. "In the event, Mrs. Evans, Lord Banallt has been notoriously hard to catch since he was recalled from Paris."

Sophie lifted her eyebrows, looking at the earl and Lady Harpenden. Banallt's eyes slid away from her. Had he been watching her?

"From what I've heard," Tallboys continued, "he's not been interested in any particular woman this last century." He shrugged. "Although..."

"Although?"

"The rumor is that he'll marry Miss Llewellyn." She did not have a good view of Miss Llewellyn from her seat.

"Rumor seems to follow him," she murmured, turning her attention to the gentleman on her left. She passed the remainder of the meal refusing to look in Banallt's direction. Eventually, the ladies left the men in possession of the table and returned to the salon, where Sophie discovered she liked Banallt's cousin, Mrs. Llewellyn, a great deal. She was a sensible woman. And Miss Fidelia Llewellyn was breathtaking. If the talk was true, she wasn't Banallt's usual sort. She was beautiful, no denying that. Sophie had never heard his name connected with any woman who wasn't, but she was plainly a lady.

The arrival of guests who had not been invited to dine increased the noise level in the parlor considerably, despite the fact that the gentlemen had still not yet come in. The news from France was on everyone's tongue. Doubtless the gentlemen were discussing the Corsican yet. She wished she were a fly on the wall in that room.

"My dear Margaret," a woman said.

Sophie, who had been looking in the direction the men would come from, didn't see the woman approach; she only heard her voice. She looked back and was shocked beyond words to recognize the woman.

"Constance," said Mrs. Llewellyn. "Good evening to you."

"We've just come from the Duke of Portland's." She was still quite beautiful. "I'm glad we're not too late to see you."

Mrs. Llewellyn put a hand on Sophie's shoulder. "Constance, you really must meet the delightful Mrs. Evans. Have you met?"

Sophie's chest constricted. Smiling was impossible. Her throat threatened to close off.

"No," Mrs. Peters said. "I've not had that pleasure." She extended a hand to Sophie. Either Mrs. Peters did not remember her, did not connect her with Tommy, or intended to brazen out their meeting. Any case was intolerable.

A door opened across the room, and the gentlemen came in just as Sophie stood up and headed for the door. It was either leave or tear out the woman's deceitful eyes.

CHAPTER SEVEN

Banallt was the last of the gentlemen to leave the dining room. Not that he'd lingered over the port or a cigar. In his opinion, Vedaelin served an inferior port, and he'd not indulged in a cigar. His clothes smelled of smoke all the same. But Sophie was out there among the guests, and if he was to be honest with himself, seeing her again had rattled him. He'd not expected that. And so he'd stayed behind longer than he ought to have while he worked out how he would respond to her. He settled on *not at all.* The maintenance of his dignity was required.

He determined that Sophie should have no discernible effect on him. She'd made her feelings perfectly clear to him at the close of last year. The least he could do was oblige her wish, and her brother's, that they have nothing to do with each other. He'd left Henrietta Street the other day painfully aware for the first time in his life that he was not going to have what he wanted. He was not, however, he'd learned, completely resigned to that unpleasant fact.

Guests had begun arriving from other engagements, and the parlor was now noisy in addition to crowded. He deliberately sought out Sophie so as to avoid meeting her. Despite the crush, he found her quickly. Her posture was achingly familiar; the shape of her head, the slope of her shoulders, the tilt of her chin. And what a shock to see her in a gown that bared her shoulders and upper bosom. No other woman drew his notice the way she did, and there were plenty of better-looking females around. She stood near the middle of the room with his cousin Harry's wife Margaret, facing the door he'd come in by. Sophie's dark-lashed eyes were fixed on a woman he'd once have pursued straight to a mattress.

Mrs. Peters stood with her back to him, so he could only imagine the quizzical expression on her face from the way her head was tipped to one side. Margaret watched Mrs. Peters with an expression that suggested whatever she was hearing from the woman was not to her liking. Sophie looked as if she'd just been insulted. He veered away from the woman, and damn it all, the image of Sophie's stricken expression stayed with him. Fidelia was on the opposite side of the room holding court with a crowd of men that included John Mercer. He ought to join Fidelia just to feed the gossip and tweak Mercer, who had pretensions where Banallt's goddaughter was concerned. And, if he were honest, to see how Sophie felt about him courting. Not flirting, but courting.

What if he was courting or flirting? Sophie Mercer Evans was none of his affair. He doubted he'd marry Fidelia, and didn't care what Mrs. Peters had said to put that dead expression on Sophie's face or whether Margaret approved or not. He and Sophie were done. He had been rejected and then warned away by her brother.

He continued deeper into the parlor, pulling his gaze from the women. Best they cut all ties between them. Sophie, blast her, had been a topic of conversation among the gentlemen during their cigars and port. Vedaelin had been charmed by her and had made no secret of it, either. Banallt doubted he was the only man to leave the room wondering if Vedaelin thought he'd found his new duchess in Mercer's sister. As for Mercer, he'd said little, and what little he did say had been, thankfully, to his sister's credit.

The fuss over her wouldn't last, he told himself. Sophie Evans was new blood in a circle of jaded men who spent most of their time with women equally jaded. His heart clenched. Damn, damn, damn. And damn again. He was done with her. Utterly done. If he had any sense at all, he'd wait for Mrs. Peters to finish with Sophie and Margaret and let "La Grande Peters," as she was called in certain circles, succeed in her pursuit of him. Or perhaps he'd allow Lady Harpenden to make progress with him. Mrs. Peters was more to his taste, but at least he liked the countess. He needed a distraction, and he'd gone far too long without sexual indulgence. Why not a mindless encounter with Mrs. Peters?

He halted when he realized he was going to walk headlong into the wall if he didn't get his mind off Sophie. The idea of taking Mrs. Peters to bed left him cold.

"Banallt," someone said. "Good to see you out and about."

"Tallboys," he said. Tallboys had been Sophie's partner at dinner. That had been a deft pairing of two fine minds. Until recently they'd not moved in the same circles. Tallboys had never been the sort to keep company with men like Tommy Evans. Or the Earl of Banallt, for that matter. What vices Tallboys had tended to keep him in better company than Banallt had once kept. "How are you?" he asked.

He didn't give a damn how Tallboys was, but the man proceeded to tell him, and that meant Banallt didn't have to stand alone, stupidly staring at a woman who did not want him. Tallboys was not married. At his age he ought to be. He ought to find himself a decent woman and retire to the country to live boringly ever after. Sophie, damn her eyes, didn't seem to have moved. He had her profile now, not her face. The arch of her nose was a glaring imperfection.

"Have you an interest?" Tallboys said in the manner of someone who has repeated a question. Perhaps more than once.

"I beg your pardon?" He had no damned idea what Tallboys had asked him. Mrs. Peters had finished talking to Margaret. Sophie was now making her way across the parlor, away from him. Away from Margaret. Mrs. Peters, on the other hand, was moving toward him. Her hips swayed invitingly as she opened a fan and waved it slowly under her chin. She was heading in his direction. God help him. He wanted to run.

"You've been staring at her," Tallboys said in a low voice. Well of course he was staring. Look at the way the woman was walking. He wasn't the only man whose attention was on those swaying hips. He was probably the only man who didn't want her any nearer. "I wondered if perhaps you felt you had a prior claim. You did meet her first, after all."

"No," he said. He tore his gaze from Mrs. Peters. "There is no prior claim." She was beautiful, but he wasn't interested. He ought to be. He wished he were. Before Sophie, he would have been. Hell, he'd have already been to bed with her and found a way to drop her if she was as tedious as he suspected. He glanced around the room, looking for Vedaelin or even Mercer, if that would save him from Mrs. Peters. What he saw was Sophie heading for the door with short, rapid steps. Head down, she had her skirts fisted in one hand.

Tallboys stepped back, hands lifted. "No need to snarl, my lord. If you reciprocate her interest, I won't interfere."

"I don't," he said. He didn't even care that he sounded curt. Sophie was moving at an angle to where he stood, but someone must have called out to her, because she hesitated, and he caught a glimpse of her face. Deathly white. And the tremble of her hand over her bosom. Then she fled. With a flash of the satin trim down the back of her gown, she was gone. "Damn," he whispered. Well. Let her go then. Frankly, she had the right idea. He needn't stay for this torture, either. He could leave while Sophie was in the retiring room fixing whatever disaster had happened to her rather shopworn gown. Couldn't Mercer be bothered to properly outfit his sister for Town?

"I thought perhaps you'd met her before tonight," Tallboys said. "You knew her late husband, after all."

Banallt stopped staring at the empty doorway and looked at Tallboys. "Late husband?" To his knowledge, Mr. Peters was on the other side of the room. He wasn't often caught flat-out stupid, and he'd just been, he realized. "Mrs. Evans, you mean?"

"Why, yes, my lord." Tallboys scanned the room. "She's absolutely charming. Not the way you prefer them, but she's got something all the same." He smiled. "I'm relieved you don't mind. The way you were staring at her tonight I thought you might."

"I was not staring at Mrs. Evans." This entire evening was a fiasco, and he really couldn't stand another moment of it. "Excuse me, Tallboys, won't you?"

Tallboys nodded. "My lord."

He dodged Mrs. Peters and left, heading for the stairs, mentally composing the excuse he would give a servant to deliver to Vedaelin. At the top of the stairs, where the corridor went one way to the ladies' retiring room and another to God knows where in the house, a soft sound stopped him.

Sophie was standing in a darkened portion of the corridor with her forearm on one of the marble columns that ran the length of the tiled walkway. Her head was hidden in the crook of her elbow.

She gave no sign of having heard him. He could walk away. Continue down the stairs and out of the house. Away from here. He ought to. He took a step in her direction even though he didn't intend to. Her shoulders heaved.

"Mrs. Evans?"

She stilled. Her forehead pressed into her arm just once before she lifted her head and looked in his direction. She opened her mouth to say something—probably, he decided, an order to leave her alone—but her breath stuttered, and her eyes...Her eyes were bleak. Broken.

"What's happened?" He was instantly cast back to Rider Hall, to the days when they'd been friends despite the relentless pull of his desire for her. He moved closer, near enough to touch her. He didn't dare. "If it's me who has upset you, please, dry your tears," he said. "I have been called away. I'm on my way out now."

She put her back to the column and stared at the ceiling. Her breath hitched again, but softer this time as she struggled with whatever it was that had shattered her. Banallt's chest shrank around his heart. "That's—" She cleared her throat and started again. "That's— It's not you," she whispered.

He stared at her as she struggled to master herself, and for the first time since he had met her, he thought she might lose the battle. "Sophie," he said. He took a breath. "Please, let me speak, and then you may either dismiss me or tell me what is the matter, as you wish. Agreed?"

She nodded. Her hands were fisted and pressed against the column at her back.

"I owe you an apology. It's not to my credit that it's taken me until now to make the attempt. That day at Rider Hall, you know the day I mean, I betrayed us both." He fought for control himself as the emotions of that day came back. "No matter the cause, no matter my state of mind, I should not have behaved as I did."

"Banallt," she said.

But he lifted a hand to stop her. "I've not lived an exemplary life." He glanced down the hall, but no one was there. "No one knows that better than you, but that day—that night of all the nights of my life, that is the only one on which I sincerely regret my behavior. I've since lain awake at night and...I imagine I behaved differently." He glanced down. "How different our lives might be if I had not treated you so abysmally. I dishonored us both. You most of all. For all that and more, for every insult and offense, and I am aware there are many, I apologize."

She chewed on her lower lip. Her hands, he noticed, were no longer fisted but flat to the column behind her. "Thank you," she said. And, God help him, something in her softened toward him.

He nodded. "If I could take it all back, I would." He hadn't righted the wrong he'd done her. Nothing would do that. "I ought to have apologized much sooner."

"It's all right."

"And now, on to tonight." A selfless act from the Earl of Banallt? Could it be true? He was actually willing to stay out of her life. Had he ever done anything so much against his nature? "Is it my presence that upset you? If it is, you needn't worry."

"That...No. Not you." She drew in a breath. "I don't belong here."

"Nonsense."

"Now I'm the one who is not being honest." She chewed on her lip again. "It's Mrs. Peters," she said on an exhale that rattled the words. She caught herself, as she did whenever strong emotion challenged her control.

Conversation from the parlor came faintly down the hall, but here they stood in private, or very nearly so. The servants weren't likely to head this way, and the retiring rooms were in the other direction. He doubted anyone would see them here, alone and in such dim and intimate lighting. "Did she say something unkind?"

"Unkind." She sniffled, a sign of how close she'd been to tears. "How could she have been unkind? Deliberately, I mean. She did not know who I was."

"Should she have?"

Her mouth worked, going from pressed thin, to parted, and back to closed. He did his best not to stare at her mouth, her full and perfect lips, the lower one just that much fuller than the upper. "Not long after you left Rider Hall the last time..." Another stuttering breath came from her, but softer than before. She tucked her hands behind her back, leaning on them, refusing to meet his gaze. So be it. Did he expect to be forgiven so easily? "Tommy came home."

He said nothing. She wore white muslin trimmed with dark blue satin. A row of tiny blue satin bows lined the neckline, some touching the pale skin of her bosom. Shadows gathered at the tucks that pulled her bodice to a tiny vee. In all the time he'd known her he'd never seen her in an evening gown. Never once with bare shoulders or with the upper curves of her breasts exposed. She was exquisite. And he would never hold her in his arms, with her body soft and pliant against him.

"He said he'd come home to stay." At last, she stopped staring at the ceiling and looked at him. His body reacted with a jolt of sexual anticipation. Misguided, hopeless, but there it was, coursing through him as if he were once more on the prowl. "He was tired of his life, he said, and he wanted me. He wanted to make a life with me." She smiled, but the corners of her mouth too quickly turned down. She looked at the floor and tugged on one of her gloves, bringing the kidskin closer to the tender crook of her elbow.

"I didn't believe him," she said. "Why should I have? You know what he was like. But he stayed at Rider Hall. He stayed home with me, and he was never once drunk. He didn't ask me for money. Nor spend the night in town. I wanted so much to believe he meant it." She bit her lower lip, and then slowly, sensuously, she smiled. He doubted she knew what she looked like with the dreamy uptilt at the corners of her mouth. "I was happy, Banallt. For the first time in...forever, it seemed, I was happy. He was the man I married, the man I fell in love with, and I fell in love with him all over again."

He let the silence stay between them. What the hell had Tommy Evans ever done to deserve such devotion?

Her head leaned against the column. "We went to visit his parents. They had several guests at the house. Down from London. We weren't going to stay long. Tommy and I had talked about going to Havenwood to see Papa and John. He knew how dreadfully I missed them."

Banallt kept his silence. If Tommy Evans had wanted to visit Sophie's family, then it would only have been to borrow money after he showed off a young wife whom he pretended to adore and who obviously adored him.

"But one afternoon I came home early from some outing with his mother. I don't even remember now what it was we were doing. And I walked in on him with Mrs. Peters. In our room. Our bed." A tear slipped off her lower lashes and headed down her cheek.

Banallt's heart dove to his feet. He saw and felt the image in his head. Sophie, believing she had her heart's desire, that her husband loved her. Her hand on the door, seeing Tommy with another woman, their bodies locked together. He felt her heartbreak. Damn Tommy Evans to hell. Banallt wasn't over her. No matter how often he told himself he was, he wasn't. If he lived to be a hundred, he'd not be over her. "I am so sorry."

"He made me love him again, and what a fool I was."

He closed the distance between them and brushed the tear from her cheek. What was he supposed to say to her when he'd been more than a little responsible for the man's many transgressions? "Sophie."

"Later, we argued terribly," she said, unaware that more tears were spilling down her cheeks. "I said a great many unkind things."

"You were angry." He was afraid she was going to break. She was trying mightily to control herself, but he knew she was at the edge. "And hurt."

"I refused to stay another night in that room. Where he'd been with that woman." She looked up. "Her eyes were closed, you know. She mayn't ever have seen me or known I came in. Perhaps Tommy never told her. I saw them, and right before I closed the door, Tommy...he looked right at me. And I could see in his eyes that he'd lied to me all along."

Banallt brushed a finger along her lower lip.

"All I wanted was for my husband to love me. Just a little."

"Sophie..."

"That night, he was killed. His mother knew we'd argued, though not why—I wouldn't tell her *that* for the world—and she blamed me. If we hadn't argued, he'd never have gone out." She looked away. "Married couples argue all the time," she said.

"She was a mother, Sophie, who'd lost her son. She must have been mad with grief."

Her eyes met his, silently acknowledging his point. She reached for his hand, holding just his fingers in hers. "Yes, that's so." She sighed. "She blamed me that Tommy got drunk that night and stayed drunk all night and killed himself riding home." She let out a breath. "If I hadn't told him to get out, he probably would have stayed. So, in a way, she was right." He watched tears pool in her eyes, and the sight tore at him. "Seeing Mrs. Peters brought it back. Even if he'd lived, he was never going to love me. I knew that, too, but I never cared. I never could believe it was so."

He pulled her into his arms, and the moment he felt her body against his he knew that he'd made a mistake touching her.

"You knew," she said into his shirt. "You knew all along he never loved me."

"Shh," he crooned. He held her while she cried, her hands against his chest. He loved her still, and there didn't seem to be anything he could do about it. He would probably love her until the day he died, a pathetic, dried-up old man married to some worthy woman who would give him his heir and a spare and would never, ever be to him what Sophie was right now and forever.

"I know Tommy's to blame for what he did, I know that," she said. "But I can't forgive her, either. She was married. She knew he was married. She knew it was wrong of her." He put his handkerchief in her hand. "I wish I'd never come here." She lifted her tear-streaked face to his. "How many other women here tonight were Tommy's lovers, too? Five? Ten? A dozen?" She crumpled his handkerchief. "I should hate him. Why do I miss him so terribly when I ought to despise him?"

He grabbed her by the shoulders. His hands were bare, and his fingers splayed onto the skin exposed by her gown. "That's quite enough out of you."

She reared back and stared wide-eyed at him.

"Sophie Mercer Evans, you are better than her. Better than this. Go back in there. She can't compare to you. She never will."

"I can't." She dissolved into tears again.

He gave her to a mental count of five, and yes, the tears stopped, exactly as he knew they would. "I'll fetch your brother," he said. "He'll take you home if that's what you want."

"Thank you," she whispered.

In the parlor, he dispatched a footman to have Mercer's carriage brought around then found Mercer and took him aside. "I beg your pardon," he said to Fidelia. "I need a word with Mr. Mercer."

"What is it, my lord?" he asked.

"Your sister is…ill." His hesitation was yet another mistake. One of many tonight. Mercer heard it and understood quite well that some other word must have been foremost in his mind. "I've called for your carriage."

Anger flickered in his eyes. "Bold of you, my lord."

He grabbed Mercer's arm, hauling him farther from curious ears. "Whatever the cause, forget about Fidelia for five minutes and take your sister home. She's in no fit condition to be seen."

Mercer took a step toward him. "What have you done?" He only just kept his voice low. "If you've harmed her, Banallt—"

He raised his hands. "I've not touched her, nor am I the cause of her distress. We barely spoke."

"Then what is the matter?"

Banallt ought to have kept his tongue. He didn't. "For God's sake, man. One of Tommy's mistresses is here, and Sophie, God help her, knows what the woman was to her husband. Why on earth she ever loved that man, let alone loves him still, I'll never understand."

"I do," Mercer said sharply.

"Then I fail to comprehend why you continue to stand here instead of looking after your sister." He ground out the words. "If you won't take her home, I shall, and I won't be responsible for the consequences of that."

"Stay away from Sophie," Mercer said. "Stay well away or—"

Banallt turned to see what had caught Mercer's attention. Sophie had come into the room. She'd obviously washed her face and re-pinned her hair. The two of them waited while she made her way to them.

"Is everything all right?" Mercer asked her with a hard glance at Banallt.

"Yes." She looked up at him grave as ever she was. "I decided you were right, my lord. I'm fine, John. Nothing's the matter."

Banallt bowed and clamped his jaws shut. "Mrs. Evans. Mr. Mercer."

"My lord," she said.

Mercer glared at him.

From the corner of his eye, he saw Reginald Tallboys walking toward them. Good, he thought fiercely. Let her fall in love with a decent man like Tallboys. Hell, let her complete the spell she'd cast on Vedaelin. Either man would do. If she was married to someone else, he could leave her alone. "Good night," he said.

CHAPTER EIGHT

Number 26 Henrietta Street, London,
MARCH 16, 1815

Sophie dreamed of Banallt that night. She had dismissed him from her life, but he was haunting her anyway. Out of sheer spite, she thought. He never did like not having his way. In her dream, Tommy had only recently died. She was poor again and living at Rider Hall, wondering how she was going to survive. The bailiff had taken away all the furniture. Rider Hall was empty, with bare windows and empty fireplaces. In reality, the house had not been stripped quite so thoroughly, but she'd felt as empty as the structure was now in her dream.

She dreamed she'd been left a single trunk in which there was nothing but a book she didn't care for, and she needed to write Banallt a note, explaining where she'd gone and what had happened. But she had no pen or ink or paper. Everything was gone. And just as she was about to cry with frustration, Banallt walked through the door, bringing with him the recollection of his lingering glances and memories of their friendship. He handed her pen, ink, and paper, and they agreed she would move into the guard tower at Castle Darmead where she could write as much as she liked. Novel after novel, if she so desired. And because she was grateful, she kissed him. For a very long time because at last she could. The kiss became more. A hungry and needy embrace. She wasn't married anymore.

When they parted for air, with her trembling in his arms, he smiled and said, "Have I told you I've remarried? To Fidelia."

Long after she'd risen in the morning, images and emotions from the dream came at her. She didn't need to write anymore, but the fact was the stories had never gone away. The difference was that now she kept them in her head rather than writing them down. As for Banallt marrying, he'd told her himself that he must. His title required it. Whoever Banallt decided to marry, she would always feel a little pang of regret, which was ridiculous. The Earl of Banallt would never be faithful.

She sat at the desk in her room on Henrietta Street and remembered all the nights she'd stayed up to write when Tommy was alive. Words that supported her. All her life, she'd made up stories. When Tommy left her without funds, she'd done the only thing she could: write her stories down. She took out paper, but instead of dashing out the history of a knight determined to reclaim his birthright, she made out a list of items the house needed and that had not been fetched from Havenwood. Paper, for one.

At half past one John came home. He burst into her room without a pause between knocking and his entry. She put down her pen. "What is it, John?"

He grinned. "You'll never guess who I've brought home with me!"

His smile was always infectious, and she smiled back. "The Prince of Wales?"

John tweaked the end of her nose. "No, Sophie. An admirer of yours."

"John."

"It's Vedaelin." He put a hand on the top of her desk and leaned over her. "Change your gown. He practically invited himself here when I told him you were home."

She lifted an eyebrow. "The Duke of Vedaelin?"

"He admires you, I tell you. Just think of it, Sophie!"

"He's a duke."

"Get dressed. Wear that green striped gown. It's the best you've got, and the color flatters your eyes. He's already got his heir, Sophie. He is free to marry for love, and last night at Cavendish Square...I promise you, I am not the only man to have remarked he was taken with you."

"He's old enough to be my father, John. He's not interested in me."

"He is, I tell you." He tweaked her nose again. "Now get dressed."

She pushed her brother away. "Be gone."

"And do something with your hair."

"Very well, John." She made a shooing gesture. "Go."

"Change your slippers, too."

"Go." She called Flora and swapped her dress for her green striped afternoon frock, even remembering at the last minute to change her slippers and tie a green ribbon in her hair. Then she went below stairs and met with the cook before she proceeded to the parlor. What if John was right and the Duke of Vedaelin wanted to court her? She wasn't sure what to think of that.

A servant brought in tea and cakes purchased from the confectioner's down the street and laid out the table. Sophie was glad to busy herself brewing tea. John's words made her look at the duke differently, and she wasn't best pleased with her brother because of it. She did find Vedaelin more than a little attractive, though. He didn't look at all his age. He might easily pass for ten years younger. He was a sensible man. Levelheaded. A bit proud, but then he was a duke, after all.

"I should like to add my thanks, Your Grace, to my brother's, for securing us such a lovely house," she said when she'd dropped sugar into his tea.

"I'm pleased if you like it, Mrs. Evans."

"We like it very well, thank you."

"Mercer," the duke said. "What plans have you to show your sister the sights?"

"Sights?" John said.

Sophie hurried to fill John's puzzled silence. "We've only just arrived, Your Grace," she said. "We've not had time to think of seeing anything."

"Have you not been to Bond Street yet?" Vedaelin smiled at them both. "If my memory is accurate, young women adore shopping."

"I'm most unnatural then," Sophie said. She kept her cup and saucer perfectly balanced. "I find shopping tedious."

John polished off his second iced cake. "My sister is more likely to make the nearest subscription library her second home."

"Indeed?" the duke said. Sophie couldn't tell if he approved of women who read or not. She'd not be able to write if she were married to him. The wife of a duke could never engage in something so undignified.

"I'm sure you'll be impressed with me," she said, hiding her thoughts behind a sip of her tea. She smiled when she lowered her cup. "This morning, after you left, John, I walked as far as Oxford Street and admired the buildings along the way." Henrietta Street backed onto Oxford Street, so she hadn't been adventurous at all.

"After having seen your home, Your Grace, I'm determined to learn something of architecture. Your home is lovely."

"Thank you." He looked pleased at that, and so did John. She was proud of herself for managing the change of subject so deftly.

"Has there been further word of Napoleon?" she asked. The duke could not possibly care to hear of her reading habits, and if he was not the sort of man who cared for women who read, then it was best to avoid that subject. "Is it true Napoleon is in Paris already?"

"Ah," Vedaelin said. His cup clicked against his saucer. "You are a woman of intellect, Mrs. Evans."

Again, whether he thought that admirable or not Sophie could not guess. No matter how much John wanted it, she wouldn't pretend she was an empty-headed female without a serious thought in her mind. Really, there was no reason at all to think the duke was being anything but polite to her. "Napoleon's whereabouts and his intentions are on everyone's mind, Your Grace. Like everyone else, I wonder if we are to go to war again."

"Yes," John answered. "We must."

"Such a disagreeable subject," Vedaelin said, "when the company is so very charming."

Sophie kept still. John's guests at Havenwood had always been political, and he'd never objected when she voiced an opinion or showed an interest in the subject. The duke had just reminded her that not all households welcomed the female point of view. "Do you think we women don't worry of such things?" she asked. "It is our sons and husbands"—she looked at John—"and our brothers who will go off to fight, after all. If there is war, not all of them will return."

"Sophie isn't like most women, Your Grace." John leaned over the tray of cakes and took two more. It's a wonder he wasn't fat. He wasn't at all, though. "She never has been, I'm afraid. Even as a girl, she was—" He caught himself. Sophie was certain he'd been about to call her odd. "—unique among girls."

The duke looked at her over his cup, fingers poised to lift. "That is abundantly plain. Tell me, Mrs. Evans, do you never wish a moment's respite from the worry?"

She set aside her tea. He was a man of another generation. His ideas about women weren't very modern. "What women wish for and what reality we face are worlds apart, Your Grace. What woman can forget her worries when the lives of her loved ones are at stake? Such a state of affairs can never be far from our minds. You've done nothing but breathe the news since it was first whispered in White-hall. But I learned of Bonaparte's escape only recently, when my brother told me. Naturally, I am curious, and anxious, to know what Britain will do in response. But, do please forgive me. You are correct. We should speak of more pleasant subjects while we may."

Vedaelin bowed his head. "With that, I wholeheartedly agree. If you do not care for shopping and you've a mind to admire architecture, then perhaps you would enjoy touring some of the great houses of London Town. What do you think of that as a pastime, Mrs. Evans?"

"I should like that exceedingly," she said. "In Duke's Head we have no Christopher Wren to admire, and Palladio never came to our corner of England, though we have a fine Norman church. Will you make me a list, Your Grace? I'll begin first thing tomorrow."

John paused in his selection of another petit four. "My sister has an appallingly methodical mind, Your Grace. Give her a task, and she'll see it through and provide you a detailed report afterward. If you give her a list of houses, expect a reckoning from her of every one she's visited and her observations of them all. Fully catalogued and indexed."

"John, really." She smoothed her skirt.

"It's so, Sophie. Don't deny it." He addressed the duke. "I've abused her talents horribly since she came back to Havenwood. It's why I've brought her to London this time. Without her there's no hope of my staying organized."

The duke leaned back in his chair. "We are but a short walk from Gray Street, and there we can see Hightower House. It's a lovely day yet. Shall we go?"

"Hightower?" Sophie asked. Her heart misgave her. "Isn't that Lord Banallt's home?"

"It is." Vedaelin nodded. "Banallt keeps other quarters in Town. Mrs. Llewellyn and her daughter are resident there for the season. The housekeeper is delighted to show the house, though, I can promise you that. Hightower is an extraordinary example of sublime architecture." His enthusiasm for the subject was comforting. He didn't object to any and all of a woman's intellectual pursuits. "If you are to study the great homes, Hightower must be on your list. What do you say, Mrs. Evans?" He smiled, and Sophie decided that she did like the duke. "Shall we walk there and permit you to make your first ledger entry?"

John said, "That would be delightful, Your Grace. Sophie, fetch your cloak."

The day was fine, and Sophie walked with her arm on the duke's. How strange it was to be thinking of him as a potential suitor. John stayed on her other side. She didn't mention to either that she knew Hightower House quite well. Banallt had once brought plans to Rider Hall. He was having the interior remodeled, and he had two sets of plans from rival architects. She'd sat with him while they discussed the merits of the two proposals. Back then, she'd thought if ever she saw the house it would be with Tommy at her side.

She felt uneasy about the visit, even though she knew Banallt would not be there. She could not help feeling she was encroaching on some private retreat of the earl's. Their own area of Mayfair was grand enough to her, but the town houses soon gave way to larger homes. From Edward Street, they took a right to James Street and from there another right onto Gray Street, which was a short street tucked between two longer ones. Hightower House took up the whole of Gray Street, from James on one end to Duke Street on the other. She recognized the exterior from the sketches Banallt had once made when he'd described his London home to her. As they walked to the entrance gate, a black carriage turned onto the street from Duke Street, Gray Street being a convenient outlet for travelers and much quieter than the surrounding streets.

An iron gate ran the length of the Gray Street side of the house, each pole tipped with a gold-painted point. The entrance gate opened onto a cobbled courtyard just large enough for a carriage to turn around in. The exterior architecture betrayed its Gothic roots. The middle, and oldest, section of the house retained medieval gargoyles on the downspouts. The central tower was flanked by Tudor-era wings. The stone was blackened with soot and further discolored where rain dripped from the eaves and gutters. A short flight of stairs led to the double front door. She knew the door was original to the house: heavy black planks crisscrossed with great iron flanges.

At the top landing, Vedaelin reached for the knocker, a roaring lion that was not original to the door. Sophie saw the teeth in the brass figure, the flowing mane, narrow eyes, lips drawn back in a snarl. He rapped on the door.

Sophie held her breath. For goodness' sake, did she expect Banallt himself to answer the door? The carriage heading for James Street was almost to the gate. The vehicle slowed. For no reason at all, her heart tripped.

The servant who answered bowed when he saw the duke. She recognized him immediately. Banallt's most singular servant had at some point, it appeared, been promoted from valet to butler. He wore black but for a white shirt and an absolutely impeccable cravat. He was unattractive and ridiculously tall. Taller than Banallt by half a head, and broader through the chest. His eyes were the color of mud and had a disturbing keenness about them. His crooked nose was flattened across the bridge. One of his ears had been shredded at the top. He looked a brawler and, indeed, had been one professionally before he came to work for Banallt.

"King," the duke said with perfect familiarity. "A pleasure to see you, as always."

"Your Grace." He spoke with a pleasant accent, almost no trace left of northern England in his speech. According to Banallt, his accent had at one time been impenetrable. King gave no sign that he remembered her from Rider Hall, even though he had been there with his employer several times.

"King?" John straightened and looked King up and down. "Not Rupert King, the great boxer? The Rupert King who fought Hampton in aught five?"

The man's muddy brown eyes lit on John with a sharp gaze. "And if I was, sir?"

"Why, then I'm pleased to meet you, that's all! I saw you fight Hampton. That was you, wasn't it?"

"Might have been, sir."

"I had ten pounds on you." John grinned. "A left to the jaw and Hampton went down like a sack of"—he glanced at Sophie—"old wheat."

"Hampton never could take that wicked left, could he, King?" said the duke.

"No, Your Grace, he couldn't: " King flexed his left hand and stared out into the street. The black carriage made the turn to Hightower House. All three of them turned to watch. A servant appeared from underneath the stairs and ran to the courtyard.

"Heigh-ho!" the coachman called as he brought his team to a halt.

Sophie found herself with the advantage of position. With just a small turn of her head she could watch King eye her and John and she could see the carriage. When the vehicle stopped, the groom put down the steps, *clack, clack.* Then came a deeper *thunk* as the mechanism fully engaged. The groom retreated to hold the head of the lead horse. Someone important was making a call at Hightower House. The caller's identity wasn't certain, because the carriage coat of arms was covered by a black lozenge. For no reason at all, Sophie's heart rattled in her chest. It couldn't be. Vedaelin had said Banallt didn't stay here. She couldn't be so unlucky.

A gentleman got out of the carriage. He dipped his head to watch his step and was, for the moment, unaware of his audience. He was not alone, for he stayed at the carriage door and immediately turned his back to the house, holding out his hand. A delicate gloved hand emerged from the carriage, touched his offered one, gripped, and then a young woman came out.

She heard John curse under his breath.

CHAPTER NINE

Hightower House, London,
MARCH 15, 1815

Sophie watched the Earl of Banallt tuck the woman's hand under his arm. Her chest constricted. Mr. Tallboys was right, then. Banallt was going to marry Miss Fidelia Llewellyn. Why should she mind that Banallt had moved on? Hadn't she expected and hoped he would?

The couple walked, arm in arm, up the stairs, and as Sophie watched them her entire history with Banallt came back. For a time, he had been her only friend during a dark and unhappy period of her life. The way he moved was familiar to her: the elegance of his clothes, the too-long hair, the eerie flatness of his eyes. She was glad they had renewed their friendship. She ought to be equally glad he had found a woman he wanted to marry. In the courtyard, the groom clung to the back of the carriage as the coachman drove the vehicle back onto the street, heading, no doubt, for the mews.

"Is it you, Vedaelin?" Banallt said, tilting his head to see who was there as he ascended the stairs with Miss Fidelia Llewellyn on his arm. The sun was in his eyes and he could not see them well, Sophie realized. He paused. "It is you. Your Grace." He grinned. "This is a pleasant surprise." Then he noticed John. "Who's that with you?"

Banallt and Miss Llewellyn came up the final stairs to join them on the landing. Sophie edged away.

"Mercer." Banallt hesitated. Only an instant. Almost not a hesitation at all. His gaze moved from John to her. His eyes shuttered, and he drew Miss Llewellyn closer to him. Sophie hoped he would find happiness with her.

"What are you doing here, Banallt, making a liar of me?" the duke asked. "I've just been telling Mercer and his sister that you are never here. And now you appear with Miss Llewellyn." He bowed to the young woman. "Charming, as always, to see you, miss. How is your dear mama?"

"Your Grace." Miss Llewellyn curtseyed. "Very well, thank you."

Banallt said, "Are you just arriving or just leaving?"

"Arriving," Vedaelin said. "And only just. The Mercers are letting a house of mine on Henrietta Street. We've walked here from there." The two men shook hands. Banallt glanced at Sophie, but she averted her eyes at the last moment and avoided directly meeting his gaze. She'd give anything to have not come here, or at least to have arrived after the carriage so they could have turned back before it was too late. "Have we come at an inconvenient time?" Vedaelin asked. The duke did not care to go, that was clear. "I'll show Mercer and his sister Hightower another day."

There was another hesitation from Banallt, but he didn't take up Vedaelin's excuse. "Nonsense." He headed for the door without another glance at her or at John. "I am delighted to see you, Your Grace. Come in, do please, come in."

King stood aside as Banallt walked in with Miss Llewellyn and Vedaelin. Outside on the landing, John gave Sophie a look she was careful to return as blandly as possible. "There's nothing for it, Sophie," he said. Strain marked the edges of his mouth. "I won't insult the duke by leaving now. Not when he's practically insisted."

"Of course not," she said.

He gestured for her to proceed him, and she went in with him on her heels. Banallt had already taken off his hat and put it into the waiting hands of the formidable King. "What am I doing here?" he repeated to the duke, smiling. A genuine smile from Banallt took your breath, and this one was genuine.

Sophie kept to the corner, out of the way as King took coats, hats, and gloves. At last, though, the monstrous butler, who she knew couldn't bear to hurt any living thing, came round to her and she had no choice but to slip free of her coat. Her arms trembled. She blocked off the emotions racing through her. This was nothing. Meeting an old friend, that's all.

Wasn't this what she'd wanted all along? For Banallt to find happiness with another woman? She looked everywhere but at Banallt and Miss Llewellyn. Veins of pale pink striated the white marble floor. The windows flanking the door were mullioned in three parts, the middle pane higher than the outer ones, with diamond panes of glass. The same pink-veined marble had been used for the columns that flanked the interior entrance to the house. Overhead, cherubim rested on clouds in a domed blue sky. To the right, past the marble columns, a staircase spiraled upward. Red and white tulips filled a Chinese vase in a marble-lined niche.

"I maintain a presence here," Banallt was saying to Vedaelin in his familiar drawl. Banallt had always been vital, and never more so than now. He was a difficult man to ignore. Sophie's heart thrummed with the force of his personality. "As well you know." His eyes moved from the duke to John and, at last, to Sophie. She kept her distance from them and wished vehemently that she could just disappear. Oh, to have that power just once in her life. She would call on it now, to be sure.

"Miss Llewellyn," John said. He hesitated before taking her hand and bending over it. He'd lost his usual smile, and Sophie couldn't help thinking he, too, must feel the discomfort of being here.

"Mr. Mercer, Mrs. Evans." Miss Llewellyn was a tall girl, but slender, and of a height that went well with Banallt's. And John's, for that matter. "I'm very pleased to see you both again." Sophie had to admit that Miss Llewellyn's manners were faultless. She turned her exquisite smile on John. She wore a white gown trimmed with pale yellow. Matching ribbons with tiny silk flowers were threaded through her dark hair. A white rosebud was pinned to her bodice. She touched the rosebud now. "Thank you for the flowers, Mr. Mercer. They were lovely."

Flowers? Sophie looked at John, astonished.

Her brother bowed. "You're quite welcome. You were a lovely partner at supper last night."

Miss Llewellyn's attention stayed on John. Sophie's brother was a handsome man; handsome enough that even a woman as lovely as Miss Llewellyn might look twice. But whatever had possessed him to send the young woman flowers? What a farce that would be if Miss Llewellyn fell in love with John. Banallt would never permit it. But if he did? She would be Banallt's relation.

"You brought them here for a tour of Hightower House, did you?" Banallt said easily.

"Yes, indeed," Vedaelin said. "Mrs. Evans has embarked on a study of London architecture. I had the brilliant idea of bringing them here to see Hightower House. There is your Caravaggio and your library to show them, too.

"And here you are." He addressed his goddaughter with rather a sharp look, Sophie thought. "Fidelia, my dear, if you wish to go to your mama, please do."

Fidelia leaned against his arm. Her cheeks had faint spots of pink. "Are you going to show them yourself, Banallt?"

"Yes."

"Then I'll stay with you, if that's agreeable."

Banallt looked at Fidelia with his eyebrows raised. "Certainly," he said.

Hightower House was beautiful beyond all Sophie's expectations. From the exquisite marble in the entrance to carved wooden walls in the corridor, the house was made to overawe. Banallt led them up the gentle spiral of the stairs and gave them a commentary on the architectural history. Inigo Jones had rebuilt the rear of the house in the previous century, and more recently, Adam had been hired for the interior.

Sophie kept a step behind the men and Miss Llewellyn, who stayed near Banallt. Although, from Sophie's vantage, she noticed the young woman looked over her shoulder at John rather too often.

The Caravaggio, *Rest on the Flight into Egypt*, hung in a drawing room three times the size of theirs at Henrietta Street. Sophie was soon lost in examining the painting. She hardly noticed when the others wandered away. She remembered when Banallt had told her he'd bought it. At the time, she'd thought he'd paid a frightful price—one that would have kept Rider Hall staffed and her in comfort for the rest of her days. The painting was lovelier than she had imagined. She could stand here for hours and not take in all there was to see. She jumped when Banallt said, "Do you admire it as much as I said you would?"

She cocked her head. "I think I do, my lord."

"The angel reminds me of you," he said, lifting a hand toward Caravaggio's barely draped angel. Sophie turned her head toward him, her eyebrows raised. "A compliment," he said. "I intend it as one and it is one. Please take it as such."

"As you wish," she said stiffly.

Banallt remained silent. His eyes searched her face. "I thought we'd gotten past our difficulties. Does it pain you so much to be near me?"

"It is...uncomfortable to be here." She glanced around. Her brother and Miss Llewellyn were conversing at the other end of the room, near a globe that John was slowly turning with the tip of his index finger. He lifted his head at something Miss Llewellyn said and made a sharp gesture. Vedaelin was sitting on a leather chair before the fireplace, hands folded over his stomach. "The duke assured us you were never here," she said in a low voice. "Had I known you would be here, we would not have presumed."

She walked away without giving Banallt a chance to reply and found herself confronted with a portrait of a woman she belatedly realized must be the late Lady Banallt. An exquisite blonde looked down from the portrait with blue eyes the color of the sky and sapphires on her ears and around her slender throat. Her smile hinted at some internal sadness. A black crepe bow still draped the frame. Her heart felt too big for her chest. Had this beautiful woman loved her husband? Had Banallt broken her heart the way Tommy had broken hers? When she turned away, Banallt hadn't moved away from the Caravaggio, but she felt his gaze nonetheless.

Banallt raised his voice to say, "I'm told Mrs. Evans is devoted to reading. Shall we discover her opinion of my library, Vedaelin?"

Before they left, she spared one last look at the woman whom Banallt had married and, for all intents and purposes, abandoned the way Tommy had abandoned her. She was right, she decided. Lady Banallt did look sad.

The library at Hightower House was exactly as Banallt had described it to her: spacious with comfortable places to sit and read and filled with thousands of books, all of which were morocco bound with a small impression of Banallt's coronet on the lower spines. His collection included novels, exactly as he had claimed. She even found hers among them. All ten of the novels she wrote during her marriage were behind glass and at eye level. How strange it was to know that Banallt had read them before he knew her. And stranger still to think he had bought the ones that came after.

"Your sister may come here anytime she pleases," Banallt was telling John. She remembered his voice, reading her words aloud. He had a marvelous reading voice. He turned to her. "Borrow whatever books you like, Mrs. Evans."

She lifted a hand to the glass, remembering the stories and the circumstances under which she had written them. Banallt came to her side again, leaning a shoulder against a panel of the shelves. "You have them all," she said.

"Yes." His head rested against the glass, his arms crossed over his chest. "The pride of my collection." He opened the glass door and reached for *The Murder of Gilling Fell*. He held it open, balanced on his palm. "I had this one already in my collection. When I read it, I never once suspected I would one day meet the authoress." He lowered his voice. "Does your brother know about your novels?"

"Of course not."

"Are you writing still?"

She shook her head.

"That seems a shame." He closed the title and took out a second one, turning pages. "Ah, the adventures of Beatrice, one of my favorites of yours."

She shut the book and took it from him. "All that is behind me." Drat his eyes. She could never look into his face without the risk of losing her soul. She replaced the book on the shelf but ran a finger down the spine, taking care not to look at him. "I don't need to pay the grocer or the butcher from my pocket anymore."

"Have you set aside pen and paper forever?" He'd managed to come quite near her, and she was trapped between the shelves and him. Not trapped. At any moment she could slide away and put a more comfortable distance between them. She touched his neckcloth. King's cravat had been perfect. Banallt's was not. Her fingers shook. "Miss Llewellyn is lovely," she said.

"Yes, she's quite beautiful. I have a dozen inquiries a month about her."

"But her heart is taken, isn't it?" Her knees were actually shaking.

His eyebrows rose. "You know?"

"I think it's a good match, Banallt."

"Do you?"

"Yes," she replied. But she was lying.

CHAPTER TEN

Rider Hall,
APRIL 27, 1812

The candlelight wavered as Sophie headed back to the room she used as her office. She jumped when her foot hit the seventh stair from the bottom and the riser creaked beneath her slipper-shod foot. That stair always creaked, but she'd let her thoughts get away from her, and she hadn't been prepared for the noise, even though she knew it was coming. A shiver of fear lingered between her shoulder blades. If ever there was a time for a ghost to appear, now was it. Despite the hour, half past two in the morning, and despite the silence in the house, there were no ghosts walking the halls of Rider Hall.

She turned the corner, her mind already back to her story. Poor Beatrice. Her young life was not going as well as it ought. And thank goodness. Her story had been stalled these past days and only just now had she worked her way past the troublesome issue of what was going to happen to the girl. She continued down the stairs and along the hallway to the room where she wrote when Tommy was at home.

So intent was she on Beatrice and her unhappy fate now that her aged aunt was dead and her fiancé was missing in Arabia that Sophie didn't notice someone else was in the room until she was halfway in. When she first saw the looming shape, her heart slammed against her chest. The sensation was a good deal less pleasant than her fright on the stairs. An instant later, which might as well have been a lifetime later, she realized the intruder was none other than Tommy's infernal companion, Lord Banallt.

His head was angled toward the lamp she'd left burning while she was upstairs attending to personal matters. He held several sheets of paper. Not just random sheets of paper, but her manuscript. And he was reading. Her manuscript! She didn't know whether to be furious or embarrassed. Both, it happened. The work was not even half done and contained much to be corrected and improved. He had no business reading without asking. She would have told him no if he had.

"I beg your pardon, my lord," she said curtly.

He turned his head toward her without moving any other part of his body. His hair gleamed black as ink, and the lamplight gave his eyes an unsettling silver glow. Gracious, was it possible for a man to be more handsome than he? Tommy was angelic, but Banallt was so darkly intense that when she looked at him she couldn't imagine thinking any other man deserved to be called handsome. "Ah," he said. "Mrs. Evans."

"Those are my personal papers, sir." She struggled to keep outrage from her voice. It wasn't easy. How dare he invade her privacy? Those were her papers. Her book. Her writing. How dare he? And her very next thought was she would be completely undone if he told Tommy she was writing. Tommy wouldn't understand. Never. And if her husband found out she was selling what she wrote? Her stomach clenched into a painful knot.

Two hours ago, Tommy and Banallt had come home from whatever carousing they'd been doing in town, with Tommy singing at the top of his lungs. They'd roused the household, had more to drink, and then Tommy had come into their room and stretched out on the bed even before his valet had arrived. Sophie left him. Let his servant get him undressed and sorted out. With her husband in another drunken sleep, she'd thought she was safe from interruption. Tommy wasn't going to wake up and doubtless Lord Banallt, too, was snoring between the sheets. So she'd thought.

"I saw the light on and thought it was your husband."

"It wasn't," she said. Banallt wasn't reading anymore, but he hadn't put the pages down, either.

He tipped his head to one side. If he was drunk, he didn't show it. He sounded and appeared perfectly sober. He couldn't be, though. Tommy had come home drunk, and surely so was Banallt, and her experience of Banallt in such a state was not agreeable. She did not want to snatch the pages from him, but she might have to. "You are up very late, ma'am. Do you not sleep at night?" he asked. All perfectly pleasant.

"Rarely." She scowled at her manuscript held in his long-fingered hands. "Those are my papers. Please put them back where you found them."

"I am used to London hours." He leaned a hip against the edge of her desk. In the light, his complexion was ghostly pale, and his eyes gleamed like a cat's. "In Town if I fall into my bed much before dawn, I've made an early night of it." He smiled, and Sophie felt a tug in her chest. For all his faults, and Banallt had a great many, he hadn't Tommy's vindictiveness. "But I daresay the same cannot be said of you."

She pressed her lips together and walked toward the desk, where she set down her candle. She did not smell liquor. Without looking at him, she picked up the pages of her story. He must think her a foolish woman, writing away in the dark of night, when no respectable lady read such novels, let alone penned them. "It is not your right, sir, to invade my privacy." She glanced at him and found his eyes steady on her. From the looks of things, he'd picked up her pages toward the middle. The most troublesome spot, too. She refused to look away from his pewter gaze. "Scribbles," she said. "Only scribbles."

"An interesting choice of word," he said mildly.

"My scribbles can be of no interest to a man like you."

"Pray tell me what you mean, Mrs. Evans."

"You'll find no verses, no lofty emotions. No Greek or Roman oratory. I write to amuse myself with lives I can never live. And if others are diverted as well, then let it be so." Those pages in his hand exposed her, opened her wide to a man she wished weren't here at all. There were two piles of paper on the desk. One consisted of the undisturbed beginning pages, the second of the overturned pages he'd read from the inch-thick set in his hands. He'd been careful, she saw, not to get her pages out of order. "It's how I pass the time, my lord."

"Mere amusements, if I may boldly contradict you, rarely keep ladies of good breeding up past midnight." Another smile quirked at the corner of his mouth. "At least not in the country."

"I don't sleep well." The words came out with genuine emotion instead of sounding distant and chilly, as she'd meant. "I never have since I came here." She didn't sleep well; that was true. He held her pages against his chest, drat the man. She could not simply take them back. "I have nightmares, if you must know."

His eyebrows rose. "Nightmares?"

"You know. The usual. Ogres in the closet She shrugged. Unpaid bills. Looming expenses—Tommy's bootmaker was especially fond of sending a representative to Rider Hall. A husband she did not see for months at a time. "Strange noises in the house. The wind. My father often complained of my overactive imagination."

"Ah," he said. He didn't sound convinced, but then, wasn't that the beauty of polite excuses? They weren't meant to be examined, only accepted as plausible.

"My lord, please." She bit her lower lip. His gaze dropped to her mouth. He wasn't drunk enough, if he was drunk at all, for her to hope she could divert him. "If you have been reading—"

"I confess I have."

"—then it's perfectly obvious what that is." She sighed as she stared out the window behind the earl. Moonlight silvered the lawn and the hedges beyond. "I work best when it's quiet." She sighed. There was no hope for it. He knew. "At night, with you and Tommy about, I cannot work in my room. So I am in here." She pinned him with her most earnest gaze. With luck, he would suffer an attack of regrets and leave Rider Hall. "Here," she said in meaningful tones, "I may have my privacy and my thoughts to myself."

"Scribbling away," he said. He did not sound in the least drunk. "In the dark of night."

"Yes."

"As scribbles go," he said, "yours are better than most." The corner of his mouth, with its full lower lip, curved as he looked at the pages against his chest. She despised him for his beauty. "This is very good." Another smile slid across his face. "Have you thought of publishing?"

There was no point in pretending she didn't know what he meant or that she'd never thought of such a thing and was flattered by the suggestion. She hadn't the patience anyway. She lifted her chin and met his peculiar tarnish eyes. She touched a finger to the desktop. Men were invariably taller than she was. Sophie was used to looking up. But Banallt was taller than most, and besides, she particularly disliked looking up at him. But she did and found herself struck anew by his dark good looks. If she were an artist, she'd paint him as Lucifer. She held his gaze and ignored the fact that he stared back. However compelling she found him, the fact remained that Lord Banallt was Tommy's friend, and Banallt's reputation was far from pleasant, as she had personal reason to know. She saw no point in pretending about that, either. With another sigh, she said, "Do you think the bills are paid from my husband's generosity and deep pockets?"

Some emotion, she could not tell what it might be, lit his eyes. "No, Mrs. Evans. I expect they are not."

She spoke over him because it occurred to her that he was mocking her. How dare he belittle her? "Because they are not, my lord. I assure you of that. I write because the bills must be paid somehow, and because even if I had a talent for farming, which I have not, it wouldn't matter. Tommy owns Rider Hall but not the land. He sold that shortly after we married."

"I know."

"Unless Tommy sends me something—from his gaming winnings, no doubt—there is no income here but what I bring in from those scribbles you cavalierly mock."

His eyebrows rose. "Mock? No, Mrs. Evans. I do not mock you." His serious reply caught her off guard. "I'm going to ask you an unforgivably rude question."

"Are you sure you ought?"

"How old are you?"

"Twenty-three."

"Twenty-three?"

"Yes."

"It was rude of me to read this without asking your permission," he said.

She eyed the pages in his hand, but not even that got him to put them down. "I should like them back, please."

"You were just a girl when you married Tommy." His eyebrows drew together. "You couldn't possibly have known anything about life."

She pressed her lips together. There he was again, mocking her. "I was in love, my lord. Head over heels in love. That was more than enough life for me."

"Mrs. Evans..."

She bowled over his silence. "Have no fear. I have learned quickly since I was married."

That too-attentive look flashed back into his eyes. He walked over to a settee with her manuscript still in his hands. "Do sit down, Mrs. Evans. It's late, and as we are both yet awake and neither one of us has yawned, let us speak a while longer. May I?" he asked, meaning, might he sit. When she waved a hand, he sat, legs sprawled so that she could not help but notice the muscled curve of his thighs. "You were in love," he said. "But no longer?"

"He is my husband, my lord."

He let his head fall back on the settee, staring at God knows what on the ceiling. When he looked back at her, his expression was unreadable. "A hypothetical, if I may."

"If I answer, will you give back my novel? I've bills to pay."

"I wonder whether you will answer to my satisfaction."

She sat sideways on the desk chair and gave him a challenging stare.

"Come closer. You're too far away." He grinned. "Just here." He pointed to an upholstered chair near him.

"Will you give back my book if I do?"

"You're a persistent woman." He leaned back and made a *sit there* motion with one hand. "No. Not yet."

She stayed where she was and crossed her ankles. She tucked her feet as far under her chair as they reached. "What is your hypothetical?"

"If you were married to me, Mrs. Evans, knowing what I am, would you be faithful?"

She made a face. "But I'm not married to you."

"Hence I pose it to you as a hypothetical, Mrs. Evans. I'm curious to know the answer." Another of his fleeting smiles flashed over his face. That smile intrigued her. He seemed another man entirely then. "Indulge me with your piquant honesty."

"Of course I would be faithful."

"Why *of course?*" He shrugged. "I would not be faithful to you."

"Marriage is a vow before God and before oneself, my lord. He cocked his head, obviously waiting to hear more. "I would not marry a man I did not love. And therefore, if I were married to you, it would be because I was in love. And to a woman in love, faithfulness is the air she breathes, not a meal she chooses. One day this, another that. Changing menus all the time because one grows bored."

"Do you still love your husband?" he softly asked.

She interlaced her fingers and forced her hands to relax on her lap. "I made a vow," she said. "And that is more than enough."

"I love my wife. But I am not faithful to her."

She lifted her gaze. He sounded oddly plaintive. Rakes did not pine for fidelity, did they? "That is nothing to do with me."

"I think it is not in my nature to be faithful. I love her. No one takes her place in my heart, but—" He frowned, and Sophie was astonished to see that he was thinking quite hard. "Why is that not enough for you?"

"How is it that you, the rogue extraordinaire, understand so little of women?"

He leaned forward. "I have a daughter, did you know that?"

"No."

"She's nearly three. There is no one in this world I love more. I would give my life for her." He settled back, his hands still on her pages. "When I became a father, I never expected that. Never. But I would. It's frightening to find oneself so vulnerable."

"I can see that," she said. Manifestly, that was true.

"There are days when I wonder who she will grow up to marry. Will she marry for love or make a political union to please her father? For which ought I to hope? Will she love her husband and be miserable or will she be happy enough in a marriage that had not, after all, engaged her heart?"

"What an odd choice you present. Love and misery or no love and happiness. Why can't a woman be in love and happy?"

He draped an arm along the top of the settee, but his eyes were intense on her face. "Are you?"

"If your daughter has even half your intelligence, and if you do not raise her to be ignorant...Do not tell me you are one of those men who think women ought to be ignorant."

"Perish the thought, madam."

"Then she will be happy in love." Sophie couldn't help but smile. How unexpected this was, to learn that Lord Banallt was a devoted parent. "Be a wonderful father to her, and she'll meet someone wonderful, my lord."

"I won't allow anything less." His eyes danced and for once did not strike her as eerie. "And yet I think, my God, if her husband does not make her happy, I'll kill him." He threw a hand into the air, describing a quick and deadly arc. "Or thrash him within an inch of his life. No man will make my little girl cry over her broken heart."

Sophie thought much better of Lord Banallt.

"Women, in my experience," he said, "are rarely happy to think their husbands stray." He turned over her pages and scanned them. "Men, Mrs. Evans, are deceitful creatures who demand fidelity of their wives while they discreetly set up a mistress or take one lover after another."

"Not all husbands do, you know," she said. "Some are faithful."

"But not I."

Neither of them, she thought, saw fit to include Tommy in that company of faithful husbands. She knew the truth, but did not *know* it, and she preferred it that way. "Perhaps you ought to set your daughter a better example, my lord."

"No doubt you're right." He stretched out a leg. They fell silent while he considered her. "You're a fine writer, Mrs. Evans."

The compliment caught her off guard. This time she really was flattered. "Thank you."

"Who will Beatrice end up with, I wonder? I burn with curiosity to know. Will it be the fiancé or the young nobleman who refuses to show her his face?"

"Perhaps Ralf, her cousin and guardian."

Banallt waved a hand. "Never. He's the villain. No heroine ever marries the villain at the end."

"Perhaps I'm writing a tragedy."

His eyes pinned her. "What name do you publish under? Not your own. I should have recognized it otherwise."

She hesitated before she answered, and he gave her a sideways look with a mischievous smile. "Very well." She frowned. "I write as Mrs. Merchant."

Lord Banallt sat up. He was still holding her pages, drat the man. *"Not The Murder of Gilling Fell?"*

"You've read it?" Her heart leaped.

He brought in his legs and leaned toward her. "Can this be so? The authoress of *The Desert Corsair* and *The Orphan of Hopewell Moor* sits before me?"

"I'm astonished," she said. Despite herself, she was immensely flattered. "You've read my books?"

"You, madam," he said, laughing, "have been responsible for keeping me up nearly twenty hours straight. I've read all your books, but for *The Peruvian Escape.* I've not found that as yet."

"That was my first."

"Yes, Mrs. Evans, you are quite my favorite authoress."

"My lord." She squeezed her fingers because she'd only now, far too late, realized what a dreadful mistake she'd made, putting her secret in the hands of a man like Banallt. Her throat closed off, and she had to take a deep breath before more words would come. She stared at her hands. What had she done, admitting anything to him, confessing even the name under which she published? He would think he knew her, and he didn't. He didn't know her at all.

"I'm not a fool, Mrs. Evans." He tsk-tsked at her. "What horror are you imagining?"

"Please." She looked up. He was still leaning forward, one hand on his knee, the other holding her manuscript pages. "Do not tell my husband."

His face went dark, and Sophie's heart raced. She'd heard the rumors about him. The absent master of Castle Darmead was no gentleman. Even here, so far from London, one heard tales. She couldn't bear to look at him, so she stared again at her lap. She wouldn't. No matter what he said or did or threatened. She wouldn't. She lifted her eyes from her lap and found him watching her. The sensation was not pleasant.

His eyes grew darker. "You would find yourself quite humiliated, not to mention badgered for money, if Tommy knew of your talent. You would indeed have a difficult time of it. If he knew."

"Then you do understand."

"Given his debts, I don't imagine he'd be able to keep the house if you weren't paying the taxes. I assume that's what you've done with the money."

"It's not as though the writing is very profitable. But an extra ten or fifteen pounds a quarter—"

"No wonder you write so quickly."

"Not the muse," she said softly, "so much as necessity." She was talking to a man who had, in all likelihood, spent that much and more in town, drinking with her husband, just tonight. A man like him would have no idea what ten pounds meant when you had to sit with the bills to decide which ones to pay this time. "Are you going to tell him?"

He shot to his feet. Her pages rattled in the air. "Do you think me so base as that?"

She stood up, too. "You've blackmailed women before."

"Have I?"

"Everyone says so."

"Well then. It's so." He dropped her manuscript on the settee and walked to her. Sophie would have retreated if her knees hadn't hit the chair behind her. He put his hands on either of her cheeks, holding her face. His skin burned hers; his eyes held her gaze and stared into her soul. "What would you be willing to do in return for my silence?"

She didn't answer.

"Well," he said, drawing out the word in an unbearably sensuous whisper. "And so. What an interesting moment this is."

What would it be like to be in the arms of a man who wanted her? Who actually seemed to admire her? She was attracted to him. What woman wouldn't be? But that didn't mean she would act on the sensations racing through her. She pulled back.

He let go of her. "Your secret is safe with me, Mrs. Evans."

She stepped back and hit the chair. He caught her upper arm, steadying her. He leaned closer. "Lovely, sad little Sophie Mercer Evans," he said in the voice of Satan himself. "When I take you to bed, I assure you, it won't be because I've coerced you. It will be because you want to be there."

CHAPTER ELEVEN

Number 5 Albion Grove, Hampstead Heath,
MARCH 16, 1815

Come now, Mrs. Evans," said His Grace, the Duke of Vedaelin. He had to raise his voice to make himself heard
over the din of conversation. They were at Mr. Tallboys's
garden fete in Hampstead Heath. John was somewhere here, but
Sophie couldn't see him from where she'd stopped to greet the duke.
A happy coincidence, meeting the duke here. Other than Mr. Tallboys and Vedaelin, she'd not seen anyone she knew even slightly.
The duke leaned closer to her. "Not a word of that was true."

She glanced in the direction of the retreating Mrs. Adcock. According to her, the Earl of Banallt, a man wicked to the very core,
was having an affair with Mrs. Peters. He would, claimed Mrs. Adcock, treat the woman badly and when he'd had his fill, leave her in
some publicly humiliating fashion, heartbroken and mired in scandal. Her information, she informed them, came from the very best
source: her own lady's maid, who had heard it directly from one of
Mrs. Peters's upstairs maids. If Banallt dared show his face here and
dared to greet her, why, Mrs. Adcock was going to give him the cut
direct. See if she didn't!

"London is no different than Duke's Head when it comes to gossip," Sophie told Vedaelin. She was proud of her cool reaction when
she learned that Banallt had been invited and might well show up.

Privately, she thought him quite up to such misbehavior, but also that he would have been more discreet up to now. Unless he really did intend to break with Mrs. Peters soon. The endings of his affairs were often the stuff of scandal.

Sophie watched Mrs. Adcock greet another couple. Her hands, glittering with half a dozen rings, flew into the air, swooping to punctuate whatever she was saying to her listeners. Repeating her gossip about Banallt's affair? Whatever the truth, Sophie did not much like the rumor. She wished she'd heard none of it. The gossip was vile. She didn't doubt Banallt was having an affair. If not with Mrs. Peters—and of course he was, the woman was exactly his type— then with some other woman who believed he was madly in love with her. Knowing him, he was probably having several affairs. She returned her attention to the duke.

Vedaelin's nut-brown hair was cut short, well above his collar. His clothing was sober and distinguished: dun breeches, chocolate waistcoat and coat. He was far from a dandy or a rake. And he would never be accused of having an affair or behaving in a manner that ill befit his rank. Sophie liked him a great deal. "Three-quarters of what one hears about Banallt is a lie, Mrs. Evans."

Sophie lifted one eyebrow but said nothing. She doubted Vedaelin knew Banallt as well as she did. "Yes," she replied, smiling a little. "But what of the one-quarter that isn't?"

He sighed and, with a hand to the back of her arm, steered her toward a quieter corner. There weren't many. Every inch of the rear gardens was occupied. His eyes were serious. "Mrs. Evans."

"Yes?"

"Your brother has told me you were previously acquainted with Lord Banallt." He lifted his hands when Sophie's eyes widened. "I know nothing more than that, I assure you."

"My brother should not have discussed me with you at all," she said. How disconcerting to think she'd been a subject of conversation between John and Vedaelin. She took a step back, but he followed, and the distance between them remained as it was. "It's mortifying, Your Grace, to know one's brother has spoken out of turn."

"I was not aware until then," Vedaelin said, "that Banallt had been acquainted with your husband. Nor that the earl brings back memories you find painful." He studied her. "My wife, the duchess, has been gone nearly ten years. I understand the heartache of loss."

She put a hand on his arm. "May I say how sorry I am for *your* loss."

Vedaelin pressed her hand. "Your brother approached me because he was worried his association with me would inevitably bring you in contact with Lord Banallt."

"And if it does?" she said, too tartly. She softened her tone. "I'm a grown woman, Your Grace. If I have reason to know he lives a less than exemplary life, though not quite as depraved as Mrs. Adcock would have it, I think I have been, and am now, quite capable of avoiding him."

"What if you cannot? Your brother has the right of it. Your temperament is too sensitive and delicate. Your loss still recent enough to cause you hurt."

Sensitive and delicate? "Then so be it." Sophie rolled her eyes. Perhaps she was, but she'd still managed to keep a household together when her husband seemed determined to spend every last penny from beneath her feet. "If I cannot avoid Lord Banallt, I won't swoon, I promise you that. I'm not so delicate as you seem to think. Nor will I show him a cold shoulder. It's perfectly possible for me to say, 'Good afternoon, my lord' or 'Yes, the weather is wet this evening. I think we shall have fog.' Honestly. John had no right to decide how I feel." And none to tell Vedaelin about it.

"Certainly, Mrs. Evans, one once heard a great deal that was not to Banallt's credit."

"Yes," Sophie said. "That's so." She was weary of Banallt as a subject of conversation, and she was now angry with Mrs. Adcock for bringing him into their conversation in such an unpleasant manner. And angrier still at John. She forced herself to smile at the duke. "If I have any delicacy at all, Your Grace, it is in how I shudder to think what will happen should Lord Banallt arrive and Mrs. Adcock be obliged to carry out her threat."

Vedaelin smiled back, some of his earlier tension dissipating with her joke. "A scandal to be sure. But as to the gossip one might hear of him these days, I've occupied his hours the better part of every day since his return from Paris. For which the government is most grateful, I assure you. Today, Mrs. Evans, we shall have no scandal from him. I keep him too busy for that."

She frowned. "May I ask why you make use of a man whose reputation is of so little credit to him? Whether what's said is true or not, I mean."

Vedaelin set a finger by his nose then tapped his temple twice. "Whatever his reputation, the Earl of Banallt is a man of extraordinary intellect and powers of persuasion."

"I'll grant you that, sir. And yet."

"Come now. If Canning and Castlereagh may shoot each other, then I thing the government will readily survive Banallt's reputation." It was the duke's turn to frown. "I should like to set your mind at ease, Mrs. Evans. Not long ago I would have refused his acquaintance. But some time ago, shortly after his wife's death, I observed a divergence between the gossip and his behavior. That divergence continues to this day."

"Mrs. Adcock notwithstanding?" she asked.

Vedaelin turned and nodded his head in the direction of a young man with a beaver hat on his head. "Do you see that young dandy there? The one with the violently purple waistcoat?"

"What of him?"

"If we're to have a scandal this season, it will come from him. Mr. Frederick Drake. Not from the Earl of Banallt."

Mr. Drake was perhaps twenty-three or twenty-four with a smile that lit his eyes. His blond curls were not long enough to be styled à la Byron, yet not short enough that he wasn't daring. He had a rather stout young lady on his arm, and it was plain to Sophie that his companion was besotted and that Mr. Drake was doing everything in his power to see that she stayed that way. And yet, she did not think he was in love with the girl. There was something familiar about Drake. "She's an heiress, isn't she?" Sophie asked.

"Miss George. Sixty thousand in the five percents, a substantial property from her maternal aunt, Lady Yelvers. And a doting father."

Sophie's heart turned. Her own dowry had not been so much greater than Miss George's, and she, too, had inherited property from her mother's side of the family. And like Miss George, she'd been dazzled by the attentions of a handsome young man. "Mr. Drake is without a fortune of his own, I collect."

"He wouldn't be the only young man in London looking to marry an heiress," Vedaelin said. "But, yes. He's rather thin in the pocket-book."

She was looking at her own past. She'd not been stout when she met Tommy, but she had certainly been physically awkward. She recognized the infatuation in the young lady's eyes, because she'd felt it herself when she met Tommy, when she was too green a girl to know when a man was sincere in his affections. "One hopes her family is paying close attention," she said.

"This, ma'am, is what comes of a girl whose reading is not strictly regulated."

She turned to a path less crowded. Vedaelin followed. "How so?" she asked.

"Horrid novels, Mrs. Evans." His expression of revulsion told her everything she needed to know about his opinion of such works.

"Good heavens. Do you truly think reading novels leads a young girl to ruin?"

"We shall hope Miss George does not come to grief." He took her hand, and they walked for some minutes in silence. "Banallt has known bitter tragedy," he said softly. "You are not, I think, aware of the extent of his personal loss." Sophie glanced away, remembering a day when her life had come crashing down around her. A day when Banallt had betrayed their friendship. "His wife's passing was a sad event," Vedaelin said. "But that was not the loss that brought him low. I don't call many men friend, Mrs. Evans, but he is one." He looked at Sophie with such tempered sorrow that she thought to herself, *Why, he quite means it!* The notion shocked her, that someone like Vedaelin should hold Banallt in such high regard.

She could not dismiss the image of Mrs. Peters in Banallt's arms and wished violently for a change in subject. "Is there some reason you're telling me this?"

Vedaelin pressed her hand between his. "Only so that you know why Banallt has earned my regard, Mrs. Evans, and my esteem. I am convinced that whatever you thought of him in the past, that poor opinion is not now justified. There is no reason for you to feel pained by his presence."

Someone called to the duke, and he pressed her hands again. "Have I helped at all?"

Sophie summoned a smile. "Yes, you have. Thank you, Your Grace." The duke took his leave of her. She'd not been standing there long when Reginald Tallboys presented himself.

"I wanted to come over much sooner," he said. "But you and the duke looked far too serious to interrupt. Have you solved the troubles of the world?"

"Yes, quite," she said. Had Banallt truly transformed himself? Her heart constricted. She did not wish to feel anything. Her feelings toward Lord Banallt were set and justified upon her personal knowledge of the sort of man he was. She had made the right decision in declining Banallt's offer of marriage. She had. His offer had not been from the heart. She lifted her head, having mastered her sudden welling of emotion. Perhaps she had not, though, for her throat felt too narrow, and she was afraid to speak.

Tallboys held out his arm and Sophie took it. "Shall we stroll farther, Mrs. Evans?"

"I should like that very much."

"That's if we can make our way through this infernal crush. I don't recall inviting so many people."

"Then your party is a success, sir."

"For an intimate gathering of two hundred of my closest friends, most of whom I don't recall meeting, yes. I've already sent my butler around to all the neighbors to scavenge more food and drink."

"I've heard no complaints of a shortage, Mr. Tallboys."

"A mercy. I see I shall have to award my butler a bonus for today's heroism."

"Have you seen my brother, Mr. Tallboys?"

Tallboys chuckled. "There are a great many lovely ladies here. Your brother is quite popular with them all, I'll have you know. Dozens of young ladies have their eye on him."

"Of course," she said. She didn't keep back the note of pride in her brother. "He's a gentleman. Handsome and jovial and one day he'll make some woman a splendid husband." He patted her arm. "Our father always said John would make a politician one day, and here he's done it." She leaned against his arm and noticed that her hand curled around muscle. "So now I must ask you, in your opinion, are any of these ladies present worthy of my brother, Mr. Tallboys?"

He laughed. "One or two perhaps."

"You must give me their names. I should like to meet them."

"Will you make an inventory?"

She laughed. "Yes, I believe I will."

Going from the terrace to the rear gardens took them nearly half an hour. She did not see John even once. But then, Tallboys was constantly stopped, and introductions had to be made, so that Sophie felt quite wrung out with all the hand lifting and knee bending and polite murmurs.

"See there?" Tallboys said, nodding toward a young woman surrounded by at least a dozen men. The crowd shifted, and she was not surprised to see Miss Llewellyn at the center. Beside her, in pride of place at her side, stood Adonis in the form of Mr. Frederick Drake. Her perfect match, nearly as lovely as she, with his booted foot propped on the metal arm of the bench on which his Aphrodite sat. His laughing brown eyes rarely moved off the young woman. He'd quite abandoned Miss George. And why not, when he was not sincere in his affections? Sophie looked at Tallboys and then back to the breathtaking young woman. He was a bold fortune hunter indeed to chase after a relative of Banallt's. "I'll wager we'll have a scandal from Mr. Drake before the end of the season," Tallboys said. "And I'll have you know, he had no invitation from me."

"You think Mr. Drake has designs on Miss Llewellyn?"

"If he dares, Banallt will tear him limb from limb." Tallboys laughed and so did Sophie. "However, that was not my reason in pointing her out. Behold, Mrs. Evans, for there sits your brother's match."

She faced Tallboys. She fisted her hands behind her back. "To my knowledge, John has not paid Miss Llewellyn any special attention. Why, they're barely acquainted." She felt a little panicky, because she remembered that John had sent Miss Llewellyn flowers. And she had worn one of the blossoms near her heart. "How can anyone predict that they'll make a match of it?"

"You've only been in London a short while," Tallboys said. "Last season was a different matter." His expression was solemn, and Sophie's heart misgave her. Was it true? Did John love Miss Llewellyn?

"What do you mean?" She bowed her head, staring at the tips of her slippers. Must everything come back to Banallt? She knew her brother well enough to know he'd never marry her when it meant bringing Banallt into the family. Not even if it meant he didn't marry the woman he loved.

"I mean that last season there was all but an understanding between them." He fell thoughtful. "I wonder what's happened?"

Sophie felt ill. "Were they very much in love?"

"That was my impression." He pulled her off the path to let a veritable herd of young ladies go past. "I don't recall inviting them, either," he said as they went past. "Lately, one hears that Miss Llewellyn and Banallt will make a match of it before much longer. If the field remains clear, I expect they will."

Sophie studied Miss Llewellyn. She was a lovely young woman, and no silly girl, either. Or course John had fallen in love with her. She ought to have realized. "I'd no idea. Really, none at all." She linked arms with him, leaning against him and taking them along the path again, and said, "Come, let's inspect the roses. They are a passion of mine. I adore gardening."

"I work very hard with the roses here. I'll be pleased to hear what you think of them."

Behind them, the texture of conversation changed. A buzz. No other description sufficed. She and Tallboys turned at the same time.

Banallt walked onto the gravel path outside and scanned the crowd. He had not come here to socialize. He wore his greatcoat and held his hat in one hand. She and Mr. Tallboys stood fifteen or twenty feet to his right, and at the moment, Banallt's attention was to his left. Looking for Miss Llewellyn? The woman he intended to marry? Whatever the source of his attraction, Sophie had ample time to study his face. On the path behind him, Vedaelin strode toward him, his expression intent.

Tallboys tensed. "Something's happened," he said.

Lord Banallt's head turned, and Sophie felt to her soul the moment when his gaze found hers. There was only a moment's pause, the space of a heartbeat, and then his gaze moved to Tallboys. He continued toward them, gripping his hat by the brim. Sophie's heart thudded hard.

"Banallt," Tallboys said when Banallt reached them.

He bowed. His mouth was tense. He looked at Sophie, and again their eyes locked and Sophie found herself trapped in his gaze. His eyes were such an odd color. "Have you seen Vedaelin?"

"Just there," Tallboys said. Banallt looked over his shoulder and saw the duke making his way toward them. "Mrs. Evans," he said turning back. As if he'd never cried in her arms. As if he'd never offered for her. So cold and distant. Exactly as she would have hoped after all that had happened between them. "Good afternoon. I hope you are well."

Sophie curtseyed. No one would guess he was a disappointed suitor. But then, he'd not really spoken to her out of love, she thought. Only vexation that he should have been dismissed by anyone. "I am, my lord. And you?"

"Quite well, ma'am." Vedaelin joined them, and Banallt's attention moved to the duke. "Your Grace." His gaze darted to Sophie, then to Tallboys, and then to Vedaelin. "Forgive me, but you are needed at Whitehall. Immediately. There is news—" Again he glanced at Sophie.

"The moment I saw you, I sent Mercer on ahead," Vedaelin said. He bowed to Sophie. "My apologies, ma'am, for sending your brother away. Tallboys, we'll need you, too, I expect."

"There is news from Rothschild," Banallt said softly in response to Tallboys's inquiring look. "Castlereagh awaits us."

Vedaelin nodded. "Tallboys, with me, if you don't mind."

"Your Grace."

"Mrs. Evans will need an escort home. See her safely to her door, won't you, Banallt? Do you mind, Mrs. Evans?

Banallt bowed. "So I anticipated," he said in a voice as dry as sand.

What could Sophie say but, "Of course not."

CHAPTER TWELVE

Seeing Tallboys starting at Sophie like some heart-sick fool sent an arrow straight into Banallt's heart. And she, of course, demonstrated no awareness whatever that Mr. Reginald Tallboys or His Grace the Duke of Vedaelin had a *tendre* for her. Her expression was sober, vivid with intelligence as always. God, what a web this was. He knew very well that Mercer was in love with Fidelia. That bit of old news had come to him months ago. Mercer, understandably, had given up hope where Fidelia was concerned. Her father had loftier hopes for his daughter. Christ. He did not care to be at the center of this tangle, yet here he was.

Banallt offered Sophie his arm after Tallboys took his leave, with more apologies to Sophie. He doth protest too much, he thought. The man was too charmed by half. He waited while Sophie watched Tallboys go. Would she take his arm, or was he to have a cold shoulder? "You are uncomfortable," he said at last. He'd not given the butler his hat nor had he put it back on when he came outside to find Tallboys looking ready to go down on one knee. He had to concentrate on not crushing the brim. "Shall I find someone else to escort you home? I can fetch Tallboys back if you like." He scowled again. He was damned if he'd send Sophie home with Tallboys. "My cousin, Mrs. Llewellyn, has a carriage here. I'm sure she'll not mind sending you home."

She took a breath. "I take it your carriage is waiting?"

"Yes."

"Then let us go." She settled into one of her unreadably calm expressions. "I don't wish to delay you with foolish errands. I'll finish scolding Mr. Tallboys myself when next I see him."

If she hadn't spoken in so fond a tone, he would have felt better to hear she'd been scolding him. As it was, she sounded on far too intimate terms with the man. They hardly knew each other. "Do they call often at Henrietta Street?" he asked. Well. And so. Of course they must. Both of them were free to call when they liked. A knife twisted in his heart.

"Who?"

"Tallboys and Vedaelin."

"From time to time. He's amusing. Tallboys, I mean. And he calls, the duke does, when he needs something of John." She didn't sound like a woman who understood the many excuses that could bring a man to her home. "Which is often."

He didn't know what to say to her after that, and so he said nothing. She walked beside him with a brisk, no-nonsense stride. Their silence was not uncomfortable. Silence between them never had been, unless she was angry with him. He let the silence continue. What, after all, did a man say to the woman who had refused his heart? Though he would allow that perhaps his had been badly offered. In such a circumstance, nothing was the perfect reply. He was aware, damn it all, far too aware, of her dainty figure at his side. He could ignore his response to her. He could. And would.

"Mrs. Evans?" a woman's voice called out. The tone shrilled in his ears. Years of experience had honed his instincts for the high-in-the-instep matron whose disapproval had just locked on him and must be voiced. He knew, therefore, what he would face if they stopped.

But Sophie stopped and so, therefore, did he.

"Mrs. Adcock. How do you do?" Sophie said.

Mrs. Adcock steadfastly refused to look at him. Such reactions were common enough from certain women. He was amused, or would have been if Sophie weren't about to be involved. "Pray tell, Mrs. Evans," she said in a voice of patently false concern, "where has the duke gone? Did I not see you with him these past five minutes?"

"The duke," Banallt said, "has been called to Whitehall." Mrs. Adcock refused to meet his gaze. Women like her lived to disapprove, and was not the Earl of Banallt a favorite target of disapproval? Deservedly or not. "As has Mr. Mercer," he added.

Mrs. Adcock's attention remained on Sophie. Ah, the cut direct. He stifled a laugh. He'd been cut dead by better women than Mrs. Adcock. "I do hope the duke has not taken ill, Mrs. Evans. Last I saw His Grace, you were with him."

"Yes," Sophie said, drawing out the syllable perhaps a moment too long. "His Grace has been called to Whitehall. As has my brother, Mr. Mercer." She lifted her chin. Somewhere between Tommy destroying her spirit and now, Sophie had learned to stand up for herself. Had she been that way when he came to Havenwood to lay his heart at her feet? Probably. He ought to have noticed and taken that into account. But then, his proposal had been too much about him and hardly at all about her. Vedaelin would do well by her. They suited. Tallboys even better. "Lord Banallt has now the unhappy task of seeing me home. And then he, too, must to Whitehall."

Mrs. Adcock laid a hand on Sophie's arm. "One so worries about undue influences."

"The duke himself asked Lord Banallt to see me home."

"One never wishes to offend, Mrs. Evans." Mrs. Adcock firmed her mouth. "I'm sure you must want to think of something else."

Sophie's chin went up. "I'm sure I don't," she said. Banallt knew Sophie well enough to understand she wasn't so much defending him as she was defending herself from Mrs. Adcock's scorn. Though he wanted to flatter himself to think she might be defending him at least a little.

"Well. I am very sorry to hear that!"

"Lord Banallt," Sophie said. "We've delayed too long. I should hate for His Grace to call you to account for any further delay."

"He did ask that I join him as soon as possible," he said mildly. He speared Mrs. Adcock with his iciest gaze and was pleased to see her blanch.

Mrs. Adcock removed her hand from Sophie's arm. "But, Mrs. Evans." She leaned in. "Ought you to be seen leaving with Lord Banallt, of all men? Is it wise?"

Sophie's hand tightened on his arm. He saw her eyes go wide and innocent. "The Duke of Vedaelin himself left me to Lord Banallt's care. Should he not have?" She didn't give Mrs. Adcock a chance to answer. Instead, she turned to him and said, "Ought I walk home, my lord, over Shooter's Hill and with rain threatening?" She stuck out a foot. "These slippers will be ruined, I'm sure."

"No, ma'am, you ought not." He reached into his pocket for his watch and consulted it. "Forgive me. Time grows short."

Mrs. Adcock sniffed and took a step back. "Mrs. Evans," she said with a darting look at Banallt. "I'm shocked by the company you choose to keep."

"Thank you for your concern," Sophie said. She curtseyed. "Good day, Mrs. Adcock." She walked away so quickly Banallt actually had to take a long step to catch up to her.

When they were walking down the front stairs to his waiting carriage, Sophie having retrieved her cloak from a servant, she exploded. Her voice remained low, but anger vibrated in her words. There was rain now, big heavy drops that hit the ground and splattered. The sky and the road were precisely the same shade of gray. "The nerve of that woman, Banallt," she said.

He raced after her, opening his umbrella and holding it over her head. He didn't think she noticed. "How dare she suggest that my brother or the duke would leave me in the care of a man whom they did not trust! How dare she insult you!" At the curb they waited for the groom to lower the carriage step. Banallt handed his umbrella to the servant. She stomped one foot on the flagstone. "Honestly," she said. "She was beyond anything."

He was rather smug about the fact that he'd brought his enclosed carriage out to Hampstead Heath rather than his phaeton, even though the morning had begun with blue skies. A stroke of good fortune, since otherwise he would not have been able to drive Sophie home. His coat of arms was uncovered, and his earl's coronet gleamed splendidly amid the gilt. When he knew he was driving here, he'd brought along four burly footmen as well. Their livery was most impressive, he thought.

She hardly gave the vehicle a glance. She was irritatingly immune to displays of position or wealth. "It's beyond anything, I tell you."

"London. Twenty-six Henrietta Street," he told the coachman. He took her hand and helped her inside, ducking a little as he generally must when a servant holding an umbrella was shorter than he was, which was most of the time. "Yes," he said, getting in after her. He sat on the backward-facing seat. The door closed, but the interior lanterns were lit, so it was not gloomy at all. "The problem," he said, setting his hat on the seat beside him and brushing off drops of rain, "with having reformed one's life is that so many others have not."

He sat across from her and thought that had they been alone like this two years ago, he would not have stayed on his seat. He leaned an elbow on the ledge of the window. Raindrops glistened in her hair. Her frock of blue muslin wasn't the least in fashion. Nor the blue ribbon twined through her hair, nor the lace-edged bow decorating her cap. Pale blue, an insipid color best suited to one's most ancient aunt, looked fetching on her. A good color for a brunette with eyes that shifted between blue and green. Despite everything, despite the silence, he felt very much at ease with her.

"Have you enjoyed London so far, Sophie?"

Her fingers spread out a pleat in the fabric of her coat. "John has been so busy with Vedaelin. Besides Cavendish Square, today is only the second time we've left the house."

The other time, evidently, having been their visit to Gray Street.

"Hampstead Heath is a pretty village," she said.

"Then you are bored."

"Not much. I've been very busy with settling us in, and John has a thousand things he needs of me. Tell me about London, Banallt." She lifted her chin, determined, it seemed, to be polite. "You've lived here for years. What is there to see?"

"London is…another world." He leaned back so that he had a better view of her face. She was one of those women, he'd long ago decided, whose appeal did not lie in repose, but in action, in the change of expression, the quick, intelligent eyes. "Town is noisy, exciting. Thrilling. You may find something of everything in the world. The poor, the rich, young, old, ugly, all that is lovely, sublime, or pathetic. Love and danger and amusements of every sort." He set a hand on the top of his hat and brushed away raindrops that weren't there. "Some you would approve of and many you would not."

"Have you met the king? Or the prince?"

"Yes. As to both. The king does not go about anymore. He is quite mad, they say. I see the regent from time to time but avoid him, as he is all too likely to ask me for a loan."

Her fingers smoothed the pleat of her coat then creased it again. "Tommy always promised to take me but never did."

"He would not have known what to do with you here." Must she constantly link him to that blasted Tommy Evans? "His notion of amusement would not have suited you."

"No doubt."

The last thing he wanted to talk about was her husband. "I've not thought of London as anything but my home for so long I've forgotten some of the very things I most love about the city."

"Such as?"

"Hyde Park, as far from Rotten Row as it's possible to be. Kew Gardens. Marylebone. King's Theatre. If I were not engaged with Vedaelin and his business, I would go to the Royal Academy several times in the month. Vauxhall amuses. Your brother should take you. Ask him. I'm sure you can persuade him. There is the opera. The ballet." He smiled. "Astley's to see Il Diavolo Antonio on the slack wire."

Her eyes turned dreamy. He imagined gazing into her eyes while she came to passion. Inappropriate, yes, but he was a man, after all, and he was not over her no matter how often he told himself that he was. "How thrilling that sounds."

"Naturally, my experience of Town is different from yours. When you do go out, you will not find the same city as I."

She frowned at him, but it was a good-natured frown. "London Bridge won't fall just because I've decided to pay a call." She put her nose in the air and looked aggrieved. "Will the Thames alter course merely because Mrs. Evans gazes upon its waters?"

"London Bridge and the Thames are on the periphery of my life in Town." He leaned toward her and caught the scent of orange water. "I do not find them entertaining. No doubt you will be at least a little diverted by Bond Street and Ackermann's, both of which I avoid like the plague. You'd be sipping chocolate and wondering if anyone would invite you to walk Rotten Row while I—I am a man, and I move in different circles."

Her eyes settled on him. "What is so urgent, Banallt, that Vedaelin and my brother must be called to Whitehall? Is it the war? Has it started?"

"Not yet."

She sighed. "Forgive my asking. I oughtn't pry."

"No fear, Sophie. I shan't tell you what I am not free to divulge."

"I didn't think you would."

He'd hurt her feelings. "Sophie."

When they arrived at Henrietta Street they listened to the coachman climb down from the box, boots clomping, breath huffing, neither of them knowing what to say to break their long silence. Sophie turned her head to the street. A moment longer for one of the grooms to see the horses were settled. Their gazes met, and this time, their silence was not so comfortable.

As Banallt waited for the step to rattle down and the door to open, he understood with a quick and inexplicable intuition that the attraction between them was mutual. He'd always known she found him handsome, but an ocean lay between a woman thinking a man was handsome and thinking she'd go to bed with him. The ocean between him and Sophie had just gotten smaller.

"Banallt," she said.

His heart leaped. "Yes?"

She leaned toward him, hands clasped on her lap. "Is there no hope for my brother and Miss Llewellyn?" How like her to get right to the point. "If 'tis true they love each other, can we not set aside our differences? Or are you determined to marry her yourself?"

"Are they in love?" he asked. The door opened with a roar of rain on the umbrella held by one of his footmen. The poor man was getting drenched, but he had his pistols tucked safely out of the way. Banallt put on his hat and stepped out. He dipped his head to avoid being hit by the umbrella and helped her down. When he felt her hand on his, he steadied himself.

"I'm told John is very much in love with her," she said.

"I've not forbidden her." He smiled. "I wouldn't dare. I'm not a fool who doesn't understand the allure of the forbidden."

She squeezed his hand. "John must feel he can't declare himself for her. Not with you and I at loggerheads. Please, let's not keep them apart."

"It's her father who ought to worry you." He took the umbrella from the footman and headed toward number 26. "My cousin has some absurd notions about whom Fidelia should marry."

"Has he?"

"You know what they are."

"And?"

"I've not made up my mind." On that subject, he refused to say more. Fidelia did not interest him, but as he watched Sophie, he thought, why not? If Sophie married Vedaelin or some other more worthy man, and if Fidelia was amenable, there were more reasons than not to marry her, chief among them the consolidation of family holdings. At the door, he bowed, and she disappeared into the house he'd been forbidden to enter.

CHAPTER THIRTEEN

Number 2 Charlotte Row, London,
MARCH 20, 1815

At eleven o'clock, Sophie had a note from John to meet him at number 2 Charlotte Row rather than wait for him to pick her up for their luncheon engagement with Vedaelin. She arrived at half past twelve, having walked from Henrietta Street with her maid, Flora. Flora went around to the back while Sophie knocked on the door of the town house, which was painted a glossy, cheerful yellow.

King answered the door, and Sophie stared stupidly at him, wondering if she'd come to the wrong place. "Mrs. Evans," the butler said. "Do come in."

"It's you, King."

"That it is, ma'am." He opened the door wider, and Sophie went in. The town house was charming. The walls were a pale green, the furniture light and long-legged. "Your brother is upstairs with the rest of that roguish crowd." He took her coat and her umbrella.

"Does Lord Banallt stay here?" she asked as she followed King upstairs.

"He keeps rooms here when Hightower isn't convenient." He paused to look over his shoulder at her. He was three steps above her, and Sophie had to look a very long way up. "This isn't his bachelor quarters, if that's why you're frowning like that." He sniffed. "I'd not let you in if that were the case, Mrs. Evans."

"Thank you for that."

"You're welcome."

King went to a parlor door from which a great deal of male conversation could be heard. He rapped his knuckles on the side of the door. In the ensuing silence, he announced her then stepped aside to let her into the parlor.

With trepidation at the thought of seeing Banallt again, Sophie went inside to confront a chaotic scene. The air stank of stale smoke, old wine, and cold coffee. Quite plainly, the gentlemen had been up all night, and furthermore, they were shocked to see her. The gentlemen who'd been sitting stood while others hurried to put on their coats. Vedaelin was seated—standing now—at a table with Banallt behind him. Banallt had been leaning over to study the papers strewn over the tabletop. A chart of the sea around France was tacked on the wall behind them.

Mr. Tallboys was here, too, as was John in a corner with a mountain of documents. She nodded at Mr. Tallboys, but no more than that. Banallt's gaze she avoided. She recognized several cabinet ministers, too. Papers, maps, and charts were everywhere, with any item at hand moved to hold down the sheets or flatten a map. A man she didn't recognize darted her a glance and began quickly turning over papers.

"Sophie," John said. He'd jumped up and was now scrubbing his fingers through his hair. "You're here."

She bent a knee. "It is past noon," she told him.

Nobody said anything.

"John," she said into that awful quiet. The back of her neck burned. "I'd never have come but for your note."

He had the grace to look abashed. "Two hours ago we thought we'd be done by now. We're not."

Vedaelin waved a hand. He did not, however, come from behind the desk. More of them were engaged in turning over or covering up the papers. "Nevertheless, Mrs. Evans, it is delightful to see you."

"Thank you, Your Grace." Sophie put her hands on her hips and surveyed the room. "I'll tell King to bring luncheon here. And order some tea, I think. When I come back, you'll have decided between the lot of you whether I may be of any assistance." She looked around. "John will confirm I have a very neat hand. If you have correspondence or other documents to be copied I should be more than happy to do so." Banallt put a hand over his mouth as if to cover a cough. She suspected not, however. "I also excel in organization. You may, however, wish to tell me that I am not needed." She let her gaze scan the room with its stacks of papers. "But I don't advise it."

She went downstairs, found King, and gave him her instructions. When she returned, John handed her a stack of papers and a portable writing desk and asked, rather sheepishly, if she minded copying them out. In another room. She didn't. She discovered a small parlor farther down the hallway that seemed a suitable and agreeable place to work. King found her a short while later to bring her tea and a plate of bread and cold meat. "Thank you," she said.

She ate some of the ham and cheese and went back to work. The documents were deadly dull. Soporifically dull. She suspected John had deliberately selected the most inane pages he could find. For a while, she amused herself by imagining she was locked in the topmost tower of a castle, forced to labor for a wicked uncle who wished to steal her secret inheritance. That worked swimmingly for a time.

The sound of the door being thrown open startled her into sitting upright. The table at which she sat was not in a direct line to the door, which was why Banallt did not see her when he strode in. In nearly one motion, he pulled off his coat and threw himself on the sofa to lie on his back, one arm thrown over his eyes. She got a glimpse of narrow hips and a flat belly. Whatever else Banallt was, he was a splendid animal. He heaved a sigh and raised his inside leg, letting his knee fall against the sofa back. His other foot stayed on the floor.

She cleared her throat to let him know he was not alone.

"Blast," he said. He snatched his coat off the floor and hastily shrugged it on. "Is that you, Sophie?" he said, buttoning his coat as he faced her.

"Yes, Banallt."

He winced. "Forgive me, I did not know you were in here."

"Why would you?" She cocked her head. "You look tired," she said.

"Yes." He scrubbed a hand over his face. "What an evening— night." He glanced at the window through which one could see sunlight. "Day."

"Have you been to sleep at all yet?"

"No."

She frowned and said, "I didn't intend to interrupt your meeting."

"You didn't." He stayed on his feet. The door gaped open because he'd not closed it when he came in. From where she stood she could see the opposite wall of the hallway and a portion of a portrait and its gilt frame.

"All the same, I felt quite the fool."

"Vedaelin admitted that you and Mercer had a positive engagement." His jaw was dark with stubble. "Thank you for sending food to us. None of us realized how the hours had gotten away from us. We were famished."

"All of you looked in need of sustenance."

He rubbed his chin. "What about you? Have you had anything to eat or drink?"

She pointed to her plate. "King brought something." Banallt's eyes glinted at the remaining food, and she smiled. "Help yourself if you care to. I couldn't eat another bite."

"I could." He walked to the table and set about making himself a sandwich.

Silence gaped between them. Sophie gathered her nerve and spoke. "I want to thank you," she said.

He turned, a thin slice of beef in hand. "For what?"

"For speaking so sternly to me at Cavendish Square. You were right to scold me." He nodded as he eyed his sandwich. "Do sit, Banallt. Eat."

He did. Sophie retreated to the sofa because the distance felt safer. "Tallboys had a great deal to say about you," he said after he'd swallowed a large bite. "You've made quite an impression on him."

"How well do you know Mr. Tallboys?" she asked. She clasped her hands on her lap.

"Tallboys?" His mouth twitched, and then the twitch became a smile. "You'll be pleased to learn I've not known him long. Only since I came back from Paris."

She returned his smile. "I don't disapprove of everyone who knew you, Banallt."

"Nevertheless."

"You do relieve my mind," Sophie said.

He laughed at the same time she did, and when they were done and both of them were smiling, she said, "Banallt, we are all right now, aren't we? As much as we can be, I mean."

His gaze settled on her. "Yes," he said at last. He wasn't telling her the truth, she thought, yet she was more than willing to accept this from him. "We are."

"I've missed you," she said. "Missed talking to you."

"As have I."

"I'm glad to be friends with you."

"It seemed like auld lang syne when I saw you here." He waved a hand at the desk. "Bent over and scribbling away. I even wondered for a moment what story you were writing."

She tugged on a fold of her skirt. "This time the material is dry as dust. I ought to write in a kidnapping just to liven things up."

He narrowed his eyes at her. "Why?"

"Why?" she said as Banallt took a bite of his sandwich. "Because I do not find a list of supplies sent to Falmouth remotely fascinating. A shortcoming of mine, I expect. You know how easily bored I am."

He tilted his head. "I mean why did you ask me about Tallboys?"

She didn't answer right away. His black hair gleamed and set off his eyes. And though he was perhaps no longer perfectly put together, his clothing was exquisite. He wore a black coat and a cream waistcoat embroidered with tiny black florets. His neckcloth was disheveled. Before her eyes, his sandwich was consumed. She watched him drink her tea. "That can't still be hot," she said.

"No." He took another swallow and put down the cup. "You take too much sugar."

"You don't take enough."

"I could eat another of those," he said, looking at her empty plate. He tugged on his cravat and managed to make an uneven loop on one side.

"For pity's sake." Sophie went to him. "Let me fix this, my lord." She unfastened his cravat and stepped back in order to refold the material with at least a halfway decent crease. "Your valet does not use enough starch," she told him as she laid it over the back of his neck and brought the ends to the front.

"He's no King," Banallt sighed.

"Why did you let him leave you as valet?" She crossed the ends, taking care to keep her edges as crisp as she could. Banallt lifted his chin.

"He wanted to move up in life. So I made him butler when mine retired. My household has never run more smoothly."

"And your neckcloths?" She pushed his chin up so she could make the next cross of the material.

"Alas, a decided turn for the worse."

She smiled to herself. "Perhaps King could give him lessons."

"He's a gentleman," Banallt said. She didn't realize right away that he meant Tallboys. "Vedaelin thinks highly of him."

"Hold still," she said. Banallt's hair brushed the backs of her fingers.

He did. For a time. "Has Tallboys asked you to marry him?"

She finished the knot and took a step back to survey her work. "You're very handsome," she said. She didn't want to answer him. She was afraid if she did it would spoil things again.

"Sophie."

She hesitated. "No. He hasn't." But she suspected he might.

"I see." He reached for his neckcloth. "He will."

"Ah!" she said, tapping his hand. "I've only just tied it. Leave it so I can admire you for five minutes."

"As you wish, madam." The laughter had gone from his eyes. He shifted on the chair and touched the pages she'd so carefully copied out. "Tallboys is from good family. Completely acceptable," he said.

"Just acceptable?"

"No," he said. "More than acceptable. He does not gamble to excess. I've never seen him drunk. He is discreet when discretion is called for. He's not mad over horses or prone to extravagance that I can see. He's amusing and not tedious in conversation. You've an excellent mind, and Tallboys will not expect you to pretend you haven't." He reached for her hand, lightly holding her fingers. "He would make you happy. It's a good match, if you want it."

On this subject, she absolutely knew her mind. "No. I do not."

"Why not?"

She saw immediately that he'd misinterpreted. "Marriage is not a state in which I wish to exist." Her stomach clenched.

"I'm sorry to hear you say that."

"John wants me to marry. He's astonishingly persistent on the subject." She stared at the toes of her boots. She ought to have worn slippers, but they would never have survived the walk from Henrietta Street to Charlotte Row.

"Not all husbands make their wives unhappy," he said. He whisked his thumb across her fingers, and she squeezed his hand in silent response. "I daresay most gentlemen are faithful to their wives, Sophie."

The corners of her mouth turned down. "I can't." She swallowed. "I simply cannot."

Banallt leaned back in his chair, and their fingers slowly slid apart. "Hm. I think you mean you will not. You've always been a stubborn thing."

"I haven't."

He laughed softly. "There was never any woman more suited to being in love and married than you."

She looked up. "That's unkind."

"Why? It's the truth. When you are in love, and do not forget that I knew you when you loved Tommy, you sparkle with life. It's irresistible. One wants to be around you just to see if the sensation will rub off." His smiled faded once more. She was sorry for it. "A woman, especially you, ought to be married. How else will you be secure?"

"You sound just like John."

"Well," he drawled. "And so."

"But I'm not in love with Mr. Tallboys. How can I marry without love?"

He crossed his arms over his chest and considered her. She recognized his expression. He was framing his reply. Whatever he said, he would be sure to make her face issues she'd rather not. "You don't love Tallboys yet? Or you don't believe you ever will?"

Sophie chewed on her lower lip. "It's not that."

"Then what?"

"I loved Tommy and that was all I had in me. There's no more."

"Nonsense."

"It's so, Banallt." She reached to adjust his cravat again. "Sometimes I think about it, that giddy feeling in your stomach, feeling as if you'll die if he doesn't smile at you. The part of me that loved Tommy like that leaves me sick." Her voice fell. "I'm nothing but ashes inside. My heart's burnt up. I've nothing to give to a marriage, Banallt."

After a bit, he smiled. "I'm sure your brother would find something to send along with you. A pound or two perhaps. And he'd give you a splendid wedding."

She reached out and tapped his shoulder. "Be serious."

"I am, darling. More serious than you'll know. You deserve a scandalously extravagant wedding. In St. Paul's. With a lovely gown to wear, and flowers for your hair. And afterward enough food to send half of London groaning to their beds."

They both looked up at the sound of voices in the hallway. Someone called for Banallt. He stood and started to say something then thought the better of it. "Well," he said. "I will leave you to your copying, Mrs. Evans. Do try to leave out the kidnapping."

"Perhaps a small robbery?" She grinned. "A stolen necklace?"

"You—"

Another voice called from the hallway. "Banallt?"

Sophie stood there, remembering the feeling of his hair brushing the backs of her hands and the way her stomach had soared. She wondered if it was possible Banallt was the reason she didn't want to marry Tallboys.

What a disaster that would be.

CHAPTER FOURTEEN

Upper York Street, London,
MARCH 30, 1815

Sophie and John arrived at Lord Harpenden's home off Upper York Street at ten o'clock at night. They were escorted to a ballroom filled with people dancing and talking and flirting. An orchestra sat at one end of the room, playing one of the more sedate country dances. Servants threaded their way among the guests carrying trays or messages, discreetly watching for mishaps to whisk away, and seeing that everything was in order. The air was heavy, and every so often someone who ought to have bathed more assiduously passed by.

She and John found and greeted Lord and Lady Harpenden, and then she stayed to speak with some of the ladies she knew from Vedaelin and Mr. Tallboys while John wandered off with acquaintances of his own. Sophie found she was quite enjoying herself. The music, the hum of conversation, the lovely men and women dancing or strolling were thrilling. She saw Frederick Drake, handsome and waiting on Miss George as if he believed she was the only young lady in the world. The poor girl was infatuated.

John came back once to see how she was doing on her own. "I'll walk with you to the punch bowl," he said.

"Why haven't you danced, John?" Sophie asked. "I've been waiting for you to."

He waved a hand. "There's no one here I care to dance with, that's all."

"That's not good of you. There are young ladies here in want of a partner."

"Vedaelin is not here yet," he said.

"John." She tapped his arm. "You must dance."

"Perhaps later," he said. He stopped when they met Lord Harpenden. The older man bowed to them and they exchanged greetings. He fell in with them, walking on Sophie's other side.

"I've just been asking John why he's not dancing," she said to Harpenden. John tensed, and his smile vanished, a reaction Sophie attributed to her remark. A moment later, though, she thought differently. Miss Fidelia Llewellyn had arrived with her mother. The stir among the young men as she came in was perfectly ridiculous. At that precise moment, Sophie had the good fortune—or was it misfortune? —to be standing with an unobstructed view of Miss Llewellyn and her mother. Fidelia scanned the room and did not stop searching until her attention fell on John. It was plain, painfully plain, now that she knew the truth, that she'd sought him out. John nodded. Very slightly, but an acknowledgment nevertheless. The girl's smile in return was breathtaking.

"John," Sophie murmured. "Go to her. Say good evening. Ask her to dance."

Her brother gave her a grateful look. "Sophie, Lord Harpenden. Will you excuse me?"

Sophie touched his arm. "I'll be perfectly all right."

Lord Harpenden held out an arm when John left. "She's a lovely girl," he said. "Now, it's not just your brother who should be dancing. Will you do me the honor, Mrs. Evans?"

She was flattered that he thought to ask. "Dancing is for young ladies, my lord."

"You're hardly decrepit," he said with a laugh.

"Do you know, Lord Harpenden, I should like very much to sit and watch the dancing."

"The next set then?"

"Now, really, my lord, how can I watch the dancers if I am among them myself?"

"May I engage you for at least one dance?"

He only asked out of politeness, and she saw no reason to inflict that burden on him. "There's a chair just there." Yes, that was a flicker of relief in his eyes. She changed their course and released his arm. "Thank you very much, my lord."

"The pleasure was mine, Mrs. Evans. You are even more of a delight than your brother." Lord Harpenden bowed. "Perhaps later in the evening I might persuade you to dance?"

"Perhaps, my lord."

When Lord Harpenden left, Sophie sat and found she had a tolerable view of the dancing. She hoped for a sight of John and Miss Llewellyn. However, Miss Llewellyn remained surrounded by men. John was not yet among them. The young woman continually scanned the room. Where on earth had her dratted brother got to? He ought to be at Miss Llewellyn's side by now.

A woman sitting to Sophie's left craned her neck in the direction of the main entrance. Sophie had ended up in a section of the ballroom populated primarily by mothers, aunts, and other chaperones of the young ladies who were dancing. She fit in quite well, she thought. She settled on her chair and tapped her toe in time with the music. Everyone around her was smiling or laughing.

"I can't see," the woman next to her said. "My, but this is a crush! Tell me, Imogen, is that him?"

"Someone's just walked in front of him," Imogen answered. The two women spoke as if they were longtime friends. With affection. Sophie tipped her head to one side and listened unabashedly. Imogen's hair was graying, but she remained a handsome woman, dressed smartly in a striped silk moire. Her companion, too, was fashionably dressed, but a deal stouter than Imogen.

The stout woman said in a breathy voice, "Who but the duke would cause such a stir?"

Who, indeed? Sophie asked herself. She admitted to herself that she was unaccustomedly nervous about seeing the duke, if he should happen to come here tonight. He'd sent her flowers as an apology for their missed luncheon at Charlotte Row. Lovely white roses that came with a note asking if she would drive out with him. He called later that afternoon and drove her out to Rotten Row. Sophie had decided she did not mind the difference in their ages. His calm demeanor settled her. She felt safe with him. He'd already lived his wild youth. His feet were solidly on the ground. He was not the sort of man to expect passion.

John had been ready to plan her wedding when she and Vedaelin returned an hour late for no nefarious reason other than the time it took them to work their way out of the traffic. As if a duke would offer for her! Though if she were ever to marry without love, Vedaelin would be a perfect choice. He wanted a companion, she fancied. During their entire drive, his greatest intimacy was to hold her hand overlong. While she had to agree with John that a drive to Rotten Row was a declaration of interest, she rather thought his criteria for love did not include a giddy stomach or breathless longing. They matched each other very well in that respect. He would do well.

The conversation beside her continued. In rather giddy tones, truth be known. "You don't suppose it could be Lord Banallt, do you, Imogen? I heard he was invited, but I never dreamed he'd dare show up. Not after his affair with that Italian woman."

"The opera singer." Yes, I know," said Imogen. They laughed and put their heads near to whisper between them. Sophie was sure, though not certain, that one of them said the name *Mrs. Peters.*

Sophie's heart skipped a beat. But then she clamped down the flood of trepidation. If Banallt was having an affair with Mrs. Peters, that was no concern of hers. He was free to live his life as he saw fit.

"I see him now," the second woman replied. She shook her head. "Not the duke."

"Nor Banallt," said Imogen. "Such a handsome, distinguished man, though. I heard he's looking for a bride." Her brother emerged from the crowd the two ladies had been examining.

Imogen tracked John. "His maiden speech in the House was a rousing success. I daresay he might do well for Lucinda."

"Yes. I think so, too."

Heavens! If John didn't find Miss Llewellyn soon, he might just find himself with the redoubtable Lucinda. But her brother seemed to be in no hurry. The orchestra was playing a lively reel at the moment. John ought to be dancing. The music made her want to dance, too, but of course she couldn't. Gallants like Lord Harpenden notwithstanding, she was too old for such foolishness. And yet, how strange, Sophie thought, to be twenty-six and attending her first dance. She'd eloped with Tommy before her official coming-out, and once she was married, there weren't any parties. Six and twenty, and she'd never danced except with her brother, who'd been horrified to be made to partner his sister during her dance lessons. In those days, she hadn't known what it was to be afraid of having nothing.

John had stopped before Miss George. Sophie repressed an urge to give John a good hard kick in the shins. If he was in love with Miss Llewellyn, why on earth was he avoiding her? He bowed and the two exchanged words while Mr. Drake scowled at him, annoyed to think he had competition. How well she knew that sort of man.

The ladies on her left kept up an amusing commentary that sometimes diverted her more than watching the dancers. She did not like Mr. Drake any better than she had when she first saw him. He was very handsome, Sophie thought, but something in the cast of his eyes set her off. When he laughed or smiled, the emotion seemed too focused, and yet not intense enough to be mistaken for deep emotion. Young Mr. Drake was a charlatan. Pretending to adore poor Miss George.

Sophie leaned to the lady on her left: Imogen. "Pray tell, do you know who that young man is?" She nodded in the direction of Mr. Drake. If her earlier opinion of the man was unfair, then these two ladies would surely know enough to set her straight.

"The handsome blond gentleman with Miss George?" her companion asked.

"Yes."

Imogen looked in Drake's direction and sniffed. "No one a'tall. His father married up, and that's a fact."

"Is that a mark against him?" Sophie asked. "He cannot help his father's marriage, after all."

Imogen held up her lorgnette and peered at Sophie through the lenses. "No, but he might have held on to the fortune he married."

She sniffed again. "Like father, like son. The boy's on the hunt for an heiress."

"He's at the right ball for that, my dear," said her companion. "Heiresses hanging from the chandeliers here."

Imogen dropped her glasses. "Mark my words, some mother and father will soon be wishing they'd watched their young heiress a little more closely. Now you take the gentleman who's just left Miss George."

"Mr. Mercer, you mean?" Sophie said.

Before Sophie could warn them of her relation to him, the other woman sighed. "Such a handsome, accomplished gentleman, he is."

"He certainly is," Sophie said, with more than a little pride.

The lorgnette came out again. Imogen had dark brown eyes, and they were suddenly very sharp indeed. "Do you know him, ma'am?"

She smiled. "He is my brother."

"Indeed?" She extended a gloved hand. "Mrs. Babington," Imogen said. They briefly touched fingers. "And this is my sister, Miss Wright."

"Mrs. Babington, Miss Wright," Sophie replied. "A pleasure to meet you both. I'm Mrs. Evans. Mr. Mercer's sister."

Miss Wright gasped and clutched Imogen's arm. "He's here! The duke. Oh, we must find a way to introduce Lucinda. We must."

Sophie turned to look. The Duke of Vedaelin had indeed arrived, and the stir on his entrance was quite something to behold. Women of all ages took notice. And why not? He was a duke without a duchess. John was so tall that she'd not realized until she saw Vedaelin in this crowd that he, too, was taller than the average man.

Imogen and Miss Wright stood up, craning for a look, whether at Vedaelin or for a glimpse of their Lucinda, she didn't know. Poor John. Set aside at the mere glimpse of a duke.

The set of dances ended and the orchestra stilled its instruments. Conversation rose as the young ladies and gentlemen left the floor, heading for chaperones or perhaps a slow stroll toward the punch bowl. Across the room from where she sat, the crowd by the wide double doors stopped its flow in and out of the ballroom. Sophie leaned forward on her chair, but her view was now blocked by dancers leaving the floor. All around her whispers began. Heads turned toward the door.

"Surely," Miss Wright said, "this commotion must mean the prince has come."

"I heard no announcement," said Imogen.

Sophie stood, too, but she was too short to see anything.

"Perhaps you missed it," said Miss Wright to her sister. "Did you hear anything, Mrs. Evans?"

"Not at all." Drat her luck in being so short. She could not see who was causing such a stir. A greater stir than Vedaelin, for heaven's sake.

Whoever it was, it was possible to follow his or her progress through the room from the reaction of the surrounding people. At last she saw him briefly. And really, it must have been her curiosity or the unfamiliar setting or her expectation that only the Prince of Wales would have sent the room into such a commotion that kept her from recognizing him. He'd stopped to speak to John and Vedaelin, of all people.

The newcomer stood with his back to her with John and Vedaelin facing him attentively. The gentleman was taller than her brother and wonderfully broad shouldered. And slender. Certainly this was not the prince. The man had dark hair. A parade of women walked past him. He acknowledged a few with a bow or nod and ignored the rest. Two broke through, though: Mrs. Llewellyn and Fidelia.

The gentleman with John and Vedaelin turned his head, giving Sophie a brief view of his profile. He was smiling, and later, when she had time to reflect on the moment, she decided his smile was why she didn't recognize him. As a stranger for those brief moments, he took her breath. Pure and simple, he was the loveliest man she'd ever seen. No wonder all the ladies wanted to catch his eye. A god had just walked into the ballroom, and mere mortal men ceased to exist.

His looks forbade despite his smile. She'd never but once before seen a face so dangerously handsome. The darkness in his expression drew her in. What lay behind that unknowable face? Something about that smile said, *Beware, I'll break your heart.* She was dying to know the color of his eyes.

—and then the puzzle was completed. Her world shifted under her feet; her stomach dropped a mile.

Not a stranger at all. Banallt.

The time in which she did not know him lasted hardly a breath, perhaps two, but so many details lived there. Claret coat, tan pantaloons, top boots, white shirt. From here, she could not see his waistcoat to judge whether he had come tonight as a dandy or a Corinthian.

Of course it was him. How could she not have recognized him? Her knees went weak, because she had never until this very moment understood how his beauty spoke to her. She watched him scan the room. Even from the distance separating them, she saw the peculiar silver irises and the pale skin set off by his inky hair. If he turned around, he would see her standing here by herself.

John said something to Mrs. Llewellyn, who nodded to him. Fidelia put a hand on John's sleeve and replied. John smiled, an unguarded smile that proved once and forever to Sophie that he was in love with Miss Llewellyn. Lord Banallt turned to greet someone else, and now he was facing her direction.

From across the ballroom, his gaze met hers, and she watched his face. Nothing in his expression changed, but they knew each other. His gaze did not move on. Not immediately, at any rate. While Sophie watched, he took his leave of John and the two women at his side. He said something to Fidelia, who gave him a smile and a nod. John caught his arm. Banallt turned back. What the two men said to each other Sophie had no idea except that neither John nor Banallt seemed pleased. Banallt addressed another gentleman. That exchange left Sophie staring at her brother and Vedaelin. Mrs. Llewellyn wrapped an arm around the duke's.

The orchestra struck the beginning notes of the next set. Banallt turned to Fidelia and held out his hand. The young woman put her hand in his. Sophie lost sight of them both in the crowd surging toward the ballroom floor. A short while later, whispers broke out on her side of the room. Sophie turned her head. On instinct? Happenstance? Or was her glance at the filling ballroom floor merely ill timed? Lord Banallt was among the dancers on the floor, and Fidelia was his partner. Mrs. Babington followed Sophie's gaze. "A striking couple, don't you agree, Mrs. Evans?"

"Yes." It was true. Banallt and Fidelia were lovely together. She was tall enough for him, and every bit as beautiful.

"Do you think he'll come up to snuff before the season's ended?"

Sophie looked away. "Up to snuff?"

"The earl, Mrs. Evans. The on dit is he'll marry the girl. The only question appears to be when."

"But I—"

"Mrs. Evans." Reginald Tallboys appeared before her. She'd been so intent on Banallt that Tallboys startled her. He extended a hand. "Will you do me the honor?"

Miss Wright leaned over and whispered, "Go on, Mrs. Evans. He's too handsome to decline!"

"You can't say no," Tallboys said. "Not with everyone watching."

"Go on!" said Miss Wright.

Tallboys gave her a serious look. "Your brother begged me to tell you that if you won't dance, neither will he."

"Unfair, Mr. Tallboys."

He grinned at her. "Yes, isn't it?"

Sophie sighed and put her hand in his. At least the country dance that was starting was one she knew she could get through without disaster. Tallboys led her to the dance floor, joining the second line of couples waiting for the music to begin: Banallt and Fidelia, John and Miss George. She and Reginald Tallboys were among the six other couples in the line. There were changes of partner as the women moved down the line of men, each woman dancing a simple pattern with each man in turn. She was, inevitably, partnered with Banallt. Her heart pounded when she placed her hand on his.

"Tallboys?" he said.

"There's nothing wrong with Mr. Tallboys."

"Agreed. I'd just thought if you danced with anyone it would be the duke."

She didn't answer, because the last thing she wanted was to humiliate herself by missing a step, and she had to concentrate. He smelled good, and his cravat, so far, was perfect. At the end of their pattern, she managed a smile and thought, when she'd moved to the next, that she'd danced quite well. She was relieved to end up back with Mr. Tallboys.

"I was wondering," he said as the dance ended, "if you would allow me to fetch you a plate when supper is served."

Before she could answer him, Vedaelin intercepted them. "Mrs. Evans," he said, bowing. "How lovely you are tonight."

"Thank you, Your Grace."

"Tallboys," the duke said. Tallboys nodded at the duke as they walked. "Will you dance, ma'am?" Vedaelin asked.

"I'd be honored," she said. Banallt was lining up to dance again, too, with Miss George. John, at last, was with Fidelia. This dance had no change of partners, just patterns that sometimes involved a neighboring couple, and she and Vedaelin were safely far from Banallt.

When she was back in her seat at last, Miss Wright tapped her on the shoulder. "Tallboys and the duke?" she said breathlessly. "Mrs. Evans, you are a triumph tonight."

"They are both friends of my brother, that's all."

Miss Wright shook a hand at her. "I saw the way Mr. Tallboys looked at you. Such cow eyes! You'll have him on his knee to you before long, ma'am."

"Really, that's nonsense." She scanned the room, hoping to see where John and Fidelia had gone. What she saw was Banallt heading toward her. All she could do was wait while her breath vanished from her lungs.

When he reached her, he bowed. All perfectly proper. Heart-stoppingly graceful. Lethally beautiful. His gaze pinned her, and she was actually dizzy. Sophie sat paralyzed for two beats of her heart and then remembered where she was and how she ought to behave. This was not a man who was safe for her. Or for any woman, for that matter. She curtseyed, crushing her fan in one hand. One of the ribs cracked underneath her fingers. "My lord. Good evening."

Beside her, Imogen and Miss Wright gaped.

He held out a gloved hand. "Come, Sophie," he said softly. "Will you dance with me?"

CHAPTER FIFTEEN

Rider Hall,
JULY 14, 1812

Banallt got down from his curricle and handed the vehicle off to the groom who appeared from the side of the house. He headed for the door, his greatcoat flapping in the breeze. Tommy ought to be out of bed by now, for God's sake. It was nearly one o'clock in the afternoon, and Banallt himself had been up since ten. He did not reach the house, however, because he caught a glimpse of white and stopped to see what had distracted him.

Ah. The delectable Mrs. Evans.

She was sitting on a swing hung from a walnut tree. One foot trailed on the ground beneath her, slowly rocking. She had her nose buried in a book and apparently no idea of the damage she must be doing by dragging her slipper through the dirt. She swung forward, blissfully absorbed by her reading. He felt an odd pang in his chest. What was it, exactly? As if he were home after many years' absence and she was the only reason he'd returned at all. Which was quite ridiculous. He did not care for Rider Hall as a place a gentleman might live, its chief defect being it was too bloody remote from the entertainment he enjoyed best.

Mrs. Evans was the rare exception to that defect of country living. She might be ridiculously prim, but she was also clever. Amusing. Kindhearted. Fascinating. Enthralling. Oh, and he wanted her.

More than any woman he'd known. He'd begun dreaming about her, too; the most explicitly erotic dreams imaginable. Even when he was in London he dreamed of her. In his dreams, she was in no way proper or prim.

He walked to the swing. Lost in the world of her book, she rocked herself forward and turned a page, completely unaware of his approach. Her clothes were very much in the country style, favoring comfort over fashion, though he would allow she had put herself together well. She wore muslin with green leaves printed in two stripes down the middle of the gown. The bodice made a heart shape of her bosom with the skin above covered by white gauze. He stopped a few feet from the swing. "Ma'am?"

"Oh!" She fumbled her book and only just saved her place.

He bowed. "Forgive me if I startled you."

"Lord Banallt." Her eyes flashed with a thousand emotions, and before he could quite put a name to any of them, the wall came down and he read nothing there at all. He'd never known a woman so frighteningly adept at hiding her thoughts from him. "What are you doing here?"

He cocked his head. "Visiting. Perhaps you don't recall that I came down yesterday with your husband."

Well. And so. She did not find him amusing. "I am aware, my lord. I mean, what are you doing here in this very spot? Outside. Are you certain your constitution can withstand the fresh air?"

He raised his hands and drew a deep breath. "No fatal effects as of yet. Be so kind, won't you, as to notify my cousin Harry Llewellyn if I should fall dead at your feet."

That got a smile from her. All sorts of fascinating things happened to her face when she smiled. "I will, my lord." He stood there, smiling at her like a half-wit. How could a woman who wasn't beautiful be, in fact, beautiful? "Surely you don't mean to tell me you want to swing?"

"Good Lord, no. I had rather not do anything so undignified for a man of my position." He walked behind her and gripped the ropes that held the swing. She twisted to look at him with a quizzical expression. He pulled back on the ropes and then released the swing. "Good book?"

She got her dangling foot up just in time. "Oh yes." She tried to hold the book and the ropes of the swing at the same time and did neither well. From the back, he noted, her bottom made an interesting heart shape where the fabric tucked beneath her. Well now. Wasn't that interesting? Stimulating, rather.

"What are you reading?" he asked.

"Who's the Murderer?"

"By...Mrs. Sleath?"

"Yes." She looked at him over her shoulder, smiling. "You do know your Romance, don't you?"

He teased her because he wanted her to smile just to confirm the effect on her features. "Proper women don't read such books."

She twisted to look at him. Light danced in her eyes, dazzling him. But then her usual gravity replaced the humor. "Considering your opinion of ladies who read and write, I should think you might hold me to a lower standard."

When she swung back, he put his hands beneath her shoulder blades and pushed. During her forward arc, she lifted her legs to try for greater height. The hem of her skirt flipped up enough to show him the tips of her slippers, one of them soiled, and two very slender ankles. Any more stimulation and he was going to have to watch the lay of his coat over his breeches. "I assure you, Mrs. Evans, I hold you to the very highest standard."

The swing arced back, and he brought it to a stop, keeping both his hands on the ropes. She bowed her head and then turned slightly so that he could see only a portion of her cheek. He released the swing and leaned against the tree trunk, arms crossed over his chest with one knee bent so the sole of his boot pressed flat against the base of the tree. "Considering the source, I'm not overly concerned," she said.

"Have you just insulted me?"

She lifted her head and looked at him. That prim little look of hers that involved her mouth going tense and a narrowing of her eyes came back. "Do you like being a rake?"

From his position against the tree, he looked her up and down and answered her honestly. "No," he said. "I don't. But I like sex, Mrs. Evans, too much to think of giving up my carnal pleasures. If that makes me a rake, so be it." He admired the pink in her cheeks. "I am discreet when necessary."

"You? Discreet?"

"I've had any number of affairs of which you've heard nothing. And never shall."

Her cheeks turned pinker yet. She didn't look away. Nor did she stand up and march back to the house, mortally offended. She had her feet planted on the ground now, and she rocked the swing back and forth just to the point of her heels coming off the ground. Forward and back. He leaned closer. He could smell her hair. Orange water, he thought.

She stood up and walked toward him, leaving her book on the swing, until she stood within a foot of his chest with her arms crossed under her bosom. "I wonder if you're all talk, my lord."

Banallt thought that if only he could hold her in his arms, she'd understand how he felt about her. Jesus, her hair was lovely even if she was a brunette. A man might pine away for want of her mouth. He uncrossed his arms and, as if he hadn't anything at all in mind, peeled off his driving gloves. She watched him warily. "Your pride will get you in trouble yet," he said, dropping his gloves into a pocket of his greatcoat. "It is, perhaps, your one great fault. You are too proud."

"Proud?" She tipped her head. "How so?"

"You know what they say, don't you?" he said in a soft voice. She was quite close enough. He took her free hand, her right, in one of his. "Your pride, darling, is standing on the edge of a precipice." She was really too small for him. But he was wild for her regardless. "If you aren't more careful with me, your pride will plunge us over the edge."

"You don't scare me." She wore yellow gloves. With great deliberation he pulled off her glove and put that in his pocket, too. Her eyes followed the motion. "That's mine."

"Not anymore." He curled his fingers around her bare hand. She had long fingers and short but strong nails. Ink stained the side of her middle finger. He turned her hand over and brushed the back of his fingertips across her palm. "What lovely hands you have, Sophie." She frowned at his use of her given name and tried to withdraw her hand. He didn't permit it. "Were you writing again last night?"

"Yes."

"And what's happened to poor Beatrice now? Has her odious cousin taken advantage?" He raised her hand to his mouth and kissed her fingertips, one after the other.

"Let go, my lord." Her eyes—very hard and unswerving—fixed on his mouth until he released her hand. Banallt was beginning to think she was immune to seduction. And yet Tommy Evans had managed it. Surely she could be brought around to succumb to him as well.

"Tell me about your story, then." He settled against the tree trunk, hands in his greatcoat pockets. He fingered her glove.

She retreated to the swing but sat facing him with her book on her lap and her toe dragging in the dirt. She let out a puff of air. "Everything sounds so foolish."

"Not to me." She wrinkled her nose at that, and Banallt found that oddly charming. She really had no idea of her gifts. Her stories enthralled him—every one that he'd read. Including the one she was working on now. "I've not your talent for words, Mrs. Evans. Anything I write is wretched beyond endurance."

She leaned forward, and he got a glimpse of the top curve of her bosom. An excruciatingly modest view to be sure. Her bosom, so surprisingly revealed by her frock, suggested the existence of more curves than he'd previously suspected. He wondered about the shape of her naked breasts, how she would fit his palm, and the color of her nipples. With her complexion, he guessed pale pink. "You write?" she asked.

"In my callow youth, I once set my hand to a story. But now?" He shuddered. "Most assuredly not. Believe what you will of me, but I've grown wise enough to know my limitations."

She frowned and leaned back. His belly went taut as she examined him. Her eyes slayed him, pulled him in to drown. "I don't understand you at all. One minute you're a rogue and a cur—"

He waggled his eyebrows at her. "A scoundrel?"

"A rake."

"A libertine?"

"A cad."

"No, Mrs. Evans." He stopped smiling. "Not that. I am never a
cad. No matter what you have heard."

"Reprobate, then."

"Quite possibly." He pulled his hands from his pockets.

"What am I to do with you?"

A dozen wickedly suggestive answers came to mind, but he kept
them back. Most unlike him. "Tell me what you've done to Beatrice.
Did she escape from the crypt or did her guardian have his way with
her?"

"Dungeon," she said. She frowned and pushed herself on the
swing again, without taking her feet from the ground. Her slippers
were going to be quite ruined. "I changed the crypt to a dungeon."

"Manacled to an icy wall?"

"Do you think that would work? It seems so cruel." She got a far-
away look in her eyes. "She escaped through a secret tunnel, but perhaps Ralf ought to put her in chains first."

"Her guardian is a cruel man, after all. And is he not already married?"

Her eyes sparkled with humor, and Banallt felt the impact in his
gut. Her eyes were nothing short of spectacular. Dark lashes, naturally, since she was a brunette, but eyes for a man to drown in.
Large, and such a luscious color in so serious and prim a face, her

eyes were a blue green shade uncannily bright. "To a woman who's left him to become a nun," she said.

"And yet he remains bound by his marriage vows. He is not free to love Beatrice."

She tilted her chin in order to look into his face. He'd never made love to a woman as delicate as she was, and he wondered if it would be inconvenient, with him awkwardly reaching for her interesting parts, or if he'd find it exhilarating. How could a man not feel his virility when his partner, with all those delicious and unexpected curves, was so dainty? Still, he did not care to worry about hurting his lover from the mere difference in their size. "But he does love her," she said. "He has no control over his heart."

Banallt snorted. "He was careless of it, then. No man with even half the wits he was born with loses his heart like that. He ought to have seen from the start the thing was impossible. A true villain would seduce her, perhaps marry her illegally—a sham ceremony—if that's what must be done to secure her person."

"Ah."

Banallt could tell from her eyes that she was wondering if his suggestion came of personal experience. "No," he replied to the question she wasn't asking. "If I wish to secure a woman's person, I don't resort to trickery. It's unsporting."

Once more her expression shut down. "And after Ralf deceives her, what then?"

"Then the bedroom doors close upon the loving, deluded bride and her faithless lover."

With the toe of her slipper, she pushed the swing forward half an inch. "You wrote a tragedy, didn't you?"

He laughed. "There's no doubt the result was a tragedy. No, I now adhere to the principles of Aristotle. If ever I put pen to paper again, I shall write a play. In three acts. Perfect in every way."

"By the end everyone is dead?" She snorted. "I wonder what Aristotle would have written on the subject of art had he read Mrs. Radcliffe." She crossed her eyes. "He would not have written anything."

"Pray tell, why not?"

She looked over her shoulder, and for a moment, a shadow passed over her face. "Because, he'd have been up all night reading straight through to the end, heart in his mouth every moment. By midday, he'd have fallen asleep and never written his treatise."

Banallt looked toward the house, too. Tommy was crossing the lawn toward them. He was hatless and barely dressed; a shirt with a cravat hanging untied across the back of his neck. Waistcoat and coat unbuttoned. Breeches respectable, boots in need of polish. Sunlight glinted off his golden curls. The man's dissipation had yet to affect his looks.

"Sophie," Tommy cried when he saw them. "There you are. I've been looking all over for you." He shot a questioning glance at Banallt. "Why the devil would you be out here?"

"It's a lovely day," Sophie replied.

"Not so loud." He put a hand to his head and winced. "I'm in a bad way this morning."

"I'm very sorry for it," she replied in a lower voice. "Perhaps you ought to have had less to drink if you don't care to rue the morning."

"It's afternoon now anyway," Tommy replied sharply. He yanked on the ends of his neckcloth. "My damned valet is useless with cravats, Sophie, you know he is. You must tie me. I can't go out like this." He dropped a hand on her shoulder and addressed Banallt.

"Why are you looking so chipper, Banallt? You drank just the same as I did last night."

"Constitution of iron," Banallt replied. In truth, he hadn't had much to drink at all, but Tommy hadn't been in any condition to know.

"Sit down," Sophie said to her husband. Banallt reached in and took Sophie's book. "Thank you, my lord." Tommy sat on the swing and slipped off his coat to give her unimpeded access to his neck. She tied Tommy's cravat quickly with a stunning result.

"What do you call that knot?" Banallt asked.

Sophie tugged a bit on one of the ends. "Neat and tidy, my lord."

"Can you teach it to my valet?"

She faced him, and he got another dose of her blue green gaze. She held out her hand for her book, which he gave to her. Jesus, she had a courtesan's eyes. "Why?"

"Never mind why." Tommy settled his coat over his shoulders and sent his wife a sour look. "Show him and there's an end to it."

Her mouth thinned. "It's not proper."

"Banallt's cravat isn't very neat." Tommy buttoned his waistcoat. "Tie his and then he can go show his bloody valet himself."

She might have turned to stone, she was so still. The color drained from her cheeks not from anger, he realized, but from embarrassment. Banallt felt another of those pangs in his chest. "Of course," she said. "Won't you sit, my lord?"

"It's not necessary," Banallt said. Was he that great a fool? This was a perfect opportunity to have her near him.

Tommy stood and slapped him on the back. "Of course it is. Can't have you going into town looking like that, can we?"

"I had rather thought we were staying at Rider Hall today."

Tommy glanced at his wife, standing with her book in her hand. "Quentin invited us to luncheon at the Stag and Thistle. I said we'd come." The Stag and Thistle housed a gaming hell in the basement and was next door to a bawdy house. Considering he wasn't getting anywhere with Mrs. Evans, he could at least slake the surface needs of his body. "Go on, Soph," Tommy said. "See if you can make Banallt presentable."

The thought of having Mrs. Evans so close to his person seemed quite a delicious encounter, but when he saw her face, he said, "If you don't mind, Mrs. Evans, I prefer King tie my cravats."

She looked rather too relieved. Mightn't she be just a little disappointed?

"I'll write out the instructions for him, my lord. Will that do?"

He bowed. "I'm sure it will, ma'am."

He and Tommy walked toward the stables. When he was certain he was out of earshot of Mrs. Evans, Banallt said, "I don't see why I should fix my cravat when I'll only have it off in an hour."

He had the feeling he'd be dreaming of Mrs. Evans again tonight. Something wicked, he thought, involving novel uses of a cravat. They visited the bawdy house after luncheon, and damned if he didn't call out Sophie's name when his crisis came.

CHAPTER SIXTEEN

Upper York Street, London,
MARCH 30,1815

Sophie placed her gloved hand on Banallt's extended palm, and his fingers closed around hers, a light touch. Proper. Nothing remarkable. They were friends. Nothing more. As the music swelled, tardy couples hurried to take their places. She was peripherally aware of Mrs. Babington and Miss Wright continuing to stare. Miss Wright clasped her hands under her chin and grinned madly.

"My lord," Sophie said. She could hardly hear herself over the pounding of her heart. Time bent around her again, and for an eternity, she imagined how lovely it would be to dance with Banallt. Completely inappropriate, but lovely. She wanted nothing more in the world than to dance with him.

"I mean to dance with you before Tallboys finds you again. Or Vedaelin. Or some other...rogue." She shook her head, and he went on, "It's only a dance. Friends may always dance with one another." Then he smiled, and her breath caught again. "Am I such a monster that you cannot have a public peace with me?"

"That's not it, Banallt."

One black eyebrow rose. How on earth did he do that? "No?"

She turned to the women at her side and decided they did not look offended to be in Banallt's presence. Quite the opposite. "Mrs. Babington, Miss Wright. May I introduce you to Lord Banallt?"

Mrs. Babington and Miss Wright offered their hands in turn. "My lord," they murmured.

Banallt inclined his head when he'd kissed the air over their hands. "Ladies. I trust you're enjoying yourselves?"

Miss Wright recovered first. "Yes, indeed, my lord. We've been delighted to meet Mrs. Evans. Such a charming young lady. Don't you agree?"

"Completely, Miss Wright." He returned his attention to her. "I hope you will not think poorly of me if I take her away from you? The waltz is next, and she is not engaged."

"Not at all," said Miss Wright. She opened her fan and waved it beneath her chin. "Not at all. Her foot's been tapping since she sat here." She sent a look in Sophie's direction. While she did that, Banallt took Sophie's hand and brought her to her feet. "She's too young to sit with old women like us." Miss Wright fluttered her eyelashes at him. "And every young woman ought to waltz with a wickedly handsome man at least once in her life, my lord. Don't you agree?"

Banallt bowed. "I cannot agree more, Miss Wright."

"Banallt," Sophie murmured.

He smiled, though perhaps smile was too charitable a word for the look that came over his face. He was all hauteur and ice-cold certainty. "There is no complicated pattern to learn. All you have to do is follow my lead."

"I'll humiliate us both," she said. "People will talk." She took a step toward him. "There will be a scandal."

"A scandal over dancing? I think not. All anyone will see is Banallt waltzing with the sister of Vedaelin's political protégé. I will be accounted astute for it, I assure you." His fingers tightened around hers, and she let him draw her onto the ballroom floor because, after all, she must mend things between them, if only for John's sake. And hers, she thought. "We will continue to be thrown together, you and I," he said, drawing her into the proper position for the waltz. "Can we not make our newfound acquaintance a public one? If only for the sake of my reputation, ma'am."

"Your reputation," she said with the slightest emphasis on the word *your*.

"You are admired for your good sense and taste. To be in your apparent good graces would be quite a coup for me. You won't be cast out of the ton merely for waltzing with me."

She was not so distracted by him that she didn't notice they were being stared at. Well, was he not the Earl of Banallt, a wicked man by a reputation he'd earned, and yet one of the most eligible men this season? An earl without a wife or an heir, still young and handsome.

"I'm hoping as well to frustrate Tallboys and all your other admirers who haven't the nerve to approach you." The music started and he looked meaningfully at the dance floor.

"Admirers?" She laughed. "I won't have any left after they've seen me try to waltz."

He leaned close enough to put his mouth near her ear and said, "Mrs. Evans. I will not permit you to humiliate us while we are dancing. Have no fear. I will get you through the ordeal unscathed and with your slippers and toes intact."

"On your head be it, my lord," she said.

Banallt nodded, and before she was ready, he swept her among the dancers, one hand holding her palm, the other pressed to her back. Her feet stuttered, but he adjusted smoothly. Though she felt awkward, they glided across the room as well as anyone else seemed to be doing. The pressure of his hands on her back and around her fingers tightened whenever he physically directed her body.

She quickly caught on to the count and pattern, and after that hurdle was bested, she and Banallt moved through the room with hardly a misstep. She felt it when she went wrong, but he always recovered easily and gracefully. Sophie relaxed, and their movements became more fluid yet. She felt herself smiling, inside and out. Dancing with Banallt was lovely. Too lovely for words.

"What are you thinking," he asked, "that's put such an expression on your face?"

She headed right when she ought to have gone left, and his arm tightened around her as he bodily pushed her in the correct direction. She frowned and tapped his shoulder. "Hush, my lord. I need to concentrate."

"Forgive me. I shan't distract you again."

And he didn't. She fell back to the joy of waltzing. Alas, though, the music ended too soon. Couples broke apart, and the noise of conversation buzzed through the room. More than a few women laughed or giggled. They'd done the right thing, she and Banallt, to renew their friendship. She was glad, fiercely glad that he was back in her life. For a very long time, he'd been her only friend, and she had missed that more than she'd realized.

Banallt stepped away from her. Only a half step, but her hand slipped off his shoulder and his palm dropped from her waist. Slowly, he released her other hand and bowed. Very properly. The other ladies curtseyed to their partners. Sophie realized too late that she ought to do the same. His attention followed her movement. When she straightened, his eyes were on her, and for a moment, she was frightened at her reaction to that dark gray gaze.

The intensity of his regard was nothing unusual for him. She'd never known his eyes to be anything but compelling. And, though his gaze burned through her, his manner was reassuringly cold and distant. "Would you care for something to drink?" he asked.

"Yes, thank you." She'd danced the better part of the last forty minutes and was parched. "I should like that very much."

As they walked along the side of the ballroom, Banallt gave no sign that he either noticed or cared that they were an object of curiosity. Doubtless, he was used to such attention. So be it, she thought. They reached the tables where the punch bowls were arranged. Three tables, each with a liveried footman in attendance.

"Orgeat?" Banallt asked. "Or ratafia? It's possible there's lemonade."

"Orgeat, if you please." Rider Hall was a world away. The rules there had been different. Their roles, their relationship to each other had fundamentally changed since then. She was not the same woman she'd been at Rider Hall, and she was beginning to think Banallt was no longer the same man.

She stared at his back while he made his way to the punch bowl. Compared to her, most everyone was tall, but Banallt towered over most of the other men nearby. His hair gleamed blue black in the light, and Sophie couldn't help but notice his body was trim. He was an athletic man. Even when he was sitting indolent on a couch or chair, he was physically intense. Just as his eyes were emotionally deep when he let down his guard. Just before a space appeared for him at the bowl, he glanced over his shoulder. His gaze met hers, and his mouth curved in a smile. Sophie felt he'd touched her someplace private. She'd missed him terribly. More than once after Tommy died, she'd found herself thinking how Banallt would react when she told him of something she'd read or heard—and she'd had to stop the thought there.

Her mind wandered off, as so often happened with her. Banallt had proposed marriage. He'd not been serious, not the way a gentleman ought to be, but all the same, had things gone differently, she might be waiting for her husband to rejoin her. What an unsettling notion. And if she had? Her chest went tight at the thought of Banallt having that level of control of her life and happiness. As a husband, he could only break her heart. Just as Tommy had.

Banallt returned with the orgeat. As he was extending it to her, another gentleman bumped him from the side. He lurched, only just saving the drink from spilling on Sophie. Some of the contents sloshed onto the floor and slopped onto his coat.

"Oy there! So sorry," said the gentleman. His booted foot landed in the spilled orgeat, and he slid. Banallt caught him by the elbow and steadied him. "Is that you, Banallt?"

"MacNaill," Banallt said. He released MacNaill to brush the liquid off his double-breasted waistcoat. MacNaill dropped a hand on Banallt's shoulder and held on, very nearly causing another spill. A sharp-eyed footman swooped in to mop up the mess, and the two men stepped out of the way. MacNaill was about Banallt's age, possibly younger, and quite obviously had overindulged in spirits. She recognized the name immediately. When Tommy was home, she'd often heard him lament that MacNaill was not here to entertain him.

"Good evening, MacNaill," Banallt said.

"Haven't ruined your coat, have I?" MacNaill hung over Banallt, though he wasn't tall enough to succeed well in the maneuver.

"No, no." Banallt sidled out of the way of the footman, but Mac-Naill kept his grip on Banallt's shoulder and moved with him. "All's well, thank you. Disaster was averted."

"I'm headed to the Golden Swan after. Do you fancy going with me?"

Banallt's expression turned about as hot as ice, not that MacNaill noticed. "No."

"Pity." MacNaill was a sloppy drunk. "Dropped all your old friends, have you? But look here, I've another complaint to lodge against you, my lord."

"Oh?" He glanced at Sophie and gave a little shrug. "Perhaps another time you'll tell me what it is. At present I'm—"

"Mrs. Peters won't give me the time of day." He shook a finger in Banallt's face. " 'Tis all your fault, I know it." Banallt's smile vanished, a fact MacNaill failed to notice until Banallt pushed free of the younger man's grip, and even then MacNaill didn't appreciate his danger.

"That is quite enough, MacNaill," Banallt said in a venomous tone. "You are speaking out of turn."

"Out of turn?" He draped an arm around Banallt. "Come now, you've been nothing but dreary since you came back. Liven up, or you'll die an old man before you're forty."

Banallt disengaged from MacNaill and set a hand to the man's chest. He pushed. "Good evening to you, MacNaill." He crossed the distance to Sophie and took her elbow in a firm grip. "Shall we find someplace less crowded?"

"Of course." She was glad, actually, to be reminded of Banallt's relationship with Mrs. Peters. It kept her from the sentimentality that had been threatening her all evening where Banallt was concerned. The lump in her throat almost didn't go down when she swallowed. She had to clear her throat. She was Sophie Mercer Evans, and no one stirred her. No one disturbed her peace of mind. Whatever Banallt chose to do in his private life needn't affect her. Why should it? Their relationship was not what it had been. "Some fresh air would be pleasant, my lord."

He frowned. *"My lord.* Must you be so formal?"

"All right then, some fresh air would be pleasant, Banallt."

"Better."

She placed her arm on his, and he led her out of the ballroom, holding her orgeat in his other hand. Not outside, which she for some reason expected, but to a withdrawing room just down the hall. "Lord Harpenden has a book I thought you might enjoy seeing." Banallt handed the orgeat to her. Overhead, a crystal chandelier cast shimmering candlelight upon the room, but Banallt struck fire to a lamp and settled it on a side table.

"Really?" she said. She took a sip of her drink. The air here was much cooler, and the door was open. No one would remark if they should be seen. "What sort of book?"

He walked to a mahogany stand on which there sat a thick volume a foot tall and nearly two inches thick. The edges of the pages were gilt. "Come, Sophie."

Banallt's voice echoed in her ears, though he'd not spoken very loud.

Come, Sophie.

Her stomach fluttered from the effect of her name uttered in his velvet-smoke voice. He summoned her blithely, and yet her body shivered with anticipation of what might happen. Nothing would happen, though. He gave no sign of having any intentions toward her at all, aside from showing her the book and providing them both a respite from the crowd. She stood beside him, orgeat in her gloved hands. She tipped her head to read the title engraved on the spine. A collection of Dutch maps, a two-hundred-year-old travel guide of the then-known world. "Yes?"

He opened the book, carefully fanning out the pages until an image appeared in the gilt edges. A pirate ship danced on the ocean waves, painted there on the edges of the pages. She caught her breath.

"Lovely, isn't it?" he said.

She bent to get a closer look. "When I was a girl, Papa had a book with painted edges like this. Not as fine as this one, but I used to make him show me until I'm sure he wished he'd never demonstrated." She glanced up and found him watching her intently. As always, his eyes drew her in, and she could look away only with difficulty.

"I brought you here for a reason," he said.

"Did you?" Her orgeat felt awkward in her hands now, and she looked around for a place to put it. Not near the book. In her current state of physical and mental frustration she'd likely knock it over and ruin the book and Banallt's waistcoat, too.

He took the glass from her and set it on the side table next to the lamp. For the space of two heartbeats, they locked gazes. "It would be unfair of me not to tell you that your brother has forbidden me to call on you."

"I beg your pardon?"

The edge of his mouth quirked. His quicksand smile was dangerously familiar. "You heard me."

She frowned and drew herself up. Not that it did much good. She still had to tilt her head to look into his face. "He had no right. Why? Why did he do such a thing?" Indeed, why, when such an instruction would doom his hopes for Fidelia? "And when?"

"When?" He shrugged. "Does it matter?"

"Of course it does. I should very much like to know if John has interfered."

He brushed at his waistcoat. "I called at Henrietta Street and was told, in no uncertain terms, that you were not at home. And would never be. Allow me to restate." His mouth quirked again, but this time there was a bitter cast to his smile. "You were not at home to me." He lifted his hands. "Sophie, don't misunderstand. I am well aware your brother refused to inform you I'd called. As to why, I don't imagine that can be any great mystery to you. He disapproves of me." He let out a breath, a quick puff of air. "Brothers often do. He wishes to protect you from me. I don't blame him, but it's frustrating, all the same, not to be able to call. I prefer an even playing field. After all, Tallboys and Vedaelin may call whenever they like."

"I'm a grown woman, not a child." She rolled her eyes ceilingward then met Banallt's gaze again. He was watching her with a thoughtful expression on his face.

"He made it plain he expected there would be rivals for your affections. He was right."

She gaped at him. "Rivals?" And then she immediately regretted her outburst. "What on earth do you mean by that? We are friends, Banallt. And friends do not have rivals. You have no competition for my affections."

"Darling," he said in a low, silky voice that ought to have set her back on her heels. He sounded like the old Banallt just now. She had the thought, quickly dismissed, that she ought to put more distance between them. She didn't. "You cannot imagine my relief."

She crossed the room and took his hand, determined to treat him as a friend. "I'll speak to John if I must. Of course you may call at Henrietta Street. Whenever you like. How dare he forbid you to call?"

Banallt stared at their hands. "Your brother wants you to remarry. For your future security, if for no other reason. I feel compelled to point out that as my countess, you would be secure."

"Banallt." She rested her other hand on his chest. "You would be an exhilarating husband for any woman. How could you not be? You're handsome and intelligent, a man of position and consequence." He interlaced their fingers, and she hurried to explain herself lest he misunderstand. "If I were to remarry, it would be to a man I know would be as faithful to me as I would be to him."

Their fingers slipped apart, and she took several steps back. "Will you accept Tallboys, then?" he asked. "When he asks."

She shook her head. "I don't imagine so."

"Why not? Because you don't love him?"

She met his gaze. When she looked at Banallt, she could hardly recall what Tallboys looked like. Her world had changed, and she had the sense she wasn't precisely certain what these circumstances required of her. Tommy was dead. And the man standing before her now was no longer a threat to her marriage or to her person. She was free to think he was the loveliest man she'd never known. She was even free to take a lover, if she liked.

The atmosphere changed. She didn't understand how or why, only that it had. Banallt hadn't moved. Nor had she. He couldn't read minds, after all. They were alone, but not private. The noise of the ball was audible. Music, laughter, people talking. The door was open, and all they'd done was come in here to look at a book. But everything had changed.

Was it she who was different? Of a certainty, she noticed the deep claret of his jacket against the embroidered bronze of his waistcoat and the way his jacket fit his shoulders, the paleness of his skin in contrast to the inky black of his hair. She was aware, viscerally aware, of a warmth deep in her body, of a longing of her body for his. Or was Banallt responsible for the change, with his pewter eyes lingering on her face? Drinking her in. Taking her places that frightened her.

He tipped his head to one side, gaze moving from her head to her toes and back, and when he was done with that long and slow perusal, he said, "Sophie, darling, come here."

And she did. Because he was Banallt. Because she was widowed now, and so was he. Because he wanted her and no one else ever had. Not even her husband. She went to him because she wanted to feel his arms around her, his hair slipping through her fingers. She wanted to know what would happen to her if she let him take her in his arms.

When she stood before him, wondering if she'd lost her senses and even whether she dared go through with whatever he had in mind, she lifted her chin and fell, lost immediately, into the tarnished silver of his eyes.

Banallt brushed her cheek with the side of his thumb. He'd taken his gloves off so his bare skin touched hers. "My feelings have not changed, Sophie." He gave a short shake of his head. "No. Please, say nothing just now. All I ask is that you give me a chance."

"To break my heart?" She didn't pull away from him.

"To prove myself." He slid his hand along the edge of her jaw, and then his fingers curled around her nape and drew her toward him. She had to take a step forward to keep her balance. His other hand slid around her waist. "If you fear for your heart, then you give me hope, and that, Sophie, is more than I expected."

"John had no right," she said.

"We shouldn't," he said. "Your brother will never forgive me."

"I'll make my own friends, thank you."

His hand slid up her spine, bringing her closer to him. Up her spine and over her shoulder until he stood with both hands cupping the sides of her face, thumbs sliding along her cheeks, his fingers spread over the sides and back of her head. "I won't promise never to make you angry. Friends sometimes argue, whether they are acquaintances or man and wife." His voice dropped. "Or something else."

Something else. Sophie was horribly aware that she longed for something else in her life. Something other than what she'd had with Tommy. For months she'd known she wanted something more. She hadn't understood what until now.

Banallt lowered his head and pulled her toward him. At the last minute, her courage failed her. She looked away. Her body wanted him, though. Desperately.

"Now, Sophie," he murmured. He put a fingertip to the underside of her chin and tipped her face so that she had to look at him. "You're no coward."

"It's not whether I'm a coward, Banallt." The words came out too breathless for either of them to pretend she wasn't under his influence. "It's whether I'm a fool to let this happen between us."

He smiled at her, and her heart dropped to her toes. "Just once in your life, Sophie, forget whatever foolishness keeps you from living. You're a passionate woman. Stop living as if you are not."

"Did you know when you arrived here tonight, I didn't recognize you?" His eyebrows lifted. "It's true." His finger slid from her chin to just beneath her lower lip. "I saw you as if you were a stranger."

"And?" He traced the bottom of her lip.

"And I thought to myself, whoever that beautiful man is, he's dangerous."

His mouth curved. "What do you think now?"

"The same."

"Your instincts have always been good," he murmured.

He meant to kiss her. She knew she ought not permit it. But she did. Because she was twenty-six years old and had never been kissed by a man who wanted her. And she wanted that. She wanted that with Banallt because he'd always been forbidden to her. Because he had never once lied to her about his desire for her.

The pressure of his fingertip beneath her chin drew her near. She looked at him from under her lashes. She wanted him to kiss her. The air thickened. Sizzled, almost. She could have leaned back, but she didn't. She wanted to know. She needed to know what it would be like.

He shifted his weight. She heard the scrape of his foot sliding on the floor, the whisper of his coat accommodating his motion until only the barest inch separated them. He touched one of her hands, they both dangled uselessly at her sides, and his fingers intertwined with hers. His eyes drifted closed; both his hands drew her nearer yet. Perilously close. But this feeling of anticipation, the giddy drop of her stomach was precisely what she wanted to feel.

Too close, Sophie thought, right before his mouth brushed hers. His breath warmed her skin. *Oh.* Only a light touch. Practically not a kiss at all.

Then, his mouth touched hers again, parting, pressing against her lips, then moving away. His fingertip moved from her chin to the side of her jaw, joining the rest of his hand, and pressing gently upward, toward him. Their breath mingled, they were so close. Their mouths touched again. He was kissing her. Lord Banallt was kissing her, and it was as wicked and soul-stealing a kiss as she had ever imagined. His mouth probed, nudging her lips apart.

Anxiety surged through her. As if he knew, he tightened his hold on her forearm. Not hard, just firm. He leaned toward her and his mouth covered hers even more firmly. She stopped comparing him to a man years gone and let herself think of him as he was now. He smelled good, she thought, and his mouth was astonishingly soft. Banallt's mouth was soft.

Time stopped, collapsed on her. During that compression of past, present, and future that might have lasted no time at all or an eternity, Sophie was incapable of thought. And when she could think again, she was without the aid of her wits. His tongue slid along the seam of her lips, and, without the slightest hesitation, she opened her mouth. His touch turned firmer; his hands tightened. His tongue moved past her lips, smoothly, intimately. Dizzyingly intimately. Her stomach did a flip-flop. The world balanced in that instant.

He withdrew, though he still held the side of her face and his fingers remained curled around her arm. He rested his forehead against hers for a moment. She heard him take a breath. He pressed his mouth to her cheek, to a spot close to her ear, then to her forehead. His fingers slipped from her face as he leaned back. But his hand on her arm slid down to enfold hers.

"I shouldn't have done that," he whispered. "I never intended to."

Was she imagining that his voice sounded as shaky as she felt? Probably. She shook her head. "It doesn't matter."

"I didn't bring you here for that," he said.

"I know that."

He laughed. "Are you going to slap me? I deserve it, I know."

"No," she whispered. She couldn't quite believe she'd let Banallt kiss her or that she'd let things get so...out of control. No wonder he'd cut a swath through half the women in London. He'd made her dizzy with wanting him. She stared, knowing he was too close to her, and that she was going to fall under his spell. If not tonight, then eventually. The only question she wished she could answer was whether the scandal could be managed when she did.

CHAPTER SEVENTEEN

Hightower House, Gray Street, London,
APRIL 2, 1815

Banallt was far too aware of Sophie. He had years of practice in not staring at a woman who interested him if his doing so might arouse suspicion. The skill he'd honed to an art form eluded him now. His present circumstances were fundamentally different than in those days. Before Sophie, his interaction with women had been, in essence, about him. His choices. His reactions. His anticipation. Back then, he didn't gaze endlessly at a woman who struck his fancy, because if he did, his seduction of her would have been thwarted by gossip or someone's interference. With Sophie, the compulsion to stare came from someplace deep inside him, and he could no more stop himself from looking at her than he could stop breathing.

The kiss they'd shared at Harpenden's ball haunted his dreams. He was afraid he'd ruined everything by kissing her like that. God, it had not been a chaste kiss at all. Oh no. He'd kissed her greedily, holding back nothing. And God save him, she had responded to him, answering once and for all the question of whether she could feel passion in his arms. In the three days since then he'd had no opportunity to learn her thoughts on ending up in his arms, then or again. A coincidence? He thought not. The moment had gotten out of hand, and he counted himself lucky she was still speaking to him.

Now she was here, by happenstance, at Gray Street. While she'd not greeted him warmly, she hadn't by any means been cold to him.

Mercer noticed him staring and was not pleased. Of course Mercer wanted to discourage him from Sophie. An earl was nothing when you thought your sister might actually be married off to a duke.

At the moment, Sophie was curled up on a sofa with her dainty pink slippers off and her feet under her legs. A book lay open on her lap, but she'd stopped reading some time ago. They were at Hightower House because Vedaelin had taken John and Sophie to luncheon at the Pulteney Hotel and from there they had come to Gray Street, where Banallt's attendance at tea had been firmly required by Mrs. Llewellyn. His was a command appearance. One supported one's family, after all, and his presence at her tea brought a certain cachet to the event. Mercer's appearance at Gray Street was for different reasons, but Banallt didn't doubt that Fidelia's presence had everything to do with it.

Now, however, tea was hours over. Many of the gentlemen had stayed past tea and made the move to this smaller, more intimate, parlor he preferred when he was not formally entertaining. His cousin and Fidelia had left some time ago to make calls. Those who stayed, which were most of the older gentlemen, dined in, King having brought in and set a table with a quite excellent dinner. Castlereagh, with his packet of dispatches from Wellington, had departed the previous hour. The vice chancellor, Mr. Thomas Plumer, had only just left for another engagement. That left Vedaelin, Mercer, and Sophie. A very cozy gathering now. Conversation continued along the same subjects, though: politics and Bonaparte, which they had discussed with Sophie soaking up everything.

Confidence in the Bourbons surviving the French crisis was low. Banallt, having been recently in Paris, had no confidence whatever that Louis XVIII would manage to keep his throne. Wellington had been ordered to leave Vienna and make his way to France. The news now was that Soult had been dismissed as minister of war on suspicion of loyalty to Napoleon. Banallt personally saw no hope of avoiding a war, and even less that Louis XVIII might actually field an army capable of standing against Bonaparte. Soult was probably on his way to the Corsican now.

"The question," said Mercer to Vedaelin, "is whether Wellington will have specie to pay the troops before morale suffers unbearably." Mercer had loosened his cravat, as had the duke, and Mercer's hair was touseled from his habit of scrubbing his fingers through his curls. "The Continental Army will be asking for money as well, mark my word on it." They were sitting at a table that had been used earlier in the afternoon to sketch out Paris and its environs. The surface was covered with sheets of paper and pencil leads. Vedaelin had drawn out various routes to Paris on one of the sheets.

"They will be paid," Vedaelin said, waving a hand. "Castlereagh has it well in hand, I assure you."

"An army fights on its stomach, but it needs cash in its pockets, too," Banallt said dryly.

"Hear! Hear!" Mercer said, lifting his wine in Banallt's direction. The second bottle was nearly empty. Banallt ordered another. Neither Mercer nor Vedaelin was aware of Sophie any longer, Banallt realized. Fools, the both of them. She'd dropped from the conversation an hour or so ago and set herself to reading on the little sofa by the fire. Vedaelin had since slumped in his chair, a fresh glass of wine in one hand. Mercer's empty one was on the table holding down a crude map of Paris and its main points of entry. Banallt had accepted a second glass of wine, but the unfinished drink was on the mantel, where it would remain, but for the time or two he might pick it up and pace with it in hand. His reputation as a hard drinker was, ironically, born of the fact that he rarely drank while his former associates drank so much they didn't recall how little he'd actually consumed. They only knew he seemed to keep a clearer head than they.

From where Sophie sat, she had a view of all three of them. He had no idea if she was watching him or Vedaelin or even her blasted brother. The book she'd fetched from his library lay open on her lap, though to his knowledge she'd not turned a page in the last hour. The sofa was at an angle from the fire, and though she could see the table where her brother and the duke sat, she had to turn to one side to deliberately watch them. Which she had done. Vedaelin was a blockhead, bringing her here and then ignoring her for hours. Mercer, too, for pity's sake. Fortunately, Sophie was nothing if not adaptable. He forced himself not to look at her.

Banallt left his chair to pace in front of the mantel and back, at a diagonal from where Sophie was, hands behind his back. Every so often he stood just so, where he could be said to have his attention on Mercer and the duke and yet have his view of Sophie remain unimpeded. The light from the fire put her face partially in shadows. She took his breath.

She was not beautiful, not by any objective standard, and yet somehow her features fit together in a way such that he could not help staring, enraptured. The years since their horrible parting at Rider Hall had sobered her. And him as well, or so he liked to think. Tonight her clothes were more splendid than usual, though. Mercer seemed to have realized at last that he needed to force the issue of a new wardrobe on his sister. Her frock was a new one, a deep blue, slightly green so as to recall her eyes, with a scalloped neckline that more than hinted at her bosom. Her taste was impeccable. Banallt, unfortunately, had dressed for a social tea. Gray breeches, top boots, blue coat, and cream waistcoat. An entirely middling bit of linen for a cravat. If he'd known he was to see Sophie, he would have found something better to wear.

As this thought entered his head, he turned during his pacing, and with his thoughts so thoroughly on her, naturally his gaze swept over her. Their eyes connected, though not in a fashion that required either of them to admit it had happened. She had been staring at him, he was sure of it. The devil! She lowered her gaze. She went back to her book, and Banallt knew he was ruined for the rest of the evening. His concentration was gone.

"Mrs. Evans," he said. "I've asked that rooms be made up for you and your brother. I'm sure they're ready now, if you'd like to retire."

"Go on, Sophie." Mercer waved a hand. Yes, now he remembered his sister. Damn the fellow. Mercer had had an afternoon in which to make eyes at Fidelia. "No need to wait up for us. We'll probably talk the night away."

She rose, tucking her book under her arm, and made her goodbyes. Vedaelin bestirred himself to take her hand and wish her a good night. If the duke wanted to win Sophie's heart, he would have to do better than this. As for Banallt, he nodded; she did the same—all very proper and cold under her brother's watchful eye—and then she was gone with the servant who came to show her the way. You'd never think he'd kissed her like he had three days ago. Jesus.

None of them lasted long after Sophie left. When Vedaelin rose, yawning, Mercer stood, too. Banallt walked upstairs with the two men, stopping first at Vedaelin's room. At the door to Mercer's room, Mercer ran his fingers through his hair. "I ought to take her home, you know."

"You may of course," he said. "Any of my carriages is at your service. But why wake her from what must now be a sound sleep?"

Mercer rested his back against the wall and sighed loudly. "All I want is that she be happy." Mercer turned his green eyes on him. "I don't doubt you would keep her safe, but how, my lord, can you ever make her happy?"

"We want the same thing for her." He smiled, but it wasn't one of his good-natured smiles.

"I won't see her in another marriage like she had with Tommy Evans. I just can't. Not for anything."

Banallt held back the obvious vaguely threatening remarks about Mercer's hopes for Fidelia. "Do you think I could persuade her against her inclination?"

"If you put your mind to it, yes."

"Then you are mistaken." He bowed. "Good night, Mercer."

Mercer frowned at him. "Good night, my lord."

Banallt didn't go immediately to his room. Instead he headed for the library to get something to read. One of Sophie's books, he decided. The last book she'd published before he'd gone and spoiled everything. First, though, he returned to the parlor to fetch his wine from the mantel. As he walked through the silent house he wondered how long it would be before he proposed to Fidelia, just to be done with things. What a jackanapes of an idea. He'd wait until Tallboys or Vedaelin convinced Sophie to remarry. Until then, he had hope.

He went into the library and found he didn't need to light a candle, because there was already one burning. Sophie was fast asleep on a leather chair. Her book, a different one than she'd had in the parlor, had fallen off her lap. He pulled up a chair and sat, wineglass in hand, contemplating her and his future. They didn't have one. Not the one he wanted, anyway. Perhaps it was time for him to court Fidelia after all. A courtship would take his mind off what he couldn't have.

Banallt finished his wine without deciding whether he ought to wake her. Better, he thought, if he called a maid to look after her. He didn't get up, though. He set his empty glass on the floor beside his chair. Her lashes were thick, a sweep of sable against her cheeks. Asleep as she was, her face lacked the lively quickness that had originally attracted him. The familiar shape of her nose made him smile. Before long, his eyes drooped, and five minutes later, he was asleep and dreaming of Sophie. His was not a polite dream.

"Wake up, my lord," said the Sophie of his dream.

He certainly wasn't ready to wake up. He'd only just got around to undressing her. Sophie shook his shoulder. He opened his eyes after the second time she called his name. For a disconcerting moment, he couldn't separate his dream from reality. But that really was Sophie leaning over him.

"You were fast asleep," she said.

Jesus. His breeches were firmly buttoned, thank God, and he was not in a fully aroused state. The muscles on one side of his back ached. He pushed himself upright. Had he been calling Sophie's name out loud? Nothing about her suggested that he had been. She wasn't laughing or, for that matter, angry. "What time is it?"

"Nearly two." She watched him the way she had at Harpenden's before he'd completely lost his head and kissed her. With something new in her eyes. His stomach fluttered with familiar anticipation. He knew women well enough to recognize where Sophie's thoughts were wandering. Well, he wasn't going to cross the lines he'd obliterated when she knew him at Rider Hall. Never. Which meant that no matter how explicit his dreams of her, he could do nothing.

"Where have John and Vedaelin gone?" she asked.

"To bed," he said shortly. "Some time ago. Come." He pried himself off his chair. "I'll see you upstairs."

Banallt wondered if he was dreaming after all. He must be, to be here alone with her, in a house so silent and empty. But then a yawn cracked his jaw, and he lost that just-awakened feeling. This was indeed Sophie standing next to him, her eyes alight, mouth curved in a smile. Why, he wondered, wasn't she asking him what he was doing asleep in the library?

He tucked her hand around his arm and took the candle-stick in the other. He extinguished the lights before they left, leaving them walking in the light of his candle. He hoped to God he'd not been calling her name in his sleep. "You'll fall asleep directly as soon as you're in your room, Sophie."

She leaned against him. "I'm sure I shall."

He was trying very hard to be good, to behave himself, but with her leaning against him like this, well. Even a saint would be tried.

They walked up the stairs arm in arm. Had he not bungled his proposal, he might be escorting his countess upstairs. If only he had given her time to understand he had changed because of her. If only he had told her he had spent the days after that final meeting at Rider Hall coming to terms with the man he was and the man he needed to become. He stopped and let go of her arm in order to open the door to her room. She waited at the door while he went inside and used his candle to light another across the room. Sophie leaned against the door frame, arms tucked behind her.

"Thank you, Banallt," she said when he stood by her.

"You're welcome."

She tilted her head to one side. "You were calling my name," she whispered. "Why?"

His stomach dropped. She was so very beautiful, and he was so very close to forgetting himself. "Even a rogue like me needs his secrets."

"Vedaelin says you've changed." She looked him straight in the face. He didn't see anything there to tell him he needed to step away. So he didn't. "Have you?"

"Perhaps not as much as I ought to have," he said after a bit.

She took a step nearer to him, into the room now. He didn't dare do any of the things that occurred to him. If something were to happen, Sophie had to take the initiative. If she did, he didn't know if he was strong enough to resist her. She reached out and touched his cravat, smoothing the top fold. "You're very handsome," she whispered. "Even with that untidy cravat."

Could any man resist the temptation in that low, silken whisper? She couldn't think he would. Sophie didn't think that highly of him. He took a step nearer. She tipped her head to look into his face, and he remembered, sharp and clear, how her mouth had felt when he kissed her.

She tugged on the end of his cravat. "Let me fix this, Banallt."

"Perhaps you should."

"Yes," she whispered.

Banallt reached past her and closed the door.

CHAPTER EIGHTEEN

The slide of wood and metal parts as the door closed was the sound of Sophie's life changing forever. In the silence that followed the soft click she could have stepped away from him. Lord Banallt let the silence grow and thus gave her the chance to object or make an excuse that would send him away. But she didn't. She didn't want to. Downstairs, he'd whispered her name while he slept. Moaned, more like it. The sound had made her feel alive. She'd made up her mind right then that she wanted to know what it would be like to have him hold her with the knowledge between them that this time there would be no stopping. Would he moan her name like that?

Banallt slid his arm around her waist until her body fit snug against his.

She'd been waiting for this all her life.

The Earl of Banallt, wicked to the core, dropped his head, and Sophie responded. Her entire body wanted this. Him. With an intake of breath before his lips touched hers, she opened her mouth under his in a capitulation to her years of suppressed desire. Her body flashed hot with need. The door held her up as he continued to kiss her, gently and yet with a leashed passion that shook her to her soul. Tonight, she would discover what it was like to be with a man who desired her.

Banallt loosened his hold on her long enough to put the candle on a table mercifully near them, and then he brought her back into his embrace, both his arms around her this time. She melted against him. Their mouths met again, and this time his kiss was a little rougher. Less controlled. Less restrained. She brought up her hand and ended up clutching his coat and pulling him closer. His tongue swept into her mouth, and her brain simply stopped reacting to anything but holding him, tasting him, making sure he didn't stop.

She slid her arms up and around his shoulders, rising on her toes. His hair, thick and cool as silk, soft as down, brushed the back of her hands. She buried her fingers in his hair, pulling his head to hers and giving herself up to their kiss and the passion that erupted from her. He wanted her; she felt his need in the grip of his arms around her and in the way his mouth fit to hers. Banallt wanted her. Knowing that made her want more. She felt as if she'd never been kissed in her life, that this was her first time.

With his arms still around her, he drew back. He lifted his hands to her face, cupping her head in his palms and brushing his thumbs along her cheeks. "Sophie," he whispered. "Sophie... Are you sure?"

"Yes."

For one chilling moment, he was every inch the cold and heartless Earl of Banallt. His hair hung straight and dark and black as pitch, and his eyes flashed with that dark light so peculiar to him. The sight threw her years into the past, when Tommy was still alive and Banallt was a dangerous man to be avoided at any cost. She pressed her spine against the closed door while he stared into her face, into her eyes with that wild expression in his gaze, and Sophie was set adrift in the pewter depths. She had no notion at all what he was thinking. Her stomach did a slow tumble, yet she knew she wouldn't change her answer. Not for anything. She wanted this. She wanted him.

Banallt pushed away from the wall, and she could not read his intentions in his face nor from the way he stood. He glanced at the door he'd closed. "It's all right," she said. She had to force herself to speak. "If you don't want this."

Just when she was certain he was going to turn away from her, he grabbed her hand and led her into the room. Toward the bed. "I want you, Sophie." His words sounded thick. "Can you really think anything else is possible for me?" He stopped walking and tugged on her wrist until he'd brought her close to him. His eyes devoured her. That was exactly what it felt like. His gaze devoured her. "Jesus," he said, "I'm in a bad way over you. It's lowering how desperate I am."

He pulled out as many of her hairpins as he could, scattering them on the floor, and kept going until her hair fell to her shoulders and down her back. "There. That's how I've imagined you." He worked his fingers into her hair and held her head fast. "From the moment I saw you—you probably think I don't remember, but I do. You standing there in the hallway, holding a lamp and looking as if you thought you might be murdered in your own home. I thought I'd been bewitched. My very own odalisque was standing before me."

Banallt kissed her again, hard and deep. Her husband had never kissed her like this, as if she were the most precious and desirable woman he'd ever held. Despite his passion, his mouth felt soft. Sinfully soft. Kissing him back was easy. He pulled away, not far at all, holding her. He turned her back to him. Brushing her hair over one shoulder, he set himself to undoing the fastenings down the back of her gown.

She bent her head, trying to steady her breathing. She wasn't an innocent. She'd been married. She knew about the intimacy to follow. She knew what Banallt would do. Her insides twisted. Banallt was used to beautiful women, and she was afraid she wouldn't meas-ure up to his other lovers. He would find her as deficient as Tommy had. A wry voice in the back of her head said, Well, then, he won't be *after* you *anymore*, will *he?* But she would have had her chance, and tonight that's what she wanted.

At the start of her marriage, Tommy had been affectionate, but it wasn't long before he stopped coming to her. Fewer than six months after their marriage, he'd left on the first of his trips to London. Each successive visit lasted longer and longer until they could hardly be said to be living as husband and wife. She'd never gotten over the conviction that she'd never pleased Tommy intimately or otherwise and that if she had, he'd not have left her.

And if Banallt wasn't pleased, either? If he left her, too? At least she wouldn't lose another husband or have her heart broken again. She closed her eyes and tried to avoid thinking about anything at all. It didn't work. When she exhaled, her breath trembled. She put her hands on her belly, trying to still the herd of butterflies there.

Banallt's hands curved over the tops of her shoulders, just above her loosened bodice, and brought her up against his body. His palms warmed her skin, and his breath came soft and damp near her ear. "You've been in my dreams for so long, now that you're real, my hands are shaking, Sophie." His laugh was a soft and velvet rumble in her ear. "I may never get you undressed: '

She turned, pressing her hands to her upper chest to keep her gown from falling away. His eyes pierced her, and the backs of her knees tingled. "You mean that, don't you?"

He hooked a finger in the bodice she held trapped against her body and pulled. "You're the most beautiful woman I've ever known. You know that's what I think. Don't pretend you don't."

"Look at me, Banallt, and say that. Really look at me." She ran a finger the length of her unfortunate nose.

"I look at you and see a woman who makes my hands tremble."

She let go of her gown. They dealt with her corset and the ties and strings that fastened her gown, until at last she stood before him wearing only her shift and stockings. The curve of his mouth was familiar, as was the dark cast to his eyes, and her heart skipped a beat as the sight brought back her habit of setting her physical reaction to him someplace far away.

"I never used to like dainty women, until I met you," he said. "But now I can't imagine anyone but you satisfying me. Only you will do."

Sophie let herself fall into the moment. She didn't want to think about the past or all the awful rumors she'd heard about Banallt, both now and in former times. She wasn't married anymore. Tommy was years dead. She was free to take a lover if that's what she wanted. This sin was one she could live with. She walked past him to the bed and climbed the wooden steps to the mattress. She sat on the bed and held out a hand to him. "Come, Banallt," she said.

He followed and pressed her against him as she kissed him. While she explored his mouth, he slid his hands underneath what was left of her clothing and undid her garters. He stopped kissing her in order to look at what he was doing. He pushed down one stocking then the other, and then he was back to drop a kiss on her shoulder. Her eyes flickered open to take in hair black as night dangling past a pale temple and neck. Banallt. This was really him. She lifted her hands and plowed her fingers through the thick locks. Her first few times with Tommy had been like this for her. Breathless, dizzying, her heart in her mouth with anticipation.

He knelt and brought her shift up and over her head. Sophie had never been undressed with Tommy, not even under the covers. "Lie back," he whispered. "I want to look at you."

She did. But she felt awkward, uncertain, and embarrassed, too. Ashamed that she would allow anyone to see her naked. She didn't know what to do with her hands, and the fact that she was nude, and he wasn't, embarrassed her. He slipped a hand behind one of her knees and brought it up.

"Spectacular," he said. She couldn't bring herself to look directly at him, but from the corner of her eyes, she saw him looking at her body. Her stomach hollowed out and yet, part of her enjoyed the wickedness. "Are you cold?"

She nodded. The fire had died down and the air had a chill edge to it that made her skin tight. A sinful light danced in his eyes, and a slow, intimate smile spread across his face. "Can you bear it just a while longer?"

She nodded. His eyes, flat, nearly dead, fixed on her, but something in her reacted to that lifeless silver. His eyes had always fascinated her. From beneath her lashes, she watched him scoot down so that his head was level with her stomach. He put his hand on her belly, spreading his fingers over her, angling them outward. His fingers curved around her hips and then to the insides of one thigh and then the other. A shiver centered very near where his hands now lingered. He rolled away, and when he reappeared in her line of sight, he lay on his side, palm propping up his head. He pushed his hair away from his face and settled a hand on her belly.

"You are very beautiful, Sophie," he said.

"You make me feel as if I am."

"Never doubt it, darling." His hand wandered up, and her breasts tightened. He drew a finger along the underside of her breasts and then, slowly, upward. Her breath hitched. She caught a glimpse of flat pewter eyes, of a lock of black hair sweeping over his forehead. The lusterless color of his eyes leaped again to that hidden gleam just before he fit his mouth over her breast. The warmth shocked her, and then the damp and the sizzle shot through her entire body. She moaned. She wasn't even sure if the sound was in her head or if she'd actually groaned. So this, she thought, was what it felt like when a rake made love to a woman. His tongue touched her nipple, and she bowed toward him. His other hand stayed splayed on her belly, pressing down. He shifted. The movement made a soft shirring sound along the top of the bed covers. His mouth teased until she thought she'd lose her mind.

A moan rose in her throat. Lord, how *undignified.* Banallt paused, then lifted his head and looked into her face. It was like seeing him for the first time. Oh heavens. The notorious Lord Banallt. A man she'd fantasized about when she was a girl and who had burst into her world when she was overwhelmed with her unhappy life and marriage, hardly living at all. Banallt. His eyes flashed like tarnished silver in the light. In a fog of passion, she slid her fingers free of his hair, down his throat to his upper torso. He scooted up the bed, leaning against the headboard with his arms upraised to clutch the top of the board.

"Come here, Sophie. Yes," he said when she was kneeling between his legs. "Just so." A corner of his mouth curved. He put his hands on either side of her neck. "Do you like being naked when I'm not?"

"I'd like to see you."

Banallt clucked his tongue. He drew his knees up, even with her sides. "Now, darling, that's not what I asked."

"No," she said. "I don't like it. It makes me wonder when, not if, you're going to leave me."

"Ah. Yes, I understand." The smoky edge to his voice made her tremble inside. "But, you see, Sophie, the thing is, I've had a particular fantasy about you. Very particular." His eyes drew her into an intimacy that shrank her universe to just her and Banallt. "It started not long after I met you. When you still disliked me simply for my association with your husband." He drew the tip of an index finger from the base of her throat to her lower belly. "While you were wishing I would drop off the face of the earth, I had this particular image of you in my head and in my dreams at night."

A shiver went down her spine. He must have felt it, because his smile deepened. "What fantasy?"

"You nude." His finger dipped in and out of her navel. "Me with all my clothes on. I'd touch you here." His palm slipped over her mons, and two of his fingers slid between her legs. "You'd be wet. Mm," he whispered. "As you are right now. And I'd slide my fingers inside you. Like so." He drew her toward him. "I'd kiss you. Like this." His mouth found the hollow at the base of her throat, his tongue dipping and swirling.

Her body softened, and she leaned toward him. How wonderful that felt. "Banallt." His name ended on a sharp intake of breath, because his fingers continued to slide in and out of her passage while another rubbed, and with each moment Sophie's body raced toward pleasure. She bowed against him, holding him, trying to open herself to him and what his fingers were doing to her.

"And then, when you're almost there, desperate to have me bring you—" He stopped. "I'd look at your face and see your eyes hazy with passion, on the very edge. And I'd lay you back." He moved forward, holding her until their bodies were stretched out on the bed again. "You'd be so soft, everywhere I touched you." Now he touched the very inside of her thigh and nudged her legs apart so he could see everything. Cool air washed along her body. "I'd bring you with my mouth," he whispered. Then his mouth was on her. There. Exactly there.

Lord, his mouth was on her, open and firm against her most inner and private parts. His lips, his tongue, the side of his face touched her, pressed against her thigh. The sensation that she was dissolving gathered inside her, stealing her wits. His hand slid over her belly, his fingers spread flat, pressing down. His other hand pushed her thigh wide, more and more, and she dropped deep into a world that did not exist unless Lord Banallt touched her.

She quivered and arched toward his mouth, and at the peak of her motion, he touched her breast, the very lightest sweep of a fingertip over her while his mouth covered her down there. His tongue flicked out. She moaned, a wanton sound that wasn't her at all. Except it was. She forgot everything but right now. The world slid away. Only Banallt was left. Only his touch, her breath. Her body opened to him, and in the very last moment in which she could think, she knew she would love him the rest of her life, just for having given her this moment.

Banallt pulled himself over her, one hand still between their bodies. "And then I'd come over you, darling, hard for you, aching for you, dying to be inside you, to have you beneath me." His hips tilted back.

"What else?" she whispered.

"Your tender skin feels my clothes, and I reach to unbutton." He bit his lower lip as his hand worked at the fastening of his trousers. "I'd push your legs apart—" The outside of his thigh pressed against hers, and Sophie sucked in a breath. His hard-muscled leg slid along hers. The buttons of his waistcoat pressed into her, and along the length of her legs the fabric of his trousers rubbed her.

"I can withdraw," he said softly. "If I did that, there's little risk you'll get with child." With his fingertip, he made a circle on her belly. "Will you say yes, darling?"

He touched the outside of her thigh, trailing a fingertip along her skin. Her breath caught. Every muscle in her body tensed. She put a hand over her mouth. His fingers moved between her legs and touched her nether hair. Her heart pounded, and her body went rigid. His hand flattened on her thigh. He drew a finger along the inside of her leg.

His body was in position. All Sophie had to do was tip her hips toward him. She did, and he was there, at her opening, sliding in, filling her, setting every nerve in her body on fire. Then he was inside her. He dropped his head and sighed into the hollow of her throat. "Sophie. God, Sophie. How beautiful you feel."

Pleasure rippled through her; something deep inside her felt ravenous. She drank him in. She'd never felt such longing, like the edge of a storm about to break. A lock of hair fell in a slash of black across his cheek. An aesthete's face, lean and hawkish. He watched her looking at him, and the corner of his lip curled. The darkness in him beckoned. Thousands of butterflies dipped and dived in her stomach. The same smile quirked at the corners of his mouth.

"Banallt," she whispered. He was inside her body, and she was beyond anything but the sensation of his movement.

"You are mine, Sophie," he said in a voice as dark as his eyes. "Mine. You ought to have told me yes the very first time I asked you. Admit we should have done this much sooner. Oh Jesus, Sophie. Maybe you do have reason to hate me, but right now at least have the decency to admit you love this."

"Yes." She let out a trembling breath. "Yes, I do love this." His eyes went soft, and when she rolled her pelvis, he arched toward her. "I used to hate you, Banallt." He leaned over her, and his hair fell over her shoulder. She twined her fingers in it and tugged. "When you left Rider Hall that night, I hated you with all my heart."

"I know. I deserved it, too." He stilled. "But now it's different. You don't hate me anymore, do you?" She shook her head. A smile spread over his face. "Good," he whispered.

Once she understood what he meant by the gentle pressure on the underside of her knee, she bent both knees, feet flat on the mattress. She closed her eyes so tight colors exploded behind her lids. He circled her wrists and brought them above her head, pinning her. And she didn't care at all, because she hadn't ever in all her life imagined feeling this way.

She freed a hand and threw an arm around his neck and pulled his head to hers. "Banallt." A low sound tore from the back of her throat, and she bowed toward him, one leg thrown over his, feeling the rasp of his clothes against her body. "More," she said. "Please, more."

Banallt answered with a movement of his own, a pushing, sliding motion into her and then over her. She felt his body, the shape of him, covering the length of her. Air came into his lungs with a gasp.

Their gazes locked. He made her feel beautiful. With him she was desired and special. The tickle in her belly spread out from her center. He studied her face while he bore down, farther inside her. His fingers spread around her thigh, sliding beneath, clutching and pulling up, and then he stopped moving. She gasped. He drew out, only a short way, and readjusted himself. He propped one elbow above her shoulder and gripped her thigh, pressing down on her, into her. He threw back his head, drew partially out of her, and then slid back in, hard enough for her to feel the friction deep inside her.

She moved, this time toward his forward pressure. He let his weight press down, into her. He pulled her thigh up and surged into her, farther and deeper, then away and back again until at last, something broke inside her. She cried out, but he came into her so fast and so far that all the air whooshed out of her lungs and cut off her groan. He pushed and pushed and still he fit. "God help me," he said. "Too soon."

He stopped moving for the space of a heartbeat. He bent his head to her shoulder and rocked his hips, pressing inside her. His hair fell forward around either side of his face, a frame of black, silky where it brushed her collarbone. "I am in paradise." His hips rocked again.

She closed her eyes tight. She felt his lips on her cheek and then on her eyelids, placing gentle kisses. He pulled nearly all the way out of her and then pressed in. "Jesus, you are tight, and I am as hard as ever I have been in my life."

He had his elbows above her, pressing the tops of her shoulders. A quiver of anticipation shot through her, wrenched her passion higher yet. She grasped for it—or maybe, just maybe, he paused long enough for her to reach for it. The quiver pooled in her belly again, as it had when he'd put his mouth on her there, as it had when he first slid inside her. She took a breath and then another, and then she stopped thinking about how impossible it was that Lord Banallt should be inside her, because all she could think of was how he filled her and how hot he felt, and how good she felt. And how wonderful he looked. How beautiful his eyes were when he looked into her face. She lifted her pelvis off the mattress and strained to meet him.

"Sophie," he whispered. His eyes darkened. "Sophie." He did what he'd promised, which was withdraw. She threw back her head and protested with a groan. He grabbed her hand and curled her fingers around him, gripping hard as he came.

After a bit, he grabbed her arm and said, "I'm not done with you yet, madam."

CHAPTER NINETEEN

The first few seconds after Banallt realized he was awake, he was aware of remarkably little. He could easily have slipped back into sleep, and nearly did, except, just there in the back of his head, there existed a niggling reason he shouldn't. What was it? Without opening his eyes, he knew it was damn early in the morning. There was very little good reason to get out of bed before the sun was up. The bedsheets formed a cocoon of warmth around his naked body. Unusual for him these days to be naked in bed, but there it was. He was naked: tired and happy in some deep and indefinable manner.

Ah. This was not his room.

A body stirred beside him, a woman, of course, and he knew she was the reason for his extremely pleasant state of existence. Nudity. Sleepiness. Happiness. He reached, pulled her close, spooning her body against his. He breathed in the scent of her and touched the warm softness of her skin. And knew.

Sophie.

She was his. Now she could not deny she was his. Now she must confront her feelings for him. He knew Sophie well enough to suspect she wouldn't. This would work between them. He'd make it work.

He tucked his chin over her shoulder and drew her closer. She sighed, a gentle sound, and her backside pressed against him. He really could fall back asleep quite contentedly. So he did. It was a joy to have Sophie in his arms and feel utterly and unashamedly happy as he tipped back into sleep.

He woke a second time to a room not as dark as before. There was still no hope of seeing the time on the clock ticking somewhere in the room. And yet, it was undeniably morning. Sophie turned in his arms and draped a hand over his waist. Her breathing changed. "Good morning," he whispered. He was a bit tense. How would she react?

She didn't open her eyes. " 'Tisn't," she murmured, wriggling close to him, with a rather predictable response from him. "Not morning at all. I'm too tired for it to be morning."

Banallt held his breath, waiting for her to whisper Tommy's name. But she didn't. He kissed the top of her head. Downstairs he heard the faint sound of servants in the kitchen. After five in the morning, but not yet six, he thought. Even so, the darkness wouldn't last much longer. Not that they needed to be up and about just yet. Bringing up the fire in the kitchen took long enough that there'd be nothing hot to eat for hours yet. "If you say so, darling."

"I do say so."

He cradled her in his arms. He was happy. Beyond happiness. Sophie was his. He knew quite well he ought to get out of bed and go back to his room while there was still a better than even chance of him getting there before anyone realized where and how he'd spent the night. He had a few moments more before the risk was too great, though, and he spent them holding Sophie, who'd fallen back to sleep.

When he woke the third time, the room was no longer dark. Dawn had certainly come and gone. He turned his head and had no trouble at all seeing the clock on the fireplace mantel. Four minutes after eight. Damned early yet, following such a late night, and yet, he was going to have a devil of a time getting out now without being seen. He sat up and scrubbed his hands through his hair.

Beside him, Sophie opened her eyes and immediately closed them again. Her hair was tangled, since the precaution of braiding her hair before they slept was simply not anything that had penetrated his pleasure-sated mind last night. Nor hers, either.

"Banallt?" Her voice was thick with sleep. "Is that you?"

Who the hell else would it be? "Yes."

She sighed. "Good."

"Go back to sleep, Sophie." He slipped out of bed, holding the sheets low to keep the cold air out and the warm in. Damn, but the chill was going to freeze his balls off.

She squinted at him and, with her weight on an elbow, partially sat up, holding, more's the pity, the sheets to her bosom. "What time is it?"

"Time for me to go."

Her attention was not on his face. She was, in fact, giving him a very long and assessing look. "You haven't any clothes on."

"Neither have you." His smallclothes had come off last. Well, yes. Of course they had, but that meant they ought to be closest to the bed. In fact, he was stepping on them now. His trousers were draped over a chair. He didn't see his coat, shirt, or stockings anywhere.

"Oh," Sophie said. A charming flush appeared in her cheeks.

"Yes," he said. "Oh."

Her eyes were sleepy, her hair mussed. Banallt wanted to get back into bed with her and hold her while they both fell back to sleep. If he did that, they would be caught out, and her brother would insist on shooting him dead and he'd have to let him, after which they would have to be married by special license. He wanted her to have a church wedding, with her brother to give her away and all his relatives in attendance.

"I ought to get up, too."

That brought him up short. "What on earth for?" He knew the moment the words came out that he'd spoken too quickly. He didn't want to sound like a tyrant. Controlling and officious. Tommy on his worst hungover morning.

"I'm usually up before eight," she said in a very bland voice. A dangerously bland voice.

Good God, but he would live the rest of his life learning how to avoid that tone of voice. He suspected he would be a better man for the lessons. "You only just closed your eyes," he said gently. From the corner of his eye, he saw his shirt hanging off the edge of a chair. He forced himself to take a breath. She sat the rest of the way up, holding the sheets to her chest, but exposing a goodly portion of her exquisite back. "Your brother and Vedaelin won't be up for hours, I'm sure. There won't be anything for breakfast yet, either."

"Oh. Oh goodness." With one hand, she pulled her hair out of her face. "This is a tangle for us, isn't it?"

Banallt stood there, and his heart felt too big for his chest. She was naked, for pity's sake. They'd spent the night making love. He wanted to again. He wanted to be certain they were all right. So far so good, but he never knew with Sophie. This was new territory for them both. He retrieved her gown from the floor where he'd let it fall. His shirt was nearby, in good condition. "I've only to make it to my room unseen, Sophie." He found her corset, too, and set that on the chair with her gown. He smoothed a few of the wrinkles from the satin. "Unless you wish to find yourself embroiled in scandal, perhaps you could help me locate my cravat. It's gone missing and it won't do to have a servant find it here."

"Banallt," she said in a low, drawn-out whisper. "I've nothing on." Her cheeks turned pinker.

"Yes," he said. He leered at her, hugely diverted by the thought. "I know."

She pointed with a bare arm. "There. By that chest of drawers."

His cravat was ruined. There was no way to resurrect it. He held up the crumpled linen. "My valet will have my hide when he sees this."

"What a scandal that would be," she said. Then she fell silent, and her gaze turned inward; he knew she was thinking about the kind of scandal that ruined reputations. Primarily the reputations of women.

He returned to the bed and sat on the edge of the mattress, still naked. "Sophie. Darling—"

"You're nothing but goose bumps." She lifted the sheets. "Get in before you freeze to death."

He slid in and shivered violently until his body warmed up. After a bit, she said, "Are we lovers now, Banallt?"

"Lovers?" He didn't want Sophie to be a lover of his. What he wanted was a permanent, legal relationship duly sanctified by the Church of England. But he knew better than to raise that subject directly. He turned onto his side and took a lock of her hair between his fingers. "If that's all I'm to have from you, Sophie, yes. We're lovers. Are you sorry?" he asked. "What a ridiculous question that is. Would you even tell me if you were?"

"I'm not sorry," she said. She wriggled under him and got a hand on his chest. "And yes, I would tell you if I were."

And then there they were, looking at one another. He leaned over her and kissed her, and damned if she didn't move toward him herself. He pulled the sheets up to his neck and drew his body over hers, using his forearms to pin the sheets around them.

"This is an extremely poor idea," he said as he bent his head to kiss her. The entire time he wondered how he was going to make this permanent between them, but then she softened against him and she kissed him back with a thoroughly distracting enthusiasm. He drew back after a while and watched her face. Her eyes slowly opened.

"You were right," she said.

"About?"

"That when I came to your bed, it would be because I wanted to be there."

He wasn't sure whether to be insulted or pleased by that. He gripped her. "I'm glad to know you wanted me, too, Sophie, have no doubt of that." He struggled to find the words that would explain everything so she'd understand. Really understand. "But what I said back then has nothing to do with now. Nothing whatever."

She stroked a hand over his head. "Your hair is so soft. I love the feeling of it against my skin."

"Stop changing the subject."

"You're very big." She had her hand on his cock at the time, so the remark was rather more complimentary than it might have been if she'd been commenting more generally.

"Witch," he said. She wasn't just holding him. Her fingers were just now being very clever indeed. He pressed his hips forward. "Go on."

"And hard, my lord." Her lashes hid her eyes. She stroked the head of his cock. "I've never in my life felt anything so wonderful as this."

One of her arms was around his waist as her eyes fluttered open. He found himself lost in limpid blue green. She wasn't his. Not legally. He could as yet lay no claim to her heart. He wanted the ceremony that would make her indisputably his. He wanted Sophie to be the mother of his children. He wanted Sophie. He wouldn't ever be whole without her. If he rushed her, he stood to lose everything.

She brought up a hand and touched his cheek. Her finger traced the line of his cheekbone, down the side of his face to his mouth and along his lower lip. "Did last night really happen?"

Banallt kissed the tip of her finger and tried not to think about her fingers around him, stroking. "I've been wondering the same myself. But, yes. It did."

"You're sure we didn't imagine it?"

His body was all too willing to prove she hadn't. All he had to do was shift his hips and he could be inside her again. So he did just that, and she let him go. She lifted her chin, pressing the back of her head into the pillow, and he surged forward.

This was different. Last night had been several of his fantasies about her combined into one. The cold logic of day had been hours away. Last night, they'd lived for a time, just the two of them, in a world no one else shared. This morning, she couldn't deny what it meant to make love with him. "This isn't an affair, Sophie," he said while he still had the wits to speak. He was rapidly approaching a point of mindlessness. "Maybe it is for you, but for me it's not."

"Banallt." His name ended on a gasp. Her hands slid down his back and she arched against him. He thought he would expire right then, before she'd come to any sort of pleasure.

"You're the only woman for me, Sophie. The only one. No one else will ever do." Underneath the covers, he planted his hands by her rib cage and concentrated on his strokes and the way her body surrounded him, and the rush of approaching orgasm took his breath and his senses and his heart. He damn near didn't withdraw in time.

Afterward, she kept her arms around his. "I'll help you dress, Banallt."

"And then go back to sleep, I hope?"

"I might just," she said. She took the duvet with her when she slid out of bed. While she helped him dress he did his best to get her to drop it. She proved too agile for that. When he was dressed, more or less, she leaned back to study the effect. "I think I could do something with your cravat," she said.

"I shudder to think of that limp strip of fabric coming anywhere near my neck. Another time, when I've fresh linens." He smiled when she smoothed his waistcoat. "I'll allow, however, that you make an excellent valet."

"Thank you." She dropped him a curtsey.

"Odd, but I've never wanted to kiss my valet before now."

"Kiss your valet?" She pretended to be horrified. "That's very wicked of you, my lord."

"I'm a wicked man, darling. And I wish to kiss my valet. For some reason, I've only just noticed her mouth is full and soft." He passed his thumb over her lips.

"Do you think she'll accept such a wicked advance from her employer?" she asked.

"Will she?" He pulled her into his arms. She had to go up on tiptoe to properly kiss him, and when he felt her body against his and her hands snaking into his hair, he groaned. He lifted his head from hers and glanced at the clock. Quarter to nine. He stepped back and stuffed his cravat into his pocket. "Sophie, I must go."

She laughed. "Very well, my lord."

"I don't like the subterfuge," he said. "I'd rather we walked downstairs together and damn what anyone says. I want to stay here, in bed with you." For years he'd had nothing but trysts. He'd planned and hoped for one with her since he first laid eyes on her, and now he wanted everything in the open. He wanted to court her openly. "I want us to be married."

Her expression clouded. "Banallt."

"Do you imagine I'd leave you at the altar?" He saw the answer in her eyes. "No," he said slowly. "Of course not. You think if we marry, I'll be unfaithful before we've had our wedding trip."

"My heart's already half broken." Her eyes glittered. "I couldn't bear it, Banallt. I couldn't. Not again. Not with you. I'll be your lover, happily. But not your wife."

He headed for the door but stopped halfway. "I love you, Sophie. I love you with my soul."

Her bare arms held up the duvet. "Don't ruin this, Banallt, please."

"I'm not a villain from one of your novels, Sophie." She stared at him, wide-eyed. "Unlike them, I can change. I have changed."

Unfortunately, she didn't believe him.

CHAPTER TWENTY

Sophie was convinced the maid who came to her room when she called for a servant knew Banallt had spent the night here. The young woman didn't say much beyond a respectful "Good morning, ma'am." She found Sophie's clothes, and minutes later another servant came to take her gown to have it ironed. As Sophie washed her hands and face, she smelled Banallt on her skin and remembered, with a shiver in the pit of her stomach, the way he'd kissed her, where he'd kissed her, the look on his face when he moved in her and how she had felt a bolt of pleasure at every stroke. If she got back into bed, she'd smell his scent there, too, and remember his voice and the way his fingers had tightened on her, how his body had felt.

While she waited for her pressed gown, Sophie put on her stockings and corset and slid on her slippers. Then she sat to let the maid work on the awful tangle of her hair. "You've lovely hair, ma'am," said the maid. She'd brought a brush and comb with her, silver backed with ivory.

"Thank you. I should have braided it before I went to bed." She watched the maid's face in the mirror. "I don't know why I didn't. I was so very tired, though."

"Some nights are like that, ma'am. Do you want me to pin your hair in any particular style?"

"Just so it's off my face and neck, thank you. My brother and I will be going straight home, I'm sure."

"Yes, ma'am."

As the maid worked, Sophie's reflection in the mirror showed the same woman she always saw. Pointed chin, too-long nose, a nice mouth, she thought, and pretty eyes. But her eyebrows were too dark and she never shaped them as she ought. Why didn't she look different, she wondered? Why did she look the same even though her life had changed completely? She was a wicked woman now. An immoral one. And she didn't much care.

Her gown came back, and she dressed quickly in her clothes from last night. Another servant showed Sophie to the morning room. John was there with the morning *Times* in one hand and a cup of coffee in the other. "Good morning, John."

"Sophie." He didn't look up from his paper.

She fetched a plate and put eggs and bacon on it. "Did you sleep well?" she asked.

"Mm, and you?"

"The same," she said as she sat down with her plate. She piled clotted cream on a scone and reached across the table to take the croissant on John's plate. He didn't notice.

Fidelia came in and John's paper came down with a rattle. He jumped up. "Miss Llewellyn."

"Mr. Mercer. Good morning." She walked to where Sophie sat. "Mrs. Evans. Good morning. I adore the scones cook makes. Do you like them, ma'am?"

"Good morning, Miss Llewellyn. And yes, very much." The girl—young lady—had Banallt's coloring, the dark hair and pale skin, but her eyes were blue as the sky. Her features were strong but tempered by a sensitive mouth. Were the rumors about her and Banallt making a match true? "I hope you're well today."

"Yes. Thank you. I'm quite well."

John came around to help her to a seat next to Sophie. "Miss Llewellyn," he said. "May I get you a plate?"

"Yes, please." She looked at John from under her lashes. Her cheeks flushed a faint pink. "Poached eggs, if you don't mind. And one of those lovely scones."

Banallt came in then, dressed in fresh clothes and a rather blandly tied cravat. Sophie's stomach shivered. She'd been intimate with him. She'd touched his naked body, and he'd touched hers. Good mornings were said all around. Sophie wasn't sure how to behave with Banallt in the room. Should she ignore him? That would be unforgivably rude, but if she didn't ignore him, she was afraid everyone would realize what had happened between them last night. His greeting to her was over before she could decide. He was absolutely unruffled.

"Good morning, Mrs. Evans. I trust you slept well." And then he moved on to Fidelia, giving her a kiss on the cheek. No one even noticed Sophie didn't reply.

She pretended she was intent on finishing her scone, but she couldn't eat. Not a bite, though it was delicious. Every time she looked at Banallt, her stomach felt like she was poised to dive off a mountaintop.

John brought Fidelia her plate and returned to his chair, which happened to end up more across from Fidelia than across from Sophie where he'd sat before. He poured himself more coffee and then left his seat again to get Fidelia the tea she wanted. Fidelia smiled at him when he handed her a cup and saucer. The two were wonderfully in love.

Banallt sat at the head of the table with his breakfast. "I'm ravenous this morning," he said to no one in particular. Sophie didn't know what to say or do or even think. She'd been to bed with the man and she was distressingly aware that she would do so again. As soon as possible.

"Has His Grace left already?" John asked.

"Yes," Banallt replied. "Before I was up. Very early this morning, I'm told."

"I'll catch up with him at Whitehall then, I expect." John shot a look at Fidelia. "Tell me, Miss Llewellyn, have you plans later this afternoon? Sophie and I were going to Gunter's." Sophie hid her surprise and managed a nod without, she hoped, anyone realizing there'd been no such engagement. John's gaze slid to Banallt and back to Fidelia. "Perhaps you and your mother might join us." He hesitated, and really, it was a very charming hesitation. "If you are not otherwise engaged, that is."

"It would be wonderful if you did," Sophie added.

Fidelia's face lit up. "I enjoy Gunter's very much. May I go, Banallt?"

He put down his coffee. "I've no objection. You may if you are free and your mother agrees."

Mrs. Llewellyn came in as Banallt was speaking. "If I agree to what?"

The invitation was made anew and accepted, and John actually gave Banallt a grateful look, which Banallt did not acknowledge. Sophie and John were to meet them at Gunter's at three since Mrs. Llewellyn and Fidelia had a call to make first.

She and John left Gray Street before eleven. They walked home, despite Banallt's offer of a carriage. Never once, by look or word or deed, had Banallt done anything to arouse suspicion that the nature of their relationship had changed. That stood to reason. He had years of experience at such things. Conducting affairs was second nature to him.

John seemed to have a lot on his mind, too. He walked with a repressed gait, as if he wished he could run rather than match Sophie's slower pace. "You're all right, Sophie?"

She looked at him. "Yes, of course. Why wouldn't I be?"

"You were very quiet at breakfast."

"We were up late last night, John. I don't know about you, but I'm exhausted."

"I thought perhaps it would be difficult for you. To be at Gray Street with Lord Banallt there."

They walked a way without speaking. "Like you," she said eventually, "I have made a treaty of peace with Lord Banallt." Her stomach churned. She was lying to her brother, perhaps not directly, but by omission. "You needn't fear for my delicacy if he happens to be near."

"I see." They turned the corner to Henrietta Street. John slowed. "It's just you seemed so unhappy when he came to Havenwood. Distraught, even." He looked at her. "Are you sure, Sophie? I wouldn't have you unhappy for the world."

"That's past now." She put a hand on his arm. "Lord Banallt and I have made up our differences." She wasn't lying. And yet, of course, she was, since she knew John was imagining something quite different from what had actually happened between her and the earl.

"You don't mind that I've asked Miss Llewellyn to join us this afternoon?"

She drew the edges of her cloak together. "If you wish to court Miss Llewellyn, John, I think you ought to."

He looked down his nose at her. "What makes you think I want to court Miss Llewellyn? An invitation to join us at Gunter's hardly constitutes an offer of marriage, Sophie. I extended a polite offer to her, nothing more."

"Well," she said carefully. "Then I think you'd best be careful with her, for it was my impression she feels differently than you." She bumped his arm with her shoulder. "I rather thought she might be in love with you. But that's ridiculous, I see that now."

John stopped short. He grabbed her shoulders. "Fidelia? In love with me? Why is that ridiculous?"

"John, you're an awful dissembler." She shook her head. "Don't think for a moment you can hide from me the fact that you are in love with her, too. It's preposterous."

"I can't hide anything from you, can I?"

"I've known for days, John."

He let out a sharp breath. "Do you mind?"

They reached their door, and she faced him on the steps. "No, of course not. But even if I did, you mustn't let that stand in the way of your happiness. Will you promise me that? I want your happiness, John, more than anything. It's plain to me that you and Miss Llewellyn belong together."

"Despite that Banallt is her godfather and her relative?"

"I don't think he would disagree with me."

"I've not made a friend of him, Sophie."

"No," she said. "You have not."

Light danced in his green eyes, but then he fell serious. "You're not the one who must face him to ask his permission, Sophie. He's the head of the family, after all."

"And what of her father?"

"I'll manage him." He broke out in a huge grin. "Somehow."

Sophie opened the door, but her brother caught the edge and held it for her. She laughed when she went inside. "I know you're up to the challenge, brother dearest."

John changed his clothes and left straightaway for Whitehall with a promise to be back in time to escort Sophie to Gunter's. She bathed, changed her frock, and spent the rest of her afternoon copying out the documents John had left for her. More bills of lading. A few letters. But her attention kept wandering to a new story. She had the perfect hero in mind. When John returned and he'd changed yet again, they walked, as the afternoon was fine. Mrs. Llewellyn and Fidelia arrived at Gunter's only minutes after they did. With Banallt. She had the opportunity to watch him without his knowing, and she learned she was still giddy over their new relationship.

Banallt took Sophie's hand and bowed over it, as proper—more, even—as he'd ever been. Then he and John went inside to order. Sophie, Mrs. Llewellyn, and Fidelia sat outside. They kept up a lively conversation until Fidelia said, "Isn't that Miss George?"

"Why, yes," Sophie said when she looked. Miss George was alone at a table, which Sophie thought odd, without even a maid for a companion, and she did not have anything to eat or drink before her.

"Her father must be inside," Fidelia said.

"Or her mother," said Mrs. Llewellyn.

From where Sophie sat, she could see a small valise at the girl's feet. Worse than the valise, which was just large enough, Sophie noted, to hold a change of clothes, was that Miss George kept craning her neck as if she were looking for someone. It was this constant checking of passersby that kept her from noticing the ladies.

Sophie leaned over and called to her. "Miss George?"

The young woman started. Her cheeks turned a violent pink. She rested a hand on her upper bosom, and her fingers drummed over her collarbone. "Oh, it's Mrs. Evans, isn't it?" Her eyes darted to Mrs. Llewellyn and Fidelia. "Mrs. Llewellyn. Miss Llewellyn. Good afternoon."

"How do you do, Miss George?" said Mrs. Llewellyn.

"Fine thank you, and you?" The words came out just as they had been drilled into her by her parents and her governess. She looked to her left again.

"Very well. Are you here with your parents, Miss George?" Mrs. Llewellyn smiled. "I've a particular question for your mother. Will she return soon, do you think?"

Miss George opened her mouth and closed it. "Why, I-I...Yes," she said. "Yes, I'm sure she will."

Sophie patted the empty seat beside her. "We're here with my brother, Mr. Mercer, and Lord Banallt. Won't you join us? I'm sure they'll bring you an ice. A lemonade, too, if you are thirsty."

"What's this?" John said, having returned from inside. Banallt was with him. A servant put lemonades and ices on their table.

"I've asked Miss George to join us, John."

John bowed. Like Sophie, he looked around for Miss George's parents or a maid and, like Sophie, saw none. His eyebrows drew together. "We should be delighted if you did, Miss George."

Banallt pulled a pound note from his pocket and handed it to the servant lingering with his now empty tray. "Another lemonade. And an ice. Have you a favorite flavor, Miss George?"

"No, thank you, sir. My lord." The girl's fingers drummed faster. "Though you are very kind to ask me."

"I do wish you would," Banallt said. "We need a woman of sense at this table."

Fidelia snorted and playfully slapped Banallt's arm.

A dreadful certainty settled over Sophie. "Is your father near, Miss George?"

"What?" Her foot hit the valise at her feet, and she winced. Not because she'd hurt herself but because she'd drawn attention to it.

Banallt studied her. "Don't tell us you've come out alone, Miss George."

"No." Her eyes went wide. "No. I wouldn't do that." She swallowed. "I haven't."

"Then do sit with us while you wait," Banallt said. "If something's gone amiss, Mrs. Llewellyn will see you safely home."

"I am not here alone," Miss George said. Her cheeks were bright red. "Mama saw someone she knew when she was a girl. A schoolmate. And she left me here to wait." Her eyes flickered over them. "Only for a moment. She did so want to say hello to her friend." She pointed. "There."

John looked, but Sophie didn't, because she'd just seen Mr. Frederick Drake walking toward Gunter's from the opposite side of the street. Miss George saw him, too, and a deeper flush spread over her chest and throat. Drake lifted a hand and then saw that Miss George was not alone. He dropped back.

"There's Mama now." Miss George popped off her chair, her valise clutched in one hand. "You see? Everything is fine. Thank you
for the ice, and the lemonade."

Mrs. Llewellyn shaded her eyes. "My dear child, where?"

Fidelia looked, too, and then sat against her chair, quiet. She
leaned to Sophie and whispered, "Mr. Drake is there. Not her mother. Everyone knows she's mad over him."

"Just there." Miss George pointed again. "She's waving at me. I
really must go or she'll be cross with me. Can you not see her?"

"Banallt," said Mrs. Llewellyn. "Will you see Miss George to her
mother?"

Sophie stood. "I shall. Please Banallt, stay here."

But Miss George was already on her way. Sophie hurried after
her. "Miss George," Sophie said when she'd caught up. She captured
the young woman's free hand. "Please don't do something you'll regret the rest of your days. Please."

"I don't know what you mean." She stopped and pulled her cloak
tight over her shoulders, trying unsuccessfully to hide her valise behind her legs. A heavy cloak, suitable for traveling.

"Reconsider this course of action," Sophie said, bending near
Miss George so she would not be overheard. "I speak from experience. Don't do this. Your future is at stake. Your happiness."

Miss George glanced away. "I see Mama now," she said. And she
hurried off, valise in her hand. From across the street, Sophie
watched Frederick Drake take a course to intercept her.

"Banallt," Sophie said when she'd returned to their table. "Please,
follow them." She thought of all the things that might have prevented her elopement with Tommy. How different her life would have

been if someone had intervened. "Prevent this. Please." She reached for him, touching a hand to his arm. "Don't let that girl ruin her life."

"Of course."

"John," she said at the last minute. "Will you go with him?"

Her brother was already on his feet.

Mrs. Llewellyn took Fidelia's hand in hers. "We'll see your sister safely home, Mr. Mercer. Have no fear."

CHAPTER TWENTY-ONE

Number 26 Henrietta Street, London,
APRIL 3, 1815

When John wasn't back by seven, Sophie assumed he and Banallt must have had to follow Drake and Miss George out of the city. In which event John might not be back until quite late. Possibly not even until tomorrow if they ended up obliged to spend a night on the road. She dined alone and afterward went to her room to finish copying out the documents John had given to her.

Her mind kept wandering off to Banallt, and how he'd gone after Miss George without hesitation. Not the act of the sort of villain she'd made him out to be all these years, was it? She gripped her pen, stilled by an awareness that hollowed out the pit of her stomach. She had never thought Banallt might refuse to go with John. The Banallt she'd known at Rider Hall might well have sat back in his chair and asked, in his familiar bored drawl, why he ought to bother rescuing a girl so obviously determined to ruin herself?

In fact, she had known in her heart he would go after Miss George. Without question. And if that were so, if she had really, honestly, known that to be true of him, why was she clinging to her conviction that he had not changed? Her hand shook and droplets of ink scattered over her page. Had she, all this time, been relying on the fact of his not having changed, in order to protect herself? If so, from what? What, precisely, were her feelings toward him? Please, she thought, let her not have left herself open to being hurt. The side of her hand brushed over the ink and smeared the page and her skin. Was it possible?

She knew Banallt. Better than anyone. He'd said as much himself. She'd seen him at his worst.

And yet.

Before her gaped a yawning abyss. If she fell into it, she would be vulnerable in exactly the way she'd been vulnerable when she'd married Tommy. She didn't want to give anyone the power to crush her like that again. But if she believed that Banallt had changed? What then?

Impossible.

She didn't have the strength to go through that again. She didn't want Banallt to break her heart.

Sophie forced everything out of her head except the document she was copying. It was a speech John intended to give in the House. He liked to have her write his final copy because, he said, she always corrected his errors and managed to throw in an excellent phrase or two for him. Her writing was also easier to read, he claimed. The ink that had splattered on the page and smeared had ruined the sheet. She balled up the page and tossed it into the fire. With a sigh, she got out a clean sheet and began anew.

The house was quiet without John at home. By the time she finished copying, it was half past nine. If John and Banallt weren't on their way home now, they must have stopped for the night. She washed up, braided her hair, and got into bed with a book.

At midnight, she admitted to herself she intended to read until she was certain John wasn't coming home. She pulled the covers around her neck and settled in. With every unusual sound, she put down her book and listened for her brother coming up the stairs. No, that distant jingle wasn't John at the mews. That creak was only the house settling. Later, it was rain on the windows and then a loose shutter on the house next door. At two o'clock, she woke with her chin pressed into the edge of her book. Her lamp was out. In her darkened room, she heard the front door open.

John, at last! But home so late. Had Banallt and John succeeded in stopping Drake? She hoped they'd managed to prevent Miss George from a disastrous marriage. She hurried out of bed, shoving her feet into her wool slippers and snatching her nightrobe from the chair. She lit another lamp and headed down the stairs, expecting to meet John, but he must still have been in the foyer for some reason. She heard voices downstairs.

"John?" she called. "Is that you?" As if it could be anyone else at this hour. She descended the rest of the stairs.

The voices stopped.

So did Sophie. Just a moment's hesitation. Only a moment. She continued into the foyer. "John?"

The entrance was dark. Their butler was there, rousted from his sleep. He wore a long coat over his nightshirt, and he'd only partially succeeded in smoothing down his hair. Another man, too tall to be John, stood with him. She smelled wet wool. Drops of water plunked onto the floor.

"Banallt?" she said.

Banallt dropped his umbrella into the stand by the door. "Forgive me," he said. He sounded tired and something else, too, but she could not fathom what that odd note was. "I'm aware it's not a decent hour of the night," he said. He meant that for the butler, who held out his hands for Banallt's things. He shrugged off his dripping greatcoat and handed over his hat. Still silent, he stripped off his gloves and dropped them into his upturned hat. He rubbed his hands together.

She didn't dare ask him anything directly. Not yet. Miss George's potential ruin was not a subject to be discussed in front of the servants.

He addressed the butler. "Wake someone, please, and have my horse seen to. It's too cold and wet to leave him outside."

"My lord." The butler nodded and reached for the pull that would summon a servant. Raindrops fell from Banallt's coat onto the floor.

"I know it's late," Sophie said to the butler. "But would you bring tea to the front parlor?" She turned to Banallt. "My lord, I'm sure you'd like something hot to drink."

"Yes." He was a dark shape melting into the doorway. He stood there, a silent figure, for too long. "Thank you, Sophie." There was a bass note in his words that trembled with some meaning she could not divine. She began to think they had not successfully intercepted Drake. "Tea is an excellent idea," he said.

"John isn't home yet," she said to Banallt as the butler left. "Were you thinking he'd made it back before you?"

He walked toward her. Another servant came from downstairs, heading for the parlor, else, Sophie was certain, Banallt would have spoken, perhaps told her that Miss George had not been rescued after all. Instead, he took her arm, his expression completely unreadable.

In the parlor, the servant had relit the fire and was just putting flame to a lantern. The room was not bright. Nor was it dim, not with Sophie's light added, for she'd brought her own lamp along with her. The servant darted a look at Banallt then at her. She ducked her head and fled.

"Miss George?" Sophie asked, sinking onto the sofa. The news must be bad indeed. Drake must have escaped them.

"She has been returned to her parents. Unharmed." Drops of rain slid down his inky hair.

"Thank goodness." She gestured to a chair, and as she did she saw the ink smears on the outside edge of her palm. As black as Banallt's hair. "Do sit, Banallt. Please."

"Sophie, I—"

Someone brought in tea, and she murmured a thank-you without registering whether the servant was male or female. The tray had two cups, a pot with the tea already added, a bowl of sugar, and some milk.

"What is it, Banallt?" She made his tea and held it out to him. He took it and stepped back.

"You were right about Drake," he said. "He intended to compromise Miss George and force a marriage on her."

"As we knew," she said. "I'm glad to hear she's safe. Did John return her to her parents? Is that why he's not here yet?"

He spread his ungloved hand over his lower face. "Sophie—" He dropped his hand and took a sip of tea. He set the cup down too hard on the saucer so that it rattled. He put down both. "I am..." Words caught in his throat. "There's—we caught up to them outside London. At an inn. They were undoubtedly headed for Scotland."

"Oh my. Thank goodness you stopped them."

He started to speak and then didn't. Instead, he seemed to catch himself, and Sophie ruthlessly tamped down the emotion that roared at her. "Your brother found them first. We were searching the inn room by room—" He touched his tongue to his lower lip. "She might have been—matters could have been much worse for her. If your brother had been a moment later—"

She leaned forward. "Miss George is all right, isn't she?"

"Sophie." He held up a hand. "Please, Sophie. You must let me speak." He held her eyes. She went still. Still as death. She knew. She knew and still she had to let him say the words. In the silence, the clock on the mantel ticked away the seconds. Her chest went numb and her arms, well, she wasn't entirely certain they were connected to her body.

"You will forever associate me with this news," he said softly. "And I—" He pressed his lips together. "Drake...had a pistol. I'm sorry, Sophie, but your brother was shot."

"No," she said. "That can't be." She didn't move. She saw his lips part, though not much. Hardly at all. He didn't speak. "Is John all right?"

He took a step toward her then stopped. "No," he whispered. "He's not."

"Please be perfectly plain, Banallt." She sat there, the scent of tea surrounding her and Banallt. With the sound of fire and the clock ticking and the patter of rain against the windows. She thought to herself that if she said nothing more, he wouldn't, either, and she would never hear what would break her heart. "Is John alive?"

"I'm sorry, Sophie. No." He took a step toward her but stopped short again. "He was dead when I got there. I heard the shot." He drew a breath. "Five minutes sooner, and I might have—"

Her mouth opened, but no sound came. Her ears refused to hear; her voice was gone.

When Tommy died, there had been such a hubbub. His mother had heard the news first, so that by the time Sophie came downstairs to see what on earth was causing such a fuss, several women were bending over Mrs. Evans and fanning her. Half a dozen men were in the room, and Tommy's body was stretched out on the couch. Someone had walked over and closed his eyes. Hardly anyone had noticed she was there.

But now, she'd heard Banallt's words and didn't know how to make sense of them. Her mind refused to understand. She swallowed hard and lifted her eyes to him. She wanted to shout that it must be his fault. That he ought to have been more careful. They should never have split up.

In two steps he was at her side. "I blame myself. And will for the rest of my life. I'd give anything if I'd found Drake first." He sat beside her and pulled her into his arms. She let him fold his arms around her. "Shall I call a doctor, Sophie? Do you need anything? My God, you're so pale." She shook her head. He rubbed her hand between his. "Your hands are freezing."

"I'm fine."

"Sophie," he whispered, sliding his arms around her. "Sophie, let me take your tears."

Gently, slowly, she softened against him, fingers clutching his coat. Some sound disturbed them, brought her out of a world in which only she and Banallt lived. She lifted her head and saw the butler, housekeeper, and other servants crowded in the open doorway. The housekeeper had a blanket around her shoulders, one corner pressed to her eyes. They'd heard the news, then. They must have known before she did.

Banallt tightened his arms around her. "The culprit was apprehended and will receive his just deserts, I assure you of that." He waited for reaction and got it, as a series of gasps and sobs and murmured prayers. "Mrs. Evans will need you all in the coming days."

She was afraid to let herself feel. Mustn't there be some mistake? John couldn't be dead. He was in love.

"The poor master!" The housekeeper sobbed into the corner of her blanket.

"I hope you can be persuaded to stay," he said to the staff. His arms tightened around Sophie's shoulders. "Regardless, your wages will be paid to you through the end of the quarter."

Sophie did a rapid calculation of the money she knew was on hand and thought that, if she was frugal, she would be able to pay their wages. But only just. And if her calculations were wrong? She would have to write. Selling a book would see her through a shortfall. But she would have to be very careful with her money.

"If Mrs. Evans is not available to give you a character," Banallt continued, "by all means apply to me. I know you've given excellent service here."

The housekeeper edged past the butler and came inside. She folded her blanket around Sophie's shoulders. "We'll stay," she said. "Don't worry yourself about that, milord. We know you'll do right by us."

"Thank you," Sophie murmured.

"Never you mind, Mrs. Evans," the housekeeper said. "Poor, poor dear. God rest your brother's soul."

Banallt pulled the blanket up higher, and Sophie reached up to hold it tight. The housekeeper bent a knee, and then she hurried out, shooing everyone away from the door and closing it softly after her.

After a time, Sophie lifted her head to him. She touched his cheek. His skin was cold. "Are you sure?" she asked. "Couldn't there be some mistake?"

"No, Sophie." His voice turned to a whisper halfway through. "I'm sorry, no."

"It doesn't feel real."

He wrapped his arms around her. "Drake will be tried, I promise you. He's been arrested." He stroked her hair. "I saw to that. And to John's body as well. I'll take care of everything."

Sophie started shaking. She couldn't stop even with the fire going and the blanket around her shoulders. She had no one. John had been her only living relative, and now she was alone.

"You'll tell me if there's anything you need?" He put his hands on either side of her face and tilted her head. "Promise me," he said. "Promise you'll tell me."

Lord help her, she kissed him. She wrapped her arms around him and kissed him, and after a moment, he kissed her back. And it wasn't a kiss between friends. Her lips clung to his, salty, desperate. When he pulled away, she said, "Stay with me, Banallt. Please. Stay and make love to me. I can't bear to be alone."

CHAPTER TWENTY-TWO

Banallt stroked Sophie's throat, his fingers pausing at the top of her chest. "Darling," he whispered. His heart was breaking. Was broken. Had been ripped to pieces since the moment he'd burst into Drake's room and saw Mercer lying on the floor. "Sophie, darling, I can't. I want to desperately, you don't know how desperate I am now, but you're in shock. You're not yourself. You don't know what you're asking."

"Don't leave me, Banallt." Her voice felt as liquid as her eyes, and her need shook him. "Please, don't leave me here alone."

"Never." He leaned forward. "I'll never leave you, Sophie. Not ever." He kissed her once and then again, more desperately. "Whatever you need," he said in a low voice.

Tears glittered in her eyes, bright in her pale face. She smiled, but the corners of her mouth trembled. "When you sound like that," she said, "I believe you."

"Believe it," he said. He brushed the pad of his index finger over her lower lip. "If you need me to stay, I will."

She lifted her face to his again, and he let her kiss him. He knew he shouldn't. But she tasted good, and he just had no control with her, and she clung to him as if she might never let go. He tried to concentrate on why he shouldn't be allowing this, but all he could think was that he needed her, too. Her hand slid down, and then slipped between them, fingers gliding down the front of his breeches, along the length of his erection.

"God, Sophie." He wanted to pull away, but he couldn't. While he watched, she freed him from his trousers and underclothing. Her fingers curled around him. Slid up the entire length of him. He propped one hand on the sofa, fisted tight, and let his head fall back, his eyes shuttered. His palm cupped her head, and his fingers, still tangled in her hair, flexed then tightened. "Jesus," he whispered.

Then, her head dipped. Her tongue touched him, and his hips lifted toward her. She took him in her mouth. Warm, and slick. His body tensed, his hands gripped her head, and she stopped.

"Sophie," he said. His voice sounded thick and gruff. "You don't have to do this. I won't leave you. I promise."

"Hush," she said. "This is what I need."

He leaned back until his shoulders hit the arm of the sofa and Sophie followed and began again. Using her mouth and tongue on him. She didn't have any pity whatever. He shifted, writhed, and clamped his mouth shut tight to keep back a shout, and all the while he had one of his hands around hers, showing her what he wanted from her and how. After a time, she pushed his fingers away because she knew exactly when to stop again and when to start. He trembled.

"Jesus, God." A moan rose up in his throat, and he moved in her mouth, wringing from her, he thought, the very last bit of pleasure to be had. After a while, when he had his breath back, he pulled her into his arms and turned them both so he leaned against the arm of the sofa with her back to his front and her bottom snug against his groin.

If she needed this from him, then she would have it. All of him. He belonged to her now and had for ages; all the months he was in Paris, he'd belonged to her. His heart. His soul. His being. He slid his hands, fingers pointed downward, from her throat to her bosom and then to the fastenings of her nightrobe. "What soft, soft skin you have." She moaned and pressed herself against him, as needy as he'd been. He left his hands there and bent his head to kiss the side of her throat. And then he brought her head back so he could kiss her again, as desperately as before. *Sophie. His Sophie. His.*

She twisted around and rose up on her knees, looking at him with eyes that killed him. "Banallt," she whispered. "I want you."

He leaned forward, and she faced him. Need vibrated between them. He spread the halves of her nightrobe. He was completely hers. Utterly in her power. He hooked his fingers into the top of her shift and tugged a little.

"Mm," he said. He no longer cared what he ought to do. He knew what he needed. But he was going to do what Sophie wanted, and since that coincided so conveniently with what he wanted, he was happy to oblige them both.

A strand of her hair dangled behind her ear, and he took it between his fingers. Upon a sudden urge, he swept her braid off her neck and pressed his mouth there. He curled an arm around her waist, pulling her against him, and then, keeping her tight to his torso, he leaned forward until her back was against the sofa and his chest hovered over hers.

She smiled—a man could live on her smile, that secret, sensual smile that took him in and captured his heart. He knelt between her legs and slid both hands beneath her chemise, curved his fingers around her lower thighs, cupping, cradling. He was hard for her already. He breathed in the orange water in her hair and on her skin. He skimmed her thighs with his palm and then slid a finger inside her, then two, stroking gently. She shifted to accommodate his hand.

"Banallt," she said, and Jesus, her voice broke saying his name. "I want you inside me now." He shifted the position of his hand. Enough. They needed this. Both of them needed this. Her eyes were on him, desolate, as if all that stood between her and utter ruin was this. The two of them. "I need you now," she said.

"Soon. In a moment," he whispered. "I promise you."

Silence gathered for a beat. She moaned softly because he had a third finger in her, caressing her, sliding in her. He could not get enough of her face; the way her imperfect features formed themselves into a face that owned his heart. He worked his fingers in her, into heat and wet. He wanted to lose himself in her, and have her lose herself in him. Her breath came ragged, and the effect on him was nothing short of electrifying. She came hard, and when it was over, he covered her body with his.

Her spectacular eyes never left his face as he slid inside her. "Oh Sophie. You are exquisite. Perfect. Better than I dreamed."

He held his breath and watched her. Her eyes slowly opened and their gazes met. He moved again. She felt slick and snug around him. Pleasure shot through him. He slipped an arm underneath her neck and the other between their bodies, around her thigh to open her for him. He rolled his hips, closing the space between their bellies. Her breath trembled with a suppressed sob. Passion? Grief? He didn't know. She tensed, but a moment later, she arched her back as he entered her. His arousal sharpened.

He palmed her breast, nipping the peak between his middle and fourth fingers. She made a sound, low, and from deep in her throat. Again, she arched into him, pressing into his belly and into his palm. Sparks settled in him. He put his mouth by her ear and whispered, "Is this what you need?"

"Yes," she said. And then her body clenched around him, and he nearly lost himself right then and there. He gave her what the moment required, which was his entire length, and not a bit of restraint. That spark leaped between them, flared hot and then hotter yet. He came fully into her, hard and fast, quick thrusts into heat and damp, and him sliding deeper into her. Harder than he thought he should. Heat and wetness surrounded him. Their bodies merged; no, he thought, he submerged himself into her.

"You are exquisite, Sophie," he said. "You must believe that." His heart pounded in his chest, slowly, unbearably hard. "Perfect. I am beyond pleasure." He levered himself up and kissed her, taking her mouth the way he took all of her, thoroughly and slowly and as deep as he could get. All the while her body moved with his, arching, straining, meeting him, taking him beyond thought or reason.

"I need you," she said. "Banallt, I need you."

He sank himself deep inside her and groaned because she was warm and wet, and he was close to his crisis. He got one hand beneath her shoulder blades and then brought her up while, in nearly the same motion, he grabbed the top of the sofa with his other hand. All pretense to detachment or restraint evaporated in the heat of her body, with the feel of her breasts against his chest. Her hair fell past her shoulders, framing her face. He pushed her nightrobe off her shoulders and stripped off her chemise.

Drawing back his head so that their eyes met, he spread his fingers downward toward where her spine curved to her backside. She put her arms around his neck, and on his upthrust, her pelvis tipped. He dipped his head and kissed the underside of her jaw. With one hand propped against the sofa back, he continued to press the small of her back with the other because it brought their bodies closer. He fit a hand to the curve of her waist. She met him, her hips tipped again. Again. And again. "Jesus," he said, whipping his head back because he could feel his approaching orgasm. "You'll break me apart."

He started to pull out, but she held his hips. "No," she said. "Don't." He stilled in her, waiting for his arousal to ramp down enough to continue without danger. He shifted onto his back. He put his hands on either side of her hips, angling his fingers around the small of her back. "Over me, like this."

She complied. Paradise again. The curve of her body from her ribs to her waist nearly sent him over the brink. With his help, she lowered herself on him. He slid in, snug as a finger in a glove. Her head drooped, and he waited, letting her adjust to the position. "Like this," he said. He grasped her hips and drew her forward. Her breasts swayed. Beautiful and lush. "Yes, like that. Sophie, you are heaven." He lifted his hands and set his palms precisely over her. She bowed toward him. He expected reluctance or even distaste, but instead, her eyes met his, glazed over with desire. He lifted his hips and pressed deep into her belly, and she didn't shrink from him or close her eyes. Instead, she rocked her hips, and he gasped at what that did to him.

She rocked on him, and he felt the exposed head of his sex caressed by her, surrounded by heat and wet. He grasped her hips and pushed down. He wasn't anything like his usual self, he recognized that much. He sat up, clutching her shoulder blades, keeping himself inside her. Her palms spread flat on his back, legs around him to accommodate this intersection of their bodies. She met him, breasts against his chest, matched his urgency. His concentration narrowed to his sex. The liquid shiver of climax approached. He stopped because it was a close thing.

She let out a groan of frustration. "Banallt, no. Don't."

"A moment," he said through his bellowing breath. "We have to be careful. I'm too close."

"Don't leave me so alone," she said. "Please?"

He never took his eyes off her when he lay her on her back and settled between her thighs to get his length in her again. He took his time because if he didn't, he would come in her. Already he was at the edge of his control. He sucked in a breath because the increasing slickness drew him deeper yet. Her breath caught, too; her eyes widened and glazed with passion. He was not entirely in control. He was not the least in control. His hand on her lower back pressed down, urging, guiding, insisting, until she had the rhythm, and he ceased to be Banallt, just as she ceased to be Sophie Mercer Evans. They were sex. They were hot and sweaty. Man and woman.

He levered up his torso, rocking into her, long and slow and then, when her knees bent on either side of him, long, deep, and fast, her with him every moment, and him chasing after his command of the encounter. He bent his head and fit his mouth over hers. She matched him beautifully. He was close. Very close to a spectacular climax. She held him tight.

"Sophie, I can't. Let go. I'm going to come inside you," he said. "Let go."

"Don't leave me, Banallt. Please don't leave me."

He was astonished he had any discipline left to him at all. His sex was eager to continue, driving him. And he was well aware that if he came inside her he'd be well within his rights to demand a marriage of her. In fact, he'd be honor bound to do so. He quivered with the effort of remaining still. He drew himself partially out and felt the spiraling drive toward orgasm. His body wound tight. He was balanced on a chasm of pleasure, tilting toward what would undoubtedly be the biggest mistake of his life. And yet, it would get him what he wanted.

"I can't do this," he said. "I won't have a bastard on you. Oh God, Sophie, don't." He threw back his head and she thrust her hips toward him. The tickle in his belly expanded, commanded his body. His balls went tight.

"Like that," she whispered. "Please, yes. Just like this. Banallt, don't stop. Like this."

He slipped over the edge into a chasm where all that mattered was rocking and thrusting. His last coherent thought was more reflex than anything else. This had to be perfect for her. Tonight of all the nights of his life, this had to be perfect. "I love you, Sophie," he said. "Oh, Sophie, I am a ruined man. I love you, and I've gone and spoiled everything by telling you so."

Her hips lifted. Her hands slid down his back to his hips and brought him forward, accepting his fever and heat. And still the pleasure wound tighter. He should have fallen by now. God, why couldn't he? And then, he crested. For an instant, he resisted the pressure and began to withdraw, but Sophie clung to him, sobbing quietly. "Stay," she said. "Stay, Banallt. Don't leave me."

"I won't," he whispered harshly. "I'm not leaving you." His climax crashed over him like a wave. Pleasure surged through him, consuming him. "I love you," he said. "I love you."

Sophie's arms tightened around him. He knew he should withdraw, but he'd gone too far. He came so hard he couldn't breathe. He shattered. Broke apart. When the world returned to him, he was still inside her. He knelt, hands on his knees.

"Oh my God," he whispered. "What have I done?"

Sophie lay amid the tangle of her nightrobe and chemise. She looked at him and said in a low, emotionless voice, "If I burn in hell for this, it was worth it."

CHAPTER TWENTY-THREE

Havenwood,
APRIL 7, 1815

The Duke of Vedaelin gave a touching eulogy at John's funeral. Banallt, Mrs. Llewellyn, and Fidelia attended as well. The service was originally to be held at St. Crispin's Church in Duke's Head, but Reverend Carson moved the gathering outdoors when it was clear there would be well over a hundred in attendance. Fifty or more people came down from London, a living copy of the peerage, Sophie thought at one point. A good many of John's fellow members of Parliament attended. At least as many came from Duke's Head and beyond. Mourners filled the inns around Duke's Head and the neighboring towns and villages. In the days just before and after John's funeral, Sophie did little but accept condolences. John had been beloved.

Banallt stayed beside her at every turn, dealing with matters as they came up, meeting with Reverend Carson or the vicar, with the casket maker and the stonemason, too. He intercepted the post and handed over to her letters of condolence, reserving for himself anything to do with arranging the burial or the reception afterward. He consulted with her on a headstone, and with Charles, the butler, about the decorations to be laid by and the hanging of mourning wreaths. A selection of her clothes were dyed black; slippers and gloves, too. Banallt had known loss. He understood her grief. But he hadn't forgiven her for what she'd done the night John was killed. He must feel she'd trapped him as so many other women had tried before her.

After the guests had gone home or returned to their lodgings for the night, Sophie walked to the conservatory and sat staring out the glass-paned walls as the sky darkened to dusk. Someone, she didn't even recall who, probably Banallt, come to think of it, had given her a black shawl. She clutched it around her shoulders trying her best not to feel anything and succeeding admirably. The damask roses were blooming again, and their scent hung heavy in the air. There had been a bowl of them in the parlor where she'd shaken so many hands. Thank goodness she'd learned when Tommy died the usefulness—no, the absolute necessity—of phrases that seemed trite until you had nothing left but the words everyone expected. Everyone said she held together wonderfully. With so much to do, so many people to entertain, and Banallt close by to prevent her from having to do anything but politely react, she was blessedly occupied, and when she wasn't, she had only to clasp a proffered hand and murmur her thanks. *Thank you for your kind words. Yes, I shall miss him, too. I'm so grateful you came.*

"Sophie?"

She moved her head in the direction of the door. She felt nothing, not even a hint of the spark she used to feel around him. She hadn't felt anything after the night John died. "My lord."

Banallt walked in. "I've been looking for you. To speak with you."

She extended her hand to him and he pressed her hand between his. "Have I thanked you for all you've done?"

"You needn't." He inclined his head in acknowledgment and released her hand. "You know that." He'd been constantly at Havenwood, but when she saw him or they were for one reason or another near enough to speak, he was solicitous and nothing more. Distant. As if they'd never been lovers at all. Sophie didn't know whether to be grateful or heartbroken. Staying numb seemed the safest choice. She didn't need to think. She didn't want to.

"Thank you for your kind words, my lord."

"Sophie." He pressed his mouth tight. "I've business to attend to in London."

She leaned against the bench. "Yes, of course." The world had not stopped merely because of her tragedy, and Banallt would not always be here to manage for her. When she first walked into his arms, she'd known there would be an end to that beginning. Now that it was here, she was grateful she felt nothing.

"I don't mean to upset you. That's the last thing I want to do." He put his hands behind his back.

"I know," she said softly.

"I'm to give evidence at Drake's trial. But when that's done, Sophie—"

"There's no need, Banallt." She clasped her hands on her lap and leaned forward. "Really, it's not necessary." She closed her eyes and breathed in the scent of roses. When she opened her eyes again, his expression was impassive. "I can't feel anything just now." She swallowed. "I've gone empty inside. There's nothing in me at all."

"That will pass," he said.

Banallt knew better than most the sort of grief that had taken her ability to feel. Was it not best to make the cut now, when she wouldn't feel the slice through her heart? "I think… I think you and I were a mistake. And I apologize, Lord Banallt, for what I did."

"No." He spoke fiercely, but Sophie could only remark the sound. The emotion behind the word remained foreign to her. "There was no mistake."

"Passion never lasts. It must burn out." She gripped her fingers and shut off the storm of emotion inside her. "It's better to end like this," she said. "It's better that we're left with fond memories rather than bitter accusations. You know, Banallt, that we would end badly, you and I."

"No, Sophie."

"You forget how well I know you." She leaned toward him. "Please. Let me have those memories. That will be worth having."

His jaw clenched. "You will tell me if there are consequences."

"There won't be."

"Do you know that for certain?"

"I'm sorry," she said, not because she felt anything but because she knew what she'd done was wrong.

"There were two of us that night." A muscle flexed in his jaw. "The fault is more mine than yours."

"There are no consequences," she said dully. How easy it was to lie. She knew no such thing, of course.

"Well. And so." He drew in a breath. "If Vedaelin proposes," he said, "will you say yes? Or will it be Tallboys?"

She lifted her chin to look at him. He meant the question seriously. "A duke," she whispered. "Can you imagine me as a duchess?" She knew she ought to feel something, but she had closed off her heart and she didn't dare risk feeling. "He won't," she replied. "He finds me too passionate. Too prone to opinion. He thinks me excessively bold."

"Has he told you that?"

"No. But he thinks it of me." She forced herself to smile. "His Grace will not propose to me. Why would he now? With John gone."

He didn't say anything for quite a while. She found the silence restful. "I don't know how long I'll be engaged with Drake's trial. I'll let you know the outcome."

"Thank you."

"This time, you'll write to me if you need anything? If anything should happen, you'll let me know?" He scowled. "Promise me, Sophie. Promise me you'll let me know."

"I'll be here, Banallt, at Havenwood. This is my home. Where I belong. I've nowhere else to go."

He took a step toward her and stopped, his mouth a slash of frustration. She said, "Frederick Drake killed my brother. You didn't. I understand that, Banallt. It's just...I miss him. I miss my brother. And I simply can't feel like this again. I can't. You know it would happen one day, between us."

"Sophie—"

"You must go and be certain that Drake is called to account for what he's done."

He nodded, and then was gone. And she didn't feel anything at all.

Sophie didn't sleep on the night Banallt left, and only fitfully on the second. On the third day, she walked to the cemetery at St. Crispin's Church in Duke's Head. The headstone was not yet in place. Only fresh-turned dirt marked John's grave. The following day, a carriage drew up in front of the house, and when she peeked out a window to look, she thought at first so fine a carriage could only belong to Banallt.

She stood there in her black-dyed gown, hands clasped hard, her pulse fluttering so that—how ridiculous—she was actually a little dizzy at the thought that Banallt had come back. But when a groom opened the carriage door and lowered the step, a woman stepped out. A stout woman followed by a man she didn't recognize at all from the glimpse she'd got of him.

Not Banallt. Her disappointment was almost as bitter as her initial reaction had been excited. He'd only done what she'd told him she needed from him. Without him, she was safe from hurt.

Soon enough a servant found her. They were Mercers. Mr. and Mrs. David Mercer. Related via a long-deceased cousin of her father's. They had never visited when she was a girl. Nor come to the funeral. David Mercer was now the eldest surviving Mercer, and Havenwood was entailed.

She looked up from the card the maid had brought her. A sliver of uneasiness slipped into her. She'd not realized until this moment that Havenwood was no longer her home. "Please tell them I'll be down directly."

"Yes, ma'am." The young woman scrunched up her face. The grimace lasted only a moment, but enough to guess the Mercers had not made a good impression on the servant. Dread worked its way around her heart.

In the parlor, Mrs. Mercer turned around at Sophie's entrance, a porcelain vase in her hand. The woman set it down, and after a lingering look at it, cocked her head at Sophie. Mr. Mercer stood by the fireplace. He was a small man, compact, with a pointed chin and sharp blue eyes.

"Mrs. Evans, I presume?" said Mrs. Mercer. Her voice was high-pitched, a tone more suited to a girl than a grown woman, though Sophie supposed she could not help her voice.

"Yes, I am Mrs. Evans." She disliked Mrs. Mercer on sight. The woman had a sharp face softened to roundness by avoirdupois. One would not stretch the truth in calling her a handsome woman. But her gaze held no kindness, none of the sort of intelligence Sophie could respond to. The coldness around her heart stayed.

Mr. David Mercer came forward and took her hand. He gave a stiff bow and retreated. "Please accept our condolences on the tragic loss of your brother, Mrs. Evans."

"Thank you." She sank onto a chair. They were here, she realized with a sickening drop of her stomach, because John was dead and Havenwood now belonged to David Mercer. "Won't you sit down, Mr. Mercer?"

He nodded, more of a bob of his head than a nod, a curt acknowledgment that she had spoken to him. "I should rather stand, but thank you nevertheless." He cleared his throat. "We received word from your brother's solicitor. We have been given to understand the reading of his will is to take place tomorrow."

"Yes. Mr. Pitt has agreed to come to Havenwood..." That was Banallt's doing, actually. He'd wanted to save her the inconvenience and expense of traveling to London. "I suppose you know that," she said. She waited for the lump in her throat to loosen. Mrs. Mercer strolled the perimeter of the room, which Sophie found quite distracting. Anger flickered through her. Was the woman totting up the value of everything in the room? "Forgive me, I'm not at my best." She speared Mr. Mercer with a firm look. "I've only just buried John."

"Tragic," David Mercer said. "Such a tragic death. He was murdered, we heard."

"Yes. I hope to hear word of the trial any day now."

Mrs. Mercer stopped and faced Sophie, which obliged her to look away from the woman's husband. "Mrs. Evans." She gave Sophie a treacly smile, which Sophie despised even more than her pacing the room. She might as well bring out a notebook and start her inventory. "You needn't worry for a roof over your head."

She stiffened. "Thank you."

The woman stared out the window. "What a pretty garden." She looked back to Sophie. "How many acres is Havenwood?"

"Three hundred and twenty-two," Sophie said.

"And how many acres do you farm?"

"I'm sure I don't know at the moment."

"Madam," Mercer said to his wife. "Your curiosity will be satisfied by and by. Mrs. Evans, if you would be so good as to show us to rooms, we would be grateful for the chance to wash away the dirt of travel."

"Rooms?" She ought to have foreseen this. Mr. Pitt would not be here until tomorrow. Naturally, the Mercers would expect to stay at Havenwood.

The Mercers exchanged a look. "Madam," Mr. Mercer said. "Whatever your brother's will says, there can be no doubt of the entailment, and I am the eldest living Mercer descendant. Havenwood devolves to me."

"Of course." John had made provisions for her, that was certain, and yet Sophie felt hollow with the conviction that she would find herself wholly dependent on the goodwill of two people whom she had despised within moments of meeting them. Such an outcome was inconceivable. John would never have left her with nothing.

The following day, John's solicitor came down from London with her brother's will in hand. Indeed, Havenwood belonged entirely to David Mercer. There were bequests to friends and maternal relatives and to several of the servants. He was generous to his valet and Havenwood's longtime butler, Charles. There was no mention of her. The Mercers exchanged looks.

Mr. Pitt put down his papers and cleared his throat. He folded his hands on the pages. "Your brother's will is several years old, Mrs. Evans," he said. "Executed when you were still married and unreconciled to your family."

Sophie interlaced her fingers and squeezed them hard. "I see."

The solicitor's attention moved to the Mercers. "In London, he gave me new instructions. Indeed, I have in my office papers in which he made substantial changes to the disposition of the property and chattel he owned outright. Under those terms, Mrs. Evans would have had no worries for her future." His mouth tightened. "He was killed before he could sign them. No young man expects to die, and I regret to say that therefore it is this document"—he tapped the pages on the table—"that controls. And in this document there is no provision for Mrs. Thomas Evans, née Sophie Mercer. His property is to be divided among the legatees specifically named therein with the residue individually to the eldest surviving Mercer male." His dark eyes moved back to the Mercers. "I am quite sure, however, that you will wish to see his desires carried out."

There was a moment of profound silence. Pitt cleared his throat and began gathering papers.

"This is all quite shocking," said Mrs. Mercer in her too-girlish voice. She fluttered a hand over her torso. Sophie knew then her premonition had been accurate. She could expect nothing from these people.

"Legal matters take some time to resolve, I do believe," Mr. Mercer said. "We never expected Mrs. Evans to be cut out entirely. You may stay here, ma'am, as long as you desire. We should be happy to have you here. Isn't that so, Mrs. Mercer?"

Sophie rose. This was all so horribly familiar. She half expected Mr. Pitt to hand her a pile of bills with a demand that she pay them immediately. "But my things remain mine, is that not so? My gowns, my personal possessions? Or do those, too, belong to the Mercers?"

The attorney frowned and straightened the papers he held. "Your personal property remains yours, Mrs. Evans. Any gifts from your brother, items you brought with you from your husband's home are yours, naturally, and remain so no matter what."

She felt as if she were going to crack open. She had very little jewelry to sell, if it came to that. All she had left, besides her clothes and her books, was her writing. And of that, she had, at present, none to sell.

Pitt put his papers into a leather case. "You have my card, Mr. Mercer, Mrs. Mercer, if you should have any questions." He looked at Sophie, then quickly away. "I'll show myself out."

The Mercers did not, after all, carry out John's last wishes, whatever they were. As Mrs. Mercer had said, if John had truly intended those documents to reflect his last wishes, then he'd had ample time in which to sign them into effect. And he hadn't. Surely, the woman said when Sophie brought herself to inquire, that counted for something. And weren't they allowing her to live at Havenwood? What more did a single woman alone need?

She hadn't, in her heart, expected them to carry out John's wishes, but she had expected them to do something. The idea of staying at Havenwood was intolerable, yet there was nothing she could do. She had no money of her own and nothing valuable enough to sell for money to make her escape from the Mercers. It might be weeks, possibly months, before she was able to remove. Until she completed and sold her story, she hadn't the funds necessary to let a flat. She had once supported herself on her writing; it seemed she must do so again.

CHAPTER TWENTY-FOUR

Havenwood,
MAY 3, 1815

Mr. Tallobys, " Sophie said when she came into the parlor where he was waiting. His timing was impeccable. The Mercers were out making a call, and for once she had the house to herself. This meant Mrs. Mercer would not be coming in to monitor her conversation or drive away her visitor with her inane conversation. She smiled, because she was genuinely pleased to see someone from their circle in London. She crossed the room to give her hand to Mr. Tallboys. "How pleasant to see you."

He stood and bowed to her. He held a bouquet of roses in his hands. "Mrs. Evans." Having bent over her hand, he looked her up and down. Doubtless he thought her black clothes drab indeed. She was thinner now than she had been in London, while Tallboys was as hale and handsome as ever. "You're well, I hope, ma'am."

"Yes, thank you."

"Here." He held out the roses with an awkward grin.

Sophie took them and breathed in the fragrance. The blood red blooms were just beginning to open. "They're lovely, Mr. Tallboys. How kind of you to think of me." Mrs. Mercer would certainly have a thing or two to say about this. Let her, she thought with a surprisingly vicious satisfaction. She would leave the flowers here for anyone to see and admire. She called for a servant to put them in water.

When she was done with her instructions, she seated herself on a chair near the fire, legs crossed at her ankles. She was aware that Tallboys's gaze had followed her the entire time. She gestured. "Do sit, Mr. Tallboys. Please."

"Thank you." He tugged on his coat and did sit. On a chair nearer to her than his last. His lovely brown eyes stayed on her. They were the color of cognac, she thought idly. "Allow me to tell you how sorry I was to hear of your brother. His loss was tragic."

"You are very kind to say so." She glanced toward the door. A maid brought in the roses, now in a crystal vase, and set them on a side table. "Thank you, Susan," she told the maid, and Tallboys beamed. She went to the roses and rearranged the blooms, leaning over to breathe in their scent again. "They're really lovely."

Tallboys, naturally, stood when she got up to smell the roses. He seemed ill at ease to her. Charles came in with tea, and they were quiet while the servant set the table for them. Sophie poured the tea while Tallboys selected a cucumber sandwich and put it on a plate.

"How is everyone in London?" she asked. She wanted to ask about Banallt but didn't know how to bring the subject around to him without seeming overly interested in the answer. He'd written her four times. All four letters remained unopened, tucked away in a box. She hadn't wanted to know anything. She didn't want the regret or the hurt or longing or any of the other emotions that would come with her reading his letters. News and gossip reached Duke's Head whether she read his letters or not. Drake had been sentenced to hang for the murder of her brother. Miss George and her family had left London, because of an illness in the family, an elderly relative they said, at whose side they must be. Banallt was rumored to be having an affair with, well, any number of ladies. A certain Mrs. P—

had been mentioned more than once. Mrs. Llewellyn had written once. That letter, too, remained unopened. She did write to Miss Llewellyn, though. She'd loved John, too, after all.

Until Tallboys, she hadn't wanted anything to do with reminders of London, but now that he was here, she found herself anxious to know more.

"Ah. Well." He bobbed his head. "London. A very great city." She smiled encouragingly. "We're getting on well enough, I think. These are excellent," Tallboys said of his sandwich. "My compliments to the cook."

"Thank you. I'll be sure to tell her. What of Napoleon? Will there be war, Mr. Tallboys? Is there any news you are able to share?" He wore his hair longer now. Nowhere near as long as Banallt's, but he no longer had the close-cut head she recalled. There was a touch of red in his hair.

"None that would settle your mind, Mrs. Evans." He crossed one leg over the other and eyed the cucumber sandwiches. Sophie passed him the plate. "Thank you. We miss you dreadfully at Charlotte Row," he said. "Without you there to keep us shipshape, we've gotten all out of sorts with one another. Vedaelin snaps at the least little thing, and nothing's where we expect to find it. Banallt says we're going to have to hire two secretaries to do the work of one Mrs. Evans."

Sophie made sure she didn't react, and then realized that no reaction would seem peculiar to him, and indeed, Tallboys was watching her thoughtfully. "I should have thought to hire myself out," she said. She could use the money.

"And of course, we are without your brother's fine mind. That is a great loss for us. We miss his voice in the House."

Her heart contracted. "You're kind to say so."

"Not just kind. It's true." Tallboys leaned forward to squeeze her hand. "He's greatly missed, Mrs. Evans."

"Thank you." She pressed his hand in return.

He sat back again, tea in hand. "The Duke of Portland held a masquerade ball t'other day. You never saw so many Roman centurions in your life."

She smiled, glad to be diverted. "That must have been quite a sight."

"There was a deluge of Athenas and shepardesses as well." He sipped from his tea. "This will amuse you." He grinned at her. "Mrs. Peters continues her pursuit of Banallt, and I'm sure it won't surprise you to know—"

Sophie jumped to her feet. Tallboys stood, too. "Oh good heavens," she said with a sharp gesture. "Do sit down. It's just, I must pace. It is a habit of mine, I'm afraid. I'm rarely still." What had she expected? That he would tell her Banallt was pining away for love of her? Tallboys slowly sat and picked up his tea again. "I'm sorry," she said. "You were telling me about the Duke of Portland's masquerade."

"Yes." He frowned. Then put down his cup and rose. "Perhaps, Mrs. Evans, it would be best if I brought myself up to the mark rather than drag matters out indefinitely."

"What do you mean?"

"I'm sure you must suspect why I've called." He clasped his hands behind his back. "I know you've been overcome with grief, but I cannot stop myself wondering if you love me as violently as I love you. Mrs. Evans, will you marry me? I understand if you cannot discuss the subject just now. You've only to tell me so. We will leave the matter for another time."

"Mr. Tallboys." She stopped pacing. Marrying was the perfect solution to her increasingly intolerable situation here. And if she must marry someone, why not Reginald Tallboys? He was a decent man. He would be faithful to his marriage vows. Even Banallt thought Tallboys would make her happy. They would be comfortable together. Something in her chest broke. It's not that he wasn't handsome. He was. His eyes were lovely, and she liked the red in his hair. They would get on well. She wasn't as numb as she'd been when John first passed away, yet she'd felt no spark of anything when she first saw him. No giddiness. No pounding heart. Until he mentioned Banallt. "I—"

"Is there any chance you might say yes?"

She stared at him. "I—" She ought to say yes. The word actually came to the tip of her tongue. "I don't know. It's very sudden, your coming here, and I've...not been myself since my brother died."

"Banallt—"

"Never mind Banallt," she said. "Banallt does not signify." She drew a deep breath through her nose, well aware that her voice trembled. "I had rather not talk about Lord Banallt, if you please!"

Tallboys fell silent and fiddled with his trouser leg. "Forgive me, Mrs. Evans, but I only meant to say that Banallt told me once I ought not give up on my hopes for you."

Her emotions clamored in her chest so that she hardly knew what she felt. "Did he tell you to come here?" Was that why Banallt wasn't here? Because he'd sent Tallboys instead? "Was this his idea?"

"No!" His cheeks flushed. "Not in the least."

"He's interfering." She was close to tears, and she could not stop the tumult in her. "I won't have any man interfere in my life. Particularly him. Let him chase Mrs. Peters." Her voice rose and she couldn't make herself stop. "I hope he catches her. They deserve each other."

"Mrs. Evans." Tallboys looked uncomfortable. "You seem to have misunderstood me. This is why one ought never gossip. I only meant to amuse you. Mrs. Peters is making a fool of herself over Banallt. Not t'other way round. It's plain to everyone but her he has no interest in her. It's his cousin's daughter everyone expects him to marry. It's all but announced from what I hear."

"Miss Llewellyn, you mean?"

"Yes. Miss Fidelia Llewellyn."

She sat down hard and held her head in her hands. Her heart crashed to her toes.

Banallt was going to marry Fidelia.

Of course. Of course he was. Why would he not? He must marry. A man like him must. Their affair was over. She had declined him and then sent him away, and she had ignored all his letters. He knew nothing of her life here. He was free to pursue any woman he wanted-ed.

"Mrs. Evans?"

She lifted her head. "John was in love with her," she said brokenly. "And Miss Llewellyn was in love with John. And I was—" She scrabbled in her pocket for a handkerchief but didn't find it before Tallboys handed over his. "He was so desperately in love with her," she whispered.

"I never meant to distress you," he said. "Forgive me. I had no idea. None at all."

"You haven't." She squeezed his handkerchief. "We would have heard the news here eventually." Somehow she managed to get control of herself. "There is Castle Darmead, you see. Not even two miles from here. Owned by the earls of Banallt, so everyone in Duke's Head pays especial attention to him. The earl's father was married here. No doubt we will have a celebration of our own when the news is official."

"And what of you, Mrs. Evans?" Tallboys asked. "Will you remarry?" He took a step forward. "Will you marry me?"

CHAPTER TWENTY-FIVE

St. Crispin's Church, Duke's Head,
MAY 7, 1815

A buzz of whispered conversation bought Sophie out of her contemplation of the hymnal on her lap. She always flipped through the pages when she arrived in church. It saved her from making conversation with anyone if she feigned absorption in the book. Reverend Carson entered, splendid in his robes, but rather than the parishioners quieting down in preparation for his sermon, they craned their necks and turned in their seats to stare at the door behind them. What on earth for? The Mercers did the same. Sophie twisted to see around the stone column between her and the door. Her stomach dropped a mile.

Lord Banallt had just come in.

That could mean only one thing. He was having the banns read for his marriage to Fidelia. The earls of Banallt were parish residents, after all. He'd had the banns read here for his first marriage, as had all the earls before him. Her fingers tightened around the hymnal. She remembered the jolt she'd felt all those years ago when she'd heard the banns called for Banallt's first marriage.

She saw him nod in the direction of Reverend Carson then walk along the center aisle, his hat in hand. His destination was the pew reserved in perpetuity for the master and mistress of Castle Darmead. Sophie faced front and kept her head down. Banallt. Her pulse thundered in her ears. Banallt was here. He came even with the pew where she sat with the Mercers. She looked because she could not help but do so. He nodded in her direction, barely a recognition. His eyes were cold and his posture haughty to the core. Every living soul in the church knew that here was a man who would never be swayed from his purpose.

Sophie, sitting with the Mercers on one side of her and the Misses Quinn on the other, was trapped. There was no way for her to slip out without being noticed.

St. Crispin's wasn't large; at most seventy people could comfortably sit inside. The population of Duke's Head had long outgrown the church, hence the second, larger church on the other side of town. But Mercers had always attended services at St. Crispin's, as did most of the landowners. To her knowledge there hadn't been an Earl of Banallt in the church since Banallt's father, and that was well before she was born.

Banallt sat in the front pew. Sophie wondered if he knew the statues flanking the Gothic entrance to the church were the viscount and viscountess who had built Darmead. The present Earl of Banallt hadn't come to church when he was here before, which occasioned a great deal of gossip about the state of his soul.

Beside her, Mrs. Mercer clutched Sophie's arm. "The Earl of Banallt? Here, at St. Crispin's!"

"Yes, Mrs. Mercer," she said with a calm she didn't feel. "That is the earl." How could such a proud man be anyone else? Mrs. Mercer knew he'd written to her, a correspondence Sophie had explained as related to Drake's trial. She dreamed of him often. Ever since Tallboys's call, she'd begun to dream he was married to Fidelia. And why would he not be? He'd told her himself his relatives hoped for the union.

"Handsome as the very devil, isn't he?" Mrs. Mercer whispered. She snapped open her fan and waved it vigorously under her chin.

Reverend Carson mounted the pulpit and greeted the congregation. Sophie registered barely a word he said. From where she sat, if she tipped her head just so, she could watch Banallt's profile. He looked every inch the aristocrat. He sat with one leg crossed over the other, back straight. His hair gleamed black in the light coming through the stained glass window commissioned by one of his ancestors. He wore dark blue today, and though she couldn't see his eyes from this distance, she knew the color made his eyes gleam unnaturally. He kept his prayer book open, one hand holding the spine. She saw his mouth move whenever the congregation was exhorted to reply.

Well. He'd not yet been struck dead. She smiled to herself. Lord Banallt in church and no lightning. Nor angels singing hallelujah, either.

Mrs. Mercer openly stared at Banallt, and the Misses Quinn sitting to Sophie's right kept up a constant whispered conversation. "Why do you think he's here? I heard Mama say he's in want of a wife. Papa says he's wicked." And then they'd giggle and their mother would hush them and five minutes later they'd start all over again. "Perhaps you'll be a countess, Alice. What if he chooses you?" More giggles. "Papa would never allow it."

The time came for the reading of the banns, and Sophie slipped into a state of dread as Reverend Carson began to read them off. Her palms sweated in her gloves. Miss Moore and Mr. Allen, for the third and final time; Miss Baker and Mr. Roberts for the first. But no

more. As the services concluded, Sophie wondered if she'd deliberately blanked out the reading of Banallt and Miss Llewellyn's names.

She looked in the direction of his pew, but he wasn't there. She
didn't see him anywhere in the church. As the parishioners filed out,
the Misses Quinn bombarded everyone with the same question: Was
that really the Earl of Banallt? Why ever was he here? When the
questions were directed at her, Sophie answered with either a nod or
something banal.

Her chest felt tight, and the longer she stayed inside the church,
the more aware she became that six of the eleven stained glassed
windows had been endowed by the earls of Banallt, and that Banallt
himself had just ten minutes ago been sitting in the ornate pew near
the nave. Mr. and Mrs. Mercer had gone outside already, expecting,
one imagined, that Sophie would follow. She extricated herself from
the young ladies—and it was mostly young ladies, dizzyingly eager
for any morsel of information about the Earl of Banallt—and went
outside.

By the time she came out into the morning sun and had given
Reverend Carson her hand, she didn't see Banallt anywhere. Nor the
Mercers, for that matter.

"Mrs. Evans," the reverend said. He clasped her hand between
his. "Good morning to you, my dear."

"Reverend." The sun was in her face, and she had to shade her
eyes to see him. "Good morning to you, too."

He pressed her hand once more then released her. Sophie walked
down the flagstone path to where she expected the Mercers would
be waiting for her, impatient at her delay. Another crowd gathered
at the gate, young men this time, all of them admiring the phaeton in

the street. A man in a home-spun wool suit held the head of the gray gelding in the traces.

Banallt stood there on the street side of the gate. He'd just shaken the hand of silver-haired Mr. Jenkins, who raised horses and owned the land abutting Darmead to the north. There was no other exit to the street. The Mercers were nowhere to be seen. She fancied herself Catherine Parr, walking her final steps at Windsor.

The earl's attention left Mr. Jenkins, and his eyes found hers, and for one exquisite moment, Sophie believed everything would come right. Foolish, foolish woman, she thought. She continued to the gate. Today, for some reason, it was harder to stop herself from feeling. Banallt turned his back to the crowd of young men and held out a hand. Mr. Jenkins beamed at her.

"Mrs. Evans," Banallt said.

"My lord." She put her hand in his and curtseyed. The shock of their contact traveled from her hand to a deep place in her body.

"Mrs. Evans," said Mr. Jenkins. "How lovely you are today."

She removed her hand from Banallt's, certain he'd felt her trembling. Why had he come? "Thank you, Mr. Jenkins. You are kind as always."

"I remember when you were just a little thing, just half as tall as you are now." Jenkins turned to Banallt. "Did you know, my lord, that Mrs. Evans, she was Miss Sophie in those days of course, used to tell the most magnificent tales of how she'd one day be mistress of Darmead?"

"Mr. Jenkins," Sophie said. Her heart sank. "I was a girl. Anything was possible then. Magic and fairy tales, that's all it was." She refused to look at Banallt, but the back of her ears itched with the knowledge that he was staring.

"When you weren't convincing my girls the castle was haunted by the ghost of a crusading knight, indeed you did, my girl."

"I believe," Banallt said, "that one of my ancestors did march on the Crusades." He leaned against the stone fence post, arms crossed over the top of the carved granite.

"Edmund," Sophie said automatically. "Edmund Llewellyn, the third viscount."

Jenkins beamed at Banallt. "I'll warrant she knows the history of your family better than anyone in Duke's Head, my lord. You'll not be surprised to learn her mother used to tell us she couldn't but think Miss Sophie would have her way." He laughed again. "I for one never doubted her."

"I was telling tales," Sophie said. "Children do, you know." How mortifying. What must Banallt think to have a country esquire matchmaking in so painful a manner? *Why was he here?* "What girl doesn't dream of growing up to marry the prince and live in a castle, Mr. Jenkins?"

Mr. Jenkins chuckled. "Not many, I daresay."

"A good tale requires enough truth to make it believable, and so I acquainted myself with as much truth about Castle Darmead as I could." The crowd around the phaeton was thinning. "How else would I balance out the rest of my inventions?" At last she looked at Banallt. "Your ancestor, my lord, was one of my more convincing ghosts. I terrified dozens of children, including my brother, though he never would admit it afterward." Her heart turned over at the thought of John. But for once the reaction was bittersweet.

"I should love to hear the tale," Banallt said. The perfect curve of his mouth sent a shiver through her with the recollection of who and what he had been to her. He reached out and tapped the tip of her nose. "I adore a terrifying ghost."

Jenkins reached for her hand. "Ah, Miss Sophie. Sometimes you look so much like your mother it breaks my heart."

"My mother was beautiful," she said. "I look nothing like her."

"You have her eyes."

"Hers were green."

"Just so. But the shape, my dear, the shape. You're a beauty in your own way, Mrs. Evans. Do not doubt that for a moment." He ended with a stern look at Banallt.

"She is, of course, a most lovely woman," Banallt said. He uncrossed his arms and touched the brim of his hat. In the light, his eyes looked darker than usual. "She does not seem to believe it."

"I look like my father," Sophie said. Panic rose up, making her light-headed and shaky limbed. She looked around for the Mercers and did not see them anywhere. Enough of this, she thought. She'd had more than enough of pretending everything was all right. If Banallt had something to say to her, then let him speak and have this over. She took a step through the gate and peered down the street in both directions. "Do you know where my cousins have gone, Mr. Jenkins?" she asked. She adjusted her shawl around her shoulders. The black shawl Banallt had given her.

"They have gone home," Banallt said.

"Home?" She faced him. "Without me?"

"I told them I'd drive you back to Havenwood." Banallt looked at the sky. "It's a lovely day to drive out. Don't you agree, Mr. Jenkins?"

"It is indeed," Jenkins said. He pumped Banallt's hand again. "Come by the Grange, my lord, and I'll show you my yearlings. I've a pair who'd be excellent in front of a phaeton one day."

"I will." Banallt held out his arm to Sophie. "Come, Sophie."

CHAPTER TWENTY-SIX

Banallt held out his arm, and even though Sophie placed her hand on his elbow, he actually hesitated, expecting her to demand that Mr. Jenkins be the one to return her to Havenwood. She didn't, despite the fact that she'd lost all color to her cheeks. Well. And so. She ought to be ashamed. Not one word from her in the days since he'd left Havenwood; no replies to his letters, no correspondence from her, leaving him wondering if her post was being intercepted or worse. "I assure you," he drawled, looking at her but speaking for Jenkins's benefit, "you'll be home in time for supper tomorrow."

Jenkins laughed, and that seemed to reassure everyone within earshot that their beloved Mrs. Evans wasn't consigning herself to a kidnapping and ravishment at the hands of the notorious Earl of Banallt. He had no illusions that the residents of Duke's Head weren't protective of Sophie. They were. To a man, woman, and child. "You'll call on us, won't you, Mrs. Evans?" Mr. Jenkins said. "My wife would dearly love to see you again. We've missed your visits, you know."

Her eyes were deceptively calm. "Yes, I will."

Jenkins beamed at her. "And bring your young gentleman with you?"

Sophie glanced at Banallt. He kept his reaction muted. "Anything for Mrs. Evans," he said with a bow in her direction. "Including presenting myself at every home in Duke's Head."

"Have you time for that, my lord?" Sophie asked, having, apparently, and thank God for it, decided it was best to follow his lead and adopt a bantering tone.

"Certainly."

"Most excellent." Jenkins grinned then cast an eye at the sky, which was at the moment a clear blue. There were clouds on the horizon, though. "Best take that drive before the weather comes in, my lord."

Ten minutes later, Banallt had Sophie at his side and his pair of grays heading east on a narrow oak-lined lane. For some time, they didn't speak. He was content with that.

"You don't really mean to call on Mr. Jenkins, do you?" she asked.

"Yes, I do. For one thing, I want a look at his yearlings."

"Why have you come back?"

"Need you ask?" He watched her face, but she was expert at hiding her emotions. A trick she'd learned while married to Tommy, devil take the bastard. "Are you with child?" She turned paler yet. Her hand clenched a handful of her cloak. "Well?" His heart thudded hard. "Sophie. This is not a question you can refuse to answer."

Her fist unclenched and clenched. "I don't know."

"When will you know?" But he'd already done a calculation of his own. If she didn't know yet, then there was reason for concern. "I thought you'd put me behind you," he said. Now was not the time to push her. Not yet. "When I heard Tallboys had been here and come back without an announcement—" What Banallt had thought was that Sophie wouldn't marry Tallboys if she was pregnant by Banallt. Either way, he needed to see her. "I came here to marry you," he said.

That made her laugh. "No, you didn't. You came here to find out if you've had a convenient escape."

He drew a breath and controlled his temper. "You know that's not so."

She gave him a stony look. "What gentleman wishes to marry a woman who won't read his letters?"

"Nor answer them," he said.

"What lady wishes to involve herself with a gentleman whose name is connected with so many lovers? Mrs. P. Lady W And I can't recall how many others." She dangled a hand over the side of his curricle and then leaned over the side, staring at the ground.

"There are no other lovers," he said.

"How fast do they go?" she asked. "The horses, I mean."

He flicked the whip, and the grays responded with a smooth canter. "They are not yet at top speed. I made nearly fourteen miles per hour when I drove here from London."

"Really?" She leaned over the side again, staring at the ground.

"Sit up, Sophie." When she did, he flicked the whip. "Too fast?"

She tilted back her head and let the wind blow past her face. His heart thumped in his chest. "Can we go faster?"

Easily. He urged more from the grays. Sophie kept her head tilted back. "We're flying," she cried.

"Not yet. Do you want to?"

"Oh yes."

Cold air blew past them and threatened to send his hat whirling away. If it went, he didn't give a damn. They reached a straight section of road, and he let the grays go. The curricle flew. Beside him, Sophie raised her arms to the sky. Her laugh vanished in the thunder of hooves and wheels. Banallt laughed, too, a deep bass rumble that ended on a whoop as he took them around a corner with hardly a decrease in speed.

When at last he slowed them down, Sophie said, "That was wonderful. Thank you for that. Thank you."

"Reckless, are you?" God, he hoped so. He wanted her body under his, wrapped around his. He wanted her breath low and on the edge of control, her voice capable of nothing but a ragged echo of his name.

"I am today."

"Have you driven before?"

"Many times." She leaned forward, hands on her lap, turning her head to look at him. "Does that shock you?" she asked, so openly curious that he realized she'd not understood what he meant. "Did you think I'd never been in a phaeton before?"

"I mean, have you ever held the ribbons yourself?"

"Oh. That." She sat back. He knew immediately her thoughts were back at Rider Hall and some recollection of her husband, that worthless bastard Tommy Evans. "No."

"I'll show you how if you like." Tommy had ignored Sophie as much as he could, and when he hadn't, he'd played a heavy hand on a woman who needed gentle treatment. Banallt presented her with the whip and with a few quick motions taught her the light touch his grays required. When she had that, he handed over the traces. She gripped the reins like a drowning man would a rope and gave him a sideways look. "You'll catch on quickly. Do as I say," he said when she tried to give them back. "Or I must conclude you are a coward." At that, her back stiffened anew, but not, this time, with disapproval. "My wife, Sophie, must be a dab hand. I can't have a ham-fingered countess driving my cattle through London."

"Shall I have a phaeton like this, then?" she asked, laughing, but not as if she believed him.

"If you like." His easy agreement got her attention. He kept a smile off his face. "Eyes on the road, Sophie. I won't allow you so much as a pumpkin with wheels until you prove you can drive without risk of breaking your neck or injuring the animals."

"Yes, my lord."

The day was fine with very little wind, despite Jenkins's worry for the weather. Excellent conditions for a drive. He slid his torso partially behind her, arms around either side of her in order to adjust her hands. Alarm flared in her eyes. Stiff as a board. In answer, he loosened his hands over hers. Christ, she was skittish.

"Like so." He pressed his chest against her back but stopped when he felt her stiffen again. "Not so hard. There. Yes. You're doing well." He lowered his head. Thank God she wasn't one of those women who favored clumps of feathers in her hats. The inner surface of his coat sleeves brushed the sides of her bosom. His balls tightened pleasantly, a natural reaction to his proximity to the woman who'd been in all his erotic dreams since the day they met. "Put your hands here. Just so."

Her frock fell in a straight line from just beneath her bosom to her hips, but her body did not. Well. And so. She had the kind of lines an artist drew to render a gown more flattering in depiction. "Relax, Sophie." He skimmed his cheek along hers and shifted closer. Soft skin. He remembered touching her, stroking her body, covering her with his, sliding inside her. He drew in a long breath. A faint scent, light, clean, and floral. "Darling," he murmured in her ear. "I cannot instruct you in the mystic skill of handling the ribbons if you sit there like a lump of cold butter."

She gave him a killing glance, but she did relax. Her back curved against his torso, and the horses settled down.

"Much better," he said. Jesus, but he wanted her. Eventually, he leaned away from her, withdrawing his hands. When she concentrated, she had the habit of sticking the tip of her tongue into the corner of her mouth. She was doing that right now, and given his state of mind, the images in his head were not polite ones. Sophie always had affected him that way, from the very first moment he set eyes on her.

She settled to the task of handling his team, and her anxiety faded, replaced by concentration and then delight. "They're doing most of the work," she said of his pair.

"An indication, Sophie, that you have got a talent for driving. You'd probably be as gifted on horseback." There went her tongue again. He spread his legs, and she was concentrating too hard to notice his thigh pressing against hers. "Do you ride?"

She spared him a glance. "We're to be married, and you do not know the answer?"

His eyebrows rose. "Are you suggesting, my darling Sophie, that you have previously told me the answer and I have failed to recall?"

"No, my lord."

"I merely assume your answer is yes, but that you have no animal of your own."

"I don't ride often." Her mouth tightened. "I did as a girl."

"Watch the turn here." He placed his hand in the small of her back. "Well done, Sophie, well done." He removed his hand, but he left his thighs spread and crowding her since she didn't seem to mind and he liked the contact a great deal. They followed the lane for another mile before coming to a narrow bridge. She gave him a panicked look, but he pretended not to notice and let her cross without remark.

"How did I do?" she said when they were over and her tongue was back behind her lips. The grays were in stride again, at ease with their guide.

"Perhaps a phaeton is in order. I'll order you one like this one."

She laughed. The first genuine laugh he'd heard from her.

He continued as if he hadn't heard her. "Considering your instructor, I expected no less." She rolled her eyes, and he was glad to see she wasn't tolerating his nonsense. The lane widened then continued straight. On either side fields stretched to the horizon. "Withypool is half a mile on," he said. And from there, just a mile and a half to Castle Darmead. "Do you want to drive so far?"

"It's a pleasant day," she said. Carefully. "But it's late. I'll be missed."

"I'll have you home in time, my word on it."

They drove in a companionable quiet. Thank goodness she was not one of those women compelled to fill every silence with inanity. Presently, though, she said, "Withypool is just around the corner."

"Let's turn around here." At his signal, she brought the curricle to a slow stop in front of a cottage with a driveway large enough to turn around in, though he was prepared to help her if she hadn't the strength in her arms. She did, and besides, his pair was well-trained.

The cottage looked empty. It was tidy, with a flagstone path, a thatched roof, and the crossbeams typical of a house built in Elizabeth's time. The flower beds were grown wild, however, and the thatch was years past replacing. Behind the cottage the fields swept out into brilliant green. "A lovely view," he said. The turrets of Darmead were visible at the horizon. As a girl, Sophie must have cut through that very field to get to Darmead.

She glanced from the house to the sky and then at last at him. "I was shocked to see you at church. I thought you were here to have the banns read."

"There's no time for banns."

"For you and Miss Llewellyn."

"Sophie." Her attention moved back to the view, and he sighed. "Sophie, look at me." She did, and for a moment his stomach threatened to fly away with his heart. Instinct told him now was the moment to take her in his arms, to touch his mouth to hers. He didn't, though. Acting on his instincts had gotten him a reputation that did him no good with Sophie. Instead, he clenched his hands into fists. "I'm not going to marry Fidelia."

"It's true," she said.

"What?"

"That I used to tell stories about Castle Darmead and your ancestors. I used to pretend I'd marry the master of the castle one day." Despite himself, he set a gloved hand to her cheek. A light touch. Her cheek turned pink. "I did tell Mr. Jenkins's daughters I would marry the Earl of Banallt one day. I was ten, I think. I absolutely believed I would."

"And that absurdity persisted until?" He kept his hand on her cheek.

She closed her eyes. "Until I married Tommy."

"I wish I'd met you first." He had no time to regret his hasty words, because Sophie's eyes popped open. Hell, but he was perilously close to kissing her. That would spoil everything.

"You'd never have looked at me twice."

"Probably not. But I'd have heard you speak and understood you were the woman for me."

Her mouth curled into a crooked smile. "I had spots. And no bosom to speak of."

"You certainly developed one later," he said. He drew a finger along the bridge of her nose. Up and over the arch. "And yet your mind was first-rate. That can't have changed." But she was right. If he'd met her when he was twenty instead of when he was thirty, he'd never have gone close enough to her to hear her speak. He was proud then, callow when it came to women, though he would have denied the accusation since in those days he'd believed sexual experience and appreciation of women were one and the same.

She curled her fingers gently around his wrist, but not, he noted, to disengage from their contact. "I was a foolish girl, Banallt."

"You are determined to disagree with me at every step, aren't you? That's vexing of you."

Her smile deepened. "And what would I have thought of you if I'd met you before Tommy?"

He put his other hand on her cheek, too. "You would have thought, there stands a man to make my pulse race," he whispered. He stroked his thumbs along her cheeks. He wished he didn't have on his gloves and that she wasn't so bloody damn wary of him now. "The Earl of Banallt and the master of Darmead. No doubt you'd have wanted to marry me straightaway. I'd only have needed to crook my finger at you."

"You ought to write a novel of your own." She drew back, but he tightened his hands on her face.

"I tried that once, as you may recall. Such a hideous failure I'll never unleash on paper again. Don't," he said, keeping his hands on her to prevent her from looking away. "Let me look at you a little longer." With his thumbs, he stroked her eyebrows, followed the strong line of her nose, and at last traced the sensitive curve of her mouth. Her eyes slowly closed. She was going to let him kiss her; he knew it because he was a connoisseur of women and their sexual responses. He didn't do it because he was afraid of what might happen if he did. He had only one chance left with her. One only.

"Let us get down and walk, Sophie."

CHAPTER TWENTY-SEVEN

S ophie put her hand in Banallt's when he came around to her side of the phaeton. She stood, and he put his hands on her waist and lifted her down. He dipped his chin toward her, but he didn't kiss her. She didn't know what she thought of that. Nor was she sure of his mood.

"Not a long walk," he said. "I don't want the horses to get cold. Perhaps just to the end of the drive and back?"

"Very well."

They said nothing to each other until they were well away from the cottage. He walked with her into the shade of a tree, and when they stood in the shadows, he touched her cheek with his free hand. The other gently held her arm.

"Did you really come here to rescue me from shame and humiliation?" Her thoughts hopped from one memory to another; her first sight of his silver tarnish eyes, an afternoon spent discussing novels. The first time his lips touched hers. The way she'd felt so alive when he held her. "After I ignored all your letters?"

For far too long, he stared into her face, and Sophie's vision darkened. "Did you even read them?"

She tried to pull away, but he didn't release her. She looked away. "I didn't dare, Banallt," she whispered.

"Why not?" He sounded calm, and that made her risk a look at him. He smiled at her. Why wasn't he angry or hurt? "Were you afraid of wretched poetry? I acknowledge you as my superior in literary matters. I wouldn't dare write you poetry."

"Be serious."

He took her hands in his. "Shall I? Tell me, then, my darling future wife, what's happened to you. Why did you fill your letter to Fidelia with nothing but lies?"

"Lies? Has she said they were lies?"

"I say they were lies. Except about your brother every single word you wrote her was a lie."

She slipped her hands free of his, and all the emotion she'd worked so hard to keep back overflowed her. Her body shook. This explosion of feelings was precisely why she hadn't read any of his letters. She didn't want to feel anything, and here she was with her numbness fading, leaving her exposed. "Why would I write anyone the truth?" The flash of heat in her words took her by surprise. "I hate it here." She managed to level out her voice. "I never thought I'd hate Havenwood. I would have said it impossible. But I do."

"Darling." He glanced back to the cottage and his horses and walked her to a bench built around the trunk of the elm. She let him draw her down beside him. "Tell me everything. How is it that you are here at Havenwood with these poor imitations of Mercers and not living independently? I was certain you'd pack up and leave if your brother's heir came here. I'd thought I'd have to track you down all over again just to make you tell me if we'd managed to make a child. Why didn't you take your inheritance and remove yourself to Yorkshire or Cumbria or some god-forsaken backwater so I'd spend the rest of my damn life discovering where you went with my child?"

"Why?" She laughed. "That's easy. Because there was no inheritance," she said.

"Of course there is." His eyebrows drew together. "Your brother had a fortune independent of the entailment."

"Yes. He did." Her throat closed off, and she bowed her head until she had herself under control. She'd not needed to control herself in a very long time. "John meant to do well by me, Banallt, but..."

"What?"

"It does no good to imagine what might have been. I inherited nothing from my brother."

He frowned. "No annuity? No trustor in charge of your money? Has your cousin stolen it from you?"

"No."

Banallt scowled until his eyebrows nearly met. "I had understood from your brother himself that you would have no worries for your future, whether you married or not." He held up a hand. "When we had such a discussion is beside the point, Sophie. In fact, he assured me that was the case."

"He did not leave behind debts, if that's what you mean."

"What did he leave you? Not nothing. He would not leave you with nothing. That's inconceivable."

"And yet he did, Banallt." Her voice rose with the anger boiling inside her, fresh, hot, and welcome. "He meant to look after me. But he didn't."

Banallt shook his head. "How could this happen?"

"According to his solicitor, the changes to his will were never executed." She let out a breath. "And so I was once again cast adrift and dependent upon relatives for every breath I take."

"You should have told me." He stood up and took two strides in the direction of the cottage then turned and walked back to her. His eyes flashed. "You should have written to me the moment you knew you'd been left with nothing."

Sophie gave him a push, but he didn't budge. "To what end, Banallt? Whether I wrote to you or not, my situation would be the same. Destitute again and dependent on the kindness of my relations."

"You are too proud for your own good." His fingers tightened on her face, and she curled her hands around his wrists and pulled down. To no avail. "Had I known, I would have come sooner than this. I thought you needed time. I never dreamed you were in straits yet again. I thought the only risk was that you were pregnant and plotting your retirement to the deep countryside."

"Hardly straits, Banallt." She let out a puff of breath and this time managed to step out of his embrace. But, she suspected, only because he let her go. "The Mercers have been very kind to let me stay at Havenwood."

He sneered. "That woman? Kind? She despises the very ground upon which you walk."

"It does not signify." She started back to the phaeton on her own. "I don't expect to be here much longer."

"Meaning?" He caught up with her and had no trouble matching her stride for stride. "Have you told Tallboys yes? You can't have."

She scowled at him. "What business is it of yours?"

"Don't pretend it isn't," he said in a dark voice.

"I have not accepted Mr. Tallboys." She took a step back. Banallt's body relaxed. She folded her arms under her bosom and hid her fists under her arms. "How could I when I don't know whether I'm disgraced?"

He grabbed her arm and leaned in. "There will be no disgrace, Sophie. None."

She pulled free. "I'll have you know I am writing again."

"In secret," he said bitterly. "And in the dark of night, I'll warrant. As if you had no other choice."

"Choice? What choice have I, my lord?" She put her hands on her hips and glared at him.

"I'd never let you give my child another man's name."

"I don't need a husband."

"That's absurd beyond belief."

"When I've sold the book," she said, looking ahead to the phaeton, "I intend to remove to lodgings elsewhere. In Duke's Head, perhaps. If I tutor some of the children—young ladies are always in need of French lessons and I think I sing tolerably well so I might add music to my repertoire of useless talents to pass on to future generations of idle young wives—I expect I'll supplement my income and scrape along well enough. I'll only have my own bills to pay."

"Scrape along. On ten pounds a year. If you're fortunate and only if you're not with child." The corner of his mouth curled.

"You've never been without more money than anyone should have, my lord. But I assure you, I have. I'll manage on ten pounds a year. I'd manage on five, if I had to. For me, that is a fortune. And I shall be happy to have the money, I do assure you again."

He turned, grabbing her hand so that she had to stop. "You wrote Fidelia pages of nonsense, lies about how pleasant it was at Havenwood. How you and Mrs. Mercer had become bosom friends. You told her you'd been to Brighton and enjoyed a bathe in the ocean. I recall the setting quite distinctly."

"I've a gift for a telling detail."

"You wrote an excellent fiction, Sophie. I only wonder that you never added in a brooding hero who lived in the next village and whom you suspected of nobility and of having a heart you felt had been cruelly treated. Or perhaps a villain with designs on your delectable innocence."

"I might have got around to it eventually." She hated that he was so much taller than she. He made her feel insignificant the way he towered over her. "Do you make it a habit to read letters that were not directed to you?"

"My dear Mrs. Evans." He loomed over her now. "Fidelia read your letter aloud. We were all touched by your description of the day your brother's headstone was placed. And Fidelia is now mad to go to Brighton herself."

"I meant to entertain, after all. I'm pleased to know I succeeded. And if she longs for Brighton, then you must take her." She was beyond rational reaction. She wasn't in a state of hysteria, but she knew she was overreacting and could do nothing to stop herself. "On your wedding trip, perhaps."

"This is absurd." He took a step toward her, and she stepped back, and he came toward her again. And by then, she found herself with her heel against a rock. If he hadn't put his hands on her shoulders she would have tripped.

"It's not absurd at all. I won't be the only woman to support herself with her pen."

"Marry me." His voice went low and harsh. His fingers dug into her shoulders. "I fail to understand this absurd conviction of yours that you must live without friends or lovers or anyone who cares for you."

"I hate it here," she said. The words came from nowhere. "I've been so terribly unhappy. I'd do anything to be free of this place. Even if it was the worst mistake of my life. Even if it meant I'd never be happy again."

"Marry me, Sophie, and you will never want for anything." He loosened his grip on her shoulder. "I don't mind if you write, you know that. You know I'd encourage you in that." He spoke dispassionately, which seemed so odd in a man making his second offer of marriage. "I'll take you away from here. You need never see the Mercers again."

"Banallt, I—I couldn't bear it."

"You'll never forgive me for that night, will you?" His mouth twisted. "I was out of my mind, you know that." His fingers tightened on her. "You know that, Sophie. You know what happened. I was not entirely myself."

"You're wrong, Banallt. You don't understand."

"Then help me understand. Make me understand."

"I can't marry you, Banallt. How can I?"

"All you have to do is say yes."

She took a step toward him, hands fisted at her sides. "Imagine that I did, Banallt."

"Very well."

"You'll be bored one day, and you'll see a woman who's lovely and I'll be miserable all over again. Trapped, just as I was with Tommy. You'll crush my heart into dust the way Tommy did."

"I am not Tommy Evans."

"I cannot live like that again. I won't!"

"Don't be a fool, Sophie."

CHAPTER TWENTY-EIGHT

Rider Hall,
AUGUST 10, 1813

Sophie came into the back parlor at such a clip that by the time she saw Banallt, it was too late to slow down. Not that it mattered. He had some nerve calling here at half past ten at night when everyone knew that only something dreadful would bring a man from London at this hour. Banallt, she well knew, had been in London. With Tommy. She came to a halt and smoothed her skirts. But Banallt never thought of those things. He'd come here never imagining the terror she'd feel at being told she'd a caller so late at night.

"What is it, my lord?" she asked without bothering to hide her annoyance at being disturbed so late.

The moment she saw his face, her heart stopped beating.

Lord Banallt stood at the fireplace, his greatcoat still on, a beaver hat in his hands. His hair was brushed back from his high, pale forehead, spreading like spilled ink to his shoulders. Cashmere trousers fit close along his legs, and one of his driving gloves poked out from his greatcoat pocket. Absurdly, she noticed the aquamarine he wore on his right index finger. A cabochon set into a heavy gold band. He seemed never to keep a neckcloth properly tied, and tonight was no exception, though a diamond sparkled at the base of the knot. Standing there in the shadows, with his dark, too-long hair and his too-pale face, he looked like a man whose life had just shattered beyond repair.

Tommy must be injured or ill or worse, she thought with a suffocating panic. Why else would Banallt come here with that broken horror in his eyes? A plate of figs, left by the day servants who ought to have known better than to leave them out, sat on the table near where she'd stopped. A stack of books from the subscription library was too near the edge. She put her hand on the table to steady herself and had to catch one of the books to prevent it from falling to the floor.

"Mrs. Evans." He took a step from the fireplace. His eyes were tortured. He'd not shaved. He wasn't untidy, but he wasn't immaculate. "Sophie."

She gripped the edge of the table. "What's happened?" she asked. She pressed a hand to her heart. "Is Tommy all right?"

He smiled, but it was the bleakest smile she'd seen in her life, and it struck cold terror into her blood. "Your husband is, to my knowledge, quite well." His voice was low and controlled. Horribly controlled. For a moment he turned back to the fireplace, but only to balance his hat on the ledge. Just so.

"Then why have you come?" she asked. Something had happened. She knew it. She knew the moment she saw his eyes that something dreadful had happened. While his back was turned, Sophie picked up the book next to the figs. It was not one of the few volumes in the house and not one from the circulating library, either, but one from Banallt's private library. He must have brought it with him. The morocco cover was engraved with his crest.

"Do you read Latin?" he asked without moving from the fireplace.

She dropped his book. "No."

"Just as well. Ovid is a rather...fast poet. I do not think you would approve. I should not have brought it. I wasn't thinking." His expression was perfectly calm, but his eyes frightened her. She found herself looking into a storm of despair. How would he survive if that storm broke?

"Why not?" She couldn't bear his eyes and so stared at the straight black hair falling to his collar. His beauty had always unsettled her. He looked as she imagined Satan had looked in the instant after he was cast forever out of heaven.

"If you read Latin, you would know." He watched her with his tarnish eyes and then walked to the table of books. "But you do not read Latin, and there I think we should let Ovid rest. Perhaps one day I will translate him for you." He took another book and inspected it, coldly controlled. "I wonder what you would think of my library, Sophie."

She let his use of her given name pass. "I'm sure it's much better than the circulating library here."

"Mm." He closed the book and said, "I like to balance the light with heavy, spice with bland. Hot with cold."

"Romance with Latin?" she said. Why was he here? The chill in her blood settled in her chest and slowly spread.

"Amour with hate," said Banallt. His hair spilled across his cheek when he turned his head toward her. As always, his eyes defied interpretation of his thoughts. The pit of her stomach clenched. With another of his reserved smiles, Banallt tapped the top of the stack of books. "I'm curious, Sophie, do you write novels to feed your reading habit? Or does your reading habit feed your novel writing?"

"Why have you come here?" She stared into Banallt's pewter eyes, her throat threatening to close, as if he'd somehow transferred to her the horror banked within those tarnished depths. She filled her lungs with air, but it didn't help, because she knew, she knew with absolute certainty, that someone had died.

"If not Tommy, then who?" she whispered. Banallt's face slid into nothing. He opened his mouth and then closed it. She went to him, against her better judgment, narrowed the distance between them, and laid a hand against his cheek. "Banallt, what's happened?" At first she thought he meant to deny anything was the matter. "You know you can tell me anything. Anything at all, Banallt."

"My daughter," he said, and then his voice cracked, and with that break emotion stormed in his eyes. He bent his head to her shoulder and put his arms around her, holding her tight. He sobbed until Sophie thought her heart would never mend itself. She held him until the worst had passed.

"What happened?" she softly asked.

His breath trembled on the way in and more on the way out. He shrugged once, a slight movement of his shoulders as he lifted his head. "Everyone said she'd be fine. The physician more than anyone, and I believed him. Children fall ill and recover all the time. But she didn't. She died in my arms, Sophie, and there was nothing I could do."

"My poor Banallt," she said. Emotion quavered in her voice, too. She knew he loved his daughter, wholly and without any reservation whatever. She wanted there to be a way to take away his devastation and there wasn't. "My heart is broken for you." She stroked his cheek. She'd never touched him like that before, and despite the unshaven face, his skin was softer than she'd imagined. "But you held her, and that must have been a comfort to her and to you, as well. She was not alone."

"I am her father," he said. "I should have been able to save her. It was my duty. She is the only good thing I've ever done in my life, and now she's gone."

"Hush," she said. Tears dammed up in her throat.

"The world stopped," he said. "And began again. Without her."

"I am here." She walked to the sofa and sat down, Banallt next to her. "Tell me," she said. "Tell me everything."

For quite a long time he talked about his daughter, the why and how and all the moments when he fell into the unconditional love of a parent for a child. During the silences, she held his hand and sometimes pulled his head to her shoulder. But after a while, he recovered himself and sat back. She stroked his cheek, brushed away a lock of hair that fell like silk across her fingers. His gaze found hers and held hers. She was aware, all too aware now, that theirs could be a lover's embrace. She stood, and his hands slid along her hips as she did. "Let me get you something to drink."

He watched her all the way to the side table where Tommy kept the brandy she never touched. How many times had she wanted to dash the bottle against the wall? The silence was altogether different now. His mood had shifted from broken to dangerous, and she was no longer certain how to behave. An intimacy had been breached. She wiped her hand on her skirt before she dared fill a glass with brandy. Banallt left the sofa. Her pulse raced at the thought that he was walking toward her, but he was only going to the fireplace. She heard the skittering of the scuttle against the bin that held the coal.

He wouldn't, she thought. She trusted him. He wouldn't presume.

The silence deepened. Banallt replaced the screen. She could not see him but knew he'd walked behind her. If she were to look at him now, she'd have to crane her neck. She took great care in stoppering the brandy. The stopper tapped the rim of the bottle and let out a perfect crystal chime.

"Are you writing still?" he asked. He wasn't as near to her as she thought. Thank God. She turned, put the glass into his hand, and retreated.

"Yes."

"Is your heroine in danger?" he softly asked.

"Yes," she replied. His voice sent a ripple of awareness up her spine. "Trapped in the ruins of an abbey with a ghost and the body of her murdered mother."

"Has she swooned yet?" His fingertips moved up and down the glass, and the light from the fireplace caught the aquamarine.

Sophie nodded.

"Why do you suppose heroines are so weak-minded as to swoon whenever they are in danger?" he asked. He took a sip of brandy, but his eyes stayed on her. She did not like the hunger she saw there.

"Convenient, I suppose." She walked to the table and went through the stack of books there, arranging them in opposite order nearer the center of the table.

"Would you swoon if you were in danger?" he said.

"I'd like to think not. I expect I shan't know until it's too late." She heard him walking again, and a moment later, he appeared beside her, one hip leaning against the table. Sophie's stomach somersaulted when he put down his glass, empty now, and crossed his arms over his chest.

His eyes were pools of shadowed silver, drawing her under the depths. "You are a very great beauty, Sophie."

"Don't," she said. "Don't bother." She summoned a smile with the hope of dispelling the odd and far too intimate mood. "You can't flatter me."

"Of course I can." His greatcoat hung open, exposing his coat and waistcoat.

"Go on then just as you like." She moved another book. "You know I am not vain enough to believe your lies."

"Lies? No lies between us. Trust me, darling," he said bitterly, "I'll never lie to you."

She laughed. "Gentlemen lie all the time."

"Gentlemen pay good money for a mistress with a figure like yours. Delicate and yet, a woman's curves." He leaned over her, which was rarely difficult for anyone, least of all him and his six feet and some inches, his hair falling forward. "Your eyes are intelligent, and your clever mind informs your every expression. An intelligent woman confident and happy in herself always attracts a man of discernment. There is no doubt of it, Sophie. You are a beautiful woman."

"It isn't true," she said tartly. "But thank you for saying it so convincingly. If it were anyone but you saying so, I might be flattered."

He pushed away from the table. "Must we constantly argue?" he said.

"Are we?"

"You are astonishingly good at disagreeing with me."

"Everyone has at least one talent, my lord."

"I wouldn't mind if you called me Gwilym."

"But I would." She started again on the books, restacking them and taking Banallt's Ovid out of the pile. If he left it behind, she'd find a Latin grammar and try her luck with a translation.

He put his bare hand over hers. The warmth of his palm startled her. "I had to come here," he said. "No one else would do. No one else will ever do."

She lifted her head. "I am so sorry."

His fingers curled around hers, and for a moment, Sophie relaxed. They would get through this moment after all, without disaster. "I thought of you all the way from London. I must be mad, I told myself. She'll not want to see me."

"That's not so."

"And here we are."

The moment crossed back into danger. His smile was wrong. Inappropriately intimate. "Don't," she whispered. She pulled her hand free of his. "Please don't."

"Why not?" he asked. "Your husband is even now in London and I daresay hasn't thought of you in weeks."

Sophie's head jerked up. "Don't," she said again, more forcefully. "You will only regret where this leads us."

"What will it take to woo you from your worthless husband?" He made a face. "No woman could be as faithful as you for no reason on earth."

She shook her head.

"Ten thousand pounds? Twenty?"

"That's quite enough." She pulled herself upright. "No more of this. You're distraught and—"

"I'm dying for want of you. Fifty thousands pounds, Sophie. That's in addition to the discharge of your husband's not inconsiderable debts."

Her heart raced. This couldn't be happening. He wouldn't do this to her. "You're mad with grief."

He laughed. "I'm mad with lust. You're not so naive that you don't understand that I want you. Come now, you know I'll treat you better than Tommy ever has or will."

"I'm married, Banallt."

"So is your husband, as I recall, and yet I left him quite happily in the tender arms of my cast-off mistress."

She lifted her hand, but he caught her wrist and pulled her toward him. "Carte blanche," he said. His face was hard, his mouth tense, and something wild came up from him and she was in an instant reminded of just how much smaller she was than him. Fear spilled down her spine, and she hated Banallt for this. For making her afraid of him.

"Get out." She shoved him hard enough that he let her go.

His eyebrows rose. "I'm quite serious about this Sophie." His gaze raked her from head to toe. "I adore you, I have since nearly the moment I laid eyes on you."

"You don't know what you're saying."

"Of course I do. I've never offered any woman carte blanche. But the offer's there for you. Only you, my beautiful, lovely Sophie. My fortune at your feet. Ruin me if you like. You've already ruined me for any other woman. You may as well complete your triumph."

She reared back. "Don't ever call here again. Do you understand me? I shan't see you."

"Don't be a fool, Sophie."

CHAPTER TWENTY-NINE

Near Withypool, one and a half miles from Castle Darmead,
MAY 7,1815

Banallt froze. He wanted to hear yes so badly that he fully believed his brain capable of manufacturing the answer he wanted, no matter the words that came out of her mouth. Her chin was pointed up so that she could look into his face. Her eyes were on his. Locked with his. She wasn't pushing him away or uttering trite phrases meant to guide his disappointment away from her answer. Could he possibly have heard correctly?

He didn't want to believe she'd said yes if she really hadn't or if she didn't mean it. His instinct to disbelieve warred with the thought that if she'd said yes, he needed to act quickly. Now. Before she changed her mind. He didn't know what the hell to do, so he just continued as they were.

Slowly, she tipped her head down until her forehead rested on his chest. Her palms were flat on his torso, but she wasn't pushing him away. His hands tightened on her shoulders as the truth washed over him. My God, she really had told him yes.

He opened his mouth to ask if she was certain then didn't. If he did, she might change her mind, and he had no intention of giving her that opportunity. Underneath his hands, her shoulders quivered. She raised her gaze to him again, and his heart plunged into the depths. She had her lower lip trapped between her teeth, and her eyes were tormented pools of blue green. His heart broke just looking at her.

She was not in love with him. He knew that. Her acceptance of him had nothing to do with the sort of desperate longing he had for her. Not that he hadn't known that the first time he proposed to her, but to have her say yes out of despair added an edge of pain to his euphoria. He knew she wasn't indifferent to him, after all, and for the moment, that sufficed to keep the hurt at arm's length. "You won't regret this," he said. "I'll see that you don't."

"I know," she said softly. But her eyes said otherwise. He knew she was thinking back to the days when he'd not been worthy of her respect, when he'd told her, far too bluntly, that it was not in his nature to be faithful and then proceeded to demonstrate exactly how reprehensible a man he was.

His chest felt too tight, but the sensation wasn't entirely unpleasant. She wasn't certain she'd made the right decision, but he was. This was right. They would be good together. "I'll make you happy, Sophie. I'll give you everything you've missed all these years." An adoring husband. A man who admired her intelligence and looked forward to the challenge of making a life with her. "I will take care of you."

"Of course," she said.

The enormity of the moment took his breath. Sophie was going to be his wife. At last. He couldn't hold back a smile.

She drew her shawl around her shoulders. "It's late, Banallt. I ought to be getting home."

When he turned his phaeton back to Duke's Head instead of making the turn to Havenwood, Sophie roused herself out of her silence. "Where are we going?"

"To St. Crispin's," he said. "I've already spoken with Reverend Carson." He inhaled deeply. "I have a special license." His hands tightened on the reins, and he had to force himself to relax. "I wish we could be married by banns, but under the circumstances, I think it best not to wait. Besides, I might be recalled to London at any time. Vedaelin's been talking about sending me to meet with Wellington when he arrives in Brussels."

"Brussels?"

"If you'd read my letters, you'd know. War is inevitable. Napoleon will never step down. Why should he when he's in possession of Paris and every day more of the French army defects to him?" He slowed the phaeton. "You asked me earlier why I came here. I'll tell you one reason now. I came because if I'm to be sent to the Continent with war about to erupt, I needed to know if there was hope for us."

"Banallt." She put a hand on his shoulder.

Reverend Carson was waiting for them at the church. The clergyman's wife was there as well as his curate, asked to be on hand in the event Banallt came back with a bride.

Banallt stood with Sophie at the altar, holding her hand until the time came to slide a ring on her finger, a gold band engraved on the inside with their given names. The words were said, their responses were given, and the vow that bound them together forever was made. They signed in turn the parish records and it was done. Sophie was his.

He drove her back to Havenwood in silence. But when he waved off the groom who came out, he handed her down and pulled her into his arms. "I love you, Sophie." He knew she didn't believe him, but he said it anyway. Because the words were true. He brought her closer and, one hand on her cheek, brushed her mouth with his. His belly went taut. How long had he dreamed of making love to her? Years. For years and years. Illicitly at first with his pleasure at the forefront of his desire, and then with the thought of her foremost. And now with her as his wife.

"Ahem!"

That didn't come from Sophie so he ignored it. She was in his arms, her mouth was soft, soft, unconscionably soft, her body warm against his. Whether she knew it or not, her torso leaned into his. She might have ruined him for other women, but she certainly hadn't affected the sorts of things he adored about women and their bodies.

"Mrs. Evans! You are home at last," said a woman's voice. A girlish voice. He lifted his head and dropped his hand from Sophie's cheek. He left his other hand on her shoulder. Mrs. Mercer stood on the path, dressed in incongruously youthful clothes for a woman of her age, her cheeks pink with outrage, a closed fan extended in her hand.

"Oh dear," Sophie said in the direction of his chest.

"My lord." Mrs. Mercer lowered her fan. "Mrs. Evans has only recently lost her beloved brother." Her mouth thinned. "It is not good of you to take advantage."

"Mrs. Mercer," Banallt said. "You shall be the first to hear that Sophie has just made me the happiest man on earth."

"I beg your pardon?" Her eyes narrowed, and she looked from Banallt to Sophie and back. "Happiest man?"

"We are married. Sophie is my countess."

"Countess?" She gaped. "When?"

"Just now. At St. Crispin's. With Reverend Carson doing the honors."

She snapped open her fan and waved it under her chin. "My good heavens. Countess? Mrs. Evans is your countess?"

Banallt bowed. "Yes, Mrs. Mercer." Sophie, he saw, was staring at Mrs. Mercer as if she'd grown two heads. "She's the reason I came to Duke's Head at all."

"Married?" She looked from him to Sophie and back several times. "Have I heard correctly? She is now Lady Banallt?"

"Ma'am," he said. "You have."

"Mrs. Evans?" Her voice slid up into an even higher register. "Lady Banallt, I mean."

"Yes," Sophie replied softly. She didn't move from his arms. Not that he would have let her. "I have at last told him yes."

Mrs. Mercer's expression softened. "I wish you both all the very best." She clasped her hands. "I hope you will be as happy as Mr. Mercer and I have been these years."

"Thank you," Banallt said. That was really very decent of her. She might be an absurd woman, but he didn't doubt the sincerity of her good wishes.

"Will you come to the house, my lord? Mr. Mercer must hear this news himself."

"Directly, ma'am. I'd like a word with him in any event."

Sophie stared after Mrs. Mercer as she walked back to the house. "I dislike her, Banallt. She grates on my nerves. She has no conversation with me except what duties she expects me to carry out on her behalf."

He laughed and pulled her back into his embrace. He was happy. His world and everything in it was perfect. "Let me kiss you, Sophie."

Sophie glared in the direction of Mrs. Mercer's retreating back. "How dare she be so gracious?"

He barked with laughter, and a moment later, she laughed, too, and then he brought her head to his so that she had to go up on her toes and hold on to his shoulders. He kissed her and knew for a fact she was not in the least indifferent to him. Letting go of her took all his reserve.

Inside the house Banallt repeated to Mr. Mercer the news of his marriage. "Lady Banallt will return to Castle Darmead with me, directly." He lifted a hand. "If you would be so kind as to see that her belongings are sent on to the castle, I would be much obliged."

Mrs. Mercer opened her fan. "We shall, my lord. You may rely upon it."

"Sophie," he said, "I'm sure you will let Mrs. Mercer know if anything has been left behind?"

"Yes, I will. Thank you, Mrs. Mercer." She licked her lips. "There are a few things I'd like to fetch immediately."

Mercer stood up. "While your wife attends to that," he said, "might we have a word in private, my lord?"

He followed Mercer to his office. He didn't wait for the other man to come to the point. "I am happy to show you the contracts drawn up when I first made my intentions known to Sophie's brother. I see no need to change them, though I invite you to offer your opinion and suggestions if you feel she is not adequately protected."

"That would be good of you, my lord. She is our relative, after all, and I am obliged to look out for her interests, despite that you have taken my wife and me quite by surprise with this news."

"I understand."

"You will also understand when I ask you to please make provisions for her in your will without delay. Her brother was remiss."

"That, sir, has been done."

Mercer clasped his hands behind his back, and for a moment Banallt was strongly reminded of John. "Her sensibilities are delicate, my lord. You never saw a woman so utterly shattered as was Mrs. Evans when we arrived at Havenwood."

"I was at her brother's funeral."

"I understand you were present when he was killed."

"I was."

Mercer pinned him with his gaze. He nodded. "Mrs. Evans—I beg your pardon, Lady Banallt—and my wife have not been bosom companions. They are, I fear, two different sorts of women, and one's wife... Ah, but you have been married before. As has she. So perhaps you both understand that marriage is not without its moments of imperfection." He poured a brandy for them both. "I'm curious, my lord, whether you intend to seek a judicial review of Mr. Mercer's bequests."

Banallt drank half his brandy before he answered. "Is that why you kept her here? I wondered."

"I'm sure I don't know what you mean."

"Why, to prevent her from pursuing the legacy her brother intended her to have." He put down the snifter with a thunk. "The late John Mercer's solicitor could hardly advise her to seek counsel on the outcome. That would have been a dereliction of his duties. Though she would eventually have thought of it herself."

"He never executed the documents."

"You ought to have seen his wishes carried out. A gentleman would have."

"To the tune of fifty thousand pounds? Or more?" Mercer's expression hardened. "I should think not. What would a woman do with such a sum of money?"

The Mercers and Havenwood were no longer his affair. He clasped his hands behind his back. "If my wife wishes to know you in future, I will not forbid her. She is free to make her own connections. But be assured, Mr. Mercer, that *I* do not wish to know you or your wife."

"But the money—"

"May you choke on it, sir."

Banallt turned on his heel and went to fetch his bride.

CHAPTER THIRTY

When Castle Darmead came into view, Sophe's stomach somersaulted. The sight was familiar to her, though she'd usually approached by the field and not the long, curving drive. She felt a pang of recognition when the phaeton passed the spot where, as a girl, she'd left the field for the graveled drive, just before the outer wall that circled the castle proper and marked the boundary of the estate. Someone had begun to clear the vines clinging to the wall. They passed between the huge black double gates that hadn't been closed in years. Smoke came from one of the chimneys in the guard tower.

When Banallt came to a stop at the top of the drive, a groom ran to the phaeton and held the horses while Banallt got down. He came around for her, but before he did, he instructed the servant that the trunk in the boot was to be brought inside to the room adjoining his. "Shall we, madam?"

She clutched Banallt's arm as they walked to the entrance. The gray stone exterior was familiar. Little had changed since she'd last been here, more than ten years ago now. She knew the structure almost as well as she did Havenwood. The front door had a fresh coat of black paint. The iron filigree that extended from the hinges across the door had been scrubbed. Her husband opened the door.

Sophie's breath hitched when he caught her in his arms and carried her into Darmead. She laughed because he tickled her. As they went in, the butler appeared from a pantry to the left. King's eyes widened when he saw her in Banallt's arms. Other than that, he was impassive. As if he saw his employer do such things every day. Inside, Banallt slowly put her down. "I promised I'd have you home before supper, Lady Banallt," he whispered.

"Ma'am," King said. Sophie slipped off her coat, and Banallt handed over his, too, along with his hat and gloves. "My lord. I trust you had a pleasant outing?"

"Yes, we had. Very pleasant indeed. And now, King," Banallt said, "you shall be the first here at Castle Darmead to know our news."

The butler tugged on his damaged ear. "Speak to my good side, then, milord." He smoothed the lay of Banallt's coat over his arm.

"Mrs. Evans is Mrs. Evans no more. I have married her." Banallt's smile lit the room, and seeing it sent Sophie's heart flying right toward him. "From this moment forward, you will address her as Lady Banallt."

King's eyes fixed on Sophie, and she felt a shock at the intensity of his assessment of her. "Married, my lord?" he said in even tones. He didn't sound the least surprised. "To this slip of a girl?"

"Yes, King," Banallt said.

King's grin broke open. "Why, then, congratulations, my lord!" King grabbed Sophie's hand in both of his and pressed hard. "Lady Banallt. I hope you know you've gone and married yourself to the best man in all of England, that's all."

She drew back her hand. The ring Banallt had put onto her fourth finger was an unaccustomed weight. She'd taken off Tommy's ring the night she saw him with Mrs. Peters, and she had believed she'd never again wear such a symbol of pain and futility. Now, her finger was once more encircled by a band of gold. Lord Banallt was her husband. The idea refused to strike her as anything but impossible. "Thank you, King," she said. Inside, she shook, and she was astonished at how normal her voice sounded. "I'm glad you think so."

Banallt put a hand on her waist and drew her close. "Gather the staff, King, so I may introduce my countess in, say, half an hour? Her things are being sent on from Havenwood. When they arrive, they're to be put in the north tower wing."

"Milord." King bowed.

His countess. My heavens. When Banallt said that, he meant her. And King would eventually turn his dark eyes on her and see she was an imposter and that her marriage was a fraud, that she didn't love him and deserved not congratulations, but contempt.

Sophie felt her life rushing headlong to the end of the world, and there wasn't anything she could do to stop it. She wished she were still at Havenwood, or anywhere but at Castle Darmead, where her past, present, and future had collided. The thought of living the rest of her days with Banallt was terrifying and electrifying at the same time. But, of course, he wouldn't stay, would he? She wasn't really going to live with Banallt. And if he was sent to Wellington...She refused to think what might happen.

Banallt led her inside, and Sophie's sense of unreality increased tenfold. In a blink, she traveled back in time to the Darmead of her girlhood. For the first time since she'd married Tommy she was someplace she belonged, someplace that wanted her, where she wanted to be. A shiver went down her spine. As a girl she'd confidently told anyone who would listen that one day she would marry the Earl of Banallt and come to live at Darmead.

And somehow she had.

She was Lord Banallt's wife. Her body felt as light as air, and her hand trembled in her husband's as he led her inside.

Long uninhabited except by a caretaking staff, Darmead retained much of its medieval character, which was why Sophie had so loved to visit as a girl. She'd been mad about history even then, always making up stories set in years long past. Visiting Castle Darmead had, for her, been like stepping hundreds of years back in time. How many dozens of stories had Darmead inspired in her girlish head? Knights in armor, dragons, Viking hordes, reivers from Scotland; in her imagination Castle Darmead had withstood innumerable assaults from villains of all kind.

Almost everything was as she recalled. The arched windows she so loved and the crossed swords hanging on the walls waiting for a warrior's hand were still there. The gray brick seemed the loveliest color in the world, and the passageway to the butler's pantry as deliciously mysterious as ever. Her head swivelled to take in the vaulted ceiling overhead and the carved wooden minstrel gallery. Darmead had always made her feel like she'd been plunked in the middle of a story she just had to tell. Well. She had been. Only this time, the story wasn't one she'd made up.

Banallt took her upstairs. Naturally, she'd been in every room in the castle multiple times, including the dungeon. Once the caretakers had gotten used to her visits and her begging for more stories about the castle and its history, they'd given her free reign. She knew, therefore, that originally and today, the rooms in this wing were reserved for family and were made up of a series of connecting rooms: the great chamber, the presence chamber, the guard chamber, a withdrawing chamber, and the privy chamber. When the first earl lived here in 1651, he'd converted the chambers to something reasonably more modern. The lord's room she assumed must be Banallt's room and was the original privy chamber. That room led to a withdrawing room, which in turn opened onto what was to be her room.

"Freshen up, Sophie," Banallt said. He squeezed her hand. "Then we'll go downstairs and meet the staff."

When she was here as a girl, all but a few of the rooms had been closed up. The rest were barely furnished, with bed hangings long gone, rugs rolled up, the furniture covered, fireplaces empty for hundreds of years. She remembered the black larch paneling that covered the walls floor to ceiling, carved with interlocking squares. The marble mantel was precisely as she recalled, columned on either side, with lozenges and the original viscount's crest carved above. The ceiling, too, was carved with the same interlocking pattern as the walls.

But she'd never seen the room furnished; her imagination had once supplied the details now before her. An azure and cream carpet, blue velvet curtains tied back with tasseled silk ropes, shuttered windows open to a view of Duke's Head, miles distant. The furniture was old-fashioned and rather dark. But there were modern touches here and there. A series of still lifes hung on the wall: fruit, flowers, a desk with sheet music. The four-poster bed was hung with brilliant blue silk and covered with a black silk coverlet embroidered with gold garlands. She would sleep in that bed tonight.

She removed her gloves to wash her face in the basin. A soft towel had been laid by. She tidied her hair and sank onto a chair by the fireplace, trying to get herself firmly grounded in what had happened. She wasn't certain she could. Her old life and her present one collided and left her not knowing whether to be giddy at being at

Darmead, glad to be away from Havenwood with its unhappy memories, or questioning her sanity for having married the Earl of Banallt. She held up her hands and watched them shake. A wedding band was on her finger. Banallt had put it there himself. She managed herself and walked through the withdrawing room. There was a door directly across from the one she'd entered through. Banallt was on the other side. She didn't knock on the door as she'd intended.

Instead, she went downstairs, where she met the housekeeper. "Welcome to Castle Darmead, Lady Banallt," the housekeeper said with the same Scottish burr Sophie recalled. Her dark curls were tinged with gray now. "Or should I say, welcome back, young lady." She clasped her hands over her apron. "I never did imagine you'd be marrying the master, Miss Sophie, yet here you are. Every inch of you Lady Banallt." She smiled. "How many times did you beg for a tour when you were still young Miss Mercer of Havenwood?"

"At least a thousand," Sophie said. She was hollow inside. She had no substance, she was empty, and if King hadn't seen her for a fraud, Mrs. Layton would. Her clear blue eyes missed nothing.

"Yes, it must have been at least a thousand." Mrs. Layton threw her arms around Sophie. "We heard about your brother," she whispered, hugging Sophie close. "I said a prayer for you both."

"Thank you."

Holding on to Sophie's shoulders, she took a step back and looked her up and down. "And now look at you. Grown up and mistress of the castle, exactly as you said."

"I never forgot the stories you told me, Mrs. Layton. I never forgot you."

"My dear. Lady Banallt. You're the same lovely girl you always were, aren't you?"

Sophie lifted her arms. "It still quite takes my breath," she said. "All of this. It doesn't seem real. None of it does."

"Ah," said a voice from above them.

Banallt walked to the front of the minstrel gallery and looked down, fiercely handsome and disreputable, what with his too-long hair and his coat unbuttoned to reveal his silver waistcoat. He put his hands on the top rail. "Lady Banallt." His eyes lingered on Sophie. "Welcome to Castle Darmead."

Sophie knew a narrow spiral staircase led from the great hall to the first tower, with landings for the minstrel gallery and then the bedchambers and on the other side, a large parlor with an enormous fireplace. More bedchambers were on the third floor, and if you climbed to the very top of the tower, you found not an observatory or an office, but a storage room full of broken furniture and bits of armor.

Her ears buzzed with the effect of seeing Banallt here. As a girl, long before she met Tommy Evans, she'd dreamed of a moment like this. Her first stories had all contained scenes much like this one. She'd constantly imagined meeting the direct descendant of the viscount who had built the original castle. He would see her, a glimpse from afar, and then a nearer one, and they would, naturally, inevitably, fall tragically in love.

Banallt disappeared from the gallery and a minute later emerged from an arched doorway at the side of the hall. The introduction to the staff was over quickly. Banallt knew every name and the position each held, whether they had been at Darmead all these years or he'd brought them with him from London or hired them on when he came here from Town. He turned his attention back to her. "The place is drafty at times. I find it's most pleasant upstairs by the fire." He bent close and kissed her cheek before she was prepared. He smelled of lemons and bergamot.

"Banallt." She managed to hide her reaction from him. She hoped. Surely she wasn't standing here next to the Earl of Banallt, married to him. His countess. Banallt understood she did not love him. Her heart would not be broken when he returned to London and, inevitably, took a lover. He would fall out of love with her one day. So long as she remembered that, they would be fine.

"We'll have tea upstairs, King," he said.

"Milord."

"We'll dine privately, I think."

"About eight, my lord?"

"Excellent."

The stairs to the parlor were so narrow they had to proceed single file. Sophie went first, then Banallt. She glanced at him over her shoulder and tried for normalcy. "My first novel was a historical romance in which a pitched battle took place on these very stairs, with knights fighting for their lives, defending the upper reaches of the castle from the depredations of a neighboring lord."

"Yes, I remember. A rousing scene. And it took place here?"

"As a girl," she said, "I was far too small to see out the windows." She stopped at one of the arrow slits in the spiral staircase. "Later I was able to see, but not easily." Since she was in the lead, their stopping meant she was nearly at eye level with Banallt. "It's exactly as I recall."

"I should be more than willing to lift you for a view," Banallt said.

For once she could look him straight in the eye. "That would be quite undignified, I should think."

He scooped her up in his arms and held her to the slit of a window. She laughed and slapped his chest. "Banallt!"

"Now is your chance, Sophie. Look." He leaned them toward the opening. "What story would you write with that narrow view of the world?"

"It's lovely," she said. Green fields sloped away from the high ground the first viscount had claimed when he built Darmead so many centuries ago. Clouds gathered on the horizon.

"Can you not see the attacking army?" he said. She put an arm around his neck to steady herself. The window opening was several feet deep and narrowed to a point less than four inches wide. "Ample space for an archer, wouldn't you say?"

"Do you think they ever admired the view as they took aim?"

Banallt held her easily. "I should hope not. That the castle still stands and remains in the possession of the Llewellyn family, I think not. The archer concentrated on his shooting."

"Do you think he laid his arrows on the ledge? Or did he keep them in a quiver at his back?"

"On the ledge, perhaps? Hm. Do you think there's room here for him to reach behind him?"

"You can put me down now," she said.

"I'd rather not." Banallt dropped a kiss on her forehead and continued up the stairs with her in his arms, though he had to walk sideways to make the turns without cracking her head on the wall.

"You'll drop me."

"I shan't." They exited to the hallway that led to their rooms with Banallt still carrying her. She had both arms around his neck by now. "Did you know, Banallt, that Henry IV is said to have visited here?"

He glanced at her and winked. "My ancestor was nearly bankrupted by his call, I'll have you know. I've seen the ledgers."

"You have?"

"My predecessor here was meticulous in his record keeping. My father set him as the example I should strive to emulate when the time came for me to manage the properties." His eyelids lowered, and Sophie saw the sweep of his thick lashes. She wanted very much to kiss him. "I shall do the same for our son."

They didn't go right to the bedchambers but rather left to the parlor. He put her down in order to open the wooden door. Someone had painted it green, which was new. When last she'd seen the door, it was brown. Sophie leaned against the wall. "I was accused of plotting to live here," she said as Banallt opened the door to let her precede him inside. "By my father and the caretakers both."

"You laid a clever scheme, Lady Banallt."

"Papa always said he expected one day he'd have to explain to the Earl of Banallt how a ten-year-old girl had come to live in his house without his permission." She smiled at the memory as she went inside. "He encouraged me, you know. He claimed it was his fondest wish that the Mercers should one day find themselves in adverse possession of a castle."

While Sophie walked the perimeter of the parlor, servants brought in tea. Banallt leaned an elbow on the mantel. The floor was covered with the same Aubusson carpet she recalled from her youth. This room, with its paintings from the days of Banallt's great-great-grandfather on the walls, had been used to entertain guests who'd come to tour the castle and grounds and who then wished for tea before leaving. The paintings had been among her favorites: hunting scenes, portraits of men and women in stiff collars and wigs, and, her favorite, St. George slaying the dragon.

Banallt grabbed her in his arms when the servants bowed themselves out. "A quick tea, Sophie, a bite to eat so as not to hurt King's feelings, and then we'll retire, yes?"

She elbowed him, but she didn't stop him when he came in close for a quick kiss.

The tea was laid out with a table of sweets and cold cuts that reminded her she was hungry. She knew how Banallt liked his tea. He preferred gunpowder black and that she found in the tin. As a girl she'd preferred gunpowder herself. Once she'd married, gunpowder black tea became an extravagance.

King knocked on the door and came just inside. In this lovely gold and red parlor, King looked more than ever like a brawler from the London stews. His black wool suit highlighted the contrast between the exquisite tailoring and his broken face. He bowed. "Milord. The Llewellyns. Are you at home, milord? Milady?"

Milk sloshed onto the skirt of her Sunday gown, once cream satin, now dyed black and already showing the effects of more frequent wear. "Drat," she muttered, snatching up a napkin to dab at her lap. She felt her cheeks growing hot.

"What the devil are they doing here?" He reached across the table and clasped Sophie's hand. "Shall I send them away?" He looked up at King, ready to do just that.

"You can't," she said. "They've come all this way."

He scowled. "Please show them in. Thank you, King." He leaned back on his chair. Sophie's stomach sank. She gave Banallt his tea and managed to pour her own without mishap. But after one sip, she put down her cup lest her trembling hand give her away.

Banallt rose, holding his saucer in one hand and his cup in another, both incongruous in his hands. He sipped from his tea, then set cup and saucer on the mantel as King returned with Mrs. Llewellyn, Fidelia, and a tall, slender gentleman she didn't recognize but who couldn't be anyone but Banallt's cousin Harry Llewellyn. Banallt whispered, "I'll have his hide, by God."

Llewellyn was in his forties with dark hair and light blue eyes. He had Banallt's pale complexion and something of his height and build, but there the family resemblance ended. He strode in, arms swinging at his side.

"What brings you to Darmead, Banallt?" said Harry Llewellyn. "Did you have a sudden longing to polish the family armor?" Llewellyn's gaze shot to Sophie then fixed on Banallt. Fidelia and her mother curtseyed to Banallt and nodded to Sophie, but neither spoke. Llewellyn held up a hand. "Margaret, take Fidelia outside. I'll want a word with Banallt."

"No," Banallt said. "They'll stay to hear what you have to say, and my answers to you."

"My lord—"

"I insist."

Mrs. Llewellyn stood well away from her husband. Fidelia was much altered from when Sophie had last seen her. She was thin and much paler, and there was no hint of a smile from her. Sophie recognized the grief that shadowed Fidelia's eyes. She'd seen it in the mirror every day since John was killed.

"A better question, Harry, is why you are here at Darmead," Banallt said in a chilling voice.

"I came all the way from Epping's Field to London only to find you not at home."

"None of which is any of your affair." He leaned an elbow on the mantel. "Not that it isn't splendid to see you."

Llewellyn stood with his head cocked, studying Sophie in her mourning black. She had put on her gloves before she went down to meet the staff, so he could not see the wedding band, and yet she itched to cover up her left hand. She felt the ring thick and cool against her skin, an unaccustomed pressure around her finger.

"Delightful as it is to see your wife and daughter," Banallt said from his place by the mantel, "I was under the impression they were happy at Hightower House. There's a great deal to do in London after all, and very little by comparison here in Duke's Head. So do tell, Harry, what's brought you here...without an invitation, when you might be escorting them to some fete or another?"

"Scandal, what else?"

Banallt picked up his tea. "Scandal. How tedious."

His cousin straightened his shoulders. "Connected with you."

"More tedious still." He waved a hand. "I should think you'd know better by now than to upset yourself over some rumor that involves me. They are often inaccurate, I warn you."

Llewellyn stood behind his daughter and rested a hand on her shoulders. He seemed a proud man to Sophie, but then his father had been the son of an earl, and, with Banallt having no son, Harry Llewellyn was first in line of inheritance. "I should think that with Fidelia in London, you would be more careful of your reputation. And with hers."

"Papa," Fidelia said softly.

"What on earth could you have heard?" Banallt spoke in a low voice that sent shivers down Sophie's spine. "Nothing true, I assure you."

Sophie was horrified to feel tears welling up. Fidelia had loved John. John had been deeply loved. The sharpness of her grief, no more the freshness of it, took her unawares. By the time she found her handkerchief, Banallt was putting his into her hand and tears burned her eyes.

"Forgive me." She took a breath and stood up to excuse herself. "I miss my brother terribly. And I—I didn't realize how—I'm so sorry."

"There, there," said Mrs. Llewellyn.

Banallt reached for her hand, and Sophie, unthinking, let him pull her to her feet and into his arms because he understood her grief. He understood how completely alone she was without her brother. They stood there, she and Banallt, hands still clasped, him with his other arm around her shoulders. Comforting her.

"I take it," Llewellyn said with a gesture at Sophie, "that this woman is the infamous Mrs. Peters?"

"Infamous?" Banallt said. "Have a care what more you say, Harry."

"Yes, infamous, by God! I come to London and what do I hear? That you have left Town, with a married woman. Whose husband is even now demanding satisfaction of you. And against all bounds of decency, I find it's true. She is here with you."

"Harry!" said Mrs. Llewellyn.

Banallt lifted a hand and Mrs. Llewellyn fell silent. "Allow me to make the introductions." He took Sophie's hand and brought it to his lips. "Sophie," Banallt said, turning to face Harry, "may I present my cousin, Mr. Harry Llewellyn."

Mrs. Llewellyn's focus moved from Sophie to Banallt.

"I'm pleased to meet you, Mr. Llewellyn," Sophie said.

"Harry, no," said Mrs. Llewellyn when her husband took a deep breath to retort.

Banallt bent his head over Sophie and whispered, "Come, it's time." She curled her fingers against his chest and in response, he stroked her back. "Margaret. Fidelia," Banallt said when Sophie lifted her head. "Even you two must be introduced anew. All of you, this is my countess, Lady Banallt."

"Banallt," said Mrs. Llewellyn. She darted a glance at her husband and then squared her shoulders. She clasped her hands, raising them to her chin. "This is extraordinary news."

Fidelia smiled for the first time since she'd come in. She pushed away her father's hand and leaned forward. "Is it true?" Sophie nodded. "How wonderfully romantic. Banallt, I am so glad for you! And you, Mrs. Evans—or, I should say, Lady Banallt." She smiled. "I'm so very happy to have you for a relation."

"Thank you," Sophie said.

"Your countess?" Llewellyn frowned. "But—"

"I know what you thought, Harry," Banallt said. "But she is the former Mrs. Evans. Sister to the late John Mercer, whom I believe you once met. So you see, what you heard was false. I did not leave Town with a married woman, but by God, I'll return with one."

"Yes. But...married?"

"This afternoon, in fact." He faced his cousin. "I'm happy to show you the marriage lines if you are thinking to dispute the legality."

"No." Llewellyn bowed. "Lady Banallt. I hope you'll accept my congratulations and felicitations."

"Thank you, sir."

Mrs. Llewellyn did not show her husband's restraint. Once Sophie became the focus of attention, she went to Sophie and, sitting beside her, hugged her. "We were devastated by your loss, truly devastated."

"Thank you for the lovely flowers you sent," Sophie told her. She was horribly aware of Harry Llewellyn glaring at Banallt. "It meant a great deal to know you thought of me."

She took Sophie's hand in hers. "Fidelia misses him dreadfully." She lowered her voice. "She's taken it hard. Very hard. I think it will do her good to see you." Mrs. Llewellyn hugged Sophie to her bosom. "This is indeed happy news. Happy news," she said. "You don't know how I've wished for this. He's been so unhappy since... Well, I'm certain you know. The moment I saw you two together I knew he'd fallen in love at last. What splendid news!" Banallt was the recipient of another embrace. Sophie, still overwhelmed by the welcome, heard Mrs. Llewellyn whisper to him, "I had so hoped you would see she was the only woman for you. Banallt, you've done well. Very well this time." And then she stepped away, and Sophie had the unwelcome thought that there were now three more people who must eventually discover that the marriage was a sham.

"I am the happiest, most fortunate man in England," he said. Sophie lifted her chin to look at him. His eyes were that eerie flat and lifeless silver that had been haunting her since the day they met. The impact of his gaze sent her pulse racing.

"Incredible," Harry Llewellyn said. "You're actually in love."

If only he knew the truth, Sophie thought.

CHAPTER THIRTY-ONE

After tea and more expressions of congratulations and sur-
prise, Banallt very slyly, or perhaps not slyly at all, gave
Harry Llewellyn a recommendation to a restaurant in
Duke's Head. Or, he told them, they could do as he planned to do
and have supper in their rooms, if they cared to stay at Darmead.
They did, as it was getting late and threatening rain. King appeared
to escort the Llewellyns to rooms, and then, Sophie was alone with
Banallt. She took one look at him and burst into tears.

"Sophie, darling," he said.

She wanted to go to him, but her feet refused to move and she
was afraid to try because her familiar world no longer existed. If she
moved from this spot, she might just vanish into thin air. But Banallt
moved the world for her, and before long, she was in his embrace.
"Your cousin wanted you to marry Fidelia." She curled her fingers
around the lapels of his coat and breathed in the scent of bergamot.
"He expected you to marry her."

"Everyone knows that. He made no secret of it." Banallt rubbed
his hands along her spine. "His hope for a marriage between me and
Fidelia was the primary reason he put off your brother."

Sophie lifted her head. "You knew?"

"I am head of the family. It is my business to know. Harry was
quick to inform me I'd a rival. It's been a favorite subject of his since
the year after my wife died." He shrugged. "I don't begrudge him
that. As such matters go, a marriage between Fidelia and me makes

sense." He tightened his arms around her, and she allowed herself to relax against him. "If I were not in love with you, Sophie, I might have gone through with it. Or if Fidelia's heart had been free to be won. But after she met your brother, there was no one else for her." He lay his cheek on the top of her head. "Her affection for him was genuine. I think they would have been happy together."

"So do I," she whispered. She blinked and something tickled her cheek. Tears, she discovered, when she swiped a hand beneath her eyes. Weeks of emotional deadness were crumbling away, and unless she found a way to stop the erosion of her control, she was going to break before the night was done. She wanted to be someplace where she would not be confronted by topsy-turvy emotions, and that meant away from Banallt. Far from Darmead.

He brushed her hair behind her ears, his fingers lingering there. "Let's go where we may be private." He took a step back, hand outstretched. She put her hand in his, and this time, her feet did move. He walked with her to her room. Her trunk from Havenwood was open at the foot of the bed. Sophie's maid, Flora, was just closing a mahogany armoire.

"Ma'am," she said. "Lady Banallt, begging your pardon."

Her presence must be Banallt's doing. Sophie hadn't arranged for her to come here. He'd thought of everything. Flora was a pretty woman, young, too, but if Banallt noticed, he hid it well.

"Flora," he said. He never hesitated calling her maid by name. He knew instantly who she was. "You are free to go tonight. I'll look after Lady Banallt myself."

"Milord." She curtseyed again. "Milady."

With Flora gone, Sophie stood in the center of the room, the tips of her fingers over her mouth. This couldn't be real, she thought.

This was Darmead, after all, the place where she'd had more foolish dreams than most girls had in their lifetimes. If this was one of her stories, Banallt would be the villain, and her marriage a sham. She knew it wasn't because she was the villain here; she had entered into this marriage without love.

Banallt went to the fireplace and added more coals. He intended to stay with her, she realized. Her husband turned. "Come, Sophie. Let's sit before the fire a while."

There was a bottle of wine and two glasses on a table along with bread, a plate of cold meats, and fruit. Banallt ignored the food as he led her to the sofa arranged before the fireplace. She sat, at once glad of a reprieve from the intimacy to come and perversely disappointed. Banallt sat beside her, but rather far away, with his back against the sofa arm and one foot on the floor, the other on the sofa.

"Shall we speak," he said, "of your long and trying day?"

"No." She looked at him, but without meeting his eyes. Coward, she thought, but she still stared at his ear rather than risk locking gazes with him. She straightened her shawl, settling it very precisely around her shoulders, and then felt foolish. The gesture gave away her unsettled state of mind. She did look into his eyes then. Yet another confusing reaction washed over her.

"You've sailed between Scylla and Charybdis, Sophie, and survived."

"Have I?"

He held out both hands as if weighing the air on his palms. "You chose between Havenwood where you were intolerably miserable"— one hand dipped below the other—"and marriage to me. A monster, yes, an infamous scoundrel, but all the same, a man who adores you."

"You're not a monster."

"Hm. The words have been used. We'll settle for scoundrel, shall we?"

"Infamous scoundrel."

"Have you made the right choice?" he asked.

"Does it matter?" she returned. "The choice is made."

He smiled at her, and Sophie's emotions went to war. She had always admired Banallt's intellect and his easy manner with her. He never had condescended to her or made her feel unworthy or insignificant. But how could she forget him arriving at Rider Hall with Tommy, drunk and with a woman who was not respectable? All the times he'd watched her with his unsettling eyes and then left with Tommy. The night he'd admitted he was unfaithful to his marriage and saw no reason to change.

"You needn't stay here," she said. His eyes went wide the moment the words burst from her. "I mean, London is more convenient for you and I am happy to stay here at Darmead. I should be very happy here, with the castle to myself."

Banallt didn't reply right away. He tipped his head ever so slightly toward the back of the sofa. "What do you suggest we do instead? Carry on a passionate correspondence via the post? I think not, darling. You've not proven yourself a good respondent."

"Your cousin mentioned Mrs. Peters." Her cheeks burned, but he wasn't looking at her and so did not see.

"For which I ought to have his head." Banallt turned toward her, his lashes partially hiding his eyes. "He spoke out of turn."

"An affair, Banallt, is nothing irreparable if both parties are aware in advance."

"Indeed?" The word dripped with ice.

"I daresay neither of us would have any deep regrets if you carried on as before. There's always been talk about you, and it needn't matter. Not between us. It didn't used to, after all."

"What else needn't matter, Sophie? Your vows to me? Because I assure you, you are wrong in that assumption." Banallt sat up and stared at the ceiling. When he looked at her again, his expression was familiarly cool. "That was uncalled for. My apologies."

"I'm only trying to find a way for us to get on, Banallt. That's all."

"You're trying to find a way for you to stay in the past," he said. "The past is dead. Let it stay that way. I don't mean for us to get on as we did at Rider Hall, Sophie." He stood, and she watched him only long enough to see him walk to the table where the wine had been left. Anger added stiffness to the set of his shoulders. She curled her legs beneath her, put her arms on the back of the sofa, and buried her face there. What a farce this night was becoming. She burned hot one moment, cold the next. She didn't want him to leave her. She couldn't bear to be near him. He was her friend. He would break her heart. Behind her closed eyes, the darkness increased. Banallt had turned down the lamp. She lifted her head, thinking perhaps that he meant to leave. The room jumped with shadows.

"What am I to do then?" she said into the darkened room. She curled in a corner of the sofa. "When I hear your name connected with some other woman's, am I to let your affair break my heart as Tommy's did? I should think that you, of all men, would prefer a wife who isn't jealous."

He was by the table with the bottle of wine and both their glasses in one hand. He rejoined her on the sofa. Not too near, but not far, either. The wine and glasses he set on a folded-up card table at his elbow. She could see his face, pale and intense, and she remembered all those times at Rider Hall before she knew him, when he was Lord Banallt only and a stranger to her, the possessor of a familiar name, and then a friend of Tommy's of whom she deeply disapproved. And somehow he'd become a friend to whom she had confessed things she'd never told anyone else. How she loved Tommy and how she kept her writing income secret from her husband.

"Sophie." He said her name softly. If her life depended on it, she could not have looked anywhere but into the flat, silver depths of his eyes. She didn't think it was possible to be more aware of him than she already was, but the next moment proved her wrong. "Darling. I must turn down your offer. I am as astonished as you. But this is a subject upon which I've had months to think. You're intelligent. You suspected my first offer of marriage was based upon my conviction that you would never consent to an affair with me and that it was desperation only for your person that drove me to offer for you."

"And the second upon a need to rescue me."

He nodded. "Far more straightforward, darling, yet hopelessly complex."

She ignored the shiver in her belly. "Meaning?"

"I love you." He reached for the wine and filled the two glasses, though he left them on the table. "I've become like you. A hopeless fool who cannot break his vows. And I did make vows to you today."

She rested her head on her arms again. "That's not like you at all."

Anger flashed over his face, quickly mastered. "On the contrary. It is precisely like me, only you refuse to see me for the man I am."

"I want us to be truthful with each other," she said. "Even here in Duke's Head we hear the rumors from Town."

"Yes, my cousin brought a particularly fine one tonight, didn't he?" He tugged on his cravat. "But it wasn't true and well you know it. I don't give a fig for Mrs. Peters or any other woman whose name has been falsely linked to mine since my return from Paris."

She said nothing.

"A scandalous number of women have delivered to me their willing persons without benefit of marriage or consideration of their vows. But never you. Not until you were free." He took up one of the wineglasses and sipped from it. "The truth, Sophie, is that I have been celibate these past months. There's been no one but you."

This was not a subject upon which they would agree. She stretched out a hand. "Banallt, come. Let's not argue. I am your wife and this is our wedding night. Whatever our reasons for marrying, we are here. We are married. And I will be faithful to my vows. You cannot doubt that."

He faced her, one leg beneath him, one foot on the floor, glass of wine in hand. "That's so, Lady Banallt." He breathed up all the air in the room, not leaving any for her. He wasn't looking away from her, and heaven knows she couldn't look away from him, not even when he leaned forward and took a stray lock of her hair between his fingers. "Like silk," he said. "Have I told you what lovely hair you have?"

"It's brown," she said. "Plain brown."

"Hardly. Your hair is brown the way the ocean is blue. How many colors is the sea? A dozen? A hundred? Such a rich color, your hair. Soft. Luxurious."

"You swore to me you were not a poet."

"I'm not." He reached behind him to return his wineglass to the table. "And yet you inspire me to such flights of desire that you transform me."

She touched his hand, drawing a fingertip from his wrist to the end of his middle finger. "Tonight you are a poet."

"That is a solid basis on which to make a life together, don't you agree? Mayn't a poet and an author find happiness?" He brushed her cheek with the back of his hand. "I mean to prove you wrong about me. You've turned me into your faithful hound."

She smiled softly. "Are you a hound or a poet?"

"Both." And then, in one fluid move, Banallt moved close to her and put his hands on her shoulders. Her skirts had ridden up when she curled up on the sofa, and, belatedly aware of the fact, she tugged her gown over her exposed ankles.

He covered one of her hands with his. "Don't."

She imagined his eyes, lifeless, black-rimmed pewter skimming over her ankles. Her belly felt tight and fluttery. She didn't want the sensation to stop, and at the same time, she couldn't bear another moment. She rested her head on her arms again and pretended, or tried to pretend, that she was unaffected. "I'm afraid, Banallt. I'm afraid of everything going wrong. I lost Tommy, and I thought my world would end. And then John died, too."

"Oh, Sophie," he said.

"I don't want to feel anything. Not anymore. I don't want to lose anyone else."

He stroked her shoulders. "You aren't alone. You never were, if only you'd believe it."

"But the duke will send you to Wellington, and there is to be war." She bowed her head and realized she wasn't going to stop the tears burning in her eyes, so what was the point of trying to hide them? "Anything might happen." She rolled her lower lip over her teeth but that didn't stop the emotion roiling in her, either. "Anything. You've been my friend. You were my friend even when I'd lost my way with Tommy. And I came to know you better than anyone. You loved your daughter so deeply, my heart did break for you, truly, and then you—"

"Insulted you."

"You were there after John died, looking after me, and now you're to be sent off to war."

"Not as an infantryman." He slid an arm around her. "They've no need of generals without experience in war, and I have none of that." He lifted her chin. "But if I'm asked to go, I will."

"I know." She didn't know how to explain her feelings to him when she didn't understand them herself. "It's just—" She threw a hand into the air. "Banallt, I don't know. I don't know anything."

"I'll not make promises I can't be sure of keeping. My will is changed. If I am killed, if my ship sinks or some fool soldier aims the wrong direction, if any of that should happen, you will not find yourself alone. That is a promise I can make you. I have family and now they are your family. Harry will look after you. And now, please, you're right. This is our wedding night. And you *are* my wife." He touched the back of her head and pulled out a hairpin. And then a second.

"What are you doing?"

"I'm not leaving this room tonight. I hope we agree. We've sent away the servant who was to help you dress for bed. Who else is left to play lady's maid but me?" He pulled more pins from her hair, and Sophie let him.

With no hesitation whatever, he smoothed out the curls the pins had made in her hair. She felt him lean close, and then his breath warmed the skin near her ear. "You've not cut your hair in a long while, have you?"

"No."

"Not very fashionable of you."

She shrugged. His fingers in her hair soothed her, and after a bit, she actually closed her eyes. Several times in the process of his work, he moved her head this way or that, so when he put a hand on either shoulder and drew her toward him, she complied. But he didn't do anything more with her hair. His hands continued to cup her shoulders. His palms slid downward to her upper arms, to her elbows, and then to her forearms with but the lightest pressure of his fingertips. And all she did in response was hold her breath. His hair brushed her cheek.

His hands left her arms and settled on her thighs, and then one palm slipped underneath the hem of her black-dyed gown. Linen and muslin rustled. She made no protest when his hands touched her bare thigh. He'd gathered up her skirts and quite completely exposed her legs. He stretched out one of her legs, trailing a finger from her calf to her thigh. His fingers, long fingers, traced a line around the top of her garter. He divested her of her stockings. The moment felt unreal. She shivered with anticipation. Her belly and lower, there, between her legs felt taut with expectation.

"Darling," he said in his familiar, wicked drawl, "legs such as these deserve prettier garters. Pink silk and Brussels lace."

"I dislike pink," she said, but how she spoke at all amazed her.

He laughed, low velvet, a sound as morbidly compelling as ever his eyes were. "In the matter of garters only my opinion is of any consequence, I assure you," he said. His palm covered the back of her thighs. "I'm going to buy you a dozen new garters, all lace and silk.

Sophie, you are luscious beyond belief. Such soft skin." His fingers slipped around to the inside of her thigh. "Darling."

His breath warmed the place where her shoulder became her neck. "You—" His fingers pressed into her, and she bowed a little. "You belong to me now." She felt his teeth nip her ear, a soft bite, a low growl that reverberated in her heart. The tautness in her belly shot through her, clear to her breasts. "You are mine, Sophie. Legally, now. Morally. Mine. Never doubt that." He withdrew his fingers, but his thumb moved along her, then his fingertips stroked, moving her into a madness of sensation. He stopped again, his palm slipping around her upper thigh to her backside. She whimpered because he wasn't touching her there anymore, and the shivering pleasure stopped. When his hand came back, she opened herself to him. "Have you ever done this for yourself?" he asked.

Since words were quite beyond her, she shook her head. Her corset, which wasn't laced all that tightly, prevented her from getting enough air, though she was uncertain if that was the cause of her light-headedness.

He gave a low laugh in her ear. "When I first met you, you were so careful of your passions and so disapproving of me. I found you quite irritatingly proper, and yet it was a matter of mere hours before you were in my most erotic dreams. Perhaps you're not really proper."

Her body and her will loosened. "I still am," she whispered. "I am a very proper sort of wife. I promise you, I am."

"You insist you are a good and proper woman," he said, arms tightening around her. "But good and proper women bore me, and you have never bored me. Not even once, so, darling Sophie, I am forced to conclude that you are not a good and proper woman at all. Are you good, darling, or wicked?"

She meant to inhale, but she had trouble filling her lungs. "I am good," she whispered. "Always good." She was going to faint. Her head swam, and she leaned against him for support.

"Yes," he murmured. "You are good. You are very good indeed. Sublime, in fact."

His fingers pressed against her, stroking, moving, and there she was, about to lose her mind to her body. She completely lost her breath.

"Let me help you, my odalisque." His arms around her were a fortress of strength. She was protected here. Revered in his arms.

"Banallt…"

"Resist the pleasure," he whispered even as he urged her into sensation. Instinct commanded, told her she was peaking toward orgasm. "Resist"

"I can't."

"If you come," he said, his voice a growl in her ear, "I'll have won."

"Oh my." She grasped blindly for him, reaching to curl her hand around the nape of his neck while with the other she gripped his wrist. "You beast. You're beastly."

"Go on."

Banallt wouldn't stop, yet he wouldn't give her what her body demanded of her, either. His hair caught between her fingers, soft as silk. "I hate you," she said. Her voice broke.

"How positively beguiling of you." His fingers slowed, and she thought she would scream with frustration.

"I despise and abhor you." She opened for him, pushed her hips forward.

"Do you hold me in contempt?"

"Yes." But the word came out in a rush of air. She tried to gasp and couldn't. Her head was spinning, reeling. She wanted.

"You disdain me," he said. "Scorn me. Contemn me." With each whispered word, he stroked harder, and then whatever else he said was lost. She could do nothing but hold him as sensation peaked, and he held her there until she thought she could not live. Pleasure washed through her, took her over, filled her so that nothing else existed, and through it all, his fingers touched, caressed, paused, and gave.

She still held him when he said, "Thank you, Sophie. You are exquisitely lovely when you come, and I should not have properly lived if I had not seen that." He turned away, though one hand remained, touching her as he reached for the wine on the table. When he came back, he extended a glass to her. His other hand slid up to her stomach, as far as her corset allowed. She was glad she wore a short corset today.

"This is my very best Bordeaux," he said. "From the Cote d'Or, and it's not to be wasted. God knows when I'll be able to get more. Drink it all, darling."

"Must you make everything sound so wicked?"

His fingers splayed over her belly, and his chin once again rested on her shoulder. "Now what kind of question is that? I thought you knew me. The answer is yes, when I mean it to be, and, sometimes, even when I don't."

"Really, Banallt." She refused the wine. She wanted a clear head tonight.

He kissed her neck and then sat beside her, this time very close. He took her glass from her and tipped his head to drink from it. He watched her face, searched her with his tarnish eyes, and this time he did not speak at all unkindly. "I suppose I ought to warn you that I have every intention of hearing you beg tonight."

"Never."

He put the Bordeaux back into her hand. "Drink up, darling, and we'll see which of us is right."

She drank in the hope that it would give her the courage. No marriage should start out with a lie between husband and wife. She had not told him the entire truth about how her marriage to Tommy had ended.

CHAPTER THRITY-TWO

Banallt leaned over Sophie and brushed her loosened hair over one shoulder. Her spectacular eyes drew him closer. He'd been bowled over by her eyes the very first time he was close enough to see them. There she'd been, standing in the corridor at Rider Hall holding up a lantern and staring at him with eyes that cut straight through him and him thinking no one could really have eyes that color. The effect wasn't any different now. It wasn't just the color but the soul that looked through to him.

"Your eyes are lovely." He drew a fingertip from the inside corner of her eye to the outside. She blinked and her lashes brushed the side of his finger. "I was always jealous of the way you looked at Tommy. Always." He smoothed the corner of her eye. "Don't frown, Sophie. I'm complimenting you. Or trying to, anyway."

"I am not frowning," she said with a lift of her chin.

"Darling." He leaned closer to whisper in her ear. "What is that I see that is quite the opposite of a smile?"

She leaned back. "I don't mean to frown."

"I want you to be happy."

"I am." Her gaze moved up and down his face. Then she reached out and tugged at the front of his cravat. Her mouth curved. "Do you know what I have been thinking lately?" Her voice went soft and liquid, and it was like fire running through his blood. "My lord."

"That my valet's skills are lacking?"

"Hm." Her tongue darted out to touch her lower lip. "It's unfair to blame him when you're the one constantly pulling at his creations."

"True."

She shifted nearer him, and he stayed still while she loosened his cravat and reached around to unfasten the knot in the back. "I've been thinking how much I should like to see you, my lord."

He quirked his eyebrows. "You may, of course, look your fill, ma'am."

Her mouth curved into a troublingly sly grin. She was up to something she thought would cause his downfall. Given the circumstances, he didn't mind in the least. "Yes," she whispered. "I'd like that a great deal."

She dropped his cravat to the floor. Her hands went to his shoulders next, beneath his coat, and kept moving back. At last, he had no choice but to oblige that very charming motion by allowing her to valet him and slip his coat off his shoulders and arms. The coat joined his cravat on the floor. His waistcoat was next to receive her attentions. She undid the buttons with care. Teasing, if he didn't know better. He reached in to secure his watch and set it on the table. She pushed off that item, too, and he let it go without a thought. He reached for his wine and took a sip. At this rate, she was going to send him up in flames.

His pulse thudded when she unfastened his braces, just the front buttons. The result, of course, was that the front of his breeches sagged away from his waist. Next, she unbuttoned the three tiny fastenings at the top of his shirt. Her fingers brushed his bare skin.

"Purely out of curiosity," he said, "how far do you intend to take this?" He hoped the answer was to be *quite far*.

"I should like to see you, Banallt." His skin prickled when she ran her fingers from his breastbone to the top of his breeches. "The way you saw me. Without anything on at all."

A most excellent reply. "You have only to ask, Lady Banallt." He took her fingers in his and kissed the back of her hand. He let his lips linger there. "The least of your desires is my certain command." He stood up, wineglass in hand. Light from the fire played over her face. He lifted the wine and watched the light through the liquid, then drank the rest. He returned the glass to the table. No more tonight. He wanted a clear head for whatever she had planned for him. He made short work of his boots and tossed them aside before he reached for his breeches and slid them off. Stockings next, then smallclothes. At last he stood in only his shirt with an erection that was making him just the slightest bit impatient. The fire warmed his back. Beneath his feet, the carpet was soft, with just a hint of chill from the floor. "Am I to continue?" he asked, hands on his hips.

She nodded. Her cheeks, he noted with satisfaction, were flushed.

He pulled his shirt over his head, and there he was, standing before his wife in a natural state. He was fully aroused. He had the great pleasure of watching her gaze track from his face downward and stop the journey just below his navel.

"Your skin is very pale," she said. "And your hair so very dark."

Banallt shrugged. And then, knowing exactly where she was looking, he curled his hand around himself. He stroked up once, then down, a little harder up than on his downstroke.

"I think," she said in a very low voice, "your body is lovely." She rested a hand on her stomach.

"Thank you, ma'am." He shifted some of his weight to one leg, and stroked himself again. Her breath stopped.

"Do you like touching yourself?" she asked. Her eyes met his and he held her gaze.

"I'd like it better if you were touching me, but yes, I do like touching myself."

She stood up. She was slipper-less and stocking-less. Her bare feet joined his on the carpet. Thank God he'd built up the fire. The air around him was warm, so long as he stayed near the fireplace. Her black-dyed gown gleamed with gray highlights in the dimness. She came in close. Close enough to touch him. Her hand was out, and he expected a touch, but she didn't. All he felt was a whisper of air as she went by. He turned with her when she walked past. "That seems very wicked of you, Banallt."

"I'm a wicked man. Does that shock you?"

"Yes." She walked behind him, but he stayed where he was. He liked the sensation of her being behind him without knowing what she was going to do. He listened to the soft swish of her skirts as she moved. The scent of orange water came to him, a scent that he'd come to associate with his wife. He flinched in surprise when she ran a finger down his naked back, from the top of his neck to the bottom of his spine. His erection pulsed, and his fingers gripped reflexively. "I don't think I've ever told you what a lovely man you are."

"No, I don't believe you have. You may if you like."

"I wish I were taller," she said softly. Her palm came to rest in the small of his back. His muscles tensed.

"I'm glad you're not. I find the difference between us to be...stimulating."

"Very lovely to look at." Her skirt brushed his calves. He drew in a breath when her arms came around his body, underneath his arms, but too high to touch his cock, more's the pity. His heart beat a tattoo against his ribs as her palms flattened over his torso. She lay the side of her face against his back and her breath warmed his skin.

"Madam," he said, holding back a laugh. "You are very bold." He tried to turn around, but she tightened her arms around him. About now would be the perfect time to put her on her back and sink deep inside her. But he was equally wild to know what she intended to do with him.

"Don't move," she said. Her voice held an odd note that had him cocking his head. "Stay just as you are. I have a confession to make."

He stilled. "I know all your secrets, Sophie."

"All but one." She slid a hand up higher, to his pectoral. Her fingernail scraped his nipple. Damn, the woman was going to send him mad with desire. Gently, her lips pressed against his back. Her other hand moved down, to his hand, the one still gripping his penis.

"Jesus," he said. He inhaled sharply. "Sophie."

"A confession about the last time Tommy and I...were intimate."

"I don't want to talk about your bloody dead husband." Would he never be free of the infernal man's ghost? "He's gone. Dead, Sophie. I am your husband now." His words rolled out in a growl. "Whether you love me or not, it's me you should be thinking of tonight."

Her body went still. "That night," she whispered. "That night, I imagined Tommy was you."

His breath caught in his chest.

"It was beyond anything," she continued. "I knew what I was doing was wrong, but I didn't stop. I wanted someone to want me the way you did. I wanted you. Without ever touching me, Banallt, you showed me the difference between what Tommy felt and what you felt for me. My own husband never wanted me. He never loved me, and I knew you wanted me. I saw you behind my closed eyes, and I pretended you were with me, making love to me instead of my husband." Her hand around his squeezed gently. "And it was wonderful. So very wonderful. He knew something was different. And when...that moment came—it never had before with us...it was your name I called out."

God in heaven, Sophie.

He closed his eyes and let his head drop back until he felt his hair touch his shoulders. "Did he hear you?"

She didn't answer right away. He heard the tremble of her breath, felt the warmth of her where she touched him. "Yes."

"Sophie—"

"Please." Her voice quavered. "Just listen. I haven't told you everything." Her hands pressed against him. "That was the night before he died. He thought I'd been unfaithful. With you. Why else would his wife call out another man's name? The thing is, he meant for me to find him with Mrs. Peters. He intended to punish me for betraying him. The next thing I knew, he was dead. With all those awful words between us."

He turned around, hands around her upper arms, holding tight in case she took it into her head to move away. "Sophie."

She looked to the side, tears sparkling on her lashes.

"Sophie," he whispered. He brought her bodily to him, pulling her hard against him. His heart spilled over. "I've brought you nothing but misery. Nothing but."

That made her look at him. "That's not so. It's just I'm not the woman you've imagined all this time: never tempted, never anything but in love with my husband."

"I knew you were unhappy." He stroked her hair. "Any fool could see you were not happy in your marriage."

"I was never immune to you, Banallt."

He pulled her to him so that she had to go up on her toes. He slanted his mouth over hers and took her lips. And she threw her arms around him, holding on so tight it was as if she was afraid he'd disappear. He swung her into his arms, and in half a dozen steps he set her down by the bed, pressing her front to the edge of the mattress and working at all the damned fastenings of her gown. Hooks and buttons and ties and all those damnable laces and fastenings that tangled in her corset and tripped up his shaking fingers.

"For pity's sake!" he burst out. "Sometimes a woman's clothes utterly confound me."

When at last she was naked down to her skin, he got his arm around her waist and lifted her bodily onto the bed. And then he joined her there, pulling himself over her, one leg cocked to the side, his hips against her thigh. He threaded his fingers in her hair and kissed her until neither of them could breathe. They parted just to get air into their lungs.

"You're so lovely," she said. "It hurts my eyes to look at you."

"When I look at you," he whispered, "I see the most beautiful woman I've ever known." Her breasts were larger than he'd imagined back in the days before he'd had reason to know. Not extravagant at all, but lush for her body. Her nipples were small, as if her breasts had grown too large for them. All this time, his prim little

Sophie with her courtesan's eyes had had a courtesan's body, too. He dipped his head to her breast.

"Closer, Banallt," she said. Beneath him she shifted her body, and her hands tightened on his shoulders. "Please."

He drew back and blew on her taut nipple. "Are you begging already?" he asked.

"Never."

"Let me remedy that." But her body trembled as he entered her, and so did his. The build to orgasm streaked the length of his cock and quivered in his balls. He rocked into her and she threw her head back, exposing her throat to him down to the top of her bosom. On either side of him, her thighs came up and pressed against him. A low moan came from the back of her throat, nearly a sob.

He wanted to drive her mad with his body, to wring her out until she couldn't think or speak or feel anything but him. Except he was the one who was mad for her. He was perilously close to finishing before he'd properly begun. Close. Too close.

"Banallt," she cried. He withdrew, and her eyes flew open. Her hands fisted handfuls of the fabric. "No."

And with her looking at him with wild eyes, he reentered her, and this time it was his voice that cried out hoarsely. He didn't understand how he could feel this way without having fallen already. "You slay me, Sophie, I swear you're killing me."

He curled an arm around the top of her head and thrust into her, hard and deep, and then they were on their sides, and her upper thigh was over his, with his hands gripping the back of her leg, with her arching her pelvis into his, her breath coming in pants, and his no better. He rolled onto his back, bringing her with him.

She closed her eyes as she sank down, and he circled her waist with his hands, thumbs angled toward her navel, his fingers pulling hard against her back. Her hands floated to her thighs, and he about died when she let her head fall back, her hair tumbling around her shoulders, brushing his fingers.

"Sophie, yes. Like that. You're killing me." She was tight around him, her skin soft and warm. "Christ, yes."

Her pelvis tipped toward him, and her head came back. Her eyes snapped open, and it was like a lightning strike between them, her eyes were so lost in him. He got her onto her back again with him driving hard inside her.

"I'm coming, Sophie, now." His body centered in his cock. Every nerve and sense in his body was here with her. "Jesus, now. More, Sophie, more. God help me. Please. I need to come. Now."

"Banallt," she whispered, and her hands slid down to his backside and brought him closer.

He reared back, holding his arms straight as orgasm raced toward him. Dimly, he thought he had to pull out, now, or he'd be too late. But Sophie held him tight, her arms around him, and he remembered she was his wife. He opened his eyes and felt her move under him, a roll of her hips toward him with her mouth open and panting, and then just a flash of her blue green eyes, and that was it. He shattered. His orgasm wrung him out. His seed spilled into her, and he damn near lost any sense of where he was.

For a while there wasn't any sound but the two of them trying to breathe, but then Sophie said, "Is it possible?" He could have sworn she was teasing. She shouldn't have the energy for that.

"What?" He lay next to her on his stomach, wrung out. Completely and utterly sated and yet thinking of the things he yet wanted to do to her.

"You did." Her voice was light, teasing even.

"What?"

"You begged, my lord."

He laughed softly. "To have you make love to me like that, I'll beg you every night of my life, Lady Banallt."

CHAPTER THIRTY-THREE

Castle Darmead,
MAY 30, 1815

S ophie?"

Sophie jumped. She'd been completely lost in her own thoughts and hadn't heard Banallt come in. The words on her page gazed guiltily back at her. She blotted her page and set down her pen before she turned on her chair.

"Yes?"

Banallt came in, leaving the withdrawing room door open. He wasn't wearing a coat, just a pair of buckskin trousers, shirt, and waistcoat. She'd been married before, yet she wasn't used to Banallt being so at home around her. But then, she'd never really lived with Tommy, had she? His neckcloth was loose, too, and his hair was getting quite long. She liked the disreputable look. "How are you this morning, Sophie?"

He held a single sheet of paper in his hand. She could see the direction written on the outside and the bit of wax left from the broken seal. Quickly, she turned her pages over and brought out a fresh sheet to lay over the stack. She was writing again, not that she would ever publish, but the story refused to leave her. She kept seeing archers standing at those arrow-slit windows, firing on an attacking enemy while upstairs a young woman stared out a tower window, her heart in her throat.

"I'm well, thank you." Quite often after they'd been apart, a sense of disbelief came over her when they were together again. Such as now. Was this wickedly handsome man really her husband? Or would he one day coldly inform her he was tired of her or tell her his legal wife had returned from Italy, not dead after all? Or perhaps their marriage was a sham. Reverend Carson would be proven to have been a fraud or to have made some egregious error in the recording of the marriage, and Banallt intended to throw her over for a Bohemian princess.

He leaned down to kiss the top of her head. She had a cup of tea on the desk, and half a scone, which she'd brought upstairs after breakfast. He picked up the cup and took a sip. "Good God, Sophie. It's stone cold!"

"Is it?" She took back the cup. "Shall I ring for fresh?"

"No."

She had the habit now of separating her relationship with Banallt into its various aspects. What they did at night and in private had nothing to do with moments like this, and moments like this were nothing to do with any other. A different Sophie made love to Banallt. That Sophie's heart could not be broken. The letter in his hand crinkled. She saw Vedaelin's signature on the page. Her heart clenched, and for a moment, she was only Sophie Mercer, and her heart was going to break. "Oh," she said. She replaced the lid on her ink. "You're going back to London, aren't you?"

"There will be war, Sophie," he said. "It's certain. Wellington is in Brussels and will soon take command of the army if he hasn't already. He's demanding cavalry and artillery and God knows what else. St. Michael himself, I shouldn't be surprised."

"Then you must go." She folded her hands on the desk. Her fairy-tale interlude was over. He was leaving her. Exactly as Tommy had done; with an excellent excuse that would not keep them permanently apart. She hadn't seen Tommy again for nearly a year. Rumors of his behavior had reached her within weeks of his departure. The occasional bill arrived from some merchant, and she dutifully forwarded it to Tommy with a polite reminder that she had no funds from which to pay for his new gloves or a horse or his six new hats. She'd dismissed the rumors that came to her as nothing but mean-spirited gossip. The thought of Banallt taking another woman into his arms sliced her heart neatly in half.

"No choice, I'm afraid." He took her scone and ate it. "We've not had much of a honeymoon," he said. "If not for Bonaparte, I would have taken you to Paris and Rome. Florence and Constantinople." His mouth curved. "Imagine the stories you would think of among the Saracens."

She forced a smile. "But I am at Darmead, Banallt. My very own castle. Is there anything more romantic?" She was a jumble of conflicting emotions. What if he did not want her so close to London? What if he wanted her to come with him?

"What sort of honeymoon is that?" he asked. "When this business with the little Corsican is over, we'll have a proper wedding trip, I promise."

"We've been private here." She stood up and began to straighten his cravat. "Will you take King with you? If you do, Darmead will need someone like him."

He lifted his chin. "You're the only one who can manage my neckcloths, Sophie. Why is that?"

"I have an artistic mind," she said. Proper neckcloths required concentration during the folding. "No starch. How am I to produce anything elegant when your linen is unstarched?"

"I like to breathe when I am at home."

"There." She tweaked the two ends of the bow she'd made. "This is much harder than it looks, you know. A la Byron is very dashing. That's all I can do with you like this."

He put down Vedaelin's letter and walked to her dresser to look at his cravat. "I feel a poem coming on," he said.

She laughed, and he came back to slip his arms around her waist. "I'm sorry to disrupt our lives like this."

"When will you leave? Not today, Banallt. It's far too late for you to leave now."

Banallt frowned. "Sophie," he said. His eyes flashed. "Have you deliberately misunderstood me?"

"Not in the least." She took a step back, uncertain of the cause of his displeasure. "Britain is going to war against Bonaparte, and you must return to London."

He drew in a breath and slowly exhaled. "I am not Tommy Evans," he said.

"I am aware, Banallt."

"Are you?"

"I don't wish to argue. I know who you are. And who you are not."

"Nevertheless, Sophie, we must return to London," he said.

"We?" She'd never thought he meant to bring her with him. The thought made her heart feel light. And wary at the same time.

"I understand you are still mourning your brother." He brushed her cheek with the back of her hand. "You needn't entertain or even go out. But you are my wife, Sophie." He hesitated. "You told me once that people will talk simply because it's me. You're right. They will." He lowered his head. "They'll talk no matter what I do, whether you stay here or come with me."

"Of that I am also aware."

"The truth is, whatever anyone decides to say or not say, I want you in London with me."

She shrugged. The image she had in her head was Mrs. Peters and the way she'd looked at Banallt. Hadn't Mr. Tallboys himself said the woman was after him and making a fool of herself? And they would return to London, where that selfsame Mrs. Peters waited for his return. "Very well, Banallt. We shall go."

"I don't wish to play the martinet, Sophie." His frown deepened. "If you aren't ready to be in public, I understand. I shan't force you to go if you'd rather not." He touched the underside of her chin and lifted her face to his. His eyebrows drew together. "What on earth is going on in that head of yours?"

She twisted away from him. "I said I'll go. Isn't that enough?"

"No," he softly replied. "It's not. Why do you insist on treating me as if I am a rogue who, having secured your fortune, now wishes nothing to do with you?"

"Why wouldn't you?" she said. She regretted the words the moment they were out.

He laughed. "What fortune of yours have I gained, Sophie, when you refuse me the only one that matters to me?"

"I'm well aware, Banallt, that I am in your debt."

He threw back his head and stared at the ceiling. "Good God," he said. "That's what you're thinking, isn't it?" He looked at her again, but she saw anger and frustration flicker behind his eyes. "That I'll go to London to gamble away my fortune. Set up a mistress or two and come home drunk every night, if I come home at all, that is."

"Haven't you before?"

"Perhaps you've not noticed my fortune is quite intact, madam. Just as it's also escaped your notice that I am rarely drunk. As for mistresses—"

She put her hands on her hips. "I knew when we married that you would not be a faithful husband."

"Sophie—"

"Please, this is quite enough, Banallt. It's absurd for us to argue about what we cannot change."

"Tell me, Sophie, what have I done to make you believe I would treat you as Tommy did? Since I came back from Paris, I mean."

"I've said I'll go with you. That ought to be enough."

"Have I been drunk? Spent a night away from here? Have creditors been knocking on the castle walls demanding to be paid? When you came to London, did you hear one word of scandal involving me?"

"As a matter of fact, yes."

"Recent scandal. Not something dredged up from the past."

"Mrs. Peters." She had the sense that she was rushing toward disaster. Out of control.

He put his hands on his hips. "What?"

"Major Haggart said she was after you. Mr. Tallboys, too."

"Tell me," he said in a tight voice, "when you have come to your senses about me."

They parted with neither of them happy. She was solidly in the right. After all, Banallt *had* lived a wicked life. She didn't need to listen to rumor to know he was no stranger to immorality. She'd seen it with her own eyes. Hadn't he spent the better part of three years trying to seduce her despite the fact that they both were married at the start? Hadn't he done all those things and worse?

She left her room not long after, feeling unsettled, at odds with the world. As if some vital part of it were missing. She found King in order to discuss their removal to London, but her mind constantly returned to Banallt. Had she been fair to him? Sophie had the uneasy feeling she hadn't been. Truthfully, since he'd come to Havenwood with his ridiculous and heartbreaking proposal of marriage, he'd behaved nothing like the man she'd known at Rider Hall. Her throat closed off.

"Ma'am?"

"Yes, King?" As with Banallt, she had to look up to see his face. The butler looked puzzled.

He cleared his throat and said, in the manner of someone who is, in fact, repeating himself, "The books his lordship sent down from London, we've just finished shelving them. Now that you're going back to Town, should we crate them up again and send them back with you?"

"What books?"

"In the library, ma'am." He smoothed the line forming between his eyebrows. "He said they were for you."

"Best show me what you mean." She followed him to the second-floor room that had the look of a withdrawing room converted to a library. And there, in the middle set of shelves, were all the books she'd written and twenty more books by authors who did not reveal their names and others who did: Mrs. Radcliffe, Eleanor Sleath, Charlotte Smith. Dozens of the favorites she and Banallt had discussed over the years were here. He'd remembered every one. She touched the bindings and pulled out the second volume of *The Nocturnal Minstrel*. Tears burned behind her eyes again. A thread of stubbornness wound through her. She would not give in.

"Ma'am? Shall we send them back to Hightower?"

She sat hard on a nearby chair and clutched either side of the book. She looked up at King. He was rubbing the top of his ruined ear. The Mercers had kept the contents of the Havenwood library, including books that had long been her beloved favorites. And he'd remembered them all.

"Lady Banallt? Are you all right?"

She looked up, barely restraining her emotions. "No," she said. "Not at all. I—I think we're done for now." She swallowed hard. "I'll call if I need you. Thank you for your help, King."

"Milady." King peered at her, and she was sure, with his piercing mud brown eyes, he'd seen right through her. Whatever he saw when he looked into her face, he bowed and left the parlor.

Quiet surrounded her, a hush that whispered of unhappiness and a life threatening to take the wrong path. The walls here were so thick one rarely heard sounds from other rooms. She could quite easily be the only woman left in the world. It was possible, she believed, that if she walked out of this room, she'd find she'd traveled back in time to the days when archers positioned themselves at the windows, hands on their longbows, eyes narrowed as they aimed at marauders attacking the castle. Or perhaps she'd walk into some other life, a not so distant past when she had been unhappy and convinced there was no other way for her to live.

During her marriage to Tommy, she'd never once thought she ought to tell him she wrote. In fact, she'd known that he must never know. Her survival depended upon her deceiving her husband. And once she was supplementing her income with her stories, meager as that income might be, she knew she could never tell her husband. Banallt had known from the start, and he hadn't derided her successes. He'd also kept her secret. Tommy never knew that she wrote as Mrs. Merchant. Tommy had taught her never to share. Never to be herself. And she had let that poison take over her life. She shivered at the life that conviction had put before her.

"Here you are."

She jumped, startled because she'd not heard anyone come in.

Banallt.

The sense that she had stepped out of time stayed with her, despite the fact that Banallt wore modern clothes. Her head felt light. The neckcloth she'd tied for him was askew again. She clutched the book on her lap. "Are we leaving tonight?" she asked.

"No. Tomorrow morning is soon enough. King said you weren't well." He knelt at her chair, pressing a hand to her forehead. "Are you all right?"

She opened her mouth, but no sound came out. She tried again. "It seems I just did this, Banallt."

"Did what?"

"Prepared for a sudden removal to London. John had political duties that called him to Town. Because of Bonaparte." She grasped Banallt's hand. Her chest tightened unbearably. "He never returned. Never came home."

"Sophie," he said softly. "Sophie, darling."

Still holding the book, she leaned forward and brought his hand to her cheek, leaning her head against his palm. "What if something happens to you, too, Banallt?"

"You've no worries for the future." He sounded distant. Cold, even.

She dropped his hand and shot to her feet. The book tumbled to the floor, and she left it there. "Is that what you think I meant?"

"You've been left destitute twice. By Tommy, then by your brother."

"But that isn't what I meant. Not at all." She pressed her hands to her cheeks, as if that would keep her from flying apart. Her body trembled and she wondered if she was going to break down right now. She was in love with him, and now she worried that she'd realized it too late. "I'm sorry," she whispered. "I'm sorry I've been so horrible to you."

He smiled and shook his head. He held out his hands. "Shh, darling. Come here. It's all right."

"But I've been horrible to you all along."

He reached for her and drew her into his arms. "Nothing I haven't deserved."

"Do you really love me, Banallt? Me? Sophie Mercer, who writes novels and imagines too much?" She licked her lips. "And who sometimes does not imagine enough?"

"Haven't I told you already?" He held her head between his hands. "I do love you, Sophie. Believe that, if you believe nothing else I say. I am your faithful hound."

She inhaled a breath that rattled in her chest. "Banallt." She stepped away and gripped handfuls of her skirts. "I feel as if I've lived a lie. I didn't want to believe you'd changed, because if you had I'd have to face the truth."

"Which is?"

"That I love you." She put her hands to her mouth. "I've been in love with you for a very long time. And if I love you, then you can hurt me, and I never wanted anyone to have the power to do that again. Especially not you." He took a step toward her, but she held up a hand. "Please, no. Let me finish. I was sitting here, before you came in, thinking that I had a choice to make. The most important choice of my life. I could go on as I have been, letting you get this close and no closer, and if I did that, you would never be able to hurt me, because I'd not have let myself love you. And we'd probably go on, getting on well enough but not as you deserved."

"Sophie—"

"Please, Banallt. Or I could risk everything and let you love me. I could love you as you deserve. And I thought, when you came in, that perhaps I was too much a coward. Because you could break my heart." She wiped away a tear. "But you brought those books here. Why?"

He shrugged. "I thought you'd want them."

"You're right." She scrabbled in her pocket for her handkerchief. "Good heavens. What if I'd stayed a coward?"

"The one thing you've never been is a coward." He put his handkerchief into her hands.

Sophie threw herself into his arms. "I love you, Banallt. I do. I have for quite a while. I'm sorry I was awful to you." She was crying unabashedly. "Please don't let it be too late."

He pulled her tight against him. "Hush, now. It's not too late." He stroked the back of her head. "Darling, we had a spat. Such things happen to a married couple. If we differ, it doesn't mean I've stopped loving you."

She put her arms tight around his neck. "I love you. I do love you." She buried her fingers in his hair and brought his head to hers. Sophie kissed him even though she was trembling. Even though she was afraid and the future was never certain. When they stopped, he kept his arms around her waist.

"You do understand, Sophie, the scandal we'll cause in London?" he asked.

"Scandal? What scandal is that?"

A wicked grin appeared on his mouth. "Among the ton, it's always a scandal when a husband and wife make no secret of loving each other. It's simply not done."

Her heart felt full. Overflowing. "Well, then, Banallt, let us cause a scandal."

ABOUT CAROLYN JEWEL

Carolyn Jewel was born on a moonless night. That darkness was seared into her soul and she became an award-winning author of historical and paranormal romance. She has a very dusty car and a Master's degree in English that proves useful at the oddest times. An avid fan of fine chocolate, finer heroines, Bollywood films, and heroism in all forms, she has three cats and two dogs. Also a son. One of the cats is his.

Visit her on the web at:
www.carolynjewel.com
twitter.com/cjewel
facebook.com/carolynjewelauthor
goodreads.com/cjewel

Awesome people sign up for my newsletter. I send one out 3 or 4 times a year, depending on how fast I'm writing

EXCERPT

INDISCREET
A REGENCY HISTORICAL ROMANCE

CHAPTER ONE

HOW EVERYTHING STARTED

This incident took place at about two o'clock the morning of September 3, 1809. The location was the back parlor of a town house owned by the Duke of Buckingham but lived in by the Earl of Crosshaven on a ninety-nine-year lease, presently in its twenty-third year. It should be remarked that Lord Edward Marrack, the younger brother of the Marquess of Foye, was in attendance that night. Lord Edward had been something of a rake until his engagement to the daughter of a longtime family friend. The Earl of Crosshaven currently was a rake.

L ord Edward Marrack refused more wine when the bottle came around in his direction. Instead, he leaned against his chair while his friend the Earl of Crosshaven raised a hand—Cross was inevitably the center of attention—and said, with significant stress, the two words, "Sabine Godard."

The other men in the room looked impressed. No one, including Lord Edward, doubted for a moment that Cross had indeed secured the person of Miss Sabine Godard.

Up to now, the young lady's reputation had been unassailable. She was an orphan who had been raised by her uncle since she was quite young. They made their home in Oxford, the city of spires, Henry Godard having been a don there and a noted philosopher until his recent retirement from those hallowed walls. She and her uncle had come to London so that Godard could receive a knighthood in recognition of his intellectual contributions to king and empire.

They had not been long in London, the Godards, but Lord Edward recalled hearing Miss Godard was reckoned a pretty girl. Very pretty and quite unavailable. She was, if he had his facts in order, her uncle's permanent caretaker, as was often the fate of children not raised by their parents. Her uncle was now Sir Henry Godard. By several large steps, quite a come up in the world for them both.

The unavailable Miss Godard had been pursued by Crosshaven. That, too, Lord Edward had heard. The Earl of Crosshaven was angelically, devilishly, beautiful. His manners were exquisite and his intellect absolutely first-rate. Lord Edward would not bother with a friendship if that were not the case. But Crosshaven, in Lord Edward's opinion, was not as familiar with discretion as he might be. Something he was proving tonight.

Though Lord Edward liked Cross exceedingly, this boast of his was infamous. Ungentlemanly, in fact. That Cross had refilled his glass far too often in the course of the evening was no excuse for his revealing to anyone that he had seduced a young woman of decent family. And, one presumed, abandoned her to whatever fate her uncle might decide was fit for a girl who strayed from what was proper.

"How was she?" asked one of the other young bucks.

Cross kissed the tips of his fingers and arced his thus blessed hand toward the ceiling. That engendered several ribald comments, some having to do with Cross's prowess in the bedroom and others having to do with Sabine Godard and what Crosshaven may or may not have taught her about sexual congress and how to fornicate with élan.

In Lord Edward's opinion, Cross, though just short of thirty, and for all his lofty titles, had now proved he had a great deal to learn about honor and decency. This evening, which had begun as a pleasant interlude with men he liked, no longer seemed very pleasant.

"A seduction," Lord Edward said to no one in particular, "when properly carried out, pleases both parties for the duration, while a break humiliates no one."

"Who says I've broken with her?" Crosshaven asked.

"I do," he replied. "And any fool with half a brain."

Crosshaven shook his head sadly. "Is this what happens to a man when he falls in love? If I didn't know better, I'd accuse you of not wanting to go to bed with a pretty young woman." He winked. "Without benefit of marriage, I mean." He gave Lord Edward a sloppy smile, then looked around the room with his glass held high in a mock toast. "To Sabine Godard."

"Hear, hear," said a few of the others. Most just took the opportunity to sample their wine.

Crosshaven took another drink of his hock, but he kept his eyes on Lord Edward as he did. He'd noticed Lord Edward hadn't joined in the toast. "Don't be such a bloody bore, Ned," he said with a roll of his eyes. "You're not married yet, old man."

"True." But in three months time he would be. God, he was weary of this, of nights like this spent drinking or whoring and living as if there weren't something more to be had from life. He wasn't married yet, but wished Rosaline was already his wife.

Lord Edward put down his glass and stood. He felt a giant. With reason. He towered over everyone in the room, standing or not. "Good evening, gentlemen, my lords."

"What?" said Cross. He was a bit unsteady on his feet. "Are you leaving already, Ned? It's early yet."

Lord Edward could not bring himself to smile to soften his disapproval of his friend's behavior. Nor could he remain silent. "I do not care to hear any lady's character shredded for the sake of a man's reputation."

Cross focused on Lord Edward, registered the slight to his honor, and said, "She's no better than she ought to be."

"True," Lord Edward said. "But the consequences of indiscretion always fall hardest on the woman. Tonight, you are lauded for your seduction of the girl, deemed ever more manly. Your reputation as a cocksman is firmly established."

Crosshaven bowed amid a few catcalls. He straightened, grinning. Lord Edward was probably the only one in the room who wasn't grinning back.

"What reason had you to prove that fact at the cost of her reputation? No one disputes your appeal to the fairer sex." Lord Edward sighed. There was no point in lecturing Cross. No point at all "Tomorrow," he said with regret soft in his voice, "Miss Godard will not find the world so pleasant a. place. That is a fate you ought to have avoided for the girl."

"She's still no better than she ought to be, Ned." He pretended to sober up, but as a drunk would do. Sloppily. "I mean no disrespect, Lord Edward. But it's true about the girt. No better than she ought to be."

He acknowledged Cross with a nod, without smiling because he was disappointed in his friend. "Nor are you."

As he walked out, Lord Edward thought it was a very great pity that Miss Godard was so thoroughly ruined. Beyond repair. Crosshaven's boast of her would be everywhere by noon tomorrow. He did not know the girl person-ally but did not like to think of the disgrace that was soon to fall on her and her uncle. They would both be touched by Crosshaven's indiscretion.

He thought it likely the newly knighted Sir Henry Godard would put her onto the street.

CHAPTER TWO

ONE YEAR AND EIGHT MONTHS LATER, GIVE OR TAKE A FEW DAYS. MAY 5, 1811

The former Lord Edward Marrack was now the Marquess of Foye and a guest at the palace of an English merchant in Buyukdere, Turkey, about twelve miles outside Constantinople. Europeans were not permitted to live in the city, and Buyukdere was a favorite summer residence for expatriates from any number of countries. Including England. A good deal of the diplomatic corps resided in Buyukdere, which overlooked the blue, blue waters of the Bosporus.

The finest woman here tonight was Miss Sabine Godard.

How strange that he should cross paths with Miss Godard so many thousands of miles from home. Foye wasn't surprised to find she was a lovely woman.

If Crosshaven had noticed her, and, quite infamously, he had, it stood to reason she would have something. She did.

Foye sat on a chair not so far from the center of the assembly that he would be thought aloof, though he'd been accused of that and worse since he'd begun his tour of countries that had the single advantage of being far from England. He was not by nature a gregarious man and was even less so now, or so he'd been told by people who had known him before- True enough. For the second time in his life, he was a changed man. What a pity he didn't like the change.

Now that he saw her before him, he understood why so many men had spoken of her looks and why Crosshaven had chosen her, it wasn't so much that she was beautiful. She wasn't quite that. A man didn't catch his breath at the sight of her. She was not a very tall woman, though from what he could see of her, her figure was a nice one. He stared at her, trying to pin down for himself the reason that she was a more attractive woman than she ought to be.

Her features were too strong for beauty in the classic sense, though anyone meeting her for the first time would think her pretty. She smiled often, and he'd watched several men stare, besotted, when her mouth curved a certain way. Her hair was an astonishing shade of gold. Curls at her temples and brow gave her an air of sweetness without being cloying, and there weren't many pretty young women who could manage that. A lace cap was on her head, a jade green ribbon threaded through the material. She wasn't beautiful, no, not that, but she was pretty. Exceptionally so.

She had something else as well, and he was determined to put a name to whatever elusive quality that was. What a shame Crosshaven had ruined everything for her. She might have done well for herself, had she stayed in London. There were any number of pretty young girls who'd married up. Some decent young man would likely have thought himself lucky to marry a woman like her. Foye couldn't help feeling at least partially responsible for the fact that she hadn't.

At the moment. Miss Godard was sitting at a table surrounded by men in uniform; sailors, soldiers of the Royal Artillery, Royal Engineers, or otherwise attached to the military here in Buyukdere. She was reading tea leaves for them and having a grand time, too. Despite her smiles, and despite the men gathered around her, she appeared unaware of the flirtatious looks and remarks sent her way, but not, he thought, unaware of her looks.

Miss Godard knew very well that men found her attractive, Foye decided. But she was not a flirt.

Her uncle, Sir Henry Godard, sat close enough to her that she could easily lean over and touch his arm should she care to. Sir Henry was deep in conversation with one of the merchants who worked for the Levant Company. The topic at hand, from what Foye could overhear, was the merits and demerits of St. Augustine. A heady subject for afternoon tea.

So far, Sir Henry had the advantage in the argument. He was a wily debater. Leading his prey to make admissions that seemed reasonable enough while in reality he was laying a trap such that when it sprang his victim would have no choice but to cede Sir Henry's entire point.

Experience had etched deep lines in Sir Henry's face and yet had taken a disproportionate physical toll on the rest of his body. His upper back was hunched, throwing his leonine head forward. His hair was that off shade of white, a yellowish silver, common to men who'd been blond throughout their adult lives. Notwithstanding the depredations of age and illness, Sir Henry was a man of considerable presence. His profession remained in his manner of speech, his temperament and even his gestures. It was easy to imagine him addressing a lecture hall of young men and terrifying them into listening at peril of their very survival.

The salon was filled with guests holding teacups and guarding plates of cakes, biscuits, and sugar wafers. There were tables piled with watermelon and bowls of sherbet in silver cups with delicate silver spoons. The merchant whose palace this was, Mr. Anthony Lucey, had invited only Englishmen and women this afternoon, though naturally men outnumbered the women, who were, for the most part wives or other relatives of the soldiers. Some of the men were longtime employees of the Levant Company who had raised families here. A pretty English girl wasn't unheard of in Buyukdere. Not by any means.

Lucey himself, a longtime friend of Foye's late father, stood in the center of the room telling a story Foye had heard before about the time he'd gotten lost in Mayfair and had mistakenly knocked on the Duke of Portland's private door. Lucey was such an excellent raconteur the tale still amused more than forty years after it had happened.

He was beginning to think, though, that he ought to go get himself introduced to Miss Godard. Just to see what she was like. Naturally, he was curious. And since he was here, if the circumstances offered, he might explain what had happened.

Foye resisted the urge to smooth down his hair. There really was no dealing with his curls. They were contrary by innate disposition, it seemed. A good match for his face, which was one of the reasons he'd let his hair grow and never cut it short again. With a face that defined "ill made" and a body that tended to intimidate by sheer size—he had always been prone to muscle—Foye was used to women looking past him or away from him. Though since he'd become Foye, that happened marginally less often.

He plucked a crisp sugar wafer from his plate and took a bite. A touch of almond, he thought, and he had a taste of bliss melting over his tongue. Lucey's cook was superb, a Neapolitan man he'd succeeded in hiring away from the Italian ambassador's residence. The story of Lucey's raid on the Italian kitchen was amusing, too. Foye took another bite of his wafer and savored it while he watched yet another lovesick young officer beg to have his fortune told by Miss Godard.

Perhaps, he thought, it was something about the way she looked at a man. Yes. Something about her eyes. And her complete disinterest. What bold young man didn't want the very woman who wouldn't have him? Given all that he and Miss Godard had in common, he ought to at least meet her. It was, however, quite plain to him that to get anywhere with the niece one must start with the uncle.

When Foye was done eating, he asked Lucey for an introduction to Sir Henry.

The old man was formidable, that had been apparent even from a distance. Closer up, he seemed no less so for all that his frailness was the more evident. He had, Foye recalled, read one of Sir Henry's treatises, the 1805 *On Hubris.*

When Lucey walked him over to the philosopher, Foye was speared by a pair of iron gray eyes that would have been at home in a man forty years his junior, they were that bright and perceptive. He did not believe it was an accident that he should think back on his university days with some sense of dread. This man would have had no compunction whatever about sending a prince packing for want of preparation. No more a mere second son—all that Foye had been in those days.

Foye bowed when Lucey completed the introduction. Already the object of much curiosity on account of his appearance, more stares came his way when his titles were pronounced. Lucey, unfortunately, knew the entire list. Marquess of Foye. Earls of Eidenderry and DeMortmercy. He was used to them now, at last accustomed to the change in his identity from Lord Edward to Foye. There were days now when he could hardly recall a time when he hadn't been Foye. His first titled ancestor had been ennobled before the reign of Charlemagne. The Marracks of Cornwall had never been viscounts. Their nobility had begun with an earldom.

It was with him that the Marrack line would end. With the death of his brother without any living children, he was the last of the Marrack men. When he died, his properties and titles would revert to the crown. What a failure to take to his grave, to leave no one to carry on the name.

"Well, well, young man," Sir Henry said, laboriously craning his neck sideways to look at him. "That is a mouthful of names."

Foye smiled despite himself. He had not been called a young man for a good many years. It wasn't as though he was old, but at thirty-eight, he wasn't a boy anymore. Godard held out a gnarled hand for Foye to take, which he did, gently. The philosopher was crippled with the gout, and his skin was hot to the touch.

"Yes, Sir Henry, it is, indeed, a mouthful." He smiled, aware of Miss Godard's attention to their exchange. Would he tell her, if the opportunity arose? He ought to but didn't know if he would. She seemed to have made a life for herself here, far from England. Why bring up what could only be painful memories for her? Because,

Foye thought, if he were her, he'd want to know the truth. "I hope you were not bored listening to all that."

"Not at all." Sir Henry bobbed his head. "I am pleased to make your acquaintance, my Lord Foye."

"The pleasure is mine, Sir Henry." Foye was aware that Miss Godard had stopped her inspection of someone's teacup—what nonsense that business was—to listen to the introduction.

Did she recognize his name from his connection with Crosshaven? Perhaps she did not know he and Cross had been friends and that Foye knew what had been done to her. Or perhaps she did, and now wondered if her reputation was to be ruined again by someone else who knew only the lies.

"Foye. Foye," Sir Henry said, tapping his chin with a finger permanently hooked into a claw. He narrowed his eyes and gave him a sideways look. "A King's College man, weren't you?"

Foye bowed. For a split second, he racked his brain for the essay he must have failed to write. "Yes, sir."

"Your elder brother, too, if I'm not mistaken."

"You are not."

"I thought so." Sir Henry grinned and nodded. "You were Lord Edward then, not Foye. That's why I didn't know who you were until you were close enough for me to see you." He pulled at a blanket spread over his lap. "Took a first in mathematics, didn't you?"

"I'm astonished you should know such a thing." It was at university that Foye had learned there were women who cared more for what he offered-when they were intimate than what he looked like in broad daylight. He'd also discovered he had a talent for pleasing his partners. He'd made himself an assiduous student of the delights to be had between a man and woman. Well. No more of that for him. Those days were long gone. He was done with that life.

Godard waved a misshapen hand. "I made it a point to acquaint myself with the names of all the young men of promise. If we were at home, I would send Sabine to find my entry on you." He smiled, and the effect was disconcertingly sly. His niece looked in their direction at the mention of her name. "I kept a ledger, my lord. I followed you in Parliament, you know. Heard your maiden speech. I am rarely, wrong in my predictions."

"Am I to be flattered by that?" Foye asked. He did not look at Miss Godard, though he burned to do so.

"I should think so. I saw you once or twice at university." He chuckled. "No mistaking you for anyone else."

He smiled again. "No, sir."

"I should think you learned early on it's better to have something here"—he tapped his temple—"than to have a handsome face. Too many young men these days spend hours primping at the mirror when they would profit more from improving their minds."

"Godard," his niece murmured. She put an arm on her uncle's sleeve in a gesture familiar enough to be habitual. Foye could easily imagine her needing to restrain her uncle's bluntness. For all Sir Henry's rudeness, he rather liked the man for it. He wasn't a pretty man, after all.

"What?" Sir Henry said, turning his torso toward his niece. "With a face like his, do you think he bothers much with enriching his tailor over his bookseller?"

"I think Lord Foye is very smartly dressed," she said.

"Thank you," Foye said. In point of fact, he was vain of his appearance. Even as Lord Edward, he had never walked out of his house without clothes that made other men beg him for the name of his tailor.

"Look at him." One thin arm shot into the air. "Do you think he spent his time at King's with his mistresses instead of in the library?"

Good God. Foye held back his shock at Sir Henry's speech. Miss Godard, too, felt the indiscretion, for her cheeks pinked up. Sir Henry didn't seem to think anything of his declaration.

"Godard." She slid a glance at Foye, and their eyes met Hers were brown. There was nothing extraordinary about her eyes, but for the intelligence there. She was no ordinary girl, he thought. "Forgive him," she murmured.

"For what?" Foye said. "It's true. I am no model of masculine beauty. I am not offended by Sir Henry pointing that out." Age had its privileges, after all; and Sir Henry had to be nearer seventy than sixty. He had decided to be amused. There was brilliance yet in the old man.

"Sensible of you, my boy."

Foye nodded to Sir Henry, but he was absorbed by Miss Godard. She was a far more interesting woman than he'd expected. All this time, whenever he thought of Crosshaven and what he'd done that night, he'd been imagining a sweet young woman, weeping for her lost reputation. Naive and mourning the infamous wrong done her. Miss Godard was hardly naive.

"Have you been in Anatolia long, my lord?" Sir Henry

"No," Foye replied.

Miss Godard was how indisputably a part of their conversation. He could not help but look at her. Her eyes were not a common brown after all, but something a more poetic man might call dark honey. From the shape of her mouth, the tilt of her eyes with their thick, dark lashes, to the sweeping line of her throat to her shoulders, she was the sort of woman who made a man think of darkened rooms and whispered endearments. He understood very well why Crosshaven had chosen her.

"I arrived in Constantinople yesterday," Foye said to Sir Henry. "And you?"

Sir Henry folded his crippled hands on his lap. "We have been in Buyukdere coming onto a month. Is that correct, Sabine?"

She answered without hesitation. "In Anatolia, forty-three days. In Buyukdere, twenty-one, Uncle."

Again, Foye felt his understanding of Miss Godard to be maddeningly incomplete. Not a woman wronged and mourning her fate. Not a pretty girl who knew and used the power her looks gave her over a man. And to speak so crisply, with such unhesitating precision. He preferred it when the people he met fell into neat categories. Irascible old man. A young woman wronged. Foye did not yet know where to fit Miss Godard.

"Twenty-one days, my lord," Sir Henry told him with a smile that conveyed his pride in the precision of his niece's recollection.

The naval officer whose tea leaves she'd been reading bid Miss Godard adieu. She nodded, said good-bye, and though the officer waited for her to say something more, she didn't. For the moment, her table was empty of a companion, yet all the other men who had been waiting for their chance found themselves dismissed without a word.

"You have an able assistant, sir." There was an awkward silence during which Foye expected to be introduced and was not. He cleared his throat and returned a bit of the older man's directness. "May I meet your niece, Sir Henry?"

"What for?" Sir Henry's eyes scalded. Foye could only thank the Lord he'd never been in one of Sir Henry's lectures when he was at Oxford. He would have quailed under that gimlet eye. Because, in truth, he had spent more time with his various mistresses than with his studies.

"Godard," Miss Godard said, firmly this time.

Sir Henry tipped his head toward her. "Very well. I suppose there's no hope for it. Sabine, will you meet the Marquess of Foye?"

She stood to curtsey but did not extend a hand to him over the very small table at which she sat. He bowed in return. "Delighted to make your acquaintance, my lord."

"My niece, sir. Miss Sabine Godard."

"Miss Godard." He was aware he was staring too hard. She was still so very young. He doubted she was much beyond twenty. Crosshaven ought to rot in hell for what he'd done to the girl

She cocked her head at him, and at that moment he would have given anything to know what she was thinking.

"Would you read my future?" he asked.

Sir Henry snorted. "It's nonsense, my lord," he said. "She knows that, too."

Miss Godard's gaze flicked to her uncle; she remained unruffled. "If he is on your list of men who will make something of themselves, Godard, I daresay he is well aware my tea reading is a nothing more than an amusing way to pass the time." She turned to him. "My lord, have you a cup you've been drinking? If not, you'll need fresh."

He pointed in the direction of the table on which he'd set his tea. "There."

"That should do." She smiled at him, but with no particular interest in him beyond what was polite and no indication that she cared anything for his title or his consequence. Or his lack of beauty, for that matter. How egalitarian of her. "I'll wait, my lord."

He returned with his nearly empty cup and sat on the chair opposite her. His legs were too long to fit underneath the table, leaving him no choice but to sit sideways or remain as he was with his thighs wide open. He turned on the chair. Miss Godard took his cup and looked into it. "Can you bear to drink another mouthful or two?"

He nodded. He would tell her, he decided. He would tell her about Crosshaven and then apologize for his role in her ruin, limited as it had been. He took back his cup, drank it nearly empty, and extended it to her.

"No," she said, refusing his cup. "Hold it just so and swirl the contents thus." She demonstrated the desired motion with her arm.

"Nonsense, all of it," Sir Henry said.

"Yes, Godard," she said without looking at her uncle. But he saw a smile lurking on her mouth. "Excellent. Now upend your cup on the saucer."

"Shall I first cross your palms with silver?" Foye asked.

"Certainly not." Her eyes, her very fine eyes, flashed with humor. There was more to Miss Godard than she meant to let on, he realized. "If I allowed you to pay me in order to learn your future, my ability to accurately assess what tomorrow and beyond may hold for you would be compromised."

"Consider the offer rescinded, miss."

Her mouth quirked. "Anyone who takes filthy lucre is no better than a rank charlatan."

Obediently, he swirled his cup and did as directed, upending the cup over the saucer. Though he did not like to admit it, she interested him. What was she? What had she become since Crosshaven? "And you, being above remuneration, are ho charlatan, I presume?"

Her smile became a direct and knowing connection with his gaze. "I am the worst charlatan in Christendom if you believe a word I say, my lord." She righted his tea and stared into it. "This is utter nonsense, as you well know."

"My future?" He sighed. "I feared as much."

Miss Godard laughed softly. "Divination, my lord. As much as I admire the great civilizations of the past, I have concluded there is a reason men of modern learning do not maintain a belief in the ancient ways. Just as there were no gods on Mount Olympus, there is no magic by which one can infer the future from random patterns made in tea leaves." She quirked her eyebrows at him. "Or the entrails of a goat, for that matter."

He very nearly laughed. Nearly. My God, she was quick witted and not afraid to show him. "Nevertheless, this"—he indicated the teacup—"is, as you say, quite a charming pastime for a lady to have."

"Thank you." She raised her voice. "You see, Godard, that I am vindicated by Lord Foye."

"What's that?" Sir Henry said.

"The marquess finds the reading of tea leaves to be an amusing occupation." She spoke so drolly and with such affection for her uncle that Foye was hard-pressed not to grin. Miss Godard handled her irascible uncle quite well.

"More the fool he," Sir Henry said.

Miss Godard lifted a hand and pressed the other to her upper bosom. "A moment of silence while I read the portents, my lord."

She could have been an actress; the gesture and tone of voice were so perfectly done. No wonder the officers vied for her attention. For one thing, she was miserly with it, and when she did look at you directly, there was so much there to see in her eyes, a man could not be faulted for wanting more. He leaned his side against his chair, his elbow over the back, and stretched out one leg while he watched her. "I believe," he said in a low voice, "that we have a mutual acquaintance."

Without taking her eyes from his cup, she replied in a soft voice, "Not a mutual friend, I am afraid. Unless you mean someone besides the Earl of Crosshaven."

"I do not."

Her expression closed off. "You have a bouquet of flowers, here." She pointed to a mass of leaves. "That signifies you are to be happy in love."

"I was," he said. "Once. But no longer."

She looked at him. "I am not reading your past, my lord, but your future."

"Happy in love?" he said, looking into her eyes. "I fear that is quite impossible."

"The tea leaves never lie," she replied.

He wriggled his fingers over his cup. "Pray continue."